CRAIG ODANOVICH

THE BLACK WIDOW TRAINER

BOOK ONE IN THE BLACK WIDOW TRAINER SERIES

Published by River Grove Books
Austin, TX
www.rivergrovebooks.com

Distributed by River Grove Books

Design and composition by Greenleaf Book Group and Bumpy Design
Cover design by Greenleaf Book Group

Publisher's Cataloging-in-Publication data is available.

Print ISBN: 978-1-63299-515-5

eBook ISBN: 978-1-934572-68-9

First Edition

To the scores of hardworking and dedicated personal trainers—men and women—and their clients.

ACKNOWLEDGMENTS

To Amy, Donna, Cheryl, Andrea, Kim, Dee, and Liz. Thank you for reading along and playing focus group.

To Melissa Messer, for teaching me so much about the mechanics of writing and putting your special touches on *The Black Widow Trainer*.

To Mike Savage for pushing me hard to continually improve the manuscript.

To my team at Greenleaf Book Group: Justin Branch, Jay Hodges, Heather Jones, Bryan Carroll, Lisa Woods, and Jenn McMurray. Your business model allows me to approach this project no differently than the many businesses I built from scratch during my career.

To Amy Evans, for taking the time to read my manuscript in its raw form. My longtime friend Greg Smith always said, "A test is worth a thousand expert opinions" and "Let the customers vote with their dollars," which is what the customers of Hastings Entertainment will be doing this fall.

To John Kuderer, for some of the cool characters you helped me think up on our long road trips, and Jenny McChesney for help on writing the synopsis in a way that drew people's attention to my work.

To Wanda Knippa Polasek (aka Comma Queen) for taking such great interest in my project and helping me with some of the mechanical editing. You have put some serious time into this project and have been a good friend.

To my dear friend Roger Davidson, you have been there from the start, giving me encouragement all along the way. Who knows if I would have made it through the early stages without your support. Misty would not be the character she is without your and Wanda's suggestions.

To my mother for supporting my efforts on this project even though the subject matter is foreign to your generation. Your unwavering support of my lifelong endeavors means more than you will ever know.

To my wife Cathie, you are as gorgeous as the first day I spotted you in my record shop in Corpus Christi, Texas, over thirty years ago. I'm sure you will have fun telling everyone which parts of the BWT books were your ideas! I can never thank you enough for the magnificent job you have done raising our four children, Jack, Michelle, Amy, and Stephen. Your kindergarten students are so fortunate to have such a caring and nurturing teacher.

Finally, to everyone I know who is wondering how a conservative-looking businessman like me could write such a wild, crazy, and fun adventure, like the Black Widow Trainer series. Here's my secret: I tapped into my seventies brain! Just because we grow older doesn't mean the same person you were in your formative years isn't lurking somewhere deep inside of you. I think too often we all let those around us dictate how we should act and who we should be as we grow older. Writing this book makes me feel twenty years old again.

I

1

A Life-Changing Event

Misty watched as the most gorgeous man she'd ever seen walked through the airport terminal, straight toward her. She felt there was nothing she could do to tear her eyes away. Even with her husband, Rob, and their friend Becca there to witness her indiscretion, she stared shamelessly at the stranger. *What a magnificent figure of a man*, she thought as she drank him in with her eyes. He had jet-black hair, light mocha skin, soft brown eyes, and the body of a model moving beneath his stylish suit. He was the most exotic-looking man she'd ever seen. She could only guess at where he came from—in Honolulu airport there was no telling where someone was from or where they were going.

Maybe he's native Hawaiian and part Japanese, she pondered. *Or German-Mongolian?* She went through a series of fantastical racial combinations, each almost fitting the bill, but always coming up short. *Whatever he is, it was God's finest hour the moment he was born.* Time seemed to slow down for her as he walked by. She studied him intently without effort, her every sense tuned to his movements. He smiled youthfully but carried himself with a maturity beyond his years. She found him an instant mix of delightful contradictions that only fed her growing interest.

Once he had passed by her, Misty felt a powerful urge to follow him.

She justified her desire, thinking, *Rob probably won't care. He followed Jennifer Aniston once when she passed us in Caesars Palace, and I didn't get onto him.* But once the stranger was around the corner and out of sight, the spell was broken. She found herself slightly out of breath and more than slightly embarrassed and turned to Becca for cover.

Misty and Rob had recently moved to Captain Cook, Hawaii, for Rob's job as a consultant for the KOA Coffee Plantation. They had kept their house in Malibu, worried that island life might be too isolating—an issue Misty faced shortly after they had arrived. Though beautiful, Captain Cook had only 3,200 residents, and she worried about being able to find enough clients.

As a personal trainer, Misty was highly recommended and carried a large client base at Elite Fitness, where she'd worked for years. Despite how excited she was for the chance to move to Hawaii and have a vacation, it was difficult to avoid thinking about how her practice had almost been to the point where she could have opened her own business. She tried to focus on adjusting to life in the tropics, but Captain Cook, with its combined lack of a good gym, a moderately stocked video store, or even one decent bar, soon wore on her patience. Growing bored and restless after only a few weeks, Misty invited Becca to visit. She then pulled Rob away from his job, convincing him that the three of them should spend time on the beautiful island of Kauai. Rob could only spare one weekend before he had to head back to the Big Island and the plantation in Captain Cook. She and Becca were not about to stop after one weekend and one island. Their next stop was Maui.

Misty checked the departures list above her head. Twenty minutes. "Come on, Becca. We're going to miss our flight if we don't get our butts in gear!" She began charging ahead of them. Then she remembered.

"Oh, Rob! Sorry!" She turned around and gave Rob a hug and a kiss. "Please be careful on your trip home. I'll call you later tonight. And thanks so much for letting us take this side trip. It's really unselfish of you."

Rob gave her a funny look and said jokingly, "Just stay out of trouble in Maui. Remember: you're on a *sightseeing* trip."

"Don't worry, Rob," Becca said, trying to reassure him. "I've got our entire week mapped out. We'll see you back home next weekend."

"Yeah, next weekend," Misty said, looking up and twirling her hair. She broke into a smile. Rob and Becca both laughed.

As she and Becca walked away, Misty turned around to see her husband one last time.

"I'll come back, promise! Love you!"

"Love you, too," he said with a wink.

Misty was just beginning to feel annoyed at loosing rock-paper-scissors with Becca over who got the aisle seat when she felt compelled to look up. She almost jumped when she saw that same ridiculously handsome stranger she'd seen earlier walking gracefully down the aisle. *This can't be happening*, she thought.

As he passed, she stretched her arms above her head, attempting to accidentally brush him with her fingers, but missed by an inch, catching only air. She pulled her arms down and folded her hands in her lap, blushing. *Now that was childish. What in the world has come over me?*

Suddenly, her nostrils filled with the pungent but bold smell emanating from his body. *My God, he smells like pure testosterone!* Excitement rolled through her body, making her shiver. Becca looked at her. "Is everything okay?"

Misty stared blankly at her before replying. "Uh, just a little cold, Becca. Would you mind pointing the air in a different direction?"

If she thought the urge to get up and follow him in the airport was strong, it was nothing compared to the urge she had now. Luckily, she came to her senses and buckled herself in so tightly she thought her legs would go numb. She felt hot, then cold, then hot again. Not only did she wish she hadn't asked Becca to turn the air vents away, she wished every air vent over the surrounding seats was pointed directly at her. She no longer felt in control of her body. It was as if the mere presence of the man had caused her circuits to go haywire.

When the plane landed, Misty asked Becca, "Why don't you get the luggage while I get in line to rent a car?"

"Sounds like a plan. I'll wait for you at the carousel."

Misty felt totally dazzled and barely heard a word Becca said. It had been a long time since she felt such a strong attraction to a man. She tried to reason with her emotions. *This is ridiculous. I'm a married woman. I have no business feeling like this.* Feeling a little more in control, she stepped up to the car rental counter.

Once Misty had the car keys in hand, she thanked the clerk, and then stepped aside so the next person in line could move up to the counter. As she attempted to pull her billfold from her purse, her driver's license slipped through her fingers. As she quickly bent to pick it up, she lost her balance but a pair of strong arms latched onto her before she fell. Awkwardly, she looked up to see who it was. It was *him*! *He was standing behind me in line the whole time.*

"I am so sorry," Misty said as she worked to get back on her feet. "I am such a klutz."

With a soft smile and a confident look, the man apologized. "No, it's my fault. I was trying to get a look at the birth date on your driver's license. Surely you can't be a day over twenty-nine."

What a charmer this guys is! she thought. She had to say something or risk looking stupid.

"Oh, this thing? I need to get it reprinted. Can you believe they messed up my birthday?" Misty wasn't great at being clever but she had to try.

He laughed. "I wouldn't bother. There's something mysterious about not knowing a woman's age."

"Ladies never tell," she replied with a wink.

Misty couldn't believe how easy it was to talk to him, and within minutes after he rented his own vehicle they were laughing and carrying on as if they'd known each other forever. That is until Becca appeared.

"Where have you been?" Becca demanded. "You were supposed to meet me at baggage claim."

She had a rolling suitcase in each hand with carry-ons stacked on top of each and a purse around her neck. A full-bodied woman with flowing red hair, she schlepped toward them, burdened with the rolling luggage. She looked almost comical. When the man shook Becca's hand, she fell under the same spell.

"Oh," she breathed. "Didn't we just see you on the plane?"

"If you just flew in from Honolulu, it's possible."

Much to Misty's surprise and her immense pleasure, Becca asked, "Hey, we're going to be with a group touring Maui until next Saturday. Why don't you join us for cocktails one evening?"

"I would love to. I'll be tied up most of the week, but how does next Friday night sound?"

"That's perfect!" Misty shouted, scrambling in her purse for a pen and paper. "I'll give you my cell number. Just text us that afternoon, and we can decide where to meet." She didn't know why she was so outgoing with this man. Part of her knew it was for Becca, who was single and desperately needed a romantic fling to top off her vacation. Another part of her wanted to see him again, at any cost, and it scared her as much as it thrilled her.

"I hear there are some fun places in Lahaina," Becca added.

"Anywhere will be nice as long as I'm in the presence of two beautiful women. You girls look like you could be a lot of fun. See you Friday." He flashed a smile at them, spun on his heel, and walked away.

Becca stared at him as he disappeared into the crowd.

Misty poked her. "Lahaina my ass. You're just thinking about his haina."

They both broke out laughing until they were almost out of breath, needing the release from the incredible tension they both felt around him.

"Well," Misty said wiping a tear from her eye. "Shall we?"

Friday morning the women left their hotel before sunrise for a sailing tour to Lanai. Once known as Pineapple Island, Lanai was still home to a large pineapple plantation. The history of the plantation had been interesting, the samples were delicious, and they even saw a few dolphins while snorkeling around the coral reef. But all they could think about was their rendezvous with the mysterious, sexy man they had met at the airport.

On the sailboat ride back, horror struck. While checking yet again for a text from Mr. Mysterious, Misty's most prized possession, her iPhone, slipped from her grasp and disappeared into the blue waters below.

Why the hell did I ever take my phone with me on a damn boat trip? If I had only left it in the room! she thought, slapping herself on the forehead.

She felt as if it were she who had sunk to the bottom of the sea, and in some ways Misty wished she had. Tonight they were supposed to meet up with the most handsome stranger on the planet, and now they had no way of receiving his text message. By the time the boat docked it would be too late to try and get a replacement.

"I am so sorry, Becca. I know how much you were looking forward to this evening. Can you ever forgive me?"

Becca seemed visibly upset. "What a crappy way to end our trip, Misty. How could this happen?"

"I know, I know. I'm sorry! We should call this trip 'Disaster in the Pacific: Shame at Sea,'" Misty offered, trying to cheer up Becca.

She couldn't blame Becca for not speaking to her for the next two hours. She didn't feel like talking anyway. Sure, it was disappointing for her, but poor Becca was single and might have had a chance with him. All Misty would miss was the thrill of Becca's score with Mr. Mysterious and some lively conversation. Despite trying to convince herself of this, she felt she was really missing much more.

Once the sailboat docked back in Lahaina, Misty and Becca decided to get a bite to eat and go up to their room. It had been a fun week sight-seeing, but those memories would be overshadowed by the disappoint-ment of their missed adventures.

After returning home to sleepy Captain Cook, they spent the next week trying to get their mysterious stranger, whom they had both started call-ing "The Man," out of their minds. Misty kept telling herself she was a married woman and that dropping her phone overboard had been for the best. Becca, however, took it much harder. She had been robbed of, potentially, the most fantastic chance meeting of her life.

The following Friday Misty headed back to Maui to attend a week-end yoga retreat at the Lancaster Hotel. Rob rarely did yoga anymore because he was so busy with work, and even Becca had backed out of the retreat, claiming that she had a cold. She probably would have sucked it up and gone if it hadn't been for the failures of the previous weekend, but she was feeling too defeated for the mental and physical challenges the trip promised. So off Misty went to Maui alone.

The Power Yoga class she attended late Saturday morning gave her the energy and relaxation she needed to hone her body and cleanse her mind of negative thoughts. When class ended around 3:00 PM she took a shuttle into Lahaina in hopes of finding a new phone. Luck was on her side. She found the newest generation iPhone along with a purple case to protect it from future falls—as long as they weren't over the side of a boat.

With her new phone in hand, Misty bounded off to catch the shuttle back to her hotel. She had decided not to make too friendly with the other class members so that she could spend a relaxing evening cozily tucked in her hotel room. A good book and room service were looking mighty nice. After she got off the bus, her phone began to beep. Startled, she thought, *That was quick.*

The message read: "Where are you guys? Thought I would try 1 more time to hook up with you before I leave Maui tomorrow AM. If you are still in town, let me know. We can all go for drinks. I'm @ the Lancaster Hotel. If you can, meet me in the lobby around 6:30."

No way! He's staying at my hotel! Could this be fate? No, it can't be fate. Becca is supposed to be here with me. I can't meet with him alone.

She sat on a park bench for a spell to think. Suddenly room service and solitude seemed tasteless and lonely. More isolation. She contemplated how stale her marriage with Rob had become. Rob was a good man, but she knew from the start she had only married him because she had felt pressure to get married. By thirty, people get married.

Rob had been a client of hers going through an ugly divorce. Misty felt sorry for him. It was a marriage of convenience, or sympathy, or whatever you want to call it. That, and Rob was head over heels infatuated with her. She told herself she would grow to love him, but now it was clear that he could not make her feel the way she felt at this very moment. To feel so entranced and excitedly nervous over a complete stranger seemed more real than anything she had felt in eight years of marriage. Misty felt guilty but finally decided that maybe there was something to learn from all of this. Tonight she was going to find out what she may have been missing the last eight years of her life. The thought occurred to her, *Maybe I'm just not cut out to be married.*

She looked at her watch. *I need to get it in gear. It's already 4:30, and I have so much to do. What am I going to wear? What am I going to tell Rob and Becca? What am I going to do with my hair?* She ran to the hotel, speaking her thoughts out loud, "At least he's staying at my hotel."

Then it hit her. *He's staying at my hotel!*

She felt her face burn in embarrassment. Here she was about to go running through the door in sweaty yoga clothes. She could pass him in the lobby!

Oh, no. She began to panic. *I never bring anything nice to wear on yoga trips! Okay, calm down and breathe deep. That's it, nice and slow, in and out.*

She used the pool entrance and got into the closest elevator. Once the doors slid shut she got her wits about her and began to laugh. She was acting like a teenager going on her first date.

I'm lucky to have this feeling again, she thought. *I need to savor the moment.* Once inside her room she madly threw off her clothes and dashed into the shower. Out of the shower, she dropped her towel to study her limited wardrobe.

Tonight all the old rules and inhibitions go out the window, she decided. *I am going to be whoever I want, and I'm not going to look back. If I've suppressed these feeling all these years, then I need to find out just who I am and how I feel.*

She guzzled a single-serving bottle of tequila from the minibar to settle her nerves and wondered, *Now where to start?*

She glanced at her body in the mirror. *Oh, yeah.* She looked down at her chest, which was usually masked by a sports bra or covered in layers of workout clothes.

You know what? I've got great boobs. Now there was a thought she hadn't had in quite a long while.

Misty was proud of her physique. Years of exercising had given her a honed, disciplined body that was essential to her success as a personal trainer. Her figure seemed to say, "I can make you look like this."

Dressing from the waist down was no problem. She had brought several nice pairs of shorts and cute sandals. Misty knew she had nice legs and was anxious for The Man to see them. The rest was going to be more of a challenge as she had brought nothing that would show off her cleavage. She had breasts to be envied in her teens and even after the last twenty years they were still a sight to behold. While married to Rob, Misty, for reasons she didn't know, had become accustomed to covering her breasts. She'd forgotten they were assets. *What the hell. It's about time I put these babies to use.*

The change in attitude felt good. She began to laugh. At that moment, laughter became her friend, and she knew it was the only thing that would get her to this meeting with enough sanity to keep from imploding on the spot.

Okay, now for the final decision. She brought out the tank top she usually wore under her workout shirts. It was nothing fancy, but she knew she looked great in lavender. After putting it on, she looked in the mirror.

Oh my, you can make out the shape of my nipples. What if it's freezing in the bar?

He might as well be looking at me without anything on. But then she thought, *Isn't that the idea?*

She gave herself a good look in the mirror and made some final nervous adjustments. Even though she'd thrown this outfit together in a matter of minutes, she liked the way she looked. *Maybe it was the tequila. On to the great unknown!*

When her elevator hit the ground floor and opened wide, Misty looked across the lobby. There he was. She was so relieved he had dressed casually in shorts and a Polo shirt. As she approached she could tell he was giving her the once-over. It was as if he could see right through every stitch of fabric she wore. To her surprise, this excited her the same way his smell had on the airplane. She crossed her fingers behind her back and hoped that everything would be okay.

He met her with a big smile, reassuring her. His salutation was a hug that released every pheromone in Misty's being and sent her floating on air. Time seemed to stop and she felt as if they were the only living souls on the planet. This was quite unlike any meeting she had ever had before. If she could only keep from giggling, she could relax and enjoy the ride.

When they got to their table, Misty began to explain, "I am so sorry we didn't call you last week. You won't believe this, but my phone fell overboard when we were taking a boat ride. I had no way of getting in touch with you. I want you to know I've felt horrible about it all week."

"So that's why I didn't hear from you. Thanks for telling me. I hesitated before sending you the text today. I figured you might not be interested. It makes sense, me being a stranger and all." He smiled, flashing a row of straight, white teeth worthy of a toothpaste commercial. "Speaking of strangers, why don't you tell me about yourself?"

She had to admit, she was flattered that he'd asked about her right away.

"Well, I'm a personal trainer by trade, and I like all types of outdoor activities. I love to travel and see the sites, you know. I've recently moved to Hawaii, and I'm really looking forward to exploring the islands. I'm actually in Maui on a yoga retreat." She explained about the yoga retreat and her life as a personal trainer. As she spoke, she realized that he was listening very attentively. "Other than that, I'm just your average girl," she finished nervously.

His eyes traced her face, hair, and shoulders, and then settled on her eyes. "Oh, I think you are anything but average, Misty." When he realized his compliment made her blush, he quickly added, "So, where is your running mate?"

"Oh, Becca's sick. She couldn't make it back to Maui. I feel bad for her because she wanted to have drinks with you in the worst way."

"That's okay because I wanted to have drinks with *you* in the worst way," he replied.

Misty couldn't stop herself from blushing. Trying to divert the attention away from herself, she said, "Let's talk about you. I don't even know your name. If you had given it to me last week, we might have been able to find you."

The Man paused before saying, "Tonight is not about me. It's about you. I come from a culture that honors and adores women. It's in my blood, but I have never come across anyone quite like you. You are bright and beautiful, but you have something—a fire inside that demands to be let out. I'm never this forward, but tomorrow I leave for home, and I may never come this way again. Tonight is eternity where you and I are concerned, don't you agree?"

Misty nodded.

"We must choose to spend it wisely. If we follow the normal protocol, we will go to dinner and know a little more about each other before we say goodnight. But if you follow me to my room, we can know everything about that fire inside you."

He pushed his chair back, stood up, and offered her his hand. It all happened so fast it caught her off guard. *His room? I can't go to his room! I'm married. I'm not that kind of person. I don't do that kind of thing.*

He didn't waver. He stood there very solidly, looking at her with his soft, knowing eyes. He seemed almost supernatural.

Where did he come from? Oh, what am I going to do?

Something in his words sounded so true that she could not deny them.

I know this is a once-in-a-lifetime opportunity, and if I don't go down this road, I may regret it more than anything, even hurting Rob. This time it has to be about me.

Before Misty could rationalize the situation any further, she felt herself stand up, almost as if she wasn't in control. The next thing she knew, she was reaching out, taking his hand, and following his lead.

2

THE ROOM

Standing at the door to the suite with key in hand, he turned and gave Misty a deep and serious stare. His eyes seemed to penetrate her very soul, calming her. Misty felt the kind of serenity she found during a Kundalini yoga class, peaceful and charged.

He spoke. "I want you to know that I will be your servant tonight, but make no mistake, this is no place for little girls."

Warmth rippled through her body like a small stone dropped into a quiet pond. She told herself on the way up that if she entered the room, there would be no turning back.

Do I jump from the cliff and join the multitude of couples that have fallen to infidelity, or do I watch this opportunity slip from my grasp forever? She already knew the answer.

"I'm a big girl."

When she entered the suite, she was amazed. More of a flat than a suite, it resembled what she imagined a high-rise in the middle of Tokyo or New York would look like. The main room had floor-to-ceiling windows. The doors to the balcony were wide open, displaying the moon's bright reflection on the sea.

It was a gorgeous night in warm Hawaii. A soft breeze stirred her hair. On the beach below, the famous torch-lighting ceremony began. With each torch lit, the view became more enchanting.

Misty breathed slowly. *Everything is so perfect. It's as if he ordered every detail from a menu provided by Mother Nature herself.*

For some reason, the fact that he could afford this suite made him seem like the real deal, not a cheat who was going to trick or rob her. Nevertheless, she started to panic, and her old insecurities began to surface. *When he makes his move how will I respond? Will he think I'm pretty?*

She had not touched anyone passionately besides Rob in over eight years, and she suddenly felt like she had forgotten how. As if he read her thoughts, The Man walked over to her, took both of her hands, and looked her squarely in the eyes.

"I want you to know that there is nothing for you to do tonight except follow my lead. I will listen to your body. No desire will go unanswered in my hands."

Misty sank into his arms. "Yes," she breathed. Then, only loud enough for the breeze to hear, "This might just be heaven."

Misty felt her breasts press against his well-developed chest while his fingers sensuously massaged the back of her neck and head, releasing her tension. Euphorically she mused, *This is ridiculous. I don't even know his name.* She wanted to express her pleasure, but words clearly could not capture her feelings. Finally, she looked into his eyes. "I put my complete trust in you tonight. Do with me as you wish."

Did I really just say that?

He took her hand and led her into the bedroom, escorting her to the bed and whispering, "There is nothing for you to plan or figure out. Simply lie down and enjoy."

As soon as Misty's back sank into the mattress, it was as if the world melted away. She followed his will from that moment on.

Hawaiian orchid–scented candles perfumed the air as their flames flickered across the walls of the room. She recognized a Sade CD playing softly in the background. She felt his strong, knowing hands slip under her back as he knelt over her. It was obvious that it was not the first time he had taken a woman this way. With surprising strength he lifted her, arching her back, leaving the ends of her blonde hair to dangle on the sheets.

His eyes seemed to look deep into her, reading her cells, her blood, as it pulsed through her body. Misty didn't know what was next, but she felt ready for anything. His warm hands explored her body, memorizing and massaging it.

Pausing his caresses, he reached under the bed and pulled out something that looked like a wand.

So that's how he cast his spell over me.

Of course, deep down, she knew the spell was cast the moment she laid eyes on him, she couldn't help wondering about what was in his hand. The wand had a flat, round surface on the end and was solid, yet looked soft to the touch. Misty had never seen one before. Well, not one like this.

Next he began to gently slide her shorts down her legs and over her feet. She was so glad she had thrown in a pair of black lacy panties. He sat down next to her and placed the flat surface of the wand over her panties where the lace became intricate and concealing. It conveniently encompassed her entire area. When he flipped the switch the wand leaped into action and let out a low, deep rumble. A heavy vibrating sensation rippled through every inch of her. At first it relaxed her, but just when she began to think this was an ordinary pleasure device, the first wave struck. A warm flush of shivers, of moist excitement, moving up her body. She'd only ever felt this from touching herself. The machine, in his hands, was able to accomplish in one minute what took her five and a lot more effort.

Misty had always wished men understood that women take much longer to get going, but, once they do, they can keep going and going like the Energizer Bunny. Her life, hell, the world, would be much better if this simple fact was understood. The days of wham-bam-thank-you-ma'am were well over. They had never begun as far as Misty was concerned. Men would be better served to listen to women's bodies and deliver. From all indications, he was in touch with this reality, and he would be capable of fulfilling all her dreams.

The waves began to come more frequently, and each new wave became more and more intense. Misty couldn't help but arch her back and raise her pelvis with every crash. And then, tsunami.

Misty fought the urge to scream in ecstasy. She'd never been a screamer, having always been too embarrassed, and now, in her attempts to hold it in, she breathed harder and harder. As the tidal wave ended she thought, *Now, that was worth the price of admission.*

Now that the first set of waves was over, his warm hands took hers, one after the other, and placed them on the wand without breaking its spell. Once in control, her hands came alive with the power of the marvelous tool. Just as Misty wondered why he placed the machine in her hands, she realized: it freed his.

He began sliding his hands under her shirt and up her ribs. His hands, placed fully on her body, made her blood simmer. She dropped the wand and raised her arms above her head, arching her back and lying fully exposed. The breasts that had all the boys drooling in college were now at the whim of his desires. Simply feeling the heat cast by his body as it leaned over hers set her nipples tingling as if he were already tonguing them. Her breasts hadn't felt so titillated since her first boyfriend, James, caressed her for the first time behind the stadium during the homecoming game.

Misty quickly glanced up and found his eyes glimmering, fixated on her glowing breasts and rosy nipples. She felt him break concentration for only a second. They were still capable of making men weak in the knees.

Why have I covered myself up all these years?

With her hands back on the wand, she found him lying on his side quietly watching her two beautiful mounds moving in rhythm to the rise and fall of her breath. With new confidence, she enjoyed him watching while she continued to master the wand.

She became so immersed in the new waves of pleasure she was creating that, for a while, she didn't realize he had moved his mouth into position to give full attention to her breasts. Man, was he good. He worked his lips around them gently, making suckling sounds in his wake. He then took the soft flesh in his mouth, tasting her. His tongue found its way around her sensitive areola and finally up to the nipple that waited full and ripe for his mouth.

When he sensed the right moment, he delicately began tugging one of Misty's nipples with his lips and the other with his left hand. And then it happened. Pressure. Release. Waves and waves of energy exploding over her and away.

He backed off and gave her time to enjoy a short respite. She thought, *It's about time my conditioning is put to good use.*

As her nipples became too sensitive he shifted his focus from her breasts to her mouth and kissed her, softly biting her lips. A moment of reality interrupted Misty's out-of-body experience. He would be flying out tomorrow, and she would never see him again. She dismissed this thought, refocused on the present, and passionately kissed him while leaving the pleasure wand wedged between her thighs to roam her mound unattended. Their kissing intensified the waves.

She climbed higher and higher on her stairway to heaven, and when she reached the top, she released a moan from the center of her being. Her record of three climaxes had just been tied, but never before had they been so intense. Her animal instincts were in charge. If he had slowed or stopped she would have taken him against his will.

While trying to control her breathing after the last orgasm, she wondered, *What could he possibly have in store for me now?*

He rose on his knees over her, stripping bare in quick, graceful movements. At that moment she realized that all three incredible orgasms had been accomplished with his clothes on. *What can he accomplish with his clothes off?*

As he crouched there on the bed in the moonlight, Misty's heart skipped a beat. Now it was coming back to her, why she had been so struck by him in the first place. His body was perfect in every way. Silky brown skin, perfect shape and proportion, and a flawless six-pack. When he freed his manhood from his tight briefs she let out a whimper. "Oh my . . ."

Misty had been with several guys before Rob, but she had never seen anyone hung like this man. She worried whether she was capable of accommodating him. *I guess we'll just have to cross that bridge when we come to it.*

In answer to her fear, he retrieved a small bottle of lubricant from the nightstand. First he gently rubbed the lubricant in his own hands to warm it before spreading it softly over both of her breasts simultaneously. He gently opened her right hand, briefly interlocking fingers with her before peeling away and leaving her open hand to receive drops from the bottle. Surprisingly, she knew exactly what to do with it. She held the wand with her left hand while polishing his male unit with her right. He grew even harder, firming like a rod of hot, polished marble in her hand. Gently exploring the tool that would soon be deep inside her was more stimulating than Misty could have ever imagined. She fantasized about the act to come while continuing to work the wand. She felt each new orgasm gradually working its way up the Richter scale and knew the best was yet to come.

He positioned himself and Misty knew the moment had arrived, but he was so large! Again he was quick to pick up on her angst. He looked into Misty's eyes, giving her a tender smile. At that moment she trusted that everything would be okay.

He moved onto his back alongside her and propped his head on a pillow. He gave her a slight grin and reached out to her. Misty could tell that he wanted her on top. She arched her hips to slide her panties down her legs and toss them off at her feet. Finally free, she rose to straddle him. Above him, she leaned forward and kissed him and said, "I trust you. Now it's my turn to please you."

He placed his powerful hands under her, supporting her careful descent onto his pulsing penis. The process was very gentle at first. Every time he took new territory, he helped her up to prepare for the next descent. It was a process of communication and trust she had never experienced with a man. Entirely inside her, he felt warm, solid, and thick.

Misty began to slide up and down faster and faster, arching her hips and feeling every bit of him from the tip to the base. There was no need for him to hold her up anymore. He was free to fill his hands with her breasts. Hungry for more, he pushed against the bed with his heels, sitting up and pulling them both backward until his back was against the headboard, so he could bend forward and reach her breasts with his mouth. As he did this he moved deeper inside her than she thought possible. She had heard about a woman's G-spot but never knew exactly where it was inside her. But, seated atop him, with both of them moving together against the headboard, they soon found it.

He went on for an eternity, rhythmically driving himself into her to the wild rotating of her hips.

How could this man have so much stamina? she thought just as she felt she would go mad from his steady pounding. Then something happened that she had never experienced before. Not madness, something more definite, and serious. His steady pumping created an intense pressure inside her that demanded release. He sensed what was happening, and just as Misty felt she was so wet and tight he would be pushed out, he braced himself against the bed and masterfully arched himself into her, deeper than ever. It hit her like a shock wave. In seconds she began quivering uncontrollably as every nerve in her body came alive. She screamed, "Yesss!" Her scream was loud and long for all the years she had been silent. It was an orgasm of fiction, of dreams, and it left her feeling as if she had lost a part of herself. Her legs felt heavy and light at the same time, like she was floating but also sinking.

All these years with Rob she had thought she had some kind of physical issue, but not anymore. Misty crumpled onto his chest and lay motionless, listening to her steadying breath. Before she passed into a deep sleep she mused, *I've just been to the moon and back.*

The moon faded and the sun broke as he lay by her side taking in the grandeur of her shape, her strong body and silky blonde hair lying over her peaceful face. He reached over and gently stroked her hair.

Misty woke to a knock on the door.

"Is anyone in there?" the maid yelled.

Misty gasped. It was time to check out of the hotel, and she wasn't even in her own room. She looked around. He was gone. There was a gift-wrapped box at her side. Misty quickly got dressed and ran past the startled maid toward her room. There, she pulled out her suitcase and hastily flung in all her belongings. Walking down to checkout, still wearing his scent, it was as if the world shone in a different light.

When the flight took off from Kahului airport, Misty stared out her window into the sea. She was sad she would never see him again. She was nervous and confused and alone. Still, she felt alive. Her senses were charged. She reached into her carry-on for the unopened box that had greeted her that morning. Inside was the wand that had awakened her body. She bit her bottom lip painfully to suppress grinning and laughing out loud. Luckily her seatmate didn't see the gift. There was also a note tucked into the box.

Misty,

I will always worship and adore you from afar. I am leaving this present in my absence to look over your every need. Men must learn that if they want women to inspire them, they must treat them as goddesses. I believe that every woman is put on Earth to help make it a better planet. Through love we can work together to make Mother Earth a better place. If a man made love to a woman every night, he would have little time to think of destroying or dominating. Thank you for teaching me last night.

Misty reflected on what he had written. After a few minutes she thought, *Whatever, I just hope this thing doesn't take some fancy-ass batteries that have to be ordered from Japan. If so, I better order a year's supply.* And with that she turned her head and fell into a deep, deep sleep.

3

NOW WHAT?

When Misty got off the plane in Kailua Kona, Rob and Becca were waiting to drive her home. She was anxious about being cooped up with them for ninety minutes. She had never been a good liar, and worried she would slip up and say something incriminating or, worse yet, come clean and put her marriage in jeopardy.

"Hey guys!" She yelled as she walked into the luggage area. "Becca, you look like you're feeling much better."

"I am. I had a nice, relaxing weekend. Caught up on some reading. How was your trip?"

"It was great. The classes were wonderful, and I had a quiet Saturday night in my room. A little alone time was all I needed."

"Ha!" Becca snorted. "I find it hard to believe that you of all people would spend a Saturday night quietly. Come on, spill the beans. Did you go out dancing? Walk on the moonlit beach?" She grinned mischievously. Misty began to feel nauseous. This is what she was afraid of, having to make up a lie on the spot that could come back to haunt her. Misty knew she had a new glow about her since last night, and she also knew she wouldn't be able to hide it from her best friend.

"Oh, I think I see my bag," Misty said and walked quickly towards the carousel.

She grabbed a bag that looked similar to hers and then set it back on the belt. She looked back at Rob and Becca and shrugged and then turned back to the rotating baggage. She shifted nervously on her heels and tapped her foot.

Oh my gosh, she thought. *I haven't felt this way since sneaking out to hang out with boys in high school. I swore I would never put myself in this situation again, but here I am!*

She caught a glimpse of her bag and quickly grabbed it and walked past Rob and Becca, motioning for them to follow her out the door. Once in the car, Misty took charge of the conversation. "Rob, what are your plans for next week?"

"I guess I'm going to take a few days off and spend it with you and Becca since Becca is returning to the States."

"What? You're going back to the States, Becca? But I thought you were going to explore Hawaii with me."

Becca looked down. "I'm sorry, Misty. I just got the e-mail Saturday. I got a great job offer in San Diego. It's just too good to pass up. I hope you aren't mad at me."

"No, Becca, I'm not mad. I mean, I'm surprised, I guess. I thought we had this all planned out."

"Sorry, Misty. I—"

"No, don't be sorry. You got a job! That's great, right? I told you you'd find something you wanted. Really, it's great!" Secretly, Misty was relieved that she would have one less person to lie to.

On the one hand, she felt that her life was spiraling a little out of control. She had a lot to think about: her marriage, what she was doing in Hawaii, who she was now that she had cheated on her husband. On the other hand, this would give her time alone with Rob to work through their marriage issues. It was not something she was looking forward to.

During the remainder of the trip home the conversation centered on Becca's new job. Misty was glad for the diversion, which took the focus away from her weekend trip. It was a struggle staying engaged in the conversation because her mind kept drifting back to the night before. She knew that there would be a price to pay for her infidelity.

She struggled with her thoughts until she rationalized her choice, convincing herself that she had not made an egregious mistake: *What is done is done. I can't change anything that happened nor do I think I would if I could. If I were truly in love with Rob, I would have resisted the temptation. Rob is a good and caring man, but I just don't seem to be madly in love with him. Who knows why we are attracted to some people and not others.*

I should have never agreed to marry him in the first place. I knew he loved me deeply. I guess I didn't want to hurt him. I should have known better. I feel bad about it, but I guess I just don't have it in me to be committed.

Arriving at this conclusion made her feel both better and worse. Deep in her mind, she knew she was tuned in and turned on for the first time in her life and that she had better drink in the freedom while it was still in the glass. But all the same, it was not an opportunity she was entirely comfortable with.

4

Just the Two of Them

Misty tried to hold it together over the next three months, but it was difficult. She settled into Captain Cook, established a routine, and tried to live normally. One night, while listening to some soft jazz and drinking a glass of wine in the living room, she realized that her feelings weren't going to change. Putting off a discussion with Rob was not the answer. She'd had a lot of time to think and figure out what was right for her, and she had decided that it was better to say something now than cause more pain in the future. She set down her wine glass, took in a deep breath, and exhaled. "Rob, I think we need to talk."

Rob looked up from the newspaper he was reading. "Okay, what is it you would like to talk about?"

Misty began her prepared speech. "I'm not sure I can handle living in Hawaii much longer. I really miss my job in Malibu. When you talked me into coming with you, I was supposed to be traveling around the islands with Becca, but now that she's gone, I don't have much to do. The last three months have been pretty lonely."

"I didn't know she would leave so early, Misty. I thought she would stay much longer."

"I know you did. I'm not blaming you or Becca. Best laid plans, you know? But the fact remains, she is gone, and I'm homesick."

"So, are you telling me you want to go back now?"

"Yes, I guess I am."

Rob was startled and hurt, but he was more concerned that he might be making Misty do something that she truly didn't want to do. He reasoned silently that asking her to stay would not help their relationship, so he acquiesced.

"Well, I guess we would only be apart five months. I can do that for you."

Things were going better than Misty expected, so she mustered up some more courage.

"Rob, there is something else I need to tell you, and I'm afraid it will hurt. I've been carrying it around with me for months now, and I need to come clean." Then she bowed her head in shame. "I had an affair in Maui the weekend I was there for my yoga retreat."

She sat nervously awaiting Rob's reaction, her breathing shallow. After about a minute, she raised her head. He was staring into space. Rob's most endearing quality was his ability to be so damn calm and rational in the face of adversity. She had little doubt that, although Rob was probably sick to his stomach, he was thinking logically, step by step, trying to get a handle on what this confession meant.

When he had run through every possible scenario, he said, "Okay, I can only assume it was a one-night stand, as I can't imagine who you would know in Maui."

"Yes, it *was* only a one-night stand."

He nodded and sighed. "I guess I can't say I'm all that surprised. I think I've known for a long time that, although we get along, you have never been in love with me the way I am with you. I probably shouldn't have pushed you so hard to marry me, but I couldn't help myself. I guess I just became addicted to you, wanted to be with you. I *still* do. You know that I do love you very much."

Misty's heart melted. She hurried with her response, wanting to get it over with. "I know this is hard for you, and believe me, it is difficult telling you this. The last thing I want to do is hurt you, but as much as I've tried, I'm unable to love you the same way you love me." It was the most honest she'd ever been with anyone, and it felt great. She walked over and sat in Rob's lap.

"So, what are you proposing, Misty?"

"I'll go back to our house in Malibu, resume training whichever clients are still available, and then we can figure out what to do when you return home. I am not asking you for a divorce right now—I'm not sure I even want that—but this is something we will have to deal with when you return. Of course, you have every right to ask me for a divorce after what I have done to our marriage."

After another few minutes of thinking, he replied, "Yes, I suppose this is the next logical step. If we can't find common ground when I return, I won't refuse you a divorce. Just promise me we will leave the lawyers out of this. I can't lose you completely. I would like to leave the door open for you to still be my friend if that's okay with you." He smiled. "A light on, so to speak."

Misty held him tight. "I would love nothing more than to be friends, Rob. That's what we do best. Listen, I want you to know that I feel really terrible about, you know, Maui. I don't deserve you being so calm about this. I would almost feel better if you'd throw some dishes or something. You have every right to hate me."

"Just let me know when you want to leave, and I will get my company to make the arrangements," he said with a weary smile, his eyes wet. "I do have every right to hate you and I am very disappointed in your actions. But at the same time I can't bear the thought of losing you. I'm going to need time to think this through." Rob left the house without saying where he was going. Misty assumed he wanted to grieve in private.

Misty cried herself to sleep that night in their bed. It wasn't a complete mystery why she had married Rob. He was one of the nicest men she had ever known—and she was hurting him.

5

Back to the Gym

It was a gorgeous summer day when Misty walked through the front door of Elite Fitness. The center was situated across from a beautiful beach. She had always loved that the facility was mostly open air. You could work out and gaze at the waves coming in under the sunset, not to mention scope out the beautiful Californian hunks surfing. Being back in familiar surroundings gave a bounce to her step, but her heart was still a little heavy over her marriage. She was anxious to cheer up by seeing some of her fellow trainers at the club.

Fellow workers and clients alike knew Misty as the top trainer at the health club, the one who made all the other toned bodies seem so—ordinary. Yet she was so approachable and so generous with a smile. Years of exercise had given Misty a honed, disciplined physique. Her body whispered, "I can make you look like this."

Heather was the first to greet her. "Hey, Misty! How are you girl? I thought you were in Hawaii."

"I was, but I'm back now. How's my fellow Minnesotan, eh?"

"Knock off the accent. In Cali you're supposed to sound like a Valley Girl. So, like, when did you get back?"

Misty laughed. "A few days ago. Just got lonely for my old friends and clients."

"Well, I can tell you your clients missed you, too. Ted's been moping around here like a lost kitten ever since you left, and Liz keeps asking about you." Heather flashed a bright smile past Misty at someone walking their way. "Look who's home, Wanda!"

Wanda lit up when she recognized Misty and came running to give her a hug. "Oh, I can't believe it's you! When did you get here?"

Before Misty could answer, Heather said, "A few days ago. Didn't you know she was coming?" Heather winked at her before adding, "I did."

Misty rolled her eyes. "Oh, stop it, Heather. I didn't tell anyone."

She looked around the club. "Hey, is that the new dance instructor? I remember talking to him right before I left."

"Sure is," Heather replied. "Hey, Ben, can you come over here?"

Ben was not only a talented dancer and choreographer, but also a world-class charmer. Dark hair, boyish looks, and a body like a wound spring. All the rich, older women made sure they signed up for dance lessons with him.

When Ben walked up, Heather asked, "Ben, do you remember Misty?"

His eyes lit up. "Hell, yeah! How could I forget the most beautiful woman at Elite Fitness?" Misty smiled, and she quickly shot the girls a glance. Those sorts of comments were sweet but sometimes hard to believe. Wanda and Heather were both gorgeous, and Misty had always felt a little inferior to them. Since The Man, however, she felt she had a special energy about her that others could sense. In the distance, over by the elliptical, she spied. "If you guys would excuse me, I need to talk to Miguel," Misty said, pardoning herself from the group and walking over to visit with her old friend. She had taken Miguel under her wing when he joined the club as a very shy twenty-two-year-old. He had always appreciated her support and had grown very fond of her.

"Hey, Miguel. How's my baby brother doing?"

"Misty!" Miguel shouted as he ran to give her a big bear hug. "I am so happy to see you. I can't believe you're back. Let's get together for dinner and catch up."

"I'd like that, Miguel. Won't Sylvia mind?" she teased.

With a grin, he responded, "No, Sylvia won't mind. She knows how fond I am of older women."

"Watch it, kiddo. I'm not that old. Okay, how about tonight? No one knew I was coming back, so I don't have any plans."

"Perfect!" he replied. "Tonight it is. I'll let Sylvia know."

"Bring her along if you like."

"No way, it's just you and me tonight."

After Misty had made her rounds at the club, she began calling her clients to let them know she was back. To her surprise they had either not hired new personal trainers or quickly insisted they would dump the new hires to reunite with her. That was exactly what she wanted to hear. By next week, everything would be back to normal—almost.

6

Back in the Fast Lane

Though happy to be home, Misty was preoccupied with Rob. They
would talk from time to time on the phone, and she could tell he
was hurting. But she kept telling herself that she was doing what was
best for her *and* Rob, and it made her feel strong in her decision. She
found refuge at the club each day by immersing herself in her job. Nights
were tough though. She had trouble sleeping, tossing and turning until
3:00 AM sometimes. Misty knew she would never get any peace until Rob
came home and they settled things, one way or another.

Six weeks before Rob was scheduled to return, Misty took on a new
client. Eddie was in his early sixties and very attractive in a distinguished
way that only men who have truly lived can be. He owned companies
all over the world and had spent considerable amounts of time in all the
places Misty wished she could go. As Eddie's workouts continued, she
became intrigued by his maturity and his experience. She looked forward to each session, finding relief from her emotional turmoil in the
presence of his wisdom.

One early morning session, Eddie was imparting some insight
learned from Theravada monks in Thailand when Misty interrupted
him. "I wish I had my life together as much as you do."

"What are you struggling with, Misty?"

She was relieved at how quickly and easily he jumped into the conversation with her, ready to listen. At first she felt embarrassed and vulnerable, but then considered that he might be the right person to talk to.

"I'm sorry, Eddie. I'm not the type of person to burden anyone else with my problems."

Eddie didn't let her off so easily. He stood up and gave her a warm sideways hug. "Believe me, I do want to know what's bothering you. It's no burden at all. Why don't we sit and have a chat at the end of our session."

After the session, she filled him in on everything that had taken place between her and Rob, leaving out her indiscretion. When she was finished, she looked at her very kind new friend and sighed. "So things are really quite a mess, don't you think?"

Eddie softly shook his head. "No, Misty. Do you think you are the first person to ever have doubts about why they got married? Don't beat yourself up. I know it's very stressful right now but hang in there. Life is a series of ups and downs, highs and lows. The higher the highs the lower the lows. You are full of life, so I would venture to guess your highs are way up there. Just be honest with yourself about your feelings. Embrace this period in your life and follow your heart. You obviously have a lot of empathy for Rob, and I'm sure he can feel it. Whatever happens when Rob gets home, just deal with it as maturely as possible, and above all, be honest with him. You owe him that. In the end, things will work out, and you will move on with your life with or without him. Such is life."

Eddie's words made her feel grounded in her decision and in her life direction. She knew that she had come to the right person for advice, but she felt she owed it to him to let him in on her darkest secret, the real trouble that made her feel so bad.

"I hear what you are saying, but maybe you'll feel differently after I add one more piece to the puzzle." Misty could tell her remark didn't seem to faze Eddie so she plowed ahead. "I was unfaithful. I had an affair when I went on a weekend trip to Maui. Now what do you think of me?"

Eddie never blinked as he said, "Affairs happen the world over. In some cultures men have mistresses on the side, and their wives are fine with it, as long as it remains discreet."

Eddie stopped to judge her mood before finishing. "Look, I'm not telling you that you shouldn't feel bad. I'm not telling you what's right or wrong. Everyone has their own moral compass they abide by, but, the way I see it, you have two choices. You can force yourself to stay with Rob the rest of your life out of duty or shame, or you can decide to deal honestly and openly with your feelings, possibly resulting in divorce. Only you can make that decision, Misty, but the sooner you deal with it, the sooner you will lose that ache in your heart and those bags under your eyes."

"I don't have any bags under my eyes."

Eddie laughed. "No, you have beautiful eyes, Misty."

After thanking him with a hug, Misty ran to the restroom to make sure she did not in fact have bags under her eyes. She was relieved to see that Eddie had, indeed, been pulling her leg.

While training Eddie one day in late October, Misty looked up to find Rob standing just inside the club entrance, looking a little lost. She looked to Eddie for help.

"Oh, I can't believe it. Rob just walked through the door. He wasn't supposed to get here until tonight. What should I do?"

He laughed and said, "That's easy. Go hug your husband."

She smiled and said, "I will just be a minute," and walked to the entrance.

Giving Rob a hug was easier than she expected. It even felt good to hug him.

"What a surprise! I thought you weren't arriving until tonight. What happened?"

"I decided to catch an earlier flight. I was going to call but decided to surprise you instead. Guess it worked."

"Yes, definitely. It's good to see you," she replied giving him another hug. She had not seen him in three months, the longest amount of time she had spent alone since they were married. Even though she was relieved to see him, she could tell that she had grown apart from him and more into herself, and it felt good.

"Look, I don't want to interfere with your session, but I've been thinking things over all the way home, and there is something I would like to run by you. When you get finished with your client, can we take a walk along the beach?"

"Sure, Rob. I'm with my last client of the day. I'll be done in half an hour, and we can go on a walk."

When Misty returned to the training floor, Eddie asked, "So, what did he say?"

"He said he's been thinking about things and wants me to walk with him after your session."

"Very well. Looks like all you need to do is hear him out and follow your feelings. Good luck."

At the end of their session, Eddie stretched his sore muscles and smiled. "Okay, you can run along to your husband now. Chin up, young lady. I'll see you in a couple of days."

She patted him on the shoulder. "Thanks, Eddie. I'll fill you in next time I see you."

As Rob and Misty walked along the beach they made small talk about their lives over the last several months. The sun was shining but the wind was cool. Rob knew how cold Misty got on days like this so he gave her his sweater. Coming upon a bench, he asked her to sit down so he could tell her what was on his mind. After getting comfortable, Rob began.

"Misty, I'm having a hard time coming to grips with us separating. I realize you're not madly in love with me, but I'd like to think you feel comfortable around me. On my flight home, I came up with a proposition for you. This may sound odd, but it's something I would like you to seriously consider. Will you promise to give it some thought?"

"Sure, I promise."

"I propose that if we can stay together, I will give you all the freedom you need. This includes sleeping with other men from time to time as long as it's only a fling. I know this sounds strange, but I really believe I can handle it. I promise I will never ask you whether you have been with anyone else and would prefer that you not volunteer the information. I'm hoping that a policy of don't ask, don't tell might work." When he was finished, Rob regarded her soberly.

Misty was taken aback. *Eddie said I would only have two options, not three.* Rob was known, even revered in some circles, for being a very logical person, but there was no way she could have expected this from him.

Five minutes passed in silence while Misty tried to envision the future he had proposed. As she tried to be like him and think logically through his proposition, she couldn't help but wonder why she was unable to be more committed to him.

Rob was an attractive man. He was a little short at five feet ten, but he was charming in an honest way. He had dark brown hair, a handsome face, and wore his prep school–style well. Rob was not powerfully built, but he kept himself in fine condition, always attracting a few glances from other women at parties and galas.

Of course, Misty thought, *the problem isn't Rob at all—it's me.*

She began to consider that she was not like other women who had always dreamed about getting married and having children. She had never been able to become totally committed to anyone or anything. She shuddered in the cold ocean breeze and pondered, *I wonder what's wrong with me?* Misty's ears picked up the sound of nearby waves, hoping they would sweep her mind clear of any negative feelings she might be harboring toward Rob.

Looking up at him, she said, "Okay, go on."

"Misty, I guess what I'm trying to tell you is that I don't want to own you. I just want to be by your side."

She was touched and reached out to hold his hand. It was warm. After some careful thought she replied, "Are you sure this is what you want?"

Rob said, tentatively, "Yes, I think so. It's at least worth a try, don't you think? If it doesn't work out, I guess we can always get a divorce later down the road." His voice trailed off.

Maybe I should give it a try, she thought. *I enjoy Rob's company, love his cooking, and I'm not fond of living alone.*

"Okay, we can give it a try if you promise one thing. If I can have a fling, it's only fair that you can as well. I'm not saying you have to, just that you have the option. I will abide by the same don't ask, don't tell rules as you. Is it a deal?"

Rob grinned and said, "I hadn't thought about that part, but what's fair is fair."

Misty smiled and said, "Well, you'll be a free agent tomorrow, but tonight I want you to pretend I'm your girlfriend and have your way with me. It's been a long three months without you in my bed."

"I hoped you would say that, Misty. Let's go home."

7

A S t a r I s B o r n

Misty was in an excellent mood when Eddie showed up for his next session. She started him on the stationary bike so they could talk. "So, things went well between you and Rob?"

"Yes, things are good, but Rob surprised me with a third option."

"Really? That's exciting! Come on, fill me in."

As Eddie pedaled, Misty told him about her walk with Rob, her feelings on commitment, and her decision to give Rob's proposition a try. When she finished, Eddie seemed pleased with her progress, but he kept his thoughts to himself.

Moving to the bench press, Eddie said, "Misty, I've been meaning to tell you that I will be heading to Zurich on business in a few weeks. I'll be gone for three full months. You've done a fantastic job over the last few months, and I'd really hate to cut the training off now."

She laughed. "So you want me to leave Rob and go to Zurich with you? Oh sure, I'll do it!"

"Okay, let's start doing some planning." Eddie was nodding, his face earnest.

"You're joking, right? I mean, Zurich, Switzerland! You want me to go with you halfway across the world? Yeah, right."

"No, I'm serious. And to prove it, I'll pay you handsomely. Go home tonight and make a list of what it would take to get you to go, and don't be bashful."

As Misty coached Eddie through a series of free weight exercises, she went over his plan. *He can't be serious*, she thought. *But he really looks serious. This is crazy. Or is it? Rob said I was free to do as I pleased. If he really meant it, he would have to agree to let me go. What if Eddie is just putting me on?*

During his cool-down stretching, Misty looked at Eddie and said, "Okay. I'll come up with a list of my demands over the weekend and bring them to you Monday."

"That's terrific!" he responded. "Just remember: don't be bashful. It's a lot to ask of you. Come up with something that will really surprise me."

Sunday afternoon while Rob went out for a run, Misty sat down at the kitchen table with pen and tablet.

Okay, Eddie boy, she thought, *I'll make out a list of demands that is so absurd there's no way you'll accept.* She started writing. "First demand: You must put me up in the nicest hotel in the city and provide a car and driver. Second: I will only conduct three workout sessions a week for no more than two hours at a time. After that, I can do as I please. Third: I am to get paid $5,000 a session and will only stay for thirty-six sessions or, in other words, three months."

She sat back and laughed out loud.

This will teach him for making such an outrageous offer. Switzerland? Ha!

Just when she was getting ready to put down her pen, Misty had another thought.

Why don't I really surprise Eddie?

She wrote, "As an added bonus, I will allow you to sleep with me once, but only once. If you can hold out until the end, we will get in all thirty-six training sessions. However, if you can't, I reserve the right to be paid in full the moment we consummate the deal, and return home early pocketing the entire $180,000."

She began laughing so hard that tears welled up in her eyes.

Even if he agreed to these ridiculous terms, there's no way he could hold out. Trying to catch her breath after a solid minute of laughter, she thought, *I can't wait to see Eddie's face when I present him with these terms. He'll think twice before he offers up anything like that again!*

Monday morning Misty couldn't wait for Eddie to show up. She thought about getting Wanda to hide in the corner and take his picture as he read her demands, but decided that would be a little over the top. When he did show up, Misty ushered him into a trainer's office, almost pushing him along.

"Okay Eddie, just remember, you said not to be bashful."

He took the document and turned straight to the signature page.

"Before I read your contract, you need to sign it."

"What? You want *me* to sign it?"

"Most certainly. That's how business is conducted. If I agree to the terms, I sign it and we have a deal."

Misty felt flustered and her face began to turn red.

This guy can't be serious, she thought. *I just said I'd sleep with him in that contract. If I sign it, I'm committed, and then I may need to be committed! Not that I would mind sleeping with Eddie, but a contract?*

Misty looked down at the floor, and shifted her weight from side to side.

Oh, what the hell. I don't have anything to worry about. No one pays $180,000 for one night, right? There is no way he will sign it.

With renewed confidence, she looked him square in the face.

"All right. Let me find a pen." She opened several of the drawers in the desk before finding one that worked.

She signed and handed Eddie the contract. "Okay, here's the pen. Now read it and let me see your John Hancock."

If Wanda had been there with a camera, she would have captured a priceless reaction on Misty's face when Eddie grabbed the contract and signed without even reading it!

He capped the pen and said, "Look, I've got a lot to do before we leave on Friday. I know I'm on a roll workout-wise, but let's scratch the other two sessions this week and get in three solid months of training in Zurich. I will send a courier with a copy of the contract later today. She will have all of your travel arrangements including hotel accommodations. I assume you asked for someplace nice to stay. If not, don't worry. I assure you it will be first class because, as the kids now say, 'that's just how I roll.' You are going to love Zurich this time of year. Hopefully there will be plenty of snow!"

And with that, Eddie walked out the door.

Misty was in shock. What was she supposed to do now? How would she tell Rob? What would she tell the management at Elite Fitness after having just returned to work?

"Oh my," she sighed. "What am I going to tell my clients?"

She wanted to get away from all of it suddenly. Of course, that was the problem. She was about to "get away" to Zurich, Switzerland.

Okay, what would Rob do? she wondered, trying to piece things together.

Watching him solve problems all these years had often been frustrating because his logical thinking was slower, more methodical. Yet here she was in a real fix that required some logical thinking. She had two hours before her next scheduled client, enough time, she hoped, to sort things out she hoped. For privacy, she went into the women's locker room, took off all her clothes, wrapped herself in a towel, and hid in the corner of the steam room.

At first she panicked over the trouble she had just gotten herself into. But after many minutes of grueling internal conflict, and just before she couldn't take the heat any longer, Misty relaxed, engulfed in a serene calm.

This might be my calling. Why am I so worked up? I'm going to Zurich with an attractive, wealthy man. Rob has offered me freedom, and I can make $180,000 for three months' work. I feel like I drew the luckiest hand in the world.

Later that night, Misty and Rob sat at their kitchen table eating saffron risotto with braised chicken that Rob had cooked. She told him the whole story.

"Yes, I know it's bizarre, but it really happened."

"But what do you know about him, Misty? I know I said to do as you please, but are you sure you can trust him?"

"Well, I think so. Heather's parents know Eddie and they have only the highest regard for him. They say he's wealthy beyond belief. What could possibly happen?"

"I don't know. He could try to take advantage of you or something."

Misty had not told Rob the entire story.

"No, Rob. I'm quite sure Eddie won't try to take advantage because—" As hard as she tried to say the words they didn't seem to be coming out of her mouth.

"Because?" Rob asked. "Because what, Misty?"

"Because in the contract it says that he can sleep with me. But, only once!"

There, she said it.

"You said he could *sleep* with you?"

"Yes, but that's as far as we're going with this. It's more like a one-night stand."

Rob felt the consequences of the offer he had made her. However, he really wanted to stand by their arrangement. Misty had clearly been happier since they had each agreed to do as they pleased, or at least, as she pleased. It was obvious that he had no choice but to go along.

"Okay, Misty. You've got me. I have no right to stop you, but just promise me you will take a personal bodyguard with you. I want to make sure things never get out of hand. It's one thing for a man to agree to a one-and-done, but, trust me, you are one very attractive woman, and he may try to keep you there. And Please . . . You're making plenty of money. Please take a friend with you, someone you trust."

"*We're* making a lot of money, honey. Remember, we are still married and what's mine is yours."

"So, does that make me your pimp?" he said too easily, too quickly.

The moment the words left his mouth, he knew he had made a mistake. Misty's face became red. Rob had clearly lashed out at his wife, and he felt all the worse for it. He rushed over to her side and held her.

"I am so sorry, love. I was just making a joke. I swear I didn't mean anything by it."

His attentions soothed her, made her feel supported in her decision. She admitted she saw the absurd humor in his comment and the direction their lives were going. Now was not the time to go ballistic. Rob had given her permission; she was clear to go. But who was she going to ask to be her bodyguard?

8

OH MIGUEL

Misty was restless most of the night, trying to figure out how to handle the situation. She desperately wanted to appease Rob as this was his only request, and he had made it out of concern for her well-being. As the sun broke through the curtains of their bedroom she knew whom she would ask to accompany her to Switzerland. He was someone who knew how to handle himself and who was a naturally great guy, and she enjoyed being around him.

When Miguel sat down at the table with Misty for lunch the next afternoon, she smiled but did not return his greeting. Finally, he said, "So what's up, *mi hermana*? You want me to take out someone who's hitting on you? No, that can't be it. The list would probably include a hundred guys." Amused at himself, he started to laugh. But the laughter quickly subsided when he saw that she was not laughing.

"Miguel, how long have we been working together?"

"Oh, probably eight years. Why?"

"Have I been good to you over those years?"

"Yeah, of course. You've been wonderful. I probably wouldn't have this job if you hadn't covered for me my first year. You taught me most of what I know. I was rough around the edges back then; growing up on the streets of South Central L.A. isn't exactly charm school, you know."

"Well, I'm going to reward you for all your hard work and ask you a favor at the same time. But first, I need to fill you in on some pretty crazy stuff."

"You know you can count on me." Miguel nodded seriously.

She told Miguel about the changes in her relationship with Rob and withheld no details about her contract with Eddie. Miguel ran his hands through his hair. She grinned and started to regret telling him so much. The boy she had practically helped raise, who thought the world of her, seeing her like this? Maybe she was making a mistake.

"Are you kidding me? You're offering me an all-expense-paid vacation to Zurich, Switzerland, and you're going to pay me as well? All I've got to do is take down anyone who gets out of line with you? It's a no brainer. I'm in."

They smiled at each other for a moment. A look of understanding passed between them. She realized that Miguel would never judge her. She had been too kind to him all these years for him not to help protect her.

Misty breathed a sigh of relief. "Well, you know, you'd have to tell all your clients, the club, everyone right away." Misty wanted Miguel to understand the seriousness of this agreement. "We're leaving Friday. Is it too short notice?"

"Hey, I said I'm in."

"Thank you so much, Miguel! I can't tell you how relieved I am. You are the only one I want to take with me. How will Sylvia handle it?"

"Don't worry. I'll handle it delicately. Trust me—I will be there for you. Just e-mail me the travel arrangements, and give me a ride to the airport."

"It's a deal."

On-board the plane to Zurich, Misty checked her iPhone one last time before takeoff. The only message was an e-mail from Eddie.

> *I finally read your contract and was pleased with every demand. What creativity! Reading your one time offer reminded me of something. One of my favorite creations of Mother Nature is a deadly spider known for weaving complex webs to trap her prey. She waits patiently at the edge of her trap. Small, beautiful, and powerful, she lies still until her prey has worked himself into exhaustion trying to escape, and only then does she finish him off with a single bite, a kiss of her venom. This spider is, of course, the black widow. And now, here I am, walking into your web. Will you deal with me like the spider with her prey, or will you let me struggle free?*

> *Godspeed to Zurich,*
> *Eddie*

II

9

Two Years Later

The morning sun broke through the clouds, spilling across the room. Misty flinched and then very slowly opened one eye. She stretched and rubbed her eyes until reality sank in. This was it. The moment she knew would come no matter how much she wished it could be delayed: the morning after. Poor Kieran lay next to her enjoying a deep sleep. Misty knew he was going to take her departure hard, but they always did.

Two years had passed since Zurich. Eddie had been so fabulous to her, and through the experience had become a mentor. He had helped her define the parameters of her new profession, and they had worked on rules that would keep her organized and safe in her job.

"Your first rule," Eddie had advised, "is to make sure you are attracted to the client before you agree to a contract. Don't agree to a client just because they live in a part of the world you want to see! Once you accept, you must never back out. If you do, your reputation will be ruined. You will never again be able to charge top dollar. Now, this is especially important: Have a background check run on each of them. That even goes for clients I send you. Your safety is the most important thing."

"That's it?" Misty had replied.

"Yes, that and work hard as a trainer. Harder than ever. Take it more seriously than before. It's important your clients feel good about themselves when the contract ends. You're selling a fantasy. You must take it very seriously to make it real for them. For a fantasy, those who can afford it will pay anything."

Eddie referred her first two clients, who taught her that, along with fantasy, they wanted challenge. She provided both. At present, no one—not even Eddie—had been disciplined enough to make it the entire three months without sleeping with her. And more than one still sent her gifts and pleas for an extended relationship.

They all want trophy wives, Misty thought as she turned to greet the stirring Kieran. He finally opened his eyes and rolled onto his side.

"Hey, Misty girl. Last night was terrific. It was everything I imagined it would be."

Gently, Misty replied, "Last night was wonderful for me as well, Kieran. You are quite a lover."

When he left the bed for the bathroom, she pulled on a robe and prepared to break the news to him. She was impressed with Kieran. He had held out for a little over two months, which was longer than any of her previous seven clients. She grew intimate with each of them, and they each felt they had what it took to make Misty forget her own life and stay with them longer. She knew Kieran would be no different. A famous Irish footballer with plenty of women at his beck and call, Kieran was used to getting what he wanted, and from every indication, he wanted Misty.

Once he settled back in bed, she took a deep breath.

"Kieran, it's time for me to go home."

"Aw, Misty, I have a beautiful day planned for us. What do you mean going off already?"

This was never easy. She liked him. She liked the last one and the one before. But she was committed only to her freedom.

"Kieran, you knew what our deal was when you signed the contract. I am your trainer until you sleep with me, and then I go home. Personally, I had hoped you would wait until the last day, but you chose otherwise and that was your prerogative."

His face rearranged. The hangdog look faded, his brow furrowed, and his mouth tightened. The look frightened Misty. She gave the wall three hard knocks and waited until she heard a knock at the front door. Kieran was wise to what had just taken place and looked even less pleased. The contract stipulated that when Misty spent the night with a client, always in a fine hotel, Miguel would stay in the room next door.

She scooped up her bag and moved toward the door. Kieran lurched forward to grab her arm with the speed and strength that had made him famous. She pried her arm from his grip and dashed out the door. She brushed past Miguel, who was already standing in the hallway outside Kieran's room, and walked briskly toward the elevator.

Miguel could tell from the look in Misty's eyes and the red mark on her forearm that it was time to earn his keep. With the toughest look he could muster, cultivated from growing up in South Central L.A., he turned to face Kieran, who was now standing in the doorway to the room. The two had become pals over the last two months, but there was no longer a trace of friendship in their eyes. They stared at each other for five long seconds before Miguel saw Kieran coming to his senses. Miguel's glare softened to a sympathetic smile. The standoff was over.

Miguel said, "Sorry, bro. Look me up if you're ever in Malibu."

10

REST AND RELAXATION

Misty peered out the window as the Los Angeles–bound plane took off from Dublin Airport. She was still learning so much from each job that she needed time to readjust to normal home life once a session ended. There was no way of predicting how attached she would become to any given client. All she knew for sure was that each time she went through the process, it took its toll. Kieran had been a lot of fun, charming and a terrific lover, but now she was ready for some time to decompress and recharge. She was also ready to catch up with Rob. Misty found that with her freedom came a deeper appreciation of her partner. That's how she and Rob saw each other these days, not as married, but as partners.

The plane was well over the Atlantic when Misty finished her bagel with cream cheese. She thought maybe now would be a good time to take some Ambien to help her relax. To prevent snoring and her fear of having a little drool roll down the side of her mouth, she only took enough to take the edge off. She was sure Miguel would be happy to be on his own for the next six hours or so.

When Misty finally came down the escalator to baggage claim in L.A., she saw Rob waiting for her. She was pleased. He looked like he had been taking good care of himself while she was away.

"Oh, Rob, I'm so happy to see you. How have you been?"

"I'm doing fine. How were your flights?"

"They were okay. I was exhausted, so I spent as much time sleeping as I could."

Tired as she was, Misty couldn't help wondering if Rob was actively seeing anyone but knew asking was not an option. As they picked up her luggage Misty thought, *Soon I will be home in my own bed.* What a wonderful thought.

On the way home Rob said, "I took the liberty of booking a week in Napa Valley at a quaint bed-and-breakfast. I hope you don't mind."

"Mind? That sounds wonderful!"

Nestled in the verdant Napa Valley and shaded by ancient redwoods, the inn was absolutely dreamy. Misty loved the English Tudor style of the inn. Its white and brown colors juxtaposed with the deep green and red of the trees reminded her of Ireland. They took a late-night swim in the hotel's beautiful backyard pool surrounded by redwoods and giant cedars. Wine tasting by day turned out to be a great aphrodisiac. One afternoon they passed a deserted old barn, pulled off the road, and explored the building and each other. They were closer than ever. Although they admired couples who could remain faithful, they felt they had customized their relationship in a way that worked best for them. Over dinner that evening they began to discuss the typical marriage.

"Rob, I know our marriage is a little different than most, but why do you think people feel like they own one another once they get married?"

"I'm not sure. Maybe they are insecure, or they fear losing their partners."

Misty puzzled over this for a moment.

"Well, maybe we are developing a model that people can follow after their kids are raised and gone. People grow throughout their lives. What guarantees both people will grow in the same direction? They don't always have the same wants and needs, so why not loosen the strings so each of them are free to experience life in the way they choose? Nothing would stop them from being together, but is it really necessary to be together all the time and know exactly where the other is at all times? You would think time spent apart would only make the time spent together that much more enjoyable."

"Well I have to admit it seems to be working out so far."

Misty and Rob were beginning to realize that the freedom they gave each other had its advantages. Instead of their marriage getting stale, their reunions were becoming more like the dates they went on before getting married.

She continued, "I keep reading that the divorce rate in this country has skyrocketed in the last few decades, and that doesn't even count the marriages that stay together 'just because.' *Just because* covers a lot of ground.

"You know, Misty, you're right. I think sometimes we lose sight of the fact that we are all individuals. We don't come out of the womb in pairs that are destined to be mates for life. We need to respect each other as individuals."

Misty added, "Maybe 'until death do us part' is actually the problem, not the solution. When you take that attitude, don't you lose the incentive to prove your love and dedication to your spouse on a daily basis? Maybe the marriage vow should read: 'We take this vow and promise to bear children if we so choose. We pledge to respect one another as individuals, so that we may live each life to the fullest.' Something simple like that, something that leaves room for creativity and customization."

Rob countered, "But this requires people to master their feelings of jealousy, and that is a tough thing to do. I have to admit, I'm still working on that one. Jealousy is very powerful and should not be underestimated."

"So you *are* still a bit jealous?"

"You know you would be disappointed if I wasn't, Misty."

"Yes, you're probably right. When are you going to give me something to be jealous of?"

"Hey now, you're not allowed to ask me that per the agreement, remember? You sound like a grandmother who can't wait for her kid to give her a grandchild."

"You're too funny. Can I have a bite of your lobster?"

The summer was coming to an end and Rob was readying to leave for a consulting job in New York City. It was just as well. The change of seasons always gave Misty the itch to hit the road again.

Okay, she thought, *I'll start going through all of the new applications so I can decide who to train next.*

She laughed to herself. *Maybe I should get a Black Widow outfit made and wear it when I'm going through the applications, like Batman preparing to go to battle with the Joker. Nah, it would be more fun as Cat Woman.*

As her reputation grew, she received more and more applications, which together created a portrait of her client base. From the Ivy League pedigrees on their resumes to their tailored suits to the exotic locations in which they were photographed, her clients were among the most rich and powerful players in the world.

She preferred to work with single men as wives often complicated the arrangement. But then, married men did have their advantages. Wives gave her more leverage, ensuring the husbands behaved. Any misstep could cost them half of their considerable fortunes. The more they were worth, the more they had to lose, so Misty usually made sure they were worth plenty. Plus, married men were less likely to fall so hard for her.

Other things came into play in her selection, like what country the applicant lived in and whether it appealed to Misty. The amount of outdoor recreation available was important to her. The client's physical attractiveness was a factor, but she always balanced that with personality. It was tricky, though. Misty insisted they send her a video explaining why they would like for her to be their trainer. This was helpful but not perfect. Actors were easier as she could rent some of their recent films and get a pretty good feel for their personality, but then again they were acting, so this method was not perfect either. Misty finally came to realize there was no perfect system for choosing the next client, but that was okay because it added a bit of uncertainty. That in its own right made the next adventure more exciting.

After several days reviewing applications, Misty realized that she kept returning to a man who lived in Denver, Colorado. He was not one of the super-rich applicants, but maybe it was time for a change. A consultant, he was always on the go, taking jobs all over the world. Maybe it was the fact that Peter lived his life somewhat like Misty was living hers that attracted her. Maybe it was the fact that he was a big guy, standing a little over six feet four and weighing a muscular 225. Maybe it was because he was single. Misty couldn't help wondering if a man that size could measure up to The Man in Maui where it counted. She had become spoiled that night and had been disappointed that none of her clients came close to matching up to his size. Misty laughed every time she heard the Aerosmith song lyrics "my big ten inch . . ." Until she met The Man, she thought that the possibility of such a length was a total myth.

After careful deliberation, Misty finally decided. She'd start in two months. With a goal on the horizon, her restless energy became focused, and she was able to enjoy the rest of her time at home.

11

MISTY MEETS THE BIG GUY

While researching upscale health clubs in Denver, Misty found one that offered all of the weight and cardio equipment she preferred that was conveniently close to Takayama Park. Running with clients was more fun than watching them on a treadmill. But her primary motivation for choosing this club was its extensive offering of group classes. If the instructors were good, she might pick up some new training techniques to add to her repertoire. The club's day spa was icing on the cake.

Since she only spent about six hours a week training her clients, she would have plenty of free time to enjoy Denver and hike in the Rockies. She looked forward to being in the fresh air, surrounded by natural beauty.

Misty and Miguel typically flew in one or two days in advance to get the lay of the land and prepare for her first session. Another rule made habit was to take her new client to dinner after the first class so they could immediately begin to develop a rapport. Because Peter struck her as a down-to-earth kind of guy, she figured a casual place might be nice. The club manager recommended a nearby bar and grill.

It was ten minutes past 5:00, and Peter had still not arrived. Misty would find he had a propensity for showing up late. He was the sort of person who tried to squeeze everything he could into each day and hated having to wait for anyone else. Of course this meant everyone else had to wait for him. At 5:15, in walked Peter. His balding hair was clipped closely, a style that to Misty suggested a high level of confidence. He had a swagger in his walk as if he didn't have a care in the world, and Misty thought she heard him whistling softly. His clear blue eyes were engaging as he met her with a grin.

"Sorry I'm late, but don't worry—I'm a hard worker and I'll always stay a little longer to make sure we accomplish our goals."

Misty shook his hand and smiled. "We're on your dime, big fella. Show up as late as you like."

Peter's face went expressionless, making her a little uneasy, but then he broke into a thunderous laugh. "Now I know I made a wise decision hiring you as my trainer, Misty. It's obvious you're not going to take any crap from me. I need someone to hold my feet to the fire. Look, I've been serious about keeping fit all of my life. Now that I'm in my mid-fifties it's becoming a little more difficult, and I need an edge. You're going to be my edge, so promise me you won't ease up. You *do* have a whip, don't you?"

"Oh, I've got a whip, big guy. Just be careful what you ask for."

True to his word, Peter worked dutifully during the first training session. He took every challenge she threw at him. Misty was not accustomed to her clients being in such good shape going into the first session, nor was she used to his level of stamina. Unless the client was a professional athlete like Kieran, they usually lived a life of overindulgence and wanted Misty to help them lose weight and get in shape. Peter was really going to be fun.

At the end of the first session she said, "Go hit the showers, big guy. You did a fantastic job today. As a reward, I'd like to treat you to dinner."

"Sounds great, Misty."

Once seated at the bar and grill, Misty looked around at the billiards and burger-joint kitsch, all the different kinds of people—blue hair, college students, businesspeople, and barflies. It was a good place to get acquainted. The menu was typical pub fair with lots of appetizers, sand-wiches, and burgers.

"Okay, you're allowed to splurge tonight. Have as much unhealthy food as you want. I heard the burgers here are the best. But starting tomorrow, I'm putting you on a strict diet."

"Hey, my diet's already pretty healthy, but you're the boss. I better get in the habit of doing what you say."

"Indeed," Misty agreed.

Peter greeted the waitress.

"Yes, ma'am. I'll have one of those double meat burgers, please, with everything on it but the kitchen sink. And the biggest basket of fries you serve. No, go ahead and make it two burgers, but bring the second one out five minutes after the first so it's hot and juicy."

The waitress raised an eyebrow.

"That a boy, Peter. Next session we're going to work off all four thousand of those calories."

While Peter ate, his eyes explored Misty's face, her high cheekbones, and almond-shaped hazel eyes. He noticed she wore very little makeup, and had skin that boasted good health; it blushed easily and was lightly sunned. She was an open book yet a total mystery.

"So, have you had enough to eat Peter?"

He wiped his chin with two fingers, and then picked up his napkin and chuckled. "Yeah, I think I might hibernate through the winter now."

"Excellent. Let's go so you can get some rest."

Over the weekend Misty and Miguel took a daylong drive through the Rocky Mountains. Their limo driver, Billy, was very knowledgeable about the towns they drove through, having grown up in the area. Misty gazed out the window as Billy pointed out the best slopes, hotels, and con-dos. The leaves were changing on the mountains, and ski season was right around the corner. Billy parked at a popular hiking trail, and the three of them began walking in the crisp air. Misty could feel her breathing become a little more labored as they made their ascent to higher elevations.

She looked at Miguel and said, "I guess when you start your hike at an elevation of two miles, it's only reasonable that it will get more difficult to breathe the higher you go!"

Billy said, "That's why other teams hate to play the Denver Broncos at home. When you don't train in high altitude it can be very difficult to make it through an entire game. If you look at the visitor's bench during the fourth quarter, it looks like an emphysema ward. There are oxygen tanks lined up behind the benches and the first thing the players do when they come off the field is strap a mask on to breathe in pure oxygen."

Misty laughed at the thought of hulking football players gasping in oxygen from little masks. On their way back down the mountain she asked Miguel, "What did you think about the Beaver Creek area?"

"I loved it. Is that where you want to set up base for ski weekends?" Miguel replied.

"Yes. Would you start booking accommodations throughout the fall and make some reservations at the restaurants Billy recommended in both Beaver Creek and Vale?"

"I'm on it, Misty."

⌀

For the next two months Misty had a wonderful time. Peter was getting in excellent shape, and she was skiing nearly every weekend.

After Thanksgiving Misty said to him, "We've been working hard for quite a while now, and you're looking terrific. Why don't we take a break and go skiing? You know, I've been going to Beaver Creek on the weekends. I thought you might enjoy making the trip with me this time."

"Oh, yeah, Beaver Creek. Great place. It's been a while for me. That sounds like fun, but I've got a good friend coming into town this weekend."

"No problemo. Bring him along."

"All right then, skiing it shall be. I have to warn you, Cody and I can get a little carried away talking sometimes. I'd hate for you to feel left out."

"Well, I won't if you include me." She gave him a look. "I like to talk, too, Peter. Anyway, it sounds like a lot of fun."

Misty decided it wasn't necessary for Miguel to accompany them so she sent him home to spend the weekend with Sylvia. She knew that Miguel realized he had a good life working with her. She paid him generously, and he got to see the world. Plus, they regarded each other as family, and they had fun together. Still, Misty knew it was difficult for him to be apart from Sylvia so frequently and for such long periods of time. Last year she had kept him away from Sylvia for a total of nine months. Miguel had told her that he had planned to ask Sylvia to marry him the fall before Misty asked him to go to Zurich. Misty doubted that either Sylvia or Miguel would want to continue spending so much time apart, especially once Miguel did decide to propose. She assumed it was only a matter of time before he would stop working with her to be with Sylvia.

12

PETER AND CODY

As they pulled up to their hotel, Misty felt like she was coming home. She had come so often the bellmen knew her by name. She preferred the deluxe suite and had managed to lock in the exact same room every weekend in December. The room had a beautiful view overlooking the ski slope. Peter and Cody decided to share a larger suite that had two separate bedrooms.

Well, I guess Peter won't be making his move this weekend. She felt a combination of disappointment and relief wrapped into one. There was nothing like the feel of a man against her skin, especially one with a raw, primal side, like Peter. When Misty had held Peter's hand earlier that week when he helped her out of the car, she felt a current running between them that had activated something in her. She figured Peter was smart and was waiting for the last day of his contract, which was fine because she was in no hurry to administer her black widow sting and scurry home. But the anticipation of being with him was somewhat maddening.

The next morning they met for coffee and sat at a table facing the slopes. A cold front had blown through, leaving more than a foot of fresh snow behind. The wind was still and the sky was clear and sunny. Peter and Cody were excited even though they were not exactly veteran skiers.

Cody drank his coffee and stared out at the slopes. Suddenly, he frowned.

"Crap! Look at how steep that hill is on the left. If there is one thing I'm certain of, it's that you will never see me coming down that slope."

"So, are you just a big wimp, Cody?" Misty teased.

"No, Misty, I'm a little wimp."

Peter added, "We don't want to slow you down, Misty. Why don't you go ahead, without us. We'll be fine."

Misty was reluctant but said, "Okay, you guys brave the mountain on your own, and I'll meet up with you at the end of the day." She took her skis down from the stand and headed toward the lift, bound for the black diamond slopes.

While waiting for the lift, Ian approached her. He was German and worked for the ski patrol. He had introduced himself to her at the top of a black diamond slope and they had chatted for a while as he provided a few pointers for handling the tricky moguls that dotted the mountainside. Since then, they had met on the slopes a few times. Ian had ropey chestnut hair that he pulled back into a handsome mess of a ponytail. His features were rugged and sun worn.

"Misty! Vhere vere you over zhe veekend?"

"Oh, I stayed here—I just decided to hit the slopes over in Vale. Good to see you, Ian!" Misty smiled. "You want to go down this one with me?" She gestured to the slope.

"Yes, of course! Zhat and so much more, Misty." She pushed off with her poles and flew down, but Ian quickly caught up to her.

While Misty and Ian tore up the black trails, Peter and Cody piddled around on the green trails. Each time the boys spotted a good-looking woman they tried to keep up with her, but to no avail. They just didn't have the skills. Later that day they ran into Misty at the intersection of the green and black trails.

"You poor guys. You look like fish out of water!" She laughed. "I'm sorry, Peter. It's just, you live in Denver, so I thought . . ."

"I know! Don't rub it in."

"I'll give you some lessons if you like."

"I would like that."

Cody chimed in, "Well, it better be soon. Peter, didn't you say Misty's only here for one more week?"

"That's right," Misty said as she and Peter locked eyes. "Well, why don't you follow me down? I know a shortcut to the hotel."

Misty slowly led the boys through the slopes until they ended up at the top of the same hill Cody said he would never traverse.

Cody took one look at the steep drop and then glared at Misty. "I rue the day I met you, girl."

Misty flashed a winning smile.

"Girl? I think you're the one acting like a girl. And a little girl at that."

"Last one down is a rotten egg!" Misty called out, and took off down the hill, laughing.

Cody looked at Peter.

"That girl is trouble. Let's figure out how to get off this mountain before she kills us."

They discussed going back but they would have had to sidestep their way up a long run. Peter got the brilliant idea of taking his skies off and trying to walk down the tree line along the side of the hill. It would have worked but the recent snow was far too soft and they became buried up to the waist as soon as they stepped off the packed snow of the skiing lanes. Cody had a better idea. "Follow me buddy, I've got a plan, but don't forget to say a prayer first."

Peter watched as he attached his poles to his skis and sent them down the hill on their own all the way past Misty.

"What in hell are you doing, Cody?" Peter yelled.

Cody looked at him with a big grin and proceeded to dive head first over the ledge, gliding on his belly down the hill and yelling "Geronimo!"

Waiting at the bottom, Misty looked up at the sound of the yell. When she caught a glimpse of Cody, her eyes widened.

Oh no, he isn't, she thought. *Maybe I shouldn't have played this trick on them.*

Cody blazed down the mountainside with his arms wide as he tried to balance himself. Misty looked away in slight panic when she realized he was about to merge with other skiers who were coming down the east slope. Trying to catch him was out of the question as Cody would have flattened her. She yelled to warn the oncoming skiers, but it was too late. Cody blew through the skiers, miraculously without injury, and then plowed into the barricade.

Misty scrambled toward him.

"Oh my God! Here, let me help you up."

Cody smiled and said sarcastically, "Thanks for all the help, Misty!"

"You scared the hell out of me!" she gasped. "It's much safer to just ski down. You would have made it. Okay, from here, it's not that far down."

They were interrupted by a bellowing "Whoop!" from the top of the hill and then, "Geronimo!"

Peter was plunging toward them. Misty shrieked. He was about forty-five pounds heavier than Cody and would certainly not make it down unscathed.

"Misty!" Ian was calling to her. "Move out of zhe vay!" Some of the patrollers were quickly forming a human barricade to protect the other skiers. Misty imagined Peter slamming into the patrollers, and she squeezed her eyes shut.

Peter's wailing ended in an "Oof!" as he slammed into the hay bale barricades. When Misty opened her eyes hay was strewn everywhere. After a moment, Peter pulled his head out of the snow and gave them a shit-eating grin. Cody let out a screaming laugh and lumbered over to help. Misty's terror turned to jubilation when she saw that Peter was unhurt. She started laughing as the two show-offs performed a victory dance in the snow.

Peter cried, "Man, that was fun. Let's do it again!" just as Ian skied up. "No, I don't sink so guys. You almost viped out half our guests!" He was peeved until Misty explained it was all her fault.

"Misty, are zhese fellows viz you?"

Misty nodded sheepishly. Ian let Peter and Cody go with a warning. The men limped back to their room with Misty, laughing and apologizing profusely the whole way.

At seven o'clock they reconvened at the hotel's fire pit to go out to dinner. They had reservations at Eli's Cabin, high up on the side of the mountain, which they would reach by a horse-drawn sleigh. The moon lit the clear night, making the sleigh ride truly memorable.

When they walked through the door of the cabin restaurant, Misty was delighted. It was beautiful inside. There was a raging fire in the fireplace, and the room was cozy and romantic, aglow with soft lighting. The dinner was fabulous as the new friends laughed and joked about what had transpired that day.

On their descent down the mountain Peter said, "Well, how about a *digestif* at Antlers Hall?"

Although Misty had been toying with the idea of tracking down Ian, she didn't want to miss hanging out with these two. "Okay, boys. Let's do it. I wouldn't miss it for the world."

13

AN ENLIGHTENING EXPERIENCE

The hotel bar was warm and inviting. They removed their jackets and settled into a trio of overstuffed leather chairs by the fireplace. The lighting was low and the smell of the burning wood was soothing and nostalgic. Peter told the server to put aside three bottles of 2003 cabernet sauvignon. When the wine arrived and the sommelier poured a taste, Peter swirled it in his glass and held it up to the firelight to peer through the lines the wine left on the inside of the glass. He brought the glass to his nose, inhaled deeply, and then tasted the wine. He closed his eyes sensually and mused, "A hint of chestnut maybe?"

"Okay, you can stop showing off now," said Cody.

Peter laughed and hastily took another sip of wine, as if he didn't actually care how it tasted.

Cody said, "Let's discuss why people have affairs."

Misty sensed her ears burning. Even though she felt secure in her arrangement with Rob and in every way enjoyed her life of one-night stands, she felt exposed to the two men before her. They were really no more than strangers. She knew it was best to say nothing so she waited for Cody to continue.

"Okay, guys, I've read about five articles on this subject, and what's amazing—"

"Five articles? Is there something you'd like to tell us, Cody?" Peter said.

"What's amazing," Cody continued, giving Peter a hard look, "is they all say pretty much the same thing. Affairs are not necessarily done by bad people or always indicative of bad relationships. Most people never intend to wind up in an affair. Things just happen. The stat that blew my mind was that at least one partner in 80 percent of marriages has had an affair. These days, it's as much women as men."

Misty couldn't resist interrupting him here. "Perhaps it's always been as much women as men, and only now do women feel it's okay to admit to it."

Peter raised his eyebrows. Cody sighed, having been interrupted yet again.

"Stop ganging up on me, okay? So, I figure that anyone who makes it to the grave without breaking their vows should probably receive a medal of honor."

"I wouldn't go that far. Maybe a silver star," Misty said.

Peter joined the conversation. "What do you think the biggest reasons are for having an affair?" He was looking directly at Misty.

"How about boredom?" she said, looking back at him. "The need to prove one's attractiveness, or possibly the search for a sense of power?"

"I think that, for a guy, it can be as easy as plain lust," Peter continued. "Men aren't as complicated as women. They can be passionate and passion can turn into lust. What more do you need?"

"Bravo, Peter," Cody chimed in. "Spoken like a card-carrying member of the Y-chromosome family."

"It's possible that many people are locked into a traditional concept of intercourse and relationships that might not actually work for them," Misty said. "Perhaps they may like diversification and find doing it the same way—or with the same person—night in and night out a little boring. Affairs have nothing to do with love. They're about sex."

Peter thought for a moment and said, "You know, you're right. The way I see it, no one has much control over their sexual desires. They just bubble up from the lower stem of the brain that houses our most primal urges."

Cody laughed while saying, "Like lizards. Right, lizard brain?"

"Cody, you can get back on topic now and leave my anatomy alone."

"All right," Cody replied. "What role does love play?"

Misty took the lead on this one. "None. I remember from my undergraduate course in human psychology that love is nothing more than a chemical reaction, just like lust. Consuming large amounts of chocolate or," Misty gestured with her glass, "a few good glasses of red wine, makes you feel the same way."

"So being in love is really like being on drugs?" Peter asked.

"I guess," Cody replied. "In that case, we're all addicts."

Misty shook her head and rolled her eyes. "You're a nut Cody."

"Here's something else for us to think about," Cody said. "What role does jealousy play in a relationship, and is it good or bad for the relationship?"

Misty responded, "Maybe a little jealousy is a good thing, as it shows you are still interested in your mate."

"That's exactly what I read in a psychology magazine the last time I was in the doctor's office," Cody replied.

"Getting your head shrunk, friend?"

Cody acted like he hadn't heard Peter. "I guess a little jealousy could go a long way toward increasing one's desirability in the eyes of your mate and possibly bringing a spark back into the relationship."

"That's positive thinking if I ever heard it," Peter said.

"I was trying to make a point." Cody sounded defeated.

Misty yawned, and then smiled at them. "This is really interesting stuff, but I'm afraid I'm ready for bed. How about we hit the sack, guys?"

Cody gave Misty a smile, but before he could get the words out of his mouth, Misty said, "I'm sleeping alone, little man."

Misty lay in her bed that night thinking about the agreement she had with Rob and if it were really possible for it to go on.

14

THE VISITOR

Bang, bang, bang! Misty woke from her deep sleep and sat up.

What was that? she thought while trying to become a little more coherent. There it was again. *Someone's knocking on my door. Why did I let Miguel go home? I wish he was next door right now.*

"Who is it?" she asked hesitantly.

"It's me, Peter. Can I come in?"

"Peter, why would you want to come to my room in the middle of the night?"

"You know why, Misty."

Once it sank in, she felt a wave of excitement.

She fumbled with the locks. When she finally got the door open, Peter was standing there in his long pajamas, his clear blue eyes gleaming.

"So, you want to call in your favor, do you?" Misty asked. "I had pretty much given up on you this weekend."

"You should know by now never to give up on me."

"Well you know, big guy, a girl learns something new every day doesn't she?" She paused. "So, what else are you going to teach me?"

Peter looked her over from top to bottom. She felt his gaze burning her skin, studying her naked body beneath her see-through nightgown.

It made her wet. This time it was Misty who held out her hand and waited for Peter to take it. Instead, Peter stepped in to close the space between them. He bent down slightly and slid his right forearm underneath the curve of her buttocks. Peter lifted Misty up until they were eye to eye, wrapping his left arm around the small of her back. With their eyes locked, Misty felt his warm breath on her face. She leaned forward and enveloped his mouth with hers.

Their kissing became hot and heavy. She reached up to hold his head steady in an attempt to dominate.

Peter pulled back and said, "This isn't the gym, Misty. I'm the teacher tonight."

"We'll see about that," Misty said airily between kisses.

Peter carried her across the room and tossed her backward onto the bed. Misty bounced twice before coming to rest. She stood up on the bed to square with Peter, who pulled off his shirt, revealing his well-defined upper body. She saw that a balding head didn't mean you couldn't have a full chest of hair. It was light brown and curly and looked soft to the touch. She wanted to rub her hands through it.

"My God, you look powerful," Misty murmured. "I'd better lie here and be a good girl."

In response, Peter laid his body over hers. Misty was pinned beneath her massive pupil. His body was a hot fire on a cold night. The heat made Misty lubricate until her wetness seeped out and ran down onto the sheets. He kissed her ravenously and she returned, equally hungry. She wrapped her lips around his tongue and proceeded to suck and lick, a sample of what she could offer his more sensitive parts.

Misty pulled her knees up to her chest, grazing his flanks with her soft inner thighs until she could grab his waistband with her toes. She pushed it down below his butt and felt Peter's penis pulsing hotly on her belly.

The tip of his throbbing tool dripped his fluid onto her chest and swam up between her breasts. She looked down and saw it pushing up on her nightgown.

All of a sudden she felt trapped beneath this hulk of a man. When she found it hard to breath, she panicked as someone claustrophobic would do.

Wanting to be back in control, she said, "Let me up, Peter." As she struggled underneath him, Peter countered, "So who's in control now?"

Pursing her lips Misty responded, "Get off me right now, you oversized gorilla!"

"Okay, I'll get off you, Misty," Peter said coolly.

He rolled over and stood at the side of her bed, pulling up his pajama pants, and then putting his top back on. Misty lay there in bewilderment.

"What the fuck are you doing, Peter?"

"I'm going back to my room."

"You're what? Why in the world would you do that? Just because I called you an oversized gorilla?"

Peter leaned down and gave Misty a warm and sensuous kiss, drinking her in. "I just came to give you a taste."

Misty was livid but wouldn't give Peter the satisfaction of knowing he had gotten to her. "Okay, little boy. Go back to your room with your buddy, Cody. I'm sleepy now, anyway."

She was still furious after he left and only slept with the reassurance that she would get him back in the week to come. When he came for her again, she'd make him beg for it.

Back in Denver, Misty and Peter continued their last few training sessions. There was some tension between them, but Misty made sure not to be too caustic. On Friday, she waited awhile for Peter to show up for the final training session. She was hoping this would be the day that Peter would complete their final rendezvous. But time came and went and Peter never showed. Just as Misty was packing her things to leave, the club manager walked over to her.

"Misty, I just received this from Peter with instructions to give it to you."

Misty took the printout from his hand.

Misty, I am so sorry. I have an emergency and have to leave right away. Please forgive me, Peter.

"Is everything okay, Misty?"

Misty realized she was frowning. "Sure, I just have a little headache is all. Thanks so much for delivering this."

Once outside she stamped her foot, clenched her teeth, and then said aloud, "That's it? I've got an emergency and I had to leave? Fuck! I don't believe this guy!"

She decided there was only one thing left to do—pack her bags and head back to Malibu.

15

GOOD GRIEF

Misty made it home for Christmas. Her dissatisfaction with Peter made Rob a lucky man. He stayed lucky all the way through the New Year.

At the end of a midday romp on New Year's Day, Rob asked Misty, "So, when are you going on the road again?"

"I thought I would head out in a few weeks. Is that okay with you?"

"That's fine."

Neither of them said anything for a few minutes until Misty broke the silence by talking about all the places she had not yet visited. She became excited and started rambling off different countries.

"Misty, dear!"

Misty froze instantly. Whenever Rob said "Misty, dear" in the tone he just used, it meant he had something to say that she probably didn't want to hear.

She rolled over on her side and propped her head up on her elbow. "What's on your mind?"

"Okay, there is no easy way for me to say this, honey. I need a big favor from you. When I was in New York I told one of my clients what you do for a living. That you were a very well-regarded trainer and that rich and famous people from all over the world line up to work with you."

Misty narrowed her eyes, but Rob trudged ahead.

"Well, my client, Will Brown, is really worried about the health of his elderly father. Apparently no one has been successful in getting him to eat right or exercise. He is *extremely* wealthy, and Will insists money is not an issue. He says he's fine with your salary demands, whatever they are." Rob gulped. "Will's father lives in New Orleans. I went ahead and told Will you would love to do it."

Misty could feel the veins in her neck starting to bulge. She lay there speechless for a solid minute, and then rose onto her elbow. "Are you out of your frikin' mind?" she yelled. "You want me to train a senile old man in that dirty southern city? New Orleans wasn't even on my 'C' list, 'dear.'" She paused, and then yelled again, "You expect me to sleep with that old fart? How could you?"

Rob quickly answered, "No, no, no. I never told him that was part of the contract. I promise. All he expects you to do is spend time with his dad and help him regain strength. Put the quality of better health into the remainder of his life. I've never complained or asked you to do anything since we came to this arrangement, but this is very important for my career. Won't you please consider it?"

Rob's statement resonated with her, and she calmed down. She thought about how good Rob had been about all of this. She felt she owed him a big favor.

Misty focused her eyes on Rob, who was holding his breath. "All right I'll do it. What's his father's name?"

Rob sighed in relief. "Charlie Brown."

"Oh, good grief!"

Because Mr. Brown was in his eighties, Misty decided that there was no need for a bodyguard on this trip. She called Miguel to tell him she would pay half his usual salary while he stayed behind in Los Angeles. She knew he would be relieved to have more time with Sylvia.

Early morning in mid-January, Misty boarded her flight to New Orleans. She may have been doing Rob a favor, but that didn't mean she was excited about it. All she knew about New Orleans was that Hurricane Katrina had ravaged it a few years back. The passenger sitting next to her was a native New Orleanian who assured her the area she would be staying in had survived just fine. This made Misty feel a lot better. She relaxed into her seat and managed to catch a few z's.

When the plane landed Misty realized that this time of year might be quite nice in New Orleans. At least that was one positive thing. She hoped there would be others. When the cabdriver drove them into New Orleans proper, her doubts melted away.

She was enamored with her hotel. Nestled between Bourbon Street and Royal, it was four blocks away from Mr. Brown's health club. Originally, Misty was frustrated that she had to use the client's health club and could not have her pick, but once she arrived at the club, she was as impressed as she was with the hotel.

The club was over a hundred years old, which Misty thought was very cool, and there were forty group classes offered every week. If that wasn't enough, it even had a bar on site. As she looked inside, she figured she would be getting to know the pub quite well. It looked like it would be a great place to go after her sessions. She felt she could use a stiff drink to unwind, so she took a seat at the bar.

The bartender looked up from the glass he was drying and greeted Misty. "G'day, love. You look like you could use a coldie."

His thick Australian accent made her smile. "No, I'm not a beer drinker, I'll have your seven-year Flor De Cana, straight. So you're from Oz, are you?"

He looked back and said wryly, "What tipped you off?"

"Well, you can take the Aussie out of the bush, but you can't take the bush out of the Aussie," Misty said flatly.

"Say, you're a live wire, aren't you, doll? My name is Sammy."

Misty introduced herself and told him she was training a client at the club. She asked, "Say, were you ever a bartender in Sydney? You look familiar."

"What were you doing in Sydney, sheila?"

"Went to visit last year on business. I stayed for several months. I really liked it there."

"Sure, I've worked at most of the top bars in Sydney over the last few years, but I decided to come to the States. I've already sampled most of the beautiful women in Sydney. Wanted to broaden my horizon, if you catch me." He winked again.

Yep. He's full of it all right, Misty thought.

"Well don't look at me buddy, I'm no sheila."

She finished her drink in one gulp and excused herself.

"Of course you're not," Sammy said patronizingly. "You'll come back, though. They always do."

In the morning Misty was ready to begin the first training session. She decided against taking the new client out to dinner. This time, all she really wanted to do was get the old codger in shape and eating right and get the hell out of Dodge.

Misty walked past the bar on her way to meet Charlie. Because the building was on Bourbon Street, the door to the bar was wide open, as were the windows, which were little more than improvised storm shutters on the ancient façade. She tried to keep her head down but couldn't resist taking a quick glance to see if Sammy was working. Sure enough, he was leaning on the bar looking straight at her. He smiled and blew a kiss. Misty shook her head in annoyance and hurried on.

As she approached her new client, her head began to swim. Charlie Brown didn't look like the cartoon character at all. He was a leering little man standing hunched over and sneering behind his long, pointy nose. Rob was very fortunate he wasn't in New Orleans right now. Of course, there was a very good chance he would feel Misty's wrath when she got back. She took a deep breath.

"Hello, Mr. Brown. I'm Misty, your new trainer, and I'm so happy to meet you," she lied.

Mr. Brown looked her up one side and down the other, surveying every inch of her body and burning it into his memory. Misty was stunned. *Now, I've known some creeps in my day, but none even close to this slime bag. I'm going to work Charlie so hard he'll be lucky to lift his head high enough to ever leer at me again.*

"All right, Mr. Brown, as you know, time is money, and we don't want to waste your son's money. So, let's get started."

"What's the rush, cutie? Will says I've got you for several months. Why don't we go over to the bar and have a drink?" Right then Misty knew she was going to earn every penny of this contract. It took some doing, but Misty convinced Charlie Brown to go straight into training with the promise of a drink at the end of each session. Luckily, he bought it.

She was amused with her cleverness. *All men need is the tiniest promise of getting laid, and they'll do anything.*

It turned out that Misty worked him so hard, she was able to go to the bar, alone. "Hit me with a double today, Sammy boy. I think I may become an alcoholic before this is over."

"Fifty-fifty you make it through, sheila. Within two weeks you will be begging me to take your mind off all this."

"Sammy, why don't you just go take a smoke break and leave me alone. I thought I told you not to call me a 'sheila.' Just leave the bottle of rum and piss off."

Sammy stalked toward the back room.

"Sorry, mate. I don't smoke cigarettes but I do need to get a few things from the back. No hurry, doll. You've got plenty of time to warm up to me." His laughter disappeared into the back of the bar.

The next three weeks were grueling. Charlie was full of piss and vinegar every single session. Misty wished Mr. Brown devoted as much time to the workouts as he did trying to cop a feel. One session he managed to cup a breast as she leaned over to help him use a weight machine.

"Mr. Brown, you are terrible!"

He had smiled proudly. Apparently it was just the reaction he was looking for.

After every session, Misty found herself sitting at the bar. Sammy helped her keep her sanity with his constant ribbing. At least he was someone to talk to.

"Was that you I saw showing off your white pointers when I walked past your hotel pool earlier today?"

"No, I don't sunbathe topless like your Australian floozies. I've got more dignity than that."

In only a few weeks' time, Sammy had worn Misty down. "All right, you win, Sammy boy. When you get off take me out on Bourbon Street. I've been here for weeks, and all I've done is go back to my room and watch *Law and Order*. I'm basically just serving out my sentence. My room is starting to feel like a cell."

"I get off at eight tonight. I know a place that serves some genuine Four X beer imported from Australia. A few of those, and you might ask me to be your cell mate." He laughed at his joke. Misty laughed too. She didn't bother sparring with him.

She finished her straight rum while watching him talk and flirt with the other customers. He had an easy charm about him that had seemed heavy-handed at first. He looked back and winked at her. Young and naturally built, Sammy's dark hair was short and curled close to his head. His face was characterized by deep smile lines and dimples, which made Misty think he was always pulling her leg, even when he was serious. Misty watched him juggle three vodka bottles, showing off to two women tourists at the end of the bar. He landed the bottles on the bar: one, two, and then caught the third and poured two shots into their drinks before spinning the bottle in his hand and placing it back in the rows of liquor. She admired his quick hands, and imagined how experienced they were. What could they do to her?

"Okay," Misty said. "Meet me at Club Hurricane at 9:00 PM. That should give you enough time to clean up. Oh, and wear something comfortable. I don't feel like dressing up tonight."

16

Out in Old New Orleans

Misty entered Club Hurricane and saw Sammy at a table set with two Hurricanes. He obviously already knew Misty was a rum drinker and the club's Hurricanes were legendary.

"Planning to get me drunk?" she asked as she sat down.

"Not at all. Cheers, love." Sammy held up his glass with a wink.

The first Hurricane went down so easily that Misty decided to order another. About halfway through the second drink, Sammy got up and started to walk off.

"Where you going there, Sammy boy?"

"Just going to take a leak. They have a trough full of crushed ice in the men's bathroom and you can write your name in the ice when you pee. I ran out of old girlfriends' names so I thought I would write 'Misty' this time."

"How romantic! Does that go over well with all your little sheilas at home?"

On his return to the table, Misty looked him over. The rum was in her head, working its amorous magic. She admired his fitted jeans and cotton pullover. He was muscular, but not in a body builder way. Sammy's muscles came from good genes and a family of longshoremen. He had done his share of heavy lifting and wore his lean muscles like a lifestyle instead of temporary achievements.

"Got your fill of swill? If so, let's hit the street. I've gotten to know the French Quarter pretty well over the last several months. I hope you like things a little on the wild side."

"Wild seems pretty good right about now, Sammy. Introduce me to Bourbon Street!"

It didn't take long for Misty to understand Sammy's idea of the wild side. Their first stop was The Ragin' Cajun's, one of the premier topless bars on Bourbon Street. Misty felt a tingle of excitement as they entered the darkened establishment.

Sammy was shocked when she told him she had never been to a gentleman's club before. He explained that his friends were all blue-collar workers. Strip joints were just a part of everyday life. He couldn't think of one other woman he knew who had never entered a strip club at one time or another. As he paid their cover, Misty started to tell him that she had a very generous expense account and would be happy to pay, but something told her that he would have taken it as an insult. Once he had their tickets, Sammy reached around and lightly held her waist. And then, with a little nudge, he escorted her into the club.

The club was electric with so many new sights and sounds that she hardly knew where to focus her attention. A sweeping majority of the patrons were men, many of whom were no doubt in New Orleans on business. After getting Misty settled, Sammy excused himself and walked over to talk to someone. While he was gone, Misty couldn't believe she felt a little intimidated. True, she was out of her comfort zone, but she suddenly felt that it was a good thing because adapting would be challenging.

There were six stages for the dancers. Men lined up in chairs along the front edge of the stages. Misty saw a dancer perform a little private dance in front of a patron. At the end of her routine the dancer turned her back to the man and shimmied down to the floor until she was squatting in front of him. She held the strap to her G-string up just enough for him to slide the cash though the opening. Snap, she released the elastic, and the bill was securely trapped along with a dozen others like it.

What a way to make a living, Misty thought. *All you've got to do is be pretty and know how to dance.* She began to realize just how pretty these women were. Absolutely gorgeous, all of them, and well endowed, naturally or not. Misty had seen lots of naked women in her health club dressing rooms through the years, but it was always a quick peek. Getting caught looking would have been supremely embarrassing. But now that it was okay to look she found she couldn't stop. *My, what fantastic bodies they have. I'll bet pole dancing is a workout! No wonder so many fitness clubs now offer pole classes.*

When Sammy returned to their table he asked, "How do you like it so far?"

"So far, so good. How much do you suppose they make?"

"That girl doing a lap dance can earn twenty dollars for a two-minute dance."

This blew Misty's mind. *Ten of those an hour and a girl could make $200. Not bad. Not bad at all.* But then Misty realized she made $2,500 an hour.

The alcohol, the exotic club, and the presence of her playful Aussie companion—mixed with her excitement at figuring how much more money she made than this high-priced stripper—combined to relax her, and she forgot her stress. Everything started to slow down for her. She was in the moment, and her senses were keen.

As Misty watched the women around her, she became mesmerized by the plethora of heavy, round breasts bouncing to the beat of the music. She felt herself getting turned on watching the women dance. She crossed her legs so that her thighs squeezed her clitoris. She sat up straight and moved her legs in various ways, massaging her moistening lips. For the first time in her life, she stared unabashedly at beautiful naked women without worrying about getting caught. Misty noticed Sammy looking at her and tried to focus on him, tried to will her attraction toward him. Just as she was in control again, she felt a presence at her left.

She turned to see a busty goddess of a woman climb into her lap and face her. The woman put her large breasts right up against Misty's face and started to move them back and forth. Numb from the rum, she froze. The dancer smelled of musk and cologne. Her breasts felt soft and natural against Misty's face. Misty was drunk, but she was close to admitting it wasn't the rum.

The dancer arched her back, lifting her breasts so that Misty could look at them. Misty had an irresistible urge to fondle and squeeze them. She began to lift her hands, but the vixen gently slapped them away and said, "No, no, that's a naughty girl. Look, but don't touch."

Enjoying the show, Sammy grinned ear to ear, but Misty didn't notice. Her mind was focused on the hot body of flesh in her lap. The dancer got up and began teasing Misty by dancing slowly and methodically as close to her as she could without coming in contact. Now Misty felt flushed and frustrated as she had the night Peter left her hotel room. She didn't like a tease. The woman leaned over to Misty's neck and began to mimic kissing her. Misty began to lift the woman's breasts toward her despite the trouble it might cause. Just then the music stopped and the dancer got up, blew Misty a kiss, and walked away.

Groggily Misty asked, "Where did she go? We never gave the girl her $20."

"Don't worry, I already paid her in advance. Bunny gets $40 a dance, and I gave her a C-note so it would be extra long. Come on, mate. Let's move on to our next adventure."

Sammy offered his arm as if asking her to trust him after the stunt he had just pulled with the dancer. Misty blushed and took it.

Sammy led them to Decatur Street. "I've got a little surprise for you. You act tough, doll, but let's see how tough you really are."

When they walked through the front door of Little Havana's, Misty shook her head. "First he takes me to a strip joint and now he wants me to smoke a cigar!"

"Hand rolled, mate. Come on, it'll put some hair on your chest so you can stand up to ole Charlie. You can handle it!"

Misty had only had a few cigarettes in her life and each time it had been when she was drinking. She always regretted the decision later. *If I don't inhale, maybe this won't be so bad.* She and Sammy picked out their cigars and lit them. They exited the humidor to stroll down Bourbon Street arm in arm, practicing blowing smoke rings and laughing like kids. The cigars they chose were very mild, so Misty actually enjoyed hers. It was a different kind of buzz than alcohol.

Just then Sammy ducked into a tiny bar that sold takeaway alcohol. He called out to the bartender, a fellow Aussie, and the two laughed like madmen and hugged over the bar. The bartender went into the backroom and returned with a couple of the Four X beers Sammy had mentioned earlier.

"Can't smoke a fine cigar without sipping on a coldie now, can you, Misty girl."

"I guess I can't come this far without going all the way."

Sammy gave Misty a mischievous grin and said, "Well, if you're really willing to go all the way."

Misty gave him a playful shove, letting him know he was out of line but she wasn't mad about it.

She had completely forgotten about Mr. Brown, about Rob, about her restlessness, and for the moment felt liberated.

"Hey! That's my hotel!" Misty said, as they were on their move down the street. "Come on up, and I'll show you my cell. It's got the greatest balcony that overlooks Bourbon Street!"

"Absolutely! What a perfect place to continue your education of Bourbon Street." Misty hit his chest playfully and looked at his always-grinning face. It struck her that he was being sincere.

Once they reached the balcony of her room, Sammy said, "Misty, rest your arms on the rail and pretend you are a fine lady of the South a hundred years ago. No, wait! First let's look through your closet and see if we can find you something they might have worn way back then."

"Looking for a bodice to rip?" Misty helped him search.

"How about this silky green thing?"

"My nightgown?"

"You wear this to sleep? What a shame! Seriously, doll. Put it on, I want a look."

Misty gave him a sideways glance but took the gown and disappeared into the bathroom. A few moments later she stepped out, purposefully heaving up her cleavage and giving him a haughty look. Sammy's jaw dropped and he collapsed back onto the window seat. Misty put her hair in a bun and put on a draping necklace with a locket that nestled between her breasts, which were now unrestricted by a bra.

She walked out to the balcony, and Sammy jumped up to follow. She leaned over the rail, closing her eyes, and imagined Sammy was dressed as a Southern gentleman. She envisioned him with long coattails standing on the street below, calling to her.

Suddenly she did hear a voice from below, but it wasn't Sammy's.

"What's it going to cost for you to show us your tits, baby?"

Misty opened her eyes to see several men looking up at her from the crowd that had gathered below. One of the men threw a string of beads up to her balcony. Mortified, she stepped back against Sammy who enveloped her in his arms, pressing her against his hardness.

"It's tradition, Misty. Don't disappoint them."

Misty's face flushed, but not with embarrassment. She was infuriated with Sammy. She tried turning to slap him, but he held her tight and whispered into her ear.

"Seriously, Misty. You may never have this opportunity again. You're as hot as any of those girls at the Cabaret. You know it. Show yourself off like you want to. You'll never see these blokes again. No worries, doll."

Misty felt her body heat up the way it had with the dancer in her lap. She did think that she was as hot as those women. She wondered what the thrill of anonymous admirers would be like.

"Okay. I'll only do it if you turn your head. Don't look. Do we have a deal?" Sammy's eyes flashed in surprise. "Yes, we have a deal."

The catcalls kept coming, and the beads kept flying onto the balcony. The crowd continued to build, and when she looked again, there seemed to be thirty people below. Misty gathered her courage and slid her gown off her left breast. When the crowd gasped and cheered, a sensation shot through her unlike anything she had ever experienced. She pulled her neckline down, letting her right breast roll out and join the other. The crowd, now numbering close to fifty, let out a roar.

She heard Sammy say, "Come on, mate, shake those darlings around a bit. You've got 'em right where you want 'em."

Misty quickly turned her head to look at Sammy. True to his word, he had his hands over his eyes. To her surprise, she felt disappointed and almost wished he would steal a peek.

Mischievously, she turned to the crowd below and started to dance and shake her breasts like the women she'd seen on stage only hours earlier. At the end of her shimmy, a hundred people were gathered, whooping and hollering like it was Mardi Gras. Thrilled, Misty turned around and jumped into Sammy's arms. He looked down at her breasts and then back into her eyes. It was now very clear to both of them what the other wanted.

Misty pushed up his chin with her fingers, hopped out of his arms, and began pulling him through the French doors toward the bedroom. He gently declined, turning her around and guiding her toward the wall. From behind, Sammy cupped her left breast in his right hand. Then he slowly slid his free hand underneath her nightgown, massaging and squeezing his way up her taut inner thigh until his middle finger discovered the wet labia of her vagina. Sammy deftly entered and moved delicately forward to her swelling clitoris, circling it and then pressing in gently. Misty stepped up against the wall and Sammy followed, his hands never missing a beat. She began to move her pelvis in unison with the motion of his fingers. The sensations of the night collided—the dancer in her lap, the crowd roaring at her exposed breasts, the alcohol, the cigar, the strapping Australian squeezing her breast and massaging her aching desire.

Misty pressed her bottom backward against his hardened penis. Sammy responded by pushing his middle finger deep inside her. Once her vagina relaxed, he added another finger, and then finally another. With long deep strokes he worked deep inside her until Misty began groaning and threatening to come.

Sammy exited her and gave her mound a squeeze. She groaned with desire. He began to massage both breasts from behind and nibbled and breathed warmly on the back of her neck. She shivered and sweated, throwing her head back to whisper in his ear, "Do me now, Sammy. Do it hard."

Sammy forcefully pulled her by the hips away from the wall until she had to brace herself with both forearms. He pulled up Misty's gown and let it rest on the small of her back. He placed his hands between her thighs and firmly pulled her legs apart. Now he had Misty in position to give her all that he had to offer from behind. He pressed and massaged the outside of her mound, running his fingers through her hair and tracing the lips of her vagina while he unbuttoned and unzipped.

She felt Sammy's heavy penis fall against her skin. She pressed into it.

He inched backward, pressing himself downward slightly and entering her cheeks before moving further downward to discover her increasing wetness. Suddenly, he thrust inside her, but then slowly worked his tool out to fully lubricate with her wetness. Then, as Misty had instructed, his thrusts became quicker, deeper, and more powerful. She had to use all of her strength to keep from slamming into the wall with each thrust. The slapping of their two bodies could be heard halfway down the hall.

"My God, you're powerful," Misty gasped. "You're giving me the fuck of my life."

Her nails scraped the wall as she came. She moaned and writhed. A second orgasm was welling up. Sammy finally pounded the wall with his fist, unloading into her as Misty screamed.

They walked backward and collapsed on the bed. The two were so exhausted they dug their way between the sheets. Blindly, Misty moved into Sammy's arms, which he wrapped securely around her. They coiled together. As sleep fogged her mind, Misty thought, *New Orleans isn't so bad after all.*

17

GETTING TO KNOW SAMMY

When Misty awoke the next morning Sammy still had his arms wrapped around her. He slept the deep sleep of a man who worked long hours. She listened to his deep, rhythmic breathing and tried to work out her emotions. Sammy was not a client, and last night she was not delivering the poisonous bite of the black widow. If anything, he was doing the poisoning, and he was really good at it.

When Sammy began to stir, Misty rolled over to look into his eyes. She wanted to be the first thing he saw when he opened them.

"Well good morning, mate," Sammy said in a scratchy voice. "Did you sleep well?"

Misty gave him a big hug. "Good morning, *mate*. You were an animal last night. I may have to refer to you as 'The Beast from Down Under.'"

"Down under, now there's an idea."

Sammy lifted the sheet and began kissing his way down her breasts and abdomen. He lingered around her mound and then slid his thick tongue into Misty's "down under." She began to groan.

"What a wonderful way to wake up." Misty said in a throaty voice. "I think we've become quite close, haven't we Sammy?" He reached up a hand and groped her breast in response.

Misty showered first and then went down to the lobby and bought Sammy a T-shirt from the gift shop. They both had the day off and she didn't want Sammy going home to change. Today she wanted him to be all hers. Back in the room she listened for his shower to stop. Then she cracked the bathroom door and stuck in her hand, offering the shirt.

"Here, I bought you a clean shirt. Go ahead and use my deodorant and toothbrush. You may have some curly little hairs stuck in your teeth from my—what do you call it in Australia—'mappa tassie' region?"

Sammy laughed heartily. "I guess that's what I get for spending time in the bush." Sammy dressed and told Misty he would take her to his favorite spots in New Orleans.

"Just put on some comfortable clothes, and we'll slum our way through the day." They started out by having beignets and coffee. After that, they strolled along the riverfront, toured the mall in the old Pearl Brewery, and wound up getting their caricatures drawn by a street artist in Jackson Square.

When it was time for lunch, Sammy took her to his favorite restaurant, which was located on Poydras Street in an old building. The chefs were famous for their Cajun cooking, and had everything from po'boys to crawfish étouffée. Their special dish was called Debris, roast beef that falls into the gravy while baking, which was offered on a plate or in a sandwich. Misty was famished from the night before and devoured a Debris sandwich.

The rest of the day was spent walking aimlessly, touring the city and talking.

"Sammy, tell me about your family back in Sydney."

"Oh, they're just normal folks."

"Normal? Then what happened to you?" she joked.

Sammy stared at her even though he knew she was only joking. She detected a hint of pain behind his smiling eyes.

"I miss my family, but I needed to get away for a while. I was supposed to marry a girl I'd known since I was little, but she backed out at the last minute. I decided to come lose myself in New Orleans. Last week I got an e-mail from my brother telling me my former fiancé left for New Zealand with another man. I guess that's why she got cold feet. So, really, I'm just telling you this to say thank you for last night. It helped take my mind off things."

"Yeah, until I just blew it by asking you questions. I shouldn't have pried. Forgive me, Sammy."

"It's not your fault, Misty. It's probably good for me to get it out in the open so I can move on."

"Well just for the record, she made a big mistake, because you are going to make one heck of a catch for some lucky girl." Seeing this side of Sammy made her feel that she owed him a sympathy lay. No, who was she kidding? She just wanted him again.

The next week, Misty approached her job with a different frame of mind. She started to joke and kid around with the old geezer and found out he was a pretty lovable guy once she quit resisting him. She made a point of giving him a quick titty brush whenever possible.

The following weekend Sammy took Misty to an old mansion on the Mississippi River. During the tour, Misty paused on the second floor balcony to look down the long drive that was lined on both sides with gigantic three hundred–year-old live oaks. She leaned over the rail, imagining what life had been like in the Old South. Of course, this time no one lined up below to catcall.

After drinking a few glasses of the mint julep served on the tour, she was up for just about anything. The julep was so potent that by the end of the tour Sammy and Misty took over for the guide and began making up details and information as they went along. The group and the tour guide were quite cool about it and laughed at their improvisations.

The tour guide kept asking the new docents, "Is that so?"

On Misty's final day at the club she went up to Sammy with a mischievous look in her eye and motioned for him to follow her. She led him into the women's bathroom.

"Are you mad, Misty? I can't follow you in here!"

"Sure you can, Sammy. If you don't, I can't give you my going away present."

Sammy looked around nervously and then said, "Well if my going away present's on the line, what the hell? If we get caught and they deport me, I'll just have to go home!" He was only half joking.

Misty wedged a chair she had stashed previously up against the door handle.

"All right Sammy, drop your trousers."

While Misty was preoccupied, Sammy patted her on the head and said, "Misty, this is the best going away present I've ever gotten and you are a—oh, my!—a very caring woman."

The following day, Sammy took Misty to the airport. Before she entered the terminal he said, "Thank you so much for putting up with me. Because of you I am pretty much over my old girl."

"You are a great guy, Sammy. You won't have any trouble finding someone new. Stay in touch. I want to know when that old girl figures out she's made a huge mistake and comes crawling back to you."

As Misty kissed Sammy good-bye, she blinked away the nagging thought that perhaps leaving him was also a mistake. Had she not been married, he was a guy she could have fallen for.

18

FLYING SOUTH FOR THE WINTER

How cool is this! Misty thought. She was stretched out in a reclining leather seat, a neat glass of rum in her hand, watching through the window as the world went by thousands of feet below. Her new client, M. G. Marquez, had sent the Gulfstream 200 to fetch her. Much mystery surrounded M. G., and she had felt uncertain about him at first, but the private jet eased her doubts and stole her heart.

The contract was going to be difficult because M.G. had made some counter-demands. He had asked Misty not to make other travel plans but to stay close to Buenos Aires, thus making her available for his social functions. She wasn't used to or entirely comfortable with a client demanding her time outside of sessions. After all, she became the Black Widow Trainer to have her own adventures, not so she could be micromanaged by some rich fat cat. Still, Misty had always wanted to visit Argentina and decided this was as good a chance as any. Besides, M. G.'s credentials were impeccable. He had been voted into the Argentinean Business Hall of Fame and came from a well-respected family. She pulled up his file on her laptop and ordered another rum from the single attendant whose sole job, it seemed, was to wait on Misty hand and foot.

M. G.'s great grandfather Ernesto Marquez, she read, had immigrated to Buenos Aires from Spain in 1889 to work as a skilled craftsman on the Teatro Colón, which was to become one of the world's finest opera houses. He had trained as an engineer in Naples, Italy, and dreamed of working on a grand building. However, before he was able to realize his dream, the main financier died and construction of the theater stopped. Stranded in Buenos Aires, he spent his evenings with architects and artists in Plaza de Mayo, drinking, talking, and dancing. There was a new dance sweeping the city—tango. Ernesto found himself night after night caught up in the drama, the rhythm, the passion of the dance, and was soon going out at night only to tango. And this is how he met Gabriella Ferarri, M. G. Marquez's great grandmother. The daughter of the Teatro's Italian financier, she stole out at night to the smoky parlor rooms of the plaza and threw her body into the passion of tango—and eventually into the passion of Ernesto Marquez.

Misty was moved by the tale of how tango became a Marquez family tradition. It was instrumental in her decision to accept the assignment. Of course, the chance to spend time in one of the most dynamic cities in South America was also very persuasive. Things in New Orleans had gotten a little out of control. When Misty caught herself e-mailing Sammy from Malibu, she knew that she was getting too close and decided it was best to leave the States for a few months, and Sammy forever. Eddie had warned her about getting close to clients, but he had said nothing about the occupational hazard of Australian bartenders. She would be more careful next time.

If she was being honest with herself, Misty's real hang-up about taking this job was the fact that all of the pictures of M. G. Marquez were shot at angles that made it almost impossible to get a clear picture of what he looked like. She could tell he had a slender build and jet-black hair that lay softly on the top of his shoulders. He seemed to have great posture and to carry himself with dignity. M. G.'s family had been wealthy landowners in Buenos Aires. However, the thousands of acres remained pasture until M. G. took control of the family finances and began to develop it one parcel at a time. He quickly became a powerhouse real estate developer in Buenos Aires and a very influential man known for inheriting his great grandfather's eye for architectural design and style.

At least Miguel was excited about the job. Buenos Aires was home to his older brother, Joaquin, and his family. Joaquin had kept Miguel on the straight and narrow after their father had passed away. They grew up in South Central Los Angeles, where they were recruited by many of the gangs. Joaquin was very strict with Miguel and monitored his activity day and night. When Joaquin landed a good job, he moved out of South Central and took his little brother with him. At the time, Miguel felt defeated and embarrassed moving away from the gangs, like he was running away scared instead of holding his own. He resented Joaquin for his embarrassment and moved out before showing his brother any appreciation for saving their lives. The trip to Buenos Aires would finally give Miguel the opportunity to make amends in person.

As they made the final descent into Buenos Aires, Miguel said, "Misty, thank you so much for taking this assignment. It really means a lot to me."

Misty was touched but wanted to keep the mood light.

"Miguel, you know I won't leave home without you. You're dearer to me than my American Express card."

Miguel laughed.

The pilot said over the intercom, "Buckle your belt and return your seat to its upright position. *Bienvenido a Argentina.*"

The sweet air hit them as soon as they walked off the Gulfstream. While waiting on their limo outside, Misty began thinking about M. G.'s request for her to not make any plans other than training. It was still troubling her—what did he have in mind? But faced with the beautiful Argentine weather, and with Miguel in especially high spirits, Misty decided to just live in the moment and see where her journey would take her.

"Miguel, isn't this beautiful?"

Miguel nodded and took in a deep breath to fill his lungs.

"Hey, I know all you can think about is seeing your brother, but just hang in there with me until I get settled, and then you can go straight to your brother's house."

"Hey, of course. I'm not gonna forget why we're here," Miguel said.

A shiny black limo pulled up in front of them. A tall, older man, seemingly of German descent, jumped out of the driver's side door and inquired, "Misty and Miguel?"

They nodded.

"I'm Tom. I'll take you to the Marquez residence."

Tom opened the doors for his passengers and then loaded their luggage into the trunk. He engaged them in small talk about the weather and the beauty of Buenos Aires and exchanged salutations with Miguel, speaking Spanish like an Argentinean.

He took them through the city, past beautiful buildings, old and new, and many gardens. It was a longer drive than Misty expected. They were hugging the coast and going south through open fields along the sea. Farther into the countryside, they turned off at a winding private driveway that led to an old stately mansion with large classical columns. The limo pulled up alongside a fountain in front of the mansion.

Tom opened the doors again and helped his passengers out. "Please leave your things in the trunk. This will not be your final destination. Gabriella would like to meet you, and then I will take you to your hotel," he instructed.

Gabriella? Could that be his wife? Misty wondered. *I thought he was listed as single in his profile.*

She started feeling nervous until Miguel said, "Man, this house looks awesome! I can't wait to see the inside."

The driver led Misty and Miguel up a long flight of steps to the second story entry. Inside, the floors were made of long tropical hardwood planks, and the interior columns were marble. Above them, the vaulted ceiling arched upwards of twenty feet. Abundant natural light filled the house through large open windows. Misty was sure this house had been built by Ernesto Marquez—it bespoke his classical taste and style that she had read about. The windows lining the wall opposite the door were filled with a vista of the Atlantic Ocean. A wonderful ocean breeze flowed through the house, making for an idyllic entrance and main living area.

Tom motioned for them to follow him. He walked briskly through the living room and out onto a large patio with a grand old swimming pool. The patio gave them the impression they were on their own private cliff jutting into the sea. Just as Misty was becoming fully engrossed in the crashing waves and the pungent scent of the sea, she noticed someone standing at the balustrade. She would have recognized that back and posture anywhere. It was Marquez. She took a deep breath and walked toward him. He looked sleek in his white linen suit, like a model, and his thick, black hair, caught in the ocean breeze, obscured his face.

"Señor Marquez," Misty said. "It was so nice of you to send your private plane for us." When the striking figure of M. G. Marquez slowly turned from the sea toward her, Misty did a double take. What she saw with her eyes refuted everything she thought she knew in her mind.

Softly and with a smile, Marquilla Gabriella Marquez introduced herself.

"Misty, how wonderful to see you. I trust your trip went well. My, you are even prettier than your pictures."

Attempting to fight reality with logic, Misty said, "Oh, you must be Señor Marquez's sister. It's very nice to meet you."

Gabriella laughed heartily. "Oh Misty, did you think I was a man? My full name is Marquilla Gabriella Marquez. My father named me Marquilla after his mother but my middle name is my great grand-mother's. I prefer 'Gabriella.' It rolls off the tongue, don't you think? I go by M. G. for business. Keeping your gender anonymous is quite convenient when dealing in the world of men. I didn't intend to fool you. I must apologize. I noticed that you had only trained men, but nothing in the contract indicated you would not take a woman. Rest assured, I will be a very dedicated client."

"There is a very good reason I only accept men. Didn't you read the final stipulation in my contract?" Misty felt tricked into coming to Argentina.

Gabriella flashed a smile of straight white teeth. "Yes Misty, I am well aware of the option." She turned to face the ocean. "As I said before, I will be a model client. You will have no problems with me. I think you will be impressed with the exercise facility I set up on the ground floor of my home. I had it equipped after talking to your people at Elite Fitness. I can assure you it will meet your standards."

Misty did not relent. She narrowed her eyes and said, "Despite how much money and effort you've spent getting me down here, I won't guarantee to accept you as a client. I can't help but feel tricked."

"You are not a prisoner," Gabriella laughed, and shook her head to dismiss the idea. "Please, take some time to think about your decision." She looked beyond Misty and Miguel to the driver. "Tom, please take Misty and her—"

"That's Miguel," Misty said. "He travels with me."

Miguel stepped forward and offered his hand. "*Mucho gusto, señora.*"

"*Igualmente*," Gabriella said as she shook his hand genially. "Tom, take Misty and Miguel to the hotel so they can start to feel at home here in Buenos Aires."

The driver moved toward Misty and Miguel and motioned for them to return to the house, but Misty did not budge. She had been so excited about coming to Argentina and had already fallen in love with Buenos Aires. Miguel had told her the city's name meant "fair winds," and the reason was obvious within Misty's first few hours there. Not even California felt this incredible.

She turned to look at Miguel. She could see he was nervous they might not stay and, once again, remembered how important a reunion and lengthy visit with his brother was to him. The job had gotten complicated. She had accepted the client and agreed to a contract. Each client furthered her reputation, which was all she really had to support this lifestyle. And she felt responsible for Miguel.

She didn't need Gabriella to tell her she wasn't a prisoner or give her permission to think about it. She looked Gabriella in the eye and said, "All right, Gabriella. If I hadn't come such a long way I would go back tomorrow. I'm going to make my decision on my own terms. I'll give you a week trial period."

Gabriella smiled slyly, her eyes twinkling. She was impressed with Misty's assertiveness but undeterred. She nodded at Tom and watched as Misty and Miguel left the terrace.

On their way down the front stairs to the car, Misty told Miguel, "You owe me one, buddy. You better spend some quality time with Joaquin pronto, comprende?"

"Thanks, boss. And yeah, I do owe you one." Miguel was relieved that they would be staying, if only for a week. Misty patted Miguel on the cheek, and they both followed Tom back to the limo.

On the long ride back to the city, Misty asked, "Hey, Tom—are you Gabriella's regular driver?"

He met her eyes in the rearview mirror. "Hey, there. Yes, I've worked for Gabriella for over ten years, and, I can assure you, you won't find a better human being than Ms. Marquez. Just give her a chance, and I'm sure you will appreciate her as much as I do."

Misty laughed. "Okay, Tom. I don't need you selling me on this too."

"Hey, don't kill the messenger." Tom winked in the rearview mirror.

"Okay, fair enough." Misty smiled and turned back to the countryside rushing past.

The car wound its way through the ancient city. Majestic classical buildings lined the narrow streets, and iron street lamps looked down on old cobblestones that had been polished by centuries of traffic. Misty could have sworn she was in a European city. She had already seen so many beautiful buildings with wrought-iron balustrades surrounding ornate marble carvings that when Tom stopped in front of one, it took Misty a few moments to realize they had pulled up to their hotel.

The carved wooden sign above the Art Nouveau doors read "Dondi." So this was the famous Argentina Tango Hotel Boutique, home to a prestigious Tango Academy. Misty had read about it in one of the magazines on Gabriella's jet, and now here it was, gloriously beautiful in white marble and dark hardwood with gold trim.

Misty was exasperated. "You've got to be kidding me. I think Gabriella and I are going to tango with our fists if she expects me to take tango lessons."

Tom hesitated before saying, "This is a high compliment. Tango is an important part of Argentinean culture and an old tradition in the Marquez family."

"I know, but . . . I make my own plans, okay?"

Tom was unfazed.

"Gabriella has paid for three lessons a week. You will be trained personally by the Academy's master trainer, Roberto Ribera."

Miguel looked at Misty.

"It won't hurt to give it a try, Misty."

She gave him a dark look.

"Don't you start on me, too," she said, turning back to Tom.

"So, I suppose you've already taken your tango lessons?"

Tom laughed. "No, señorita. I spent my life in the navy. Tango lessons were not part of our training." Tom grinned in the mirror. "But I've got a feeling you are going to be really good at it."

Misty was anxious to check in and see the inside of the grand hotel. She was tired and hungry and a little pissed off. What she needed more than anything was a shower, a stiff drink, and a few minutes alone. Tom led them into the hotel, which was more of a mansion, and arranged their rooms. He told her that he would return tomorrow after breakfast to take her to the Marquez mansion. After he and Miguel brought the baggage in, Tom left with a quick bow.

Despite the day's big surprise, Miguel was anxious for other reasons. He was excited and nervous to see his brother, and he also knew Misty well enough to stay out of her way until she'd had an opportunity to settle down. She was a strong woman, but the responsibility of performing at the top of her game all the time as a trainer and businesswoman was greater than anything Miguel had ever had to deal with. He knew that it wore on her, even if she didn't admit it.

When Miguel left her, Misty spent the next hour touring the hotel and, to her surprise, fell in love with it. The hotel had been built at the turn of the century and was both stunning and darling. It made her feel like she was in one of those old black-and-white movies. After having a nice dinner of local *locra* stew and a few glasses of petit verdot in the bar, Misty retired to her room and settled in for a good night's sleep. Despite the long day, the meal put her in a good mood. She was in Buenos Aires, after all. Perhaps fair winds *would* blow her way. As she headed up to her room she mused, *Maybe things will look better to me in the morning.*

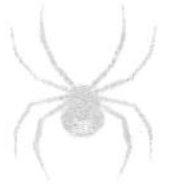

19

FIGURING OUT GABRIELLA

Misty awoke under a down duvet and linen canopy. Despite the halcyon atmosphere of her luxury suite, Misty's waking thought was wrought with anxiety. *Christ. He's a woman!*

A knock at the door interrupted Misty's brewing dread. She pulled on a robe to answer the door. Tom stood there, holding two large shopping bags in each hand.

"Morning Tom. What's in the bags?"

"No idea. Gabriella just asked me to deliver them. I'll be parked in front of the lobby to take you to the Marquez house."

Misty nodded, accepted the bags, and shut the door. The bags were full of expensive athletic outfits. Misty tried on several yoga pants and tank top sets, then some running shorts and a windbreaker. They all fit and were interchangeable lavenders and olive greens with black. She admired one of the outfits in the mirror and wondered uneasily if her size and style had been so transparent to Gabriella during their five-minute meeting.

                    Craig Odanovich

The midmorning sun cast a golden glow on the Marquez mansion, making the already impressive home appear ethereal. When the car stopped, Misty stepped out into the morning sun and breathed in the ocean. It was invigorating

Gabriella's exercise room was a screened veranda outfitted, as the lady of the house had said, with premier workout equipment.

Misty spotted Gabriella walking through the garden toward the exercise room. Her skin glowed under a light perspiration. She was stunning. Her small but muscular frame walked tall at five feet eight and was powered by long, lean leg muscles. She had inherited her Italian mother's olive skin, which beautifully complemented her jet-black hair. Her eyebrows arched over dark brown eyes, making her look alert and intelligent.

She lifted her face up to the veranda and waved to Misty, smiling warmly. Gabriella's full lips and button nose made a striking combination. Misty's gaze followed Gabriella's long neck to her sports bra, which hugged her small, firm breasts. Her bare abdomen suggested she was a woman accustomed to working out, as did her lean legs and firm bottom.

Though she wouldn't have called it sexual, what Misty felt was undeniable. An attraction. Entranced, Misty greeted her new client.

"Good morning, Gabriella. You seem to be in great condition already!"

"Misty, you are too kind. It's good genes from my father. I look like I'm in shape, but I'd like you to help me attain the level of strength and endurance you command. Oh! I see you are wearing one of the outfits I sent you. Beautiful."

Misty's face brightened.

"Yes, I adore the clothes. Thank you, that was very thoughtful."

Gabriella walked over and turned on the amplifier that drove eight speakers and put in a CD.

"I hope you like Latin music. I find it sets a nice tempo." The room filled with the sound of a lively bandoneón, a small, square accordion popular in Argentinean tango. Gabriella swung her hips sharply in rhythm.

"Whatever turns you on, Gabriella. Rather, I mean, whatever motivates you to work hard."

Gabriella raised an eyebrow as she saw Misty's face flush.

"So, um, tell me what sort of strength you want to acquire. I mean, do you want to build muscle or focus more on flexibility and stamina?" Misty asked.

"Well, tone and definition are important. I want to look strong, but still very—"

"Feminine?" Misty offered.

"Exactly. Graceful like a dancer, but strong. And I want to feel like . . . I want to have control. I want to feel like I can do anything!" Gabriella paused. "You know, I rather admire *your* body, Misty."

Misty glanced away, her face burning. She had heard these words before from other female clients—*I like your figure, make me look like you, Misty.* But the words had never triggered this response in her.

She skipped her standard thank-you after receiving Gabriella's compliment and went straight to the diagnosis.

"Well, I'm a big advocate of yoga, myself, and I'd like to incorporate some Pilates into our sessions. For weight training, we'll use small weights with lots of reps, alternating with abdominal training. And for a final cardio . . ." Misty trailed off as the ocean breeze pushed through the screens, lightly stirring both women's hair. "To finish up our sessions, let's do a twenty-minute run on the beach."

Gabriella looked pleased. She moved her hips, softly this time, as a new tango track began. Misty had little doubt Gabriella was a very good tango dancer. It seemed to be the root of her gracefulness. Suddenly Misty wanted nothing more than to attend tango lessons, to move like Gabriella moved.

They rolled out their yoga mats, and Misty instructed Gabriella through a long, slow exercise. She watched as Gabriella raised and lowered her limbs, undertaking the strenuous movements and positions with discipline.

Later, as the two slowed to end their jog on the beach, Gabriella said, "Thank you, Misty. I can tell I made a wise choice. You are a fantastic trainer. To show my appreciation, I would like to help you get to know our beautiful city. I'll be your tour guide in the evenings and on the weekends."

They walked through the door, and Gabriella turned to the stairs leading to her bedroom. Misty was accustomed to being in control of her time outside of sessions. She was excited about Gabriella's offer, but she didn't like being told instead of asked. She began to protest but decided not to. Instead, she watched Gabriella ascend the stairs in silence.

The next day Misty went for her first tango lesson. She was standing on the hardwood floor in the dance studio when a very bubbly Roberto Ribera walked in.

"My, my, my, Misty. You are so beautiful. I rarely get such a wonderful ball of clay to mold. I can't wait to get started."

"Ha, two clay feet, you mean. I don't know the first thing about tango. You better be as good of an instructor as they say if you think I can be molded into an accomplished tango dancer."

"You have such a free spirit, dear. If I can bottle it, you will become magnificent."

Roberto spent the first session introducing Misty to exercises for developing her posture. She placed a book on her head and began to walk across the room. How many times had she seen someone do this in a movie or on TV? She began to laugh and had to reach up and steady the book. By the end of the week, she could definitely feel a difference in her ribs and spine. *All right, I'm ready for the catwalk*, she laughed to herself at the end of her Friday class.

Saturday morning Misty woke to the sound of her cell phone. "Misty, this is Gabriella. I hope I didn't wake you."

"Oh, no, Gabriella. I was just lying here waking up. What's on your mind?"

"Well, I wanted to let you know I will be by in an hour to pick you up. We have a wonderful historic area south of town called San Telmo. I thought we could spend the day there. I'll meet you in the lobby in an hour, *querida*."

When Gabriella hung up Misty fought her annoyance at feeling controlled. She focused on how fantastic Gabriella's plan sounded. *If she had only asked, I would have said yes. Why couldn't she ask?*

Just then there was a knock on the door. It was Tom, holding several shopping bags.

"Well, Tom, have we been shopping again? Maybe I'll buy you a little dress to wear so you can blend in with the other women shoppers and get the full shopping experience."

"Very funny. I hope you don't mind if I forget to laugh. Just doing my job, and I'm not exactly thrilled about it. You know I don't buy this stuff, don't you? I wouldn't have the foggiest idea of what to get you. Here, just take it, and let me go pick up Gabriella so we can come back to get you."

Misty grinned at him. "You know I'm just pulling your leg, don't you."

"Yes, and you seem to be enjoying it. I'm so happy I'm amusing to you. Shall I have Gabriella add piñata to my job description?" Tom smiled genteelly to ensure that Misty understood he was joking.

An hour later, when the car pulled up to the hotel entrance, Misty came out in a skirt and blouse chosen by Gabriella. It was another beautiful day, and Misty felt especially upbeat in her new clothes.

Inside the limo, Gabriella said, "You look wonderful, Misty. I hope you like your outfit."

"Yes, Gabriella, you have good taste in clothes," Misty said, failing to strip all the annoyance out of her tone. "Do you enjoy picking out clothes for other people?"

Misty's curtness was not lost on Gabriella, and Misty could tell she was a little hurt.

"Misty, I was an only child and my mother always showered me with gifts. As you know, I am not married, and I don't have children to dote on. I know it's a silly need of mine. If it bothers you, I will try to resist the urge to buy you clothes."

"I'm so sorry." Misty was suddenly disappointed with her insensitivity. "I misspoke. I think it was a very thoughtful gesture, and I truly love wearing new clothes. Please don't think I'm anything but grateful."

When she saw Gabriella's face brighten, she breathed a sigh of relief and added, "I am so looking forward to our day together. I can't wait to experience San Telmo. You are such a gracious host."

Misty settled into the seat and told herself to relax. She was along for the ride.

20

SAN TELMO

Visiting San Telmo was like stepping back in time. For several hours Misty and Gabriella walked along cobblestone streets lined with magnificent antique shops. They arrived at historic Dorrego Square just in time to observe a troupe of tango dancers. The men wore white long-sleeved shirts with black vests and black pants. The women were dressed in tight, colorful dresses.

"Oh, Gabriella, look at how graceful they are! This is fantastic. I had no idea how exciting the tango could be. And to think you have me signed up with one of the best instructors in South America."

"Roberto is world renowned. You don't think I would let you spend three months in Buenos Aires and miss learning tango?" She squinted through the sun into Misty's eyes. "I spoke with Roberto this morning. He thinks you are doing great. Now follow me. I have something exciting to show you. I hope you like jazz." Gabriella reached out and took Misty's hand and led her down the sidewalk.

As the women approached the Jazz Club, Misty saw a sign advertising the Buenos Aires Jazz Festival. She could hear the frenetic melodies of trumpets and drums from inside the club and even down the street.

"Misty, you are lucky to be in Buenos Aires this time of year. The Jazz Festival is one of my favorite events."

For the rest of the afternoon they drank wine, ate crackers and cheese, and listened to the most remarkable jazz Misty had ever heard. She didn't know much about jazz but the afternoon educated her ear to the many different styles and forms played in Buenos Aires. She found that she had developed a new love for the music. She had not felt so relaxed and happy in a long time. Being in San Telmo reminded her why she had chosen this job: to travel to new and interesting places, to learn and grow, and, most of all, to be happy.

By the time the sun was setting behind the classical storefronts of the old city, Tom drove them to a small Middle Eastern restaurant with tables covered with beautiful, dyed fabrics instead of the usual white linen. Misty later found out that it was almost impossible to get reservations at Ting Al Amal. Gabriella seemed to be connected all over the city. The entire dining experience was sensational. From the fragrant tea to the diverse flavors of the selections on the *mezze* plates, she had never experienced food with so many textures, smells, and flavors.

After dinner Tom and Gabriella drove Misty to her hotel. As Misty got ready to exit the car, she gave Gabriella a sincere hug and thanked her for the wonderful day. As they embraced Misty noticed how wonderful Gabriella smelled. She had the scent of musky flowers and the sea, something sensuous and powerful hiding a delicate reserve. Misty thought that maybe she held Gabriella in the embrace a moment too long. She broke the embrace, thanked her again, and stepped into the street.

"*No es nada, mi dulce.*" Gabriella winked and pulled the door closed. The limo drove off and disappeared around a corner. Misty felt unbalanced, her head swimming as if she had drunk too many glasses of arrack at dinner. She felt something like embarrassment at feeling intoxicated by Gabriella, or maybe it was just the evening. Whatever it was, she felt good.

Over the next week Gabriella made every training session, even though she was also busy entertaining some very important clients from Spain.

Her clients wanted to develop a European-style outdoor shopping mall that had living quarters above the retail space. The Spanish knew that Gabriella had control over the last parcel of land in the large urban barrio of Palermo, which was just big enough to accommodate their mixed-use development. Both Gabriella and her distinguished clients had been trying to outdo each other in an attempt to get the upper hand in negotiations. After spending almost two weeks with Arturo and Benito, Gabriella had deduced that they were both womanizers with a thing for blondes. This gave her the opportunity she was waiting for.

At a café in Palermo Viejo, over lunch with Arturo and Benito, Gabriella said, "Gentlemen, this is your final weekend in our fine city, and I would like it to be a memorable one. Why don't you accompany my friend and me to the world-renowned Teatro Colón opera house this weekend? You do like the opera, don't you?"

Arturo and Benito didn't seem enthused until Gabriella produced a picture of Misty. Once the men got a look at Misty's blonde hair and fine features, they took the bait.

Arturo said, "Oh, we love the opera, don't we, Benito?" He gave Benito the photo. "We wouldn't miss it for the world. When will you be picking us up?"

"I will be in touch."

Gabriella watched the two walk off looking like schoolboys in their matching brown suits, absorbed in an animated conversation. No doubt they were hedging bets and conducting hardball negotiations regarding who would get to sit next to Misty. Gabriella smiled at her handiwork.

21

DINNER

Driving his car to Amelia's through the crisp Californian night with the windows down, Rob felt a taste of the supposed freedom he had arranged with Misty. He knew he was free to be with other women, but it wasn't something he was accustomed to. At first he thought he would take the high road, but over time, it had become more and more difficult to deal with Misty's frequent absence. They had always been intimate; it had been a large part of their relationship and how they communicated. Two to three months was really pushing the envelope when it came to abstinence. As Rob walked up the steps to Amelia's townhome, he wondered how he would act if an opportunity too good to refuse presented itself.

Amelia opened the door and greeted him. The sweet and spicy smell of Thai food flowed out of the house. The aroma was rather fitting for Amelia's looks as well. Rob found her attractive during his coffee runs, but she never looked this good standing behind the howling espresso machine at Java Joe's.

"Rob, is something the matter?"

"Why no, I'm just a little intoxicated by the delicious smells coming from your kitchen! I have to admit, I've been eating out almost every night." Rob paused and looked her in the eye, "Or maybe it's just because you look so beautiful tonight."

It was the first real compliment Amelia had received in a long time, since before her divorce. It seemed surreal to her, a man she liked at her doorway saying nice things.

"Well," she paused a beat to keep things ambiguous. "I hope you like things spicy. Why don't you come in and make yourself comfortable. Can I get you a beer?"

"A beer sounds really good right now. How 'bout I clean up the kitchen after dinner to help pay my way." That brought a smile to Amelia's face.

It was Rob's first time eating pad thai, and he thought it was delicious. It was an aromatic blend of spicy, sweet, and sour flavors, garnished with lime and cilantro. He was halfway through the meal and a bottle of Riesling before he realized he was eating tofu.

Well, try something new every day, he thought.

"I hope you don't mind me asking this question, but what exactly does your wife do, and why is she away so often?"

Rob bit his fork accidently and winced.

He responded thoughtfully, "Misty is a very talented and renowned personal trainer. She's in high demand. About four times a year she travels to visit a client and train him for anywhere between one to three months."

"Him? Is it always a him?"

"Yes," Rob said slowly. "And always rich and powerful. Once you start working in certain circles, it pays to stay connected. Misty has a very niche business."

"But Rob, don't you worry about her being seduced by one of these clients?" This time Rob spilled the wine as he refilled his glass. As soon as the words left her mouth, Amelia wanted to retract them. She was quick on the trigger, however, and immediately started to apologize.

"Oh, Rob, I'm so sorry. Where are my manners? I guess I've been living alone for so long I just don't remember how to be polite to guests. You don't have to answer that question, of course."

Rob laughed nervously.

"It's totally okay. I mean, it's an obvious question to ask. Misty is very attractive."

Amelia's heart sank slightly.

"I've been alone quite often myself, and these are issues I've been needing to address for a while. Honestly, it has been somewhat difficult for me since agreeing to let Misty take these assignments, and although it didn't bother me at first, I'm beginning to question my decision from—" Rob paused and chose his words carefully. "When I think of Misty being alone with those powerful men, I always come back to the fact that I believe Misty is a professional and everything that happens when she is gone will be solely business related."

He was proud of himself. He knew that Misty sleeping with her clients technically *was* business. But that was the part that bothered him. Rob still believed that if Misty slept with her clients it was not because she was in love with them. It was just business. But if he slept with Amelia it would be because he wanted to and would have nothing to do with business.

"Well, I admire your trust in your wife, Rob. You are really a strong person." Rob was indeed admirable, but Amelia wondered how satisfied he was with his marriage. The confident tone in his voice contradicted the sadness in his eyes.

They finished off the wine and opened up a few beers for dessert, feeling playfully naughty about it. They continued to talk, but about things less personal than the past, and before they knew it, it was after midnight. As they said good-bye, Amelia looked Rob in the eye and said, "I just want you to know that I had a wonderful evening, and you have a standing offer to come back for a home-cooked dinner anytime you want." And with a grin she added, "I can cook Italian, too."

Rob reached out and took Amelia's hands and flashed her a smile.

"I hope you mean it. A home-cooked meal is hard to come by these days."

22

Night at the Opera

The next morning, Rob's phone rang.

"Rob! I miss you. How's your day going?"

"Hi, Misty. I'm so glad you called. The day's, you know, going. Got my morning americano and thinking about watching golf this afternoon. Phil Mickelson is having a pretty good tournament and you know how much I like Phil."

"Sounds like a packed day."

Rob could hear laughing, cars rushing, and someone shouting in Spanish in the background.

"Guess what I'm getting ready to do? In thirty minutes I will be taking my ninth tango lesson. Aren't you proud of me?"

"Tango lessons? That's the funniest thing I've heard all week. You? You're a rough-and-tumble girl. You sure you haven't been in the sun too long?"

Rob broke into heavy laughter until he caught himself. "Misty, are you still there? You sure are quiet." He was beginning to feel that he was not handling the conversation well.

She responded flatly, "You are so funny, Rob. I've got to go. Enjoy your afternoon."

Talking to Rob both angered Misty and motivated her to try harder at tango that morning. Roberto remarked after their lesson that she had really channeled the *pasión* of tango, words she had found encouraging.

While showering in her room after class, Misty thought about how she would prove to Rob that she was more refined than a simple rough-and-tumble girl. *I'm more than just an athlete. I can be as refined and elegant as anyone—even as sophisticated as Gabriella, if I put my mind to it!* Misty didn't really believe that last part, but it made her feel good to think it. Learning the tango proficiently in three months was like becoming an accomplished gymnast in three months—impossible. It was the hardest thing she had ever done. For a while she thought she might be doing it for Gabriella, but now she knew she was doing it entirely for herself.

There was a knock at the door just as she was stepping out of the shower. She grumbled about the rotten timing as she wrapped a towel around her dripping wet body and opened the door.

"Gabriella, what are you doing here? Is something wrong?"

Gabriella stood dumbly in the doorway staring at Misty, her eyes wide and glazed. After a second she snapped out of it. Misty stood with her head cocked to the side, her long blond hair dripping onto the carpet.

"Oh, Misty, I'm so sorry I caught you at a bad time. Please go back to the bathroom and get dressed. What I have to tell you can wait." Misty laughed at Gabriella's awkwardness and went into the bathroom to change. While she dressed, they continued their conversation through the bathroom door.

"Misty, the reason I came by was to tell you we are going to the opera tonight. The Teatro Colón is one of the top five opera houses in the world, and I would never forgive myself if you didn't get a chance to see it before leaving. You do like the opera, don't you?"

Misty turned on the hair dryer to buy herself some time to think of a response. She had never been to an opera nor had she ever wanted to attend one. But as she watched herself in the mirror, she realized she was being childish. It wasn't like she had any other plans, and everything Gabriella had arranged for them so far had been a lot of fun.

Misty switched the hairdryer off and was about to accept the invitation graciously when a thought shot through her head like a bolt of lightning. "But Gabriella, I have nothing to wear!"

"Oh, Misty! Don't you know me by now? Haven't I provided you with clothes for everything we've done so far? The only reason I didn't bring you an evening gown is that it will be much more fun to let you pick it out. But before that, we're going to visit my good friend Pino. He runs the most wonderful salon, and I just know you will love what he can do with your hair."

"You always think of everything."

"I'm so glad you are excited. There is one more thing I should tell you; I am working on a rather large real estate deal, and you will be helping me entertain my clients, Arturo and Benito. The more flirtatious you are, the better chance I will have in my negotiations. Is this something you would feel comfortable doing?"

Misty thought, *Did Gabriella just ask me if I would do something instead of telling me? Now that's a pleasant surprise.* She smiled and nodded.

As they walked out the door she gave Gabriella a mischievous grin.

"Not to worry, girlfriend. I'll have them eating out of my hand before the evening is over. This is going to be fun. Maybe I'll even save you enough money to pay for all the things you're buying me. I can't wait to pick out my new gown." Misty could tell she had just made Gabriella's day.

23

At the Teatro

When Misty and Gabriella strode slowly across the marble flag-stones of the grand lobby of the Teatro Colón, all eyes—not just those of Arturo and Benito—were on them. Gabriella wore a daringly cut Emanuel Ungaro hand-painted gown that accentuated her beautiful upper torso and long elegant neck and hugged her sleek body all the way to the floor. Her olive complexion and black hair complemented the maroon, beige, and light-gold pattern.

As beautiful as Gabriella looked, Misty was even more spectacular. The sight of Misty's long golden hair draped just above the back of her Carlos Miele jet-black, full-length gown was stunning. The gown was just as sleek as Gabriella's and Misty thought it made her seem as long and lean as she had ever looked. Plus, the low-cut dress magnificently accentuated her breasts. Gabriella intentionally bought Misty an under-sized gown just so she did not leave anything to chance in the attempt to distract her oversexed clients. If the great designer Carlos Miele could see Misty in his work of art, he would have thought she looked every bit as beautiful as his celebrity clients.

Arturo and Benito had been staring at them as they moved through the crowd, but it wasn't until the women were right upon them that their faces fell.

"Ga-Ga-Gabriella?" Arturo stuttered in disbelief. Benito stood there, dumb as a post, trying to process what he was seeing. He'd only seen Gabriella in suits tailored to translate her curves into masculine lines.

"Gentlemen, I would like you to meet my personal trainer and good friend, Misty. She has been kind enough to spend three months in Buenos Aires training me. I hope I can count on the two of you to help show Misty a good time tonight. *Mi amiga no habla español, ¿está bien?* So, English, guys. Okay?"

They nodded stiffly and stood tall, looking as much like gentlemen as they could.

Benito didn't waste a moment greeting Misty as if she were royalty. His English accent was good, but the words didn't come out right.

"I am very placed to seat you."

Misty stifled a laugh. Arturo not so subtly nudged his friend out of the way and took Misty's hand. He raised it to his lips and kissed it.

"Pay no attention to my associate. I am Arturo Jose Carlos De Los Parlotes De Amadeo, and this is," he glanced at his friend, "this is Benito." Gabriella raised an eyebrow at the two men acting like children to impress the new girl at school.

Gabriella strategically placed Misty's seat between Arturo and Benito She sat on the other side of Arturo; he was the more stubborn of the two, and if she could talk to him after Misty had softened him up, she'd have a better chance of getting her way in the negotiations later. Gabriella only needed Benito to behave himself so that he didn't make Misty want to go home early. Gabriella had a long night planned for the four of them. The real savior of the evening, however, was the opera house itself. Once seated before the grand proscenium, the two men's persistent posturing ceased.

Misty, to her surprise, was absolutely enthralled by the Teatro Colón. Magnificent didn't come close to describing the opera house. Even though the balconies rose four stories above them, the rich interior and warm lighting made the large space intimate. Paintings on the ceiling surrounded the largest and most beautiful chandelier Misty had ever seen. All she could see was elegant gold everywhere, and one look at the woodwork made her understand why it had taken so long to build. The woodwork was also one of the reasons that construction had, at one point, stopped: they ran out of money. Had they not run out of money, delaying the project for a whole year, Gabriella's great grandparents would not have met, and she wouldn't be one of the wealthiest people sitting in the Teatro.

Halfway through Verdi's *Aida*—the very same opera that opened the Teatro a hundred years before—Gabriella realized things were not going as she had planned. Her three guests were mesmerized by the facility but totally underwhelmed by the opera. It was becoming obvious she had made a huge miscalculation and was in danger of losing the upper hand in her negotiations. Of course two rowdy boys and a wayward American woman wouldn't swoon for the opera. She needed to get the blood pumping in the two Spaniards, or it was going to cost her a lot of money. She needed to come up with Plan B.

Gabriella dabbed away a tear as the curtains closed on *Aida*. The performance was divine, moving and beautiful. She looked at her three guests, two of whom were asleep. Misty was relieved to see the velvet hit the stage. Gabriella stood and nudged Arturo with her foot. He jumped awake, startled. Misty took the clue and woke Benito.

"I guess the opera isn't for everyone," Gabriella said. "But don't worry. I know a place with a more exciting type of theater." She could see Arturo and Benito instantly revive.

24

SMOKIN' HOT

When they walked through the front door of the Caliente Cabaret, it became clear to Misty why the boys were so excited about going. The place was alive with women of every nationality and shape. The club's interior was dark but richly decorated with fine fabrics, leather, and red accents. From the outside, the place had not been much to look at, but inside it was sparkling with energy and far more charged than the club she had experienced in New Orleans, and the total opposite of the refinement she had experienced only forty-five minutes earlier when rubbing shoulders with the sophisticates at the opera. The cabaret could only be described as opulent.

Gabriella leaned over and whispered to Misty, "Don't let the crowd fool you. Some of the richest and most powerful people in Argentina frequent this club. A high-ranking dignitary stopped by last month and the rumor is he had a thing for one of the Cali girls, Andrea Rincón. Apparently he laid down $1,000 to spend five minutes with her! Andrea is Argentina's top adult movie star, but I've known her since she was a little girl, and she's extremely smart. Her mother was my parents' personal chef for several decades. She used to come over and swim in our pool. By the time she was sixteen my mother had to ask her mother politely to not bring her over to swim anymore as my father had a heart condition, if you know what I mean. If Andrea is working tonight I'll introduce you to her, but right now we need to get Arturo and Benito distracted so I can try to negotiate the price of my land."

"And just how do you propose we do that?"

"Follow me. We need to get into character."

Misty wasn't exactly sure what she meant by "getting into character," but she was ready for a change of pace after snoozing through the stuffy Italian opera. Gabriella took Misty by the hand and led her past darkened tables of men and women whispering and laughing and shouting, past the garishly lighted bar with its hundred bottles of liquor, and past the shining stage of acrobatic dancers into the dressing area.

There were maybe a dozen girls in various stages of dress and costume, some wearing feathers, others ornate lingerie, and some nothing at all. At first Misty and Gabriella weren't noticed, but the amount of clothing covering their skin gave them away. A girl wearing a brightly colored mask of feathers and sequins, and not much else, gasped when she saw Gabriella.

"Doña Marquez, what are you doing here? We didn't know you were coming."

All the girls in the dressing room gathered around Gabriella, hugging her and kissing her cheek. What Misty didn't know was that Gabriella was a silent partner in the club, but she was very low key about it. She had acquired a stake in the business as repayment for a debt and had grown to love the women who made the cabaret what it was.

One of the girls commented on Gabriella and Misty's beautiful gowns. "*Que lindo!*" she whispered, touching the fabric delicately. Another girl reached out and stroked the material of Misty's dress while whispering in Spanish. Misty was a little startled as other women began touching her. Reading Misty's facial expression, Gabriella smiled and said, "Come on, follow me. I'll save you from all of these wild women!"

Gabriella pulled Misty through the dressing room.

"Poor girls. Most of them are from the very poorest areas of South America. Andrea's family fled Columbia when she was a small child. I like to think of the cabaret as a refuge."

She took Misty into Andrea's private dressing room. She closed the door behind them so they were alone. The room was more like a large walk-in closet, with a few stuffed leather chairs and a large vanity with a collection of makeup and animal masks made with real fur hanging from them. Gabriella walked over to a rack of clothing and began rifling through it.

"I keep a change of clothes here for emergencies," she grunted as she shoved a large swath of clothing out of her way. "Our gowns have to go, chica." Misty half expected her to pull out a slutty minidress or something else one of the dancers might wear. Instead, she pulled out a dark pinstriped suit.

"Uh, Gabriella?"

"Playtime is over for me. I need Arturo and Benito to see me as a businesswoman so that they will respect me when I take their *cojones* in this real estate deal."

She threw the suit over a chair and went to another rack of clothing and costumes. "You, however, must be as *caliente* as possible." She drew a dark-red scrap of fabric from the rack and tossed it over her shoulder to Misty.

"Put that on. We've got to get back out there before those boys run off." Gabriella began to unzip the back of her dress. Misty looked at the fabric in her hands and held it up in front of her, figuring it was some kind of dress—a very short dress. As she started looking for a place to change, Gabriella called to her.

"Misty, I can't get this zipper. Can you help me?"

"Sure." Misty put the red garment down and walked over to her. As she unstuck the zipper, the light silk of Gabriella's Emanuel Ungaro gown fell to the floor, revealing smooth olive skin, lean feminine shoulders, and a narrow waist widening to firm, round buttocks. Misty paused, stunned.

She is really gorgeous, she thought. *Her body looks like a work of art.*

"Admiring your handiwork?" Gabriella asked, looking over her shoulder.

"You're beautiful."

"*Gracias*. Now, let's get dressed." She winked at Misty.

Misty tried to concentrate on getting herself into the dress Gabriella had picked out for her. She didn't realize until after it was on that she had to take off her bra for it to really work. When she had herself straightened out, she took a look in the vanity mirror. She was wearing a flowing piece of red cloth that fell from her shoulders in an open V all the way to her pelvis where it gathered in a small skirt just covering her underwear. It was as if she was wearing nothing and yet was very nicely dressed. She was exposed from her neck all the way past her belly button, but the dress passed over her nipples, revealing the curve of her breasts. She had to admit it was sexy and classy.

Gabriella, meanwhile, was buttoning the links on her French cuffs and tying back her hair. She looked powerful and sultry, the suit hanging perfectly on her tight body. She looked Misty up and down and nodded. "Perfect. Let's go."

When the women walked up to Arturo and Benito's table, the effect was the same as when they had met the Spaniards at the opera house.

"*Doña* Gabriella!" Arturo gasped. Already Gabriella's plan was working.

Standing in front of the boys with her hands on her hips, Gabriella said, "Sorry we were gone so long. We wanted to get into something a little more comfortable." Arturo was speechless for the first time that night and Benito openly stared at Misty's bare torso through the crimson folds of her dress.

Strangely, his stare didn't make her uncomfortable. She actually liked wearing something so revealing. She thought, *Gabriella needs my help so why not have some fun with it. I enjoyed driving the boys wild in high school. Handling the Spaniards should be no different.*

Misty sat down next to Benito and took a sip out of his drink while looking him in the eye over the rim. She touched her lips demurely and brought her hand down softly on his leg.

"Benito, you've been here for a while. Which one of those hot ladies would you like to have? I think that little number in the red thong thinks you're cute." He stared wide-eyed at her and coughed.

Misty deftly slid her hand into the inside pocket of his jacket and drew out his money clip. She snapped a hundred-peso note from the clip and held up the crisp bill, motioning to the girl in the red thong, who expertly twisted off the pole and strutted toward them. Benito offered no resistance and looked from the dancer to Misty and back again, smiling.

She wanted to please Gabriella by making sure Benito did not escape, but she was pretty sure she didn't have much to worry about. Benito wasn't going anywhere. Misty wouldn't admit to herself that she was enjoying the lap dance nearly as much as Benito. *My God this woman is beautiful*, she thought. *Look at her golden skin. There isn't a blemish on it.*

As the dancer brushed Benito's face with her nipples and leaned forward to put his face between her breasts, she knelt on her knees over him, moving rhythmically to the music. She turned and looked down at Misty. Her eyes were confident and hungry. Misty was mesmerized.

Misty's lips tingled and her tongue seemed to burn when the dancer leaned over and gave her a long, wet, open-mouthed kiss. Misty moved her hand up the Spaniard's leg and stroked him through his tight pants. He was already straining against them. The feel of his warm hardness on her hand made Misty instantly wet.

Suddenly Benito moaned quietly and asked the dancer to get off. Embarrassed, he got up and walked quickly toward the men's restroom. The girl in the red thong didn't leave, though. She threw a leg over Misty and knelt on top of her. The sweet smell of sweat mixed with perfume filled Misty's lungs and took control of her senses. She began fondling the woman's breasts. This wasn't New Orleans; the girl let Misty touch her all over. Misty never knew caressing another woman could feel so different. It was nothing like touching herself or touching a man. She felt dangerous, her senses heightened, wanting for more.

What am I doing? This is embarrassing. I hope Gabriella hasn't noticed.

Misty breathed a sigh of relief when she turned to find Gabriella in a deep discussion with Arturo. She gave the girl the hundred pesos and pressed her hands lightly against her thighs, directing her to get off. And then she was gone, back into the crowd. Misty's heart was still racing.

Gabriella was at her wits' end. The plan was for Arturo to fall for Misty, but now he was beginning to take a serious interest in Gabriella. If Arturo made a pass at Gabriella and she rebuffed him, the entire night and possibly the entire real estate deal would fall apart. What had looked like an easy trick before was now looking like more trouble than it was worth. She caught a glimpse of Andrea out of the corner of her eye.

"Arturo, I've got something I need to do. I'll be right back."

"*Bien*, Gabriella. I'll be right here when you return."

Gabriella strode across the cabaret to Andrea and touched her on the shoulder. She turned around in surprise.

"*Mi hermana!* How are you? You are much too beautiful to be in a place like this," Andrea said playfully.

"I could be better. Andrea, you look stunning tonight."

Indeed, Andrea did. She was wearing the nicest, longest dress in the place. Many years ago Gabriella had coached Andrea to dress like a lady in order to attract higher-paying clients. "It's just good business sense," Gabriella had said.

"Me? Look at you, Gabriella. Who are you trying to impress? What's her name?"

"I need your help. Listen, I've got a Spanish bull over there who needs to be put down. You up for it, *matadora?*"

Andrea looked through the crowd at Arturo sitting in his tailored suit, drinking rum.

"He looks like an absolute beast. Just my type." She paused, pursing her lips. "I have to ask. What's the occasion?"

"My big plan was to soften this guy up on a real estate deal. However, things aren't going according to plan, and now he thinks I'm on tonight's menu. I'm not going to sleep with him just to make a little more money, but if I don't, it might kill the deal."

"So your dominatrix routine is finally paying off?" Andrea laughed, stroking Gabriella's pinstriped arm.

"I will make sure it's worth your time, *hermanita.*"

"You know I would do anything for you Gabriella. *De nada.* We are like family. Besides, there's nothing I like more than taming Spaniards."

"You have my undying appreciation. You know you're going to own this place some day."

Andrea winked and walked toward Arturo.

When Gabriella found Misty, she was leaning against the wall and seemed to be in a fog.

"Oh, Gabriella, I'm so sorry. I'm afraid I just embarrassed Benito, and I feel really bad about it."

"Don't worry. I just made a colossal mistake that probably makes yours look minor by comparison. I'll tell you about it later, and by then we can both have a good laugh. That is, if I didn't blow my real estate deal."

"Well, what do we do now?"

"Hopefully nothing. Let's just stand here and pretend to talk while I monitor the situation for a moment."

From a distance the girls observed Andrea make her moves on Arturo. Andrea was a sex bomb in the classic sense. Well-endowed with voluptuous hips, she had long black hair that hung down her flawless brown skin past her shoulders. She had the face of royalty and the confidence to back it up, even though she was from a family of poor farmers. The years working for Gabriella had sharpened her wit so that no one could ever mistake her for just a pretty face.

Benito came lumbering out of the men's room. It was getting late, and he was tired. All he wanted to do was go back to the hotel. When he approached the table, he got his wish.

Arturo did not want anything to ruin his chances with Andrea, so the moment he saw Benito he said, "Why don't you go back to the hotel? I want you fresh for tomorrow's meeting. I may be out late tonight, so I'll just see you in the morning."

Andrea chimed in, "Yes, Benito, I can assure you Arturo will be out late tonight." She began kissing Arturo's ear.

Gabriella sized up the situation and made her move. When she and Misty dropped by the table, Gabriella pretended to be startled.

"Arturo, what are you doing?"

"Gabriella, this is—" he searched for a creative answer, "an old friend of mine. I haven't seen her in several years and would like to catch up on things. I hope you don't mind."

Looking slightly hurt, Gabriella replied, "I guess I understand. But I had hoped to finish our negotiations tonight."

"Negotiations?" replied Andrea. "I just love rich businessmen. Are you a rich businessman, Arturo?"

Arturo was speechless a moment as he contemplated what to do. He was bad at improvising and was worried Gabriella would start to figure out he was blowing her off for a woman he had just met. He thought Gabriella might get upset and either raise the asking price so high he would have to back off or just kill the deal. But the liquor and the women had softened his resolve. He only wanted Andrea now.

"Gabriella, I've been thinking. If we can get this settled right now, I will raise my offer from 12 million euros to 12.5."

As soon as the words were out of his mouth, he began to regret his offer. He tried to think of a way to retract it but it was too late.

Gabriella looked Andrea in the eyes and said, "Why yes, Arturo is a rich and powerful man, and you are a very lucky girl. Arturo, because I like you, I'm going to accept your offer. Please take out your BlackBerry and send me a confirmation e-mail. I would like to put this deal to bed tonight."

When Arturo hesitated for a moment, Andrea said, "Oh this is so exciting. But let's make it quick, because I'd like to put something else to bed tonight." Arturo hurriedly composed the e-mail.

Grabbing the device from his hand, Andrea pushed the Send button and giggled.

Gabriella gave Arturo a sly grin. "It was a pleasure doing business with you, Arturo. Let's go, Misty. I'm starting to get an appetite." Arturo had the look of someone who had just witnessed a car wreck.

When Tom pulled up to the Tango Hotel, Misty hugged Gabriella tightly.

"Oh, Gabriella. I had such a wonderful night. It was a blast. Thank you so much."

"No, thank you, Misty. Now get some rest because I've got a lot more fun things planned for us, chica."

As Misty entered the elevator she realized how much she was beginning to enjoy Gabriella's company. For some reason, however, the thought made her tense and nervous in a way that she couldn't fathom, as if she couldn't trust her enjoyment. Misty went up to her room, disrobed, and went to sleep, hoping the uneasiness would subside by morning.

25

FUN IN THE SUN

Over the next month, Misty made incredible progress with her tango lessons, while Gabriella transformed her body into incredible shape. Both women were ecstatic about their accomplishments. Typically, Misty's relationship with her clients was a one-way street. She rarely interacted with them outside of the scheduled training sessions, using them strategically to build sexual tension—as well as muscle tone—until her client completed the contract early and Misty could go home early and fulfilled. This was always a great source of satisfaction, but still one-sided. Now with the tango lessons, Misty was sharing the experience with Gabriella, as each woman had a vested interest in the progress of the other. A strong bond was beginning to form that gave Misty a warm feeling of trust and friendship.

Misty was lying in her bed one morning when she heard a knock on the door. She cracked the door open and saw Tom standing there with yet more bags in his hands. "Tom, what have you got for me today? Is it something good?"

"Oh, now you like me bringing you gifts. My, haven't we changed?"

"Okay wise guy, go ahead and rub it in. I guess I have become accustomed to the gifts, but don't tell Gabriella."

"So, you think I'm Gabriella's spy? Put me on your payroll, and I'll be a double agent."

"The only double I'm going to give you, Tom, is double trouble if you don't give me my presents."

He chuckled and set the bags on the bed.

When she opened them, she found eight bathing suits that were all skimpy. Inside was a note that read, "I hope you like the swimwear. I know they don't have much material but I thought you would want to blend in on the beaches of Rio de Janeiro. We leave tonight."

Rio de Janeiro! She kept saying the name over and over in her head. *I'm going to Rio de Janeiro! What a wonderful way to spend a weekend!*

Tom could see Misty was preoccupied so he let himself out without saying good-bye.

The excitement turned to apprehension once Misty started trying on her presents. She had never exposed so much of herself in public. When she put on the bottom of her thong bikini, she was aghast. Over half of her pubic hair was exposed. *My word, this just isn't going to work. I can't go out in public wearing this.*

Just then the phone rang.

"Before you say anything, darling, I need you to understand that everyone on the beaches in Rio will be wearing skimpy swimwear. Some won't even be wearing tops. Besides, no one will even know you so this is your big chance to live on the wild side. What do they say in the States? What happens in Vegas stays in Vegas? Well just substitute Rio for Vegas. And don't worry about that other little thing. I'm picking you up in a few minutes, and we are both going to get a Brazilian wax." Gabriella hung up.

The thought of being naughty around perfect strangers excited Misty the way it had excited her to expose herself to the crowd in New Orleans.

When she got into the car with Tom and Gabriella, she looked at them and shook her head. Tom was doing everything he could not to grin, but he was having a hard time.

Misty said, "Tom, not one word out of you today, got it?"

Gabriella grinned but quickly stopped once she got a darting glare from Misty.

They rode in silence for some time before Gabriella held out her hand to Misty. "Here, you might want to take some Tylenol with codeine if this is your first time."

"Does it hurt that much?"

Gabriella smiled but did not answer.

Misty was still apprehensive when she lay down on the table in her private room at the Wax-on Wax-off salon. A sweet-faced young woman came in and immediately made her feel more comfortable.

"Hi, I'm Gracie, and I'll be taking care of you. Gabriella told me this is your first time. Don't worry. I will be very careful. I even brought you a paper thong so you won't get embarrassed."

Once Misty put on the paper thong, she relaxed. Gracie took one look and said, "Oh! I thought you would be a little more blonde." Gracie ran her hands through the hair on Misty's head and said, "We will be leaving some hair, just a strip. Would you like me to dye your pubic hair as blonde as your hair?"

"Why not?" Misty laughed. "Well, I guess the cat's out of the bag now."

The process over the next half hour was both interesting and a little painful. First, Gracie put on talcum powder. Next, she applied the hot wax, which didn't burn nearly as much as Misty had anticipated. Then, Gracie placed cloth over the wax. Once the wax cooled, she pulled the hair out with quick jerks, being careful to always pull against the natural grain of Misty's hair. When it was all over, Misty looked down and was happy with the results. She knew she would never do this in the States but this weekend she wasn't going to be in the States. She was going to be on the beaches of Rio! She felt excited all over again.

Misty, Gabriella, Miguel, and Tom boarded the Gulfstream and flew overland to Rio. The weather was perfect, and Misty could look down and enjoy the beautiful countryside. As they approached the private runway, Misty could see the famous Christ the Redeemer statue. It gave her goose bumps. It had always symbolized Rio to her in movies and pictures, and now she was really there.

Miguel was equally excited. He had spent two months with his brother's family making up for lost time. Things were now squared away, so he was free to focus on other parts of the trip. Gabriella was very happy to have Miguel with them as Rio de Janeiro could be dangerous. Crime in the *favelas* surrounding the safe tourist areas often spilt over with deadly consequences. Having both Tom and Miguel by her side comforted Gabriella.

On their final descent, Misty asked, "So, Gabriella, what do you have in store for us this weekend?"

Tom and Miguel's ears perked up. They were both hoping it included a lot of time on the beaches. Miguel, in particular, pictured himself in a bathing suit with his muscular upper body glistening in the sun. With his sunglasses on, he could look a little menacing in the event that some guys wanted to give Gabriella and Misty trouble. Tom could be a pretty intimidating figure himself. His amiable personality contrasted his six feet two height and solid build of 220 pounds. He had been the fleet heavyweight boxing champion in the U.S. Navy and looked every bit like someone who could hold his own in a brawl.

Tom's German ancestry cursed him with naturally pale skin in a country of sun, and Miguel chided him. "Now Tom, be sure to put on lots of suntan lotion throughout this trip. You know it's illegal to bring lobsters into Argentina from another country."

Tom shook his head.

"I thought we would go to a local salsa bar tonight to watch the salsa dancers. This is the heart of salsa country, you know. They say it was started by a slave who became a free woman. She taught locals the dances she had learned in Africa," Gabriella said.

Miguel, given to superstition, said enthusiastically, "Maybe we'll be able to feel her spirit tonight." Misty frowned at him and shook her head.

Gabriella said, "Tomorrow we will all spend the day at the beach. You are probably thinking Copacabana, due to the song, but I prefer the beach at Ipanema."

"Wasn't there an old song that went something like—" Miguel broke into song, "The girl from Ipanema goes walking . . . something, something?"

Gabriella nodded. "Tomorrow night I thought we would hang out on the beach and watch the sun go down."

Tom sighed audibly, and Miguel seemed to become antsy at the thought of sitting in the sand making small talk. Gabriella expected this and was ready with a remedy. "Don't worry, guys. I didn't take you as the sunset type, so I reserved a table at the local bar. I hear it's very popular with single women." Gabriella rolled her eyes a little, slightly annoyed at having to babysit grown men.

Miguel smiled and said, "We're always willing to do our part in, um, scouting out the place. Right, Tom?"

"I thought you boys would enjoy that. Don't worry; I've got you on my speed dial. If anything looks suspicious, you will only be minutes away. Besides, there's supposed to be pretty good security on the beach at night."

"There's only one piece of bad news," Gabriella said, her tone turning apologetic. "I have an important board meeting to attend Sunday afternoon, so we will have to head back early Sunday morning."

Gabriella was pleased with how she had, yet again, organized a good time for her friends.

Typical of South America, where people sometimes don't often eat dinner before ten in the evening, the salsa club was just starting to stir when they arrived at nine o'clock. This gave Gabriella enough time to give Misty a crash course in salsa dancing. Misty watched Gabriella as she slowly walked through the basic steps. Misty instantly fell in love with the dance, but she knew it was out of her league this trip. If only she had been learning the salsa along with the tango! *Maybe on one of my future assignments*, she thought.

Misty ordered her usual Flor de Cana straight up while the men drank Skol beers one after the other. Sadly, the wine and bourbon selection at the bar was poor, and Gabriella was having a tough time deciding on what to drink, so she decided to take a sip of Misty's.

"That is really good, but the rum is just a touch too heavy for me."

"Not a problem, Gabriella. This one is aged seven years, but they make a five-year and a four-year, which are a little sweeter."

Gabriella tried the five-year and wound up ordering a bottle. While they were sipping on their rum and waiting for the club to start grooving, Gabriella explained to Misty that salsa is an act of seduction and reverence from the man toward the woman. Misty felt this made the dance even more desirable and now really regretted not knowing it.

By ten thirty the mood in the club started to crank up, and the dance floor was filling up with well-dressed men and women who looked like frequent guests.

Just as Gabriella was scanning the crowd for a good dance partner, Miguel tapped her on the shoulder. "May I have this dance?"

Both Gabriella and Misty looked up at him, shocked.

"Miguel!" Misty gasped. "I've known you for eleven years, and you never told me you could salsa."

"Well, Misty, maybe there's a lot you don't know about me." He raised an eyebrow and took Gabriella's hand.

So off Gabriella and Miguel went. Misty watched the pair for an hour and became a little jealous. Even though it was immediately obvious that Miguel wasn't telling the whole truth about knowing how to salsa—he had the basic idea, but not all the moves—the two of them looked like they were having a blast. Misty felt like the odd one out. Well, maybe she and Tom, who had moved down the bar to sit next to her, were the odd couple out.

"I just love watching Gabriella dance, don't you? She is so graceful and coordinated. I could watch her for hours."

Misty enjoyed watching Gabriella as well, and it was frustrating not to be able to dance with her. She had been watching her nonstop the whole evening. She and Gabriella had become so close, doing everything together, and now they were separated. Having a close friend at last after all these years was wonderful, but somehow her relationship with Gabriella didn't feel complete.

Misty switched her attention to Tom from time to time, to keep him company, but she preferred watching Gabriella spin and dance under the multicolored lights of the dance floor, her skirt flying and her arms raised, her eyes closed and her hair wild. She was beautiful.

26

SURF'S UP

"Tom, I think we're ready to go," Gabriella said after breakfast. "Flag down a taxi?"

"Sure thing, Gabriella."

"Are you guys excited?" Gabriella asked.

Miguel replied, "Are you kidding me? I didn't sleep a wink last night thinking about all the lovely ladies I saw at the club. I can only imagine what today's going to be like."

"I think my feelings are hurt, Migs. So, you think Gabriella and I are just chopped liver?"

"Are you kidding me? You two are the hot babes I'm talking about! I usually only see you when you're wearing regular clothes and workout stuff. I'm sure you are both wearing something very provocative underneath those baggy beach dresses. Don't worry about anything happening to you today. I'm going to keep my eyes on you all day long."

"Gross, Miguel. You pervert. Maybe Gabriella and I will just stay covered up all day." Misty picked up her beach bag, huffing. Gabriella flashed Miguel a smile, enjoying the ruse.

Once they settled in with their beach chairs and oversized umbrella, Misty walked to the edge of the pounding surf so she could look up and down the long curve of Ipanema Beach. The beach was situated in an inlet of pure blue water. Beachgoers were arriving nonstop, and soon there would be thousands. Hundreds of brightly colored shade umbrellas dotted the beach into the distance. She noticed the downtown Rio skyline only blocks away. It provided a backdrop of high-rise structures: tall office buildings mingled with scores of condominiums.

Misty followed the beach line with her eyes all the way to the far end, where Sugar Loaf Mountain loomed. The large hill was like a dragon lying down to protect the beach with its head jutting out to sea. The sand was hot between her toes, and the cool water lapped against her heels. She was mesmerized by the beauty of the beach and of Brazil.

Seated under the shade of their umbrella, Miguel and Tom were mesmerized as well.

"Hey Miguel, do you see that one? Oh, wait, look at that one over there!"

"Tom, slow down or you'll get bloodshot eyes."

"Don't worry, Miguel. I've been training my eyes for years."

Miguel had never quite seen swimwear like this. One girl had on a sideless metallic nano G-string suit that looked like a single piece of Lycra stretched from her pubis, over her breasts, to the back of her neck. Miguel couldn't understand how it stayed on. But it was the girl with the black onyx V-string and cage top that really got the guys going. The top only had three strings per breast that came together at each nipple. There wasn't much left to the imagination.

"Hey Tom, you're going to scare the fish away if you don't close your mouth," Miguel said. "Let's walk over to that vendor and get you some sunglasses."

"I've been in the game a lot longer than you, young man. But, it is a very sunny day. Gabriella, we will return in a moment."

"I think I can take care of myself for a few minutes, guys." Gabriella laughed at their overprotectiveness.

Tom and Miguel came back just as Gabriella was removing her beach dress. Miguel was stunned by her choice of swimwear. The entire swimsuit was made out of fishnet. "Hey Tom," Miguel whispered under his breath. "You can see Gabriella's nipples through the fishnet." There was no response from Tom, who looked shocked.

If the men had a chance to recover themselves, it was too soon because Misty stripped off her beach dress next. Misty's 35C-25-35 dimensions filled her black tank bodysuit to the brim. The suit looked like it was painted on and covered her firm full breasts like a second skin, the thin material peeling back in a V away from her chest, baring her ample bosom. Just as they were beginning to appreciate the front of the suit, Misty turned around and bent over to pick up some suntan lotion. That's when they got a good look at the scooped back and high-cut sides. A small string of fabric ran between her two well-defined buttocks, exposing the black widow tattoo on her right cheek.

Miguel thought it appropriate that any client seeing the tattoo would be seeing Misty for the last time. He realized he would never be able to look at her the same way again, and that if he wanted to be professional, he needed to work on putting this sight out of his mind. He turned his thoughts to Sylvia and looked out to sea.

Tom, however, had no qualms about looking, especially since his eyes were hidden behind his newly purchased sunglasses. Gabriella, too, was unashamed in her appreciation of Misty's body. She gazed at her over the top of her novel, her eye tracing her friend's figure. For her, it was the realization of a small fantasy that had started the minute she bought the bathing suit for Misty back in Buenos Aires.

"Misty, why don't we go for a walk along the beach and enjoy the sights?"

"Sounds great. I'd love to see more of the beach."

Miguel interjected in a serious tone, "Tom and I will walk the beach a dozen yards behind you."

"Thanks Miguel."

Gabriella and Misty walked for a good twenty minutes, establishing a comfortable distance between themselves and the men following behind. When Gabriella was sure they were no longer in earshot, she said, "So Misty, how are your tango lessons coming?"

"Well, you'll just have to wait to find out," Misty teased.

Gabriella enjoyed the teasing and was happy that Misty felt comfortable enough with her to be playful.

"What's your story, Misty? Where do you come from, and how did I end up paying you so much money to play with me in South America?"

"It's really not that interesting of a story."

"Everyone's story is interesting. Please tell me yours."

Misty pondered for a moment before responding. "I have never told anyone my story before. In fact, it's somewhat painful, and I guess I've buried it away from myself."

"I promise whatever you tell me will be in the strictest confidence, and I will not judge you. Girlfriends are not in the business of judging."

"Thanks, Gabriella. You are probably the only person on earth I feel comfortable telling it to." She took a deep breath. "Okay, here goes nothing. I grew up like any midwestern girl in rural western Minnesota. My parents owned a farm outside of Hancock. I was an only child, and my parents gave me plenty of attention. To the best of my memory, Mom was always in a good mood and very much in love with my father. Dad was usually working on our farm or in town going to city council or school board meetings. He was considered a pillar of our community. One day when I was only eight years old, I was playing with one of my friends in town when my grandparents came to pick me up."

At this point Misty stopped abruptly. Tears formed in her eyes. Gabriella was wise enough not to say anything. The men were gaining on them, and both Miguel and Tom looked concerned. Gabriella motioned for them to stop. They halted, looking confused.

Misty cleared her throat and resumed her story. "While Gramma held me in her arms, Gramps told me that my parents had been driving back from Minneapolis early that morning when a drunk driver plowed into them head-on. They were killed instantly. I remember feeling like I was in a movie or something—that it wasn't real. The perfect little world I knew had instantly changed. Fortunately for me, I had two wonderful grandparents to look after me later. I think they fantasized they were raising my mother all over again. I looked and acted a lot like her, so they were simultaneously raising me and grieving for their daughter at the same time." She looked up at Gabriella with wet eyes and laughed nervously.

"I guess I've blocked out a lot of these memories. They've always been too painful to deal with. My grandparents lived in Alexandria,

Minnesota. It was and still is a really small town. To take my mind off things I threw myself into sports. Soccer, basketball, volleyball, track and field—I did it all. I spent my summers at our cottage on Lake Minnewaska where I filled the days fishing with Gramps, boating, skiing, and even going on long hikes hunting for arrowheads on different farms in the area. The big treat was taking the speedboat to a small beach just outside the little town of Starbuck and getting a chocolate hand-dipped ice cream cone from the local soft serve joint. I guess I kept myself busy so I would never have time to think about my parents or miss them."

"Oh, Misty," Gabriella said, her voice catching. "I had no idea this would be such a sad story. Just remember, strength comes from adversity, and now it's becoming obvious why you are such a strong person. Please go on, but only if you want to." They began walking again.

"I might as well finish. This feels somewhat liberating. My dad had a sister who lived in Malibu, California. For a girl growing up in rural Minnesota, this sounded glamorous, so I left home to attend the University of Southern California and get a physical education degree. After graduating, I decided not to teach but to become a personal trainer. It was the one-on-one contact that I loved most.

"When I was twenty-seven, Rob hired me as his trainer. I got caught up in all the trouble he was having with his first wife and felt sympathetic. When they divorced, I became his rebound girlfriend. I'm not exactly sure why I finally decided to marry him. I know we were close at the time but I still don't know if I ever truly loved him. Over the years I've gradually wanted more and more freedom, and I've always felt guilty for it. I really did want to be a good wife, but my desire for independence is too strong, I guess. I don't think it has anything to do with Rob. I would probably be this way no matter who I married."

Gabriella gave her a big hug and said, "At least you are being honest with yourself. Look, it's human nature to beat ourselves up over not being like everyone else. Just because you don't fit into the mold society has built for you doesn't mean you are broken. You are one of a kind, Misty, and that's why I love you. If the Creator had wanted us all to be exactly alike, then we would be exactly alike, right?"

"So, you don't think there's anything wrong with me?"

Gabriella wrapped both arms around Misty and held her tight.

"Absolutely not! How could I ever think that about you when you're exactly like I am?"

Misty buried her wet face into Gabriella's hair and felt relieved to be accepted by someone she respected so much.

Exactly like I am? she thought. *So, I'm not the only person who feels this way!*

For the first time in many years, she didn't feel alone.

Later that afternoon Misty and Gabriella were sitting next to each other in a beach tent Gabriella had rented, watching through the tent opening as the sun met the ocean. The sunset was just to the left of Sugar Loaf Mountain and the sight was breathtaking. They were all alone on a practically deserted stretch of beach.

Miguel and Tom were a few minutes away in a restaurant, rehydrating and waiting to spring into action if their employers called for help. But, on a peaceful night like this, violence of any kind seemed unlikely. Rio seemed much safer than they had expected.

"Misty, would you like another glass of wine?"

"Sure, but just one more."

After drinking the wine, Misty couldn't resist resting her head on Gabriella's shoulder. Gabriella gently twirled Misty's hair in her fingers. When the sun had simmered below the waves, darkness set in. It was then that they noticed the moon was already out, riding low on the horizon.

In the growing darkness, the moon illuminated the shoreline and glistened across the breaking waves. Gabriella knew that this was the perfect moment to show Misty how she really felt, and she kissed her softly on the mouth. Without thinking, Misty responded to the warmth of Gabriella's moist mouth by opening her own. How sweet and delicate Gabriella's mouth felt. *Everything Gabriella does is so gentle, not rough like a man.*

Misty's breathing quickened as she became more and more aroused. She didn't resist when Gabriella gently tugged at the top of her bathing suit. Gabriella slowly kissed her way from Misty's mouth to her neck.

Misty became wet as her breasts heaved up and down. Gabriella covered them with delicate kisses, finally settling on an erect nipple.

This feels so good, Misty thought. *A woman seems to know how to arouse me more than a man. Oh my God, a* woman! *Maybe I should stop her, but I'm not sure I want to.*

Misty came alive and took control. She pushed Gabriella onto her back and kissed her passionately. Misty wasn't sure what she was doing or what she would do next, but it felt good. After kissing Gabriella firmly on the mouth, she pulled her top down to fondle her taut breasts. Touching her made Misty's mouth water, so she placed her mouth on Gabriella's breast and licked her nipple with a teasing tongue. As Misty began sucking on Gabriella's nipple, the girls heard someone running in their direction. They quickly pulled up their tops while frantically trying to separate. Miguel's eyes had a wild look to them as he entered the tent.

Once he saw everything was all right, he said, "Why did you call me?"

"Call you?" Gabriella shouted. "We didn't call you!"

"Yes you did!" Miguel replied, confused.

Tom arrived, breathing heavily. When he saw the girls were in no danger he bent over, grabbed his knees, and began to take large breaths.

"Tom, tell Gabriella you heard the call and the strange noises coming from the phone."

Tom replied in short bursts, "Yeah . . . I . . . I . . . shit, I heard 'em."

Gabriella suddenly realized her phone was on the ground between her and Misty. One of them must have inadvertently speed-dialed the guys. She shook her head, realizing how much time and effort she had put into this and how close she had come to consummating her relationship with Misty.

"What's the matter Gabriella?" Tom finally asked when he had caught his breath. All Gabriella could do was laugh. Her laughter made everyone relax a bit. "What a comedy of errors," Gabriella said. "I guess we should take the hint and fold the tent. Come on, we've had a terrific day at the beach. Let's all go back to the hotel and get some rest. We have an early flight in the morning. I need to make sure I'm well rested for my board meeting tomorrow afternoon in Buenos Aires."

Just before they departed, Miguel turned to Tom and asked, "Are you ready to go, old man?" Tom was not amused.

27

BUENOS BOUND

They barely spoke to each other during the return flight to Buenos Aires. Gabriella had her head buried in paperwork for the emergency board meeting she had scheduled to ratify the land deal with Arturo. Although she had an e-mail from Arturo that stated the agreed-upon terms, she did not trust him. Her plan was to maneuver quickly and take Arturo by surprise, before he could figure out a way to back out. She preferred to think of it as catching him with his pants down, even though she was the one who had pulled his pants down, in a way.

Misty spent most of the trip staring out the window trying to make sense of the night before. In a few months' time she had gone from feeling tricked by Gabriella's deliberate attempt to hide her gender to being willingly seduced by her. What would have happened if Miguel had not interrupted? The answer was both dizzying and exciting. Never had she felt so confused about who she was. As they deplaned at Jorge Newbery Airport, the overcast, windy weather made Misty instantly miss sunny Rio. Gabriella waved to the driver of a private car who was waiting for her on the tarmac and then said to Tom, "Take Misty back to her hotel and then Miguel to his brother's."

Gabriella looked at Misty for a moment and then took her hands into her own. "Are you okay?"

Misty focused on the polished tarmac, which was almost the same color as the stormy sky. She nodded slowly. Gabriella put a finger under Misty's chin and gently lifted her head until their eyes met.

"I had a wonderful time and hope you did too. Please get some rest today." She broke into a warm smile. "We have a couple big weeks of training left. I'll see you Monday, okay?" Misty smiled slightly.

"*Bueno, mi amiga.*"

Misty watched Gabriella's long frame walk to the car and step inside. The car drove off.

"*Vámonos,*" Tom yelled. "Let's get you two home."

When Misty got to her room, she crawled into bed. After a few hours lying there contemplating her situation, she got the urge to call Rob just to hear his voice. A woman answered tentatively, "Hello?"

Misty heard Rob in the background: "Who is it, Becca?"

"Becca?" Misty shouted. "What are you doing there?"

"Oh, Misty, it's you! Rob, it's Misty calling."

Misty didn't hear any response from Rob.

"What am I doing in Malibu you mean? I decided to visit some friends and thought I would stop by to see Rob. I sure wish you weren't on the road. But then, when aren't you?" Becca laughed.

Becca's passive-aggressiveness stung Misty into silence.

"I'm sorry, Misty. I didn't mean it that way. But it's true. You *are* on the road a lot these days."

When Misty didn't respond, Becca said, "Here, why don't I give the phone to Rob."

"Thanks."

"Misty! I'm so glad you called. Wasn't it nice of Becca to drop by before she heads back to San Diego?"

"Sure, it's fantastic. So, how's Becca doing, Rob?"

"She's doing great, aren't you, Becca?"

Misty didn't know why she had a knot in her stomach. She convinced herself it had more to do with her weekend than with Becca hanging out with Rob. She decided to change the subject.

"Rob, I really was just calling to let you know I had a wonderful weekend in Rio."

"Rio?" he gasped. "Like, Rio de Janeiro?"

"*Exactamente*. It's just a short flight from Buenos Aires."

"Your Spanish is sounding great! So, it was a quick weekend getaway?"

"Yes." He seemed distracted, and Misty assumed it was due to Becca being there. The thought irked her.

Tell Becca I miss both of you. I'm late for a manicure, so I've got to run. I'll call again in a few days."

"Okay, Misty. Thanks for calling." Misty watched Rob's picture fade on the call screen of her iPhone. She lay back and put a pillow over her head, hoping things would be clearer after a nap.

After Rob hung up, Becca asked, "So, what's really going on? Why is Misty gone all of the time? Are you two getting along?"

Misty and Rob had decided not to tell anyone about their arrangement, and Rob wasn't sure he wanted to start now, even though he had always been comfortable telling Becca what was on his mind. Their history was a long one, and although she and Misty were good friends, the reality was that Rob and Becca seemed to communicate on a different level. They were both businesspeople, and they shared interests in politics and current affairs. They could talk for hours about tax legislation or international politics, or just chat about future plans.

Misty was not that sort of person. She had always prided herself on being a real "carpe diem" type, living for the moment. Rob just assumed she was tuned out to the world on a certain level. Long-range planning was not in her vocabulary and keeping up on current events meant checking what the temperature was going to be each day. Rob accepted this about her, but he also wished that their conversations were not limited to only the things Misty was interested in, never what Rob wanted to talk about. Becca had always given him the outlet he needed when wanting to discuss and contemplate deeper issues. But he knew that discussing his marriage with Becca was going to start a conversation he didn't think he had the energy to finish.

"Of course, Becca. Misty's private practice is doing really well right now, and she often gets clients who live in other countries. It's a great opportunity for her. I know that she doesn't do it as much for the money as for the travel. In a few years she'll settle down, I'm sure."

"Hmm. I guess you can handle it for a few more years." She paused. "But don't you get lonely while Misty is gone?"

Rob looked at Becca and said nothing. "I'm sorry. It's not any of my business. It's just that I care about both of you," Becca said.

"No, that's okay. It was a legitimate question. Listen, don't worry about me. I'm getting by just fine."

"If you say so, Rob. If you get lonely and need someone to talk to, just let me know, and I will come up for the weekend to keep you company."

"Thanks, Becca. I'll keep that in mind."

As she was walking out the door, she turned and said, "Just remember, I'm here for you if you ever need me."

Rob continued to stare out the window as Becca's car disappeared down the street. Within a few minutes his thoughts drifted to the only question that seemed to comfort him: *I wonder if Amelia will be working the morning shift at Java Joe's tomorrow?*

28

TWO CAN TANGO

Misty's three-month stint in Argentina was drawing to a close. She and Gabriella had been more businesslike than usual during their recent training sessions as neither one had the courage to discuss the night on Ipanema Beach. Confrontation was not Misty's style, so she had become content with just letting it go. For Gabriella, it was a totally different story. She had wanted a trainer for the physical challenge and the discipline it would teach her. She could have picked anyone, but she chose Misty because of her unique contract. Gabriella could have many women in Buenos Aires, but when she saw Misty's RFP and heard rumors from previous clients about how great the Black Widow Trainer was in bed, she wanted Misty only. Misty was beautiful, strong but shy, and had a kind of naiveté that made her seem invulnerable to the ugliness of the world.

On the second to last day before the end of Misty's contract, when the girls were tired and sweaty at the end of the workout, Gabriella asked Misty, "So, tell me about your tango lessons. Is Roberto taking good care of you?"

The question lifted Misty's spirits because she was proud of what she had accomplished. "Yes, Roberto's been terrific, and you wouldn't believe how much I've learned."

"I know, Misty. Roberto called me yesterday bragging about your progress. He said you are one of the fastest learners he has ever seen. You're a natural!"

Misty laughed. "Well, I'm a fast learner for someone who doesn't have much dancing experience. I'm really excited about how far I've come." She quickly added, "Gabriella, don't you want to see me dance?"

This was the opening Gabriella had been waiting for. Without hesitating, she said, "I would love to watch you dance."

Misty was overcome with excitement and giggled briefly before becoming embarrassed. She really wanted to impress Gabriella.

"I have one more class with Roberto tomorrow. Maybe you could come watch."

"That would be fun, but I have a better idea. Saturday night I have reservations at a quaint tango bar." She paused, and then added, "Well, I have reserved the entire establishment, to be more precise."

Misty's eyes opened wide, giving Gabriella a sense of her excitement.

"You'll love it. The bar only has twelve tables. They mainly cater to tourists, but I have a standing arrangement with the proprietor to rent out the club one Saturday every two months. It actually works out well because I hire my own staff, which frees up his staff to get a Saturday night off. It's what you call in the States a win-win situation."

"So, what are we going to wear?" Misty asked excitedly, knowing full well that Gabriella would come up with something very special.

"I'll send Tom to pick you up Saturday morning, and we'll go shopping. You're going to look stunning. Oh, also, when we come to get you in the evening for our date, would you mind having your bags packed?" She smiled mischievously. "I know you are not leaving until Monday, but I would like you to spend the weekend with me at the mansion. If you ever come this way again, which I hope you do, I would insist that you stay at my home, so we might as well make the change now."

Misty was struggling for a response when Gabriella added, "I will be very hurt if you turn down my invitation." Misty warmly agreed.

When Tom pulled up at the bar, Misty was intrigued. It was on the bottom floor of a three-story historical building situated at the intersection of two cobblestone streets. At night the old gas globe lamps cast a warm golden light over the stones of the building and the polished metal of the ancient trolley rails. Even though the bar had only been around since the seventies, the building was at least a hundred years old. When the girls entered, Misty felt as if she had gone back to another time. It reminded her of something she'd seen in a Humphrey Bogart film. The diagonal black-and-white floor tile was pitted and worn from decades of dancing. Rich, dark wood contrasted with light-colored walls painted with Art Nouveau designs. The small round tables were intimately lighted by single candles. Misty got goose bumps. She heard a familiar voice and turned around.

Roberto greeted them: "Welcome ladies. Gabriella, I have taken care of everything. You have the place to yourselves, and we have situated your table in the far right corner tucked just out of view from the street per your instructions. Your personal chef is in the kitchen putting together a wonderful but light meal starting with chilled spinach salad with mandarin orange slices and a vinaigrette dressing. For the main course we have prepared some fresh Mahi Mahi ceviche accompanied by grilled vegetables."

"That all sounds wonderful, Roberto," Gabriella replied. "But are your best dancers here to entertain us while we eat?"

"Absolutely, Doña Marquez. Please take notice of the space to the right. I have made preparations for a small band. You will be listening to live music tonight."

"Excellent, Roberto! You have certainly outdone yourself, my friend."

"I hope you don't take this the wrong way, Gabriella, but I have gone out of my way because this is Misty's opportunity to show you how well she has learned the tango, and I wanted to make everything perfect for her, too."

Gabriella turned to Misty and lightly stroked her cheek.

"Yes Roberto, we want to make sure this is a night Misty will always remember."

The dinner was wonderful but the martinis the bartender brought were even better. Misty was not usually a martini drinker, but she had to admit it was the perfect accompaniment to the ceviche.

"These martinis are heavenly. I think I'm already getting a little buzzed."

"Don't worry. You'll be dancing that buzz off a little later," Gabriella said, and took another sip.

Toward the end of dinner the band came in to set up. They were a trio of older men dressed in fine Argentinean clothing, and their instruments looked like they were older than all of them combined. The bandoneón started up slowly, and then a guitar joined, followed by a violin. They played softly, providing excellent background music to the meal.

Misty could tell the dancers were about ready to start when the tempo of the music picked up. The dancers, four of them in two pairs, took to the floor. The band switched seamlessly into a rousing tango song, and the dancers began the slow, intense, and beautiful theatrics of tango under the warm lights of the bar. They were magnificent and so was Misty's third martini. She became lost in watching the dancers as they locked into a perfect rhythm of passion and music. She felt her body awaken and her soul become filled by the energy of the tango.

Misty looked at Gabriella and mouthed, "This is absolutely incredible." Gabriella reached out and squeezed her hand in agreement. After an hour of watching, the male lead broke from his partner's embrace, walked up to Misty, and held out his hand. She quickly looked at Gabriella for reassurance. Gabriella smiled and patted Misty on the back.

"You'll be amazing, trust me. You are the fastest learning student Roberto has ever seen. Trust yourself and feel the tango from the music and your partner. Remember: *pasión*!"

And with that Misty took the dancer's hand and walked to the dance floor. He was tall and handsome, his black hair slicked back, his tailored clothes fitting him tightly. His scent, a blend of sweat and cologne, was invigorating. He looked into her eyes and nodded before drawing her close on beat with the music. Her body immediately responded in time to the dance. She quickly lost herself to the tango as they spun around the dance floor, the music and the heat of her partner's body close to hers driving her to dance with a passion and lust that she had never experienced in practice and had never felt before.

The first song ended, and Roberto stood up clapping his hands.

"Bravo! My little American beauty, bravo!" She wiped sweat from her brow and grinned widely.

Misty spent the next hour having the time of her life. It was as if she were dancing on a mountaintop. As she changed lead partners from one Argentinean hunk to the next, she refocused long enough to wonder how Gabriella liked her dancing.

Where is she? Misty wondered as she looked the room over. At first disappointed, Misty quickly convinced herself that Gabriella had just gone to the bathroom and would be back to cheer her on any time now.

Her new dance partner whispered softly, "Who are you looking for, my dear?"

"Gabriella! You're my lead?"

"Did you think I would miss an opportunity to dance the tango with you?"

What a sight the two made. Misty had on a classic tango dress, short with long tight sleeves and red sequins. Gabriella was dressed in a sleek black Hugo Boss men's suit that accentuated the clean long lines of her body. Her jacket was complemented by a dark red shirt and red handkerchief. Gabriella's hair was tucked into a stylish black hat with a red band. Misty could not take her eyes off her.

She looked into Gabriella's deep brown eyes, and the two smiled warmly. Gabriella said, "Now, really show me what you can do."

For the next half hour the two were on fire. Misty was a blur with high leg kicks and rapid twists from side to side. Gabriella used some of the strength she had gained from her private workout sessions to hold Misty as she arched her back and let her head drop toward the floor. Roberto and the whole tango troupe clapped along.

Unlike ballroom dancing, the Argentinean tango relies heavily on improvisation. More and more Gabriella challenged Misty, leading her through ever changing patterns. Finally, she challenged Misty with "dueling feet" actions.

My God, I feel sexy, Misty thought. *I wish Rob could see me now. Something tells me he wouldn't be laughing.*

Finally the women were beginning to wear down. Misty felt like she had just run a half marathon. The tango troupe was amazed with Misty's stamina and they murmured in satisfaction. They had never seen a newcomer dance so strongly for so long. At the end of the night, Roberto brought Misty and Gabriella a dozen roses each.

After they drank some water and took time to catch their breath, Gabriella said, "Come on Misty, why don't we go home, put on our swimsuits, and jump into the pool to cool off?"

Misty responded ecstatically, "That sounds like a wonderful idea. I'd love to wash the night off me."

Misty and Gabriella thanked Roberto, the dancers, and the wait staff, who had long since put up the chairs and were drinking glasses of wine, still beaming with pleasure at the amazing show. Gabriella translated the dancers' comments and praise and they joked with them until Tom brought the car around. Outside the night was quiet and still, and they both felt like they had stepped out of another world into the night air.

29

THE MOMENT OF TRUTH

Gabriella was first to exit the car upon returning home. "Tom, you've had a long weekend so why don't you go ahead and take the rest of the night off. I'm confident we won't need your services this evening."

"Thank you, Gabriella, I could use some shut-eye, but don't hesitate to call if something comes up."

Misty lingered in the car.

"Thanks for all the hard work this weekend, Tom. I'm pleased you and Miguel get along so well. This can be a very lonely job for Miguel when he doesn't have anyone to hang with."

"No problem, Misty. Miguel is a great guy, and I enjoy his company as well, even if he can run faster than me."

Misty laughed and said, "Well, I'm sure you would have been giving him a run for his money in your day, old man. Then again, he may have been in diapers when you were in your prime." She gave him a wink. "See you tomorrow."

"Okay, Misty. Get some rest."

When Misty finally got out of the car, Gabriella had already climbed the long stairway and was about to enter her front door.

A soft sea breeze met Misty when she walked onto the back patio. The sound of waves crashing in the distance mixed with the smell of the salt air filling her lungs and she thought, "This is going to be a great way to relax and wind down."

She caught a flash of naked flesh out of the corner of her eye and looked to the pool. Misty walked closer and saw the Hugo Boss suit crumpled on the ground beside a pile of women's lingerie. Gabriella was treading water, with her naked silhouette darting back and forth beneath her. She pulled her wet hair back from her face, her eyes sparkling in the aqua light of the pool. Misty quickly turned around and walked to the railing and looked out over the ocean.

She said nervously, "Gabriella, it's so beautiful out here. I can see the waves crashing on the shore."

"I know! The waves are almost as beautiful as the ones on Ipanema Beach last weekend." Gabriella's voice was bright from the night of dance and drink. Misty also felt intoxicated. She was confused but excited. She didn't know whether to tear off her dress and leap into the pool or jump over the rail and escape to the sea.

In a confident voice Gabriella said, "Misty dear, please turn around and look at me."

Misty stood there trying to figure out what to do.

Again Gabriella said in a much softer tone, "Love, please look at me."

This time Misty turned around but would not look up.

"Misty, come here my darling."

It was obvious to Gabriella that Misty was struggling and that calling to her again would not help. She smiled fondly and did a back flip under the water. She shot to the other side of the pool, giving Misty time to think. After several minutes, Misty walked to the edge of the pool, but still she refused to look at Gabriella. Just as Gabriella was beginning to fear she had made a terrible mistake, Misty began to unzip the back of her dress. It dropped to her feet. Misty stood in the pale light from the pool in her bra and underwear. She slowly unlatched her bra and pulled her arms out from the straps and let it fall to the ground, atop her dress.

For a while, Misty hugged her breasts with both arms and held them tight as if she were embarrassed or ashamed. Gabriella fought the urge to give any further instructions. Finally, to Gabriella's delight, Misty freed her breasts and pulled down her panties. When Misty finally lifted her head and met Gabriella's eyes, she was no longer timid. Her stare was that of a woman who knew exactly what she wanted. Gabriella realized this could actually be the moment of truth she had so desperately hoped for.

Misty's dive split the water and she resurfaced in Gabriella's arms. She hugged Gabriella tightly before backing away to make eye contact. Gabriella traced the shape of Misty's face with her eyes while running a hand through her hair.

Gabriella broke the silence: "I've dreamt of this moment ever since I met you on that very first day. I've wanted you so badly, but I was sure being with another woman would be something new to you. All I could hope for was that when the time came, you would have an open mind."

"You know me pretty well. This is all new to me. I never would have thought I could feel this way about another woman, and to be honest with you, I have no idea what to do next."

"I know. Just follow my lead, like when we tangoed."

Gabriella opened her mouth and kissed Misty. The girls were right back where they left off the night in Rio. This time, Gabriella prayed there would be no one running in to ruin her night. Misty immediately remembered how pleasurable it was to kiss Gabriella. A few minutes later she could feel Gabriella's fingers massaging her clitoris under the water. Misty's breath quickened and her legs opened, inviting Gabriella in. Gabriella's fingers expertly found their way inside her. She penetrated her deeply with her fingers, her hand clasped over her mound, stimulating her clitoris at the same time as she went in and out of her. As Misty began to come she wrapped her arms tight around Gabriella's neck. The next thing she knew her body was quivering violently. She seemed to be coming apart at the seams. Gabriella was breathing as hard as Misty, their bodies locked together, sleek and weightless in the water. She felt Misty's orgasm with her whole body, and it only made her want more.

When Misty regained her composure, she looked up to Gabriella and smiled drunkenly. "What are you going to do to me next?"

With a mischievous grin Gabriella said, "Sit on the side of the pool, and I'll show you." Misty smiled back.

She lifted herself out of the water and leaned back with her arms behind her, arching her back. Gabriella coaxed her legs open with gentle kisses, slowly kissing her way up the insides of her thighs. Misty felt Gabriella's hot tongue lick her vagina. Gabriella's face was soft as silk against Misty's legs and she could not tear her eyes away from Gabriella's red tongue darting in and out of her pink flesh. For a while Misty stroked Gabriella's hair with her hands, but soon the warm feelings were getting so intense that she had to lie back on the pool deck. She lifted her legs and brought them down to rest on Gabriella's shoulders. The feeling of Gabriella's tight, hot, sleek body wrapped in her own heightened Misty's ecstasy.

Gabriella responded by running a hand up Misty's belly to her breasts, massaging them in rhythm with her rapid tonguing of Misty's clitoris. After Misty's fourth orgasm, she was so hungry to taste Gabriella that she pulled her onto the pool deck and got on top of her, kissing her passionately. Misty worked her way down Gabriella's body with her tongue and hands. Gabriella felt so good under Misty's body: her skin was perfectly smooth and taut over her lean frame. Returning to look Gabriella in the eyes, Misty kissed her lips while grinding herself against Gabriella, feeling her entire body with hers. Her hand slid down to Gabriella's mound, exploring her friend's wet vagina. It was then that Gabriella realized Misty was the lover she had envisioned her to be. Misty made love to her until she couldn't take it any longer and fell on top of her panting.

Misty lay beside her lover, stroking her hip and tracing her thigh.

"Gabriella, I'm a little nervous about going down on you. I'm not sure what to do."

Gabriella smiled and whispered, "It's okay, lover. I don't want you to go down on me until you are ready. Let's go find some dessert in the kitchen and crawl into bed."

Misty was relieved. She had never felt so little pressure from a lover. "God, that sounds great! I hope you have plenty of ice cream because I'm starving."

They wrapped themselves in giant plush bath towels and walked into the house.

When Misty opened the freezer door she asked, "What's this?"

"It's a caramel ice cream called dulce de leche. Just eat it from the carton, lover."

Misty and Gabriella filled their large bowls and retired to Gabriella's luxurious canopy bed. After nestling into the dozen pillows and soft duvet, Misty took her first bite of what was about to become her new favorite ice cream.

"This is absolutely divine. I think I might miss this more than you when I get back home," Misty said with a little twinkle in her eye. Gabriella puckered her lips and scrunched her nose, pretending to be mad. Misty cracked up.

"Well, just so you don't miss your precious ice cream more than me, I'll let you in on a little secret."

"Secret? "

"All you have to do is go down to your local grocery store and buy some. Häagen-Dazs makes a pretty good version of dulce de leche."

"Well isn't that handy," Misty replied. "Can I go down to my local grocery store and get some of you too?"

"Sorry, that would not be possible." They both laughed.

Misty took a large bite of ice cream and pulled the spoon out of her mouth slowly. Gabriella watched Misty intently as she tongued the remaining ice cream from the spoon. Their towels had come off, and they were naked on the bed. Misty then used her spoon to scoop up some of the dulce de leche that had melted and began to drizzle it onto one of Gabriella's breasts. She began to lap up the ice cream ever so slowly.

Gabriella laughed softly and began to stroke Misty on her head, saying, "That's a nice kitty. Oh my, what a nice kitty."

After Misty cleaned the cream she moved on to Gabriella's nipple, sucking on it gently. She gave it a little bite and said "Meow!"

Gabriella squirmed and moaned quietly, "Bad kitty."

Misty kissed Gabriella softly between her breasts and then slowly moved the kisses down, down, down. This caught Gabriella by surprise but it wasn't long before she lay her head back onto the comfy pillows, looked up at the ceiling, and let her eyes roll back in her head. Misty kissed Gabriella's mound and around the sweet lips of her vagina and then let her tongue protrude from her lips as she gave Gabriella's clitoris a short, quick, scaredy-cat lick. Misty's licks became a little quicker, longer, and stronger. Soon she was in a rhythm and Gabriella was squirming. She ran her fingers strongly through Misty's hair and pulled her closer into her. When Gabriella started to moan and move her hips to the rhythm of Misty's tongue, Misty felt as turned on by being in control as she did by the beautiful woman under her spell. Before her lay one of the most powerful women in Argentina; she was wealthy, sophisticated, and sexy. Gabriella had her hands locked onto the bedpost behind her head and was grinding her hips while Misty firmly held her buttocks. Misty was creating a steady crescendo as if she was conducting the most orchestrated orgasm the world had ever known. Finally Gabriella exploded and the symphony came to an end with the crashing of cymbals. Misty was certain Gabriella's scream could be heard throughout the entire house. When Gabriella's heavy breathing subsided, Misty crawled up and laid her head on her lover's heaving chest. Gabriella reached up to turn out the lights and then wrapped her arms around Misty while kissing her gently on the top of her head. They held each other until they passed into sleep.

30

THE MORNING AFTER

Misty woke first to a heartbeat and second to the vision of a woman's perfect breast. She didn't want to wake up Gabriella, so she lay quietly, recalling the events of the night. Her initial feeling of shame quickly gave way to excitement, lust, and, finally, contentment. With her arms wrapped around Gabriella's warm body, Misty closed her eyes and fell back to sleep.

When Misty awoke again, she was ready for a shower. She slipped gently from the bed. When she reached the doorway, she glanced back at Gabriella. The image of her half-naked lover sleeping contentedly was soothing to Misty. She began to realize just how fond she had become of her, and for the first time, she regretted having to fly back to the States. But at the same time, she could not imagine staying. She was the Black Widow Trainer forever and had no power to become someone else. Staring at her lover, she wondered, not for the first time, if there was something missing from her heart, if she would ever feel complete with a person.

After an invigorating hot shower, she dressed and went to the kitchen. To her surprise, her lover was already there. Gabriella's face lit up at the sight of Misty.

"I see you found the shower. Now, how about a cup of hot coffee?"

Misty gave Gabriella a peck on her cheek before taking the coffee. They enjoyed their coffees while searching for the right words. Finally, Gabriella broke the silence.

"Misty, there is no need to discuss last night if you don't feel like it. I just want you to know that everything I did was sincere and from the heart. I live a very full life and my job keeps me occupied most of the time, but after spending the last three months with you, I realized you bring me great joy, and I wanted to express it in the most intimate way possible. I can't remember if I told you I loved you last night, but if I did, I was telling you the truth. I do not want you to misunderstand the meaning. I admire you. I love that you are self-sufficient and dedicated to your craft of helping others feel better about themselves. I wish I could be more like you. I will certainly miss you when you are gone, but I know I can never make you mine. I think both of us are too independent to allow someone else to own or control us." Gabriella paused to give her words time to sink in and then said, "Can we just be good friends?"

Misty's heart was warmed by Gabriella's honesty. She had worked so hard to win her approval, and now she had something better, her love. Gabriella's pragmatic approach and honesty lifted her spirits. She smiled and looked into Gabriella's eyes intimately.

"Friends. Forever," Misty said.

They made plans to spend the day at Bosques de Palermo and tour the rose garden. They agreed to enjoy each other's company and see where things went.

31

HELLO, AMELIA

On the Monday morning Misty was to return, Rob made his morning coffee run. He didn't spot Amelia immediately, and he began to worry she wasn't working. Just as he was about to place his order with another barista, Amelia came to the bar from the back.

"There you are! I thought that maybe you were off today."

"Oh, you know I always work Monday mornings, Rob. My, you seem happy to see me."

"Does that surprise you? Listen, when you take your break I'd like to visit if that's okay."

"Sure, I would love to, but I won't get my next break for an hour."

"Oh, that's not long at all. I'll just read a paper and enjoy my coffee until you're ready."

Amelia was relieved. She had been worried that he wouldn't be able to wait. She was so preoccupied with wondering what Rob wanted to say that she ruined the next customer's double chai soy latte. It was going to be a long hour.

Just before the clock struck nine, Amelia slipped into the back, put on some fresh lip-gloss and smoothed down her hair. She kept telling herself not to get too excited. Rob seemed different this time, much more open and engaging, and it made her nervous.

As Amelia walked toward him, Rob couldn't help but notice just how attractive she was. He'd always noticed her appeal, but he had never fully looked at her before. She was probably five feet six, small and athletic, with long dark brown hair that framed her pixie face. Her flashing hazel eyes exuded energy and curiosity. Her skin glowed, the complexion of an angel.

He flashed a smile at her when she walked up. "Well, hello gorgeous. How's your day going?"

Amelia blushed. Rob waited for her to settle into her chair and then said, "I'm really sorry I haven't taken the time to visit with you more since the night you cooked dinner. I've been pretty busy with work, but that's no excuse. After all the trouble you went to that night, you deserve better."

"Well it's good to know you've finally come to your senses. Just don't let it happen again buddy," Amelia joked.

She let him feel like a fool for a few seconds before breaking into a big smile and laughing. "I got you! I wish you could have seen your face, Mr. Business Guy. I hope you conceal your emotions better than that when negotiating your consulting fees."

"Maybe you should negotiate my fees for me. You could make me a rich man."

Rob suddenly became serious. "Listen, Amelia. I guess the real reason I came in today was to let you know that Misty will be arriving from Argentina late this evening."

Rob's statement took the wind out of Amelia's sails. His next few words would determine whether her bubble would totally burst.

"Yesterday, I began to realize how much I enjoyed your company at dinner, and I consider you a good friend, but while Misty is home we will only be able to visit when I'm here for coffee in the morning."

Amelia immediately responded, "How long will Misty be home?"

"I'm not sure. Misty is the one who decides when she will take on another client, and she makes that decision when the mood strikes her."

"I see," Amelia replied. "I'm happy for you, Rob. I know it must be hard for you being away from Misty for so long, and I'm sure you will want to make up for lost time. So is that all you wanted to tell me? I should get back to work."

Knowing he might be on the verge of losing Amelia, Rob said, "No, I wanted to tell you that I'm going to miss you, and I would very much like to come over for dinner when she leaves." He smiled.

Amelia let Rob's statement settle in before responding, "Let's discuss that when she's gone." Rob felt a little hurt as Amelia began to walk away. But after just a few steps, she came back and gave him a kiss on the cheek.

"That's so you don't forget me," she said.

32

TIME TO GO

Tom pulled up to the Marquez mansion at noon on Monday. He found Misty out back by the pool taking a last look at the Atlantic Ocean. She had become very fond of Gabriella's place, and she was imagining what it would feel like to live there.

"*Buenos dias*, Misty. Are you ready to go home?"

While still staring out to sea, she replied, "Yeah, I suppose so."

Tom could sense she was sad to leave, so he moved the conversation along. "Okay, the plans are to pick you up first, then Miguel, and finally Gabriella. She's at the office, but she'll break away to see you off." He loaded her baggage into the limo and waited in the car as she took one last look at the sea.

They rode in silence until they picked up Miguel. It had been a week since Misty had seen him, so they talked and caught up while Tom drove downtown to Gabriella's office.

After Gabriella joined the group, they drove to the airport. Misty would miss the four of them together, riding through the beautiful city. They had all been on so many adventures, big and small, in the three months they had known each other. Misty knew that she was closer to Tom and Gabriella than she had ever been to a client before and wondered again, as she had briefly that morning, how committed she was to being the Black Widow Trainer—or if she even had a choice. When they arrived at the airport, Tom and Miguel began making trips, carrying luggage from the limo to the airplane. This gave Gabriella a moment to say good-bye to Misty in the privacy of the limo.

Misty said, "Gabriella, I don't know how to thank you. I feel like I came down here a girl and am leaving a woman."

"You are my new best friend, and I am going to miss you. Please come back to me, Misty, even if it's just for a few weeks at a time. *Mi casa es tu casa*. You are welcome here anytime." Gabriella then placed something over Misty's head.

When Misty looked at the key on the end of the twenty-four carat gold chain, Gabriella said, "That is a key to my house. I also want you to know that it doubles as the key to my heart." Gabriella's joking grin faded until she could barely disguise her sadness.

Misty responded by wrapping her arms around Gabriella, who gently rocked her back and forth and whispered, "*Mi amore*."

Misty knew she could trust Gabriella unlike she could trust anyone else, even Rob. It was a kind of love she could not put a name to, but already it ached in her heart. She pulled back and discreetly wiped the tears from her eyes.

After one more round of hugs, Misty and Miguel climbed the ladder to the jet door. Just before entering, Miguel looked back at Tom and said, "Don't consider this good-bye. Something tells me we will be coming this way again. Better get in shape because we're going to have another foot race when I come back."

Within minutes, the Gulfstream was roaring down the runway. Misty looked back at the taxi apron and spotted Gabriella's stark figure in her black suit standing near the limo. She wondered if they would ever be together again.

33

HOMEWARD BOUND

As the Marquez Gulfstream jet approached LAX International Airport, all Miguel could think about was Sylvia. He had gone three full months without seeing her. The relationship he was able to rebuild with his brother, and the chance to get to know his sister-in-law and two nephews, made him feel that the time spent away from Sylvia had been worthwhile. But now that he was headed home, Sylvia was the only thing on his mind. Only two more hours and he would be holding her in his arms.

Misty's thoughts were not as focused. Rob was not the only person on her mind. Yes, she wanted to see him, but the nervous, excited feeling she normally got when she was about to see him after a long assignment was absent. She decided she was burned out. Even though the thought of her night with Gabriella kept creeping into her head, Misty refused to give it any credence. She kept telling herself that Gabriella was just a very close friend and that what had happened between them, although remarkable, was nothing more than a fling. She also told herself that she was probably not the only woman to want to experiment and that she had done nothing out of the ordinary.

Rob and Sylvia were standing together when they caught a glimpse of Misty and Miguel coming toward them from baggage claim. Rob fed on Sylvia's excitement to keep him enthused about seeing his wife again. He had agreed to the unique arrangement with Misty at a time when he could not bear the thought of living without her. Misty had been such an improvement over his needy and selfish first wife that Rob had convinced himself his life would be miserable without her. But he was beginning to entertain the notion that he could possibly put his life together without Misty, even though he knew he still loved her very much. When Misty gave him a big hug, however, all he could think about was her naked body lying next to him.

"Hey Gorgeous!" Miguel yelled as he approached Sylvia. "How's my baby?"

"Your baby is very happy to see you," Sylvia replied as she wrapped him in her arms. "I can't believe you left me for three whole months. You better be here for a while, or I'll have to chain you to the bed."

"I'm game. Don't worry baby, Misty promised we won't go out again for two whole months."

Sylvia was thrilled.

Misty and Rob were still in an embrace when Miguel said, "So long, guys. I hope you don't think it's rude, but we're out of here."

"See you later!" Misty and Rob yelled in unison, and then Misty said, "Thank you for everything, Miguel. Enjoy yourselves, and I'll touch base with you in about six weeks."

"Six weeks?" Rob replied. "Are you going to be around for a while this time?"

"Yep, I've decided it might be a good idea to slow down so Miguel and I can spend time with our loved ones. Do you have a problem with that?" she said with a grin.

"I certainly don't. Let's get home."

The next morning, Rob woke and got up to make a pot of coffee, accepting that he would begin the day without an americano. When Misty woke up, they went into the living room and settled into their easy chairs to catch up.

"So, tell me all about your three months in Argentina."

"It was really something special. Miguel spent much of the time with his older brother and his family, and I concentrated on my tango lessons, of course."

Noticing the distant look in her eyes, Rob replied, "Oh yes, you told me about those, didn't you? I seem to remember making fun of you at the time. I guess it just struck me as a little funny. I'm sorry. It's just that I have never known you to be interested in learning how to dance."

Misty paused for a moment before responding. She needed to let any negative emotions from the memory of the phone conversation subside. This was not the time to show anger and, after all, Rob did apologize.

Noticing the pause, Rob quickly added, "Are you still upset that I laughed at you when you told me you were taking tango lessons?

"I guess just a little, but that's okay because it motivated me to prove you wrong. I have never worked harder or been more proud of myself and the results. Gabriella and I had a terrific time dancing just before I left."

"Gabriella?" Rob replied. "Gabriella? Who is Gabriella?"

Misty froze. *Oh my*, she thought. *Rob doesn't know about Gabriella.*

When she didn't reply, Rob asked, "Is this someone you met while you were down there? I don't remember you saying anything about a Gabriella."

Taking a deep breath Misty said, "Rob, Gabriella was my client."

"Your client was a woman? You never told me you would work for a woman." Rob became silent, as if thinking about how a woman might take advantage of Misty's unique contract.

After giving it some thought, Rob gasped. "Misty! What about the agreement you have with your clients? Oh my God, did you sleep with her? Did you have sex with a woman?"

Misty said, "Rob, first of all, you know better than to ask a question like that. Remember what we agreed? Don't ask, don't tell. Second, do you think I would sleep with a woman?" She secretly prided herself on her quick thinking.

"I'm not accusing you of sleeping with a woman, it's just, well, you know."

"Rob, the agreement. And besides, what's the big deal anyway? You act like it's somehow worse than me sleeping with a man. What is the real issue here?" Misty had never been so assertive with Rob, and it felt good. She was surprised at how offended she felt at his prying. She felt a rush of anger flow over her, but it quickly dissipated.

Rob rubbed his temples and sighed. "You're right. I retract my question and apologize for insinuating that you may have slept with a woman. Plus, it's none of my business."

Misty had just dodged a bullet, but she wanted to move away from the entire discussion so she left her own La-Z-Boy, walked over to Rob's chair, and climbed onto his lap. After giving him a kiss on the cheek, she wrapped her arms around him and laid her head on his shoulder. Her affections made Rob feel better and like less of a prick for asking so many questions.

"Oh, I forgot to tell you that Becca e-mailed me last night," he said. "She wanted to know if we would like to take a bike trip with her from Malibu to San Diego on Highway One this weekend. We could spend a few days in San Diego before you and I took the train back home. Becca said that she misses us all being together and thought August would be perfect for making the trip."

Glad that Rob had changed the subject, Misty quickly replied, "That sounds like fun." She smiled and rested her head on his chest, feeling right with her world again.

III

34

SHE SAID WHAT?

Tuesday evening after dinner, Misty decided to surprise Rob by taking the trash out to the curb for the morning pickup. She knew she was not normally very helpful around the house—home had become a place of relaxation and rest away from her work—but she felt that she owed Rob a little effort. Was it guilt from being gone so often, or maybe her affair with Gabriella? Either way, doing little things around the house was making her feel better. As she was dumping Rob's small office trash can with the rest of the trash, Misty noticed writing on a Java Joe's coffee cup:

Robster,

Coffee, tea, or me? Just kidding, cutie. Have a wonderful day!

Amelia

Misty wondered if Rob had actually started something on the side or if this Amelia just thought he was cute. When she walked back into the living room and saw Rob reading the paper, she almost said something but then remembered what she had told him the night before. *I know I can't say anything, and Rob has every right to be getting a little on the side, but I can't help but wonder what she looks like. Maybe I'll go for a latte after Rob gets his coffee tomorrow morning*, she reasoned to herself.

While Rob was on his coffee run the next morning, Misty called the Java Joe's nearest to their house.

"J. Joe's, this is Jacob speaking."

"Hello, Jacob. Can you please tell me if Amelia is working today?"

"I'm sorry, there's nobody by that name working here. Maybe she works at our store across the highway. Would you like the phone number?"

"Yes, that would be great."

She wasn't sure why she agreed. It did not make sense for Rob to go to that store. He would have to drive past the Cross Creek location in heavy morning traffic to get to the West Malibu location. Misty called anyway and asked the lady who answered if Amelia was working.

"She is, but she's busy right now. Can I give her a message?"

"That's okay," Misty replied. "I'll just text her."

Now Misty was curious. *He must really like Amelia to go to such effort*, she thought.

The line was extremely long that morning, but waiting gave Misty extra time to figure out which of the baristas was Amelia. Most of the staff were college-age men. Just as she was about to give up, a very attractive woman popped out from behind the espresso machine. It didn't take Misty long to surmise that the woman was probably Amelia. She had a sweet, wholesome face, and if it were not for her long, dark brown hair, she could have doubled as Misty's sister.

When Misty reached the cash register the woman politely asked, "Can I get something started for you?"

"Yes, you can," Misty replied. "I'll take a large nonfat vanilla latte."

With a genuine smile the woman responded, "I don't know why you need a nonfat latte—I don't think you have an ounce of fat on you. You are in terrific shape."

Misty was caught off guard. *Now that's dirty pool*, she thought. *I didn't come here to like her.* She hoped this wasn't Amelia.

"You are so kind, what is your name?" Misty asked.

"I'm Amelia. Thanks for asking."

Amelia held up the empty cup in one hand and a pen in the other.

"So your name is—?"

"Misty," she replied as she focused squarely on Amelia's face.

Amelia almost dropped her pen when she heard the name. She wrote it down anyway, her pen skipping off the cup when she wrote the *y*. She could feel Misty looking at her as she struggled to gather the courage to look up. She finally did so with a careful smile. The two women stared at each other. Misty was prettier than Amelia had imagined and more strongly built as well.

Amelia thought about how Misty could kick her ass in a fight. She shook the notion out of her head.

The man behind them interrupted the silence. "Come on ladies, time's wasting."

Misty glanced around and saw they were holding up the line. "It was nice to meet you, Amelia. Next time you see Rob, tell him this store's coffee is much sweeter than Cross Creek's." She spun around and headed for the door.

Amelia called after her, "Pleased to meet you."

Misty raised her hand "thanks" with the flippancy of one driver to another in traffic, and walked out without her latte.

35

THE AFTERMATH

The next morning, Misty was in the shower after an early run when she heard Rob yell, "I'm going for my morning cup of joe. Would you like me to bring you anything?"

Oh crap, Misty thought. *He's going to see Amelia and she will tell him about yesterday.*

Misty shouted over the rushing water, "No thanks, Rob. I, um, I love you. Drive carefully."

After Rob left, Misty planned for his line of questioning when he returned. She would be sitting in an easy chair pretending to read a book. Her face flushed. She felt foolish for being so sneaky and was upset with herself for engaging in conversation with Amelia. All she had wanted was a quick look at the woman who had written the note on Rob's cup. It started out innocently enough, but once she saw how attractive Amelia was, she just got a little carried away. Misty knew it was not in the spirit of their agreement. Now there was nothing she could do except sit and wait for Rob to return and hope for the best.

Even with Misty home, Rob was looking forward to his usual encounter with Amelia. He had become as addicted to her smile as the four shots of espresso in his americano. He was standing in line when Amelia finally noticed him.

Uh-oh, Rob thought. *Why does Amelia look so troubled? Have I done something wrong?*

Amelia quickly walked over to her manager and whispered something into his ear. The next thing Rob knew, the manager took Amelia's place in line and she motioned Rob to the table with a "Reserved" sign on it. Before Amelia joined Rob, she made two venti americanos and loaded them with four shots of espresso each.

"Amelia," Rob said as she approached the table. "Is everything okay?"

"Oh, nothing too serious, I hope."

Amelia had decided to downplay the meeting with Misty.

"So, how much do I owe you for the coffee?" Rob asked lightly.

"Don't worry, it's on me." Amelia blew the steam from her cup while trying to figure out how to explain what had happened between her and Misty.

"Rob, Misty came in yesterday about an hour after you."

"She did. How did you know it was Misty?"

"Well, I just thought I was chatting with a customer when she asked for my name, which happens less often than you'd think. She ordered a latte, and I asked her name to write it on the cup. She told me. I'm sure I looked a little startled. She looked at me as if she knew exactly who I was, Rob."

"But how could she know anything about you?" Rob murmured. "Are you sure she knew who you were?"

"I'm sure, Rob, because before she left she said to tell you that this store's coffee is sweeter than Cross Creek's."

Now it all became clear to Rob. Misty had found the coffee cup in the trash with Amelia's message written on it. *I'm busted, now. How am I going to explain myself to Misty?*

But then Rob reminded himself of their agreement. He was not only allowed to date Amelia, he also had every right to sleep with her if he chose to.

"Is everything okay?"

"Oh, sorry, Amelia. I just needed a moment to think about what you said. Yes, everything is okay. Don't give it a second thought."

Amelia blew on her coffee some more. "So how is everything okay if your wife caught me flirting with you and came down here to confront me?"

"Confront you?" Rob asked quickly. "Was Misty upset? Did she upset you? Tell me if Misty was rude to you, and I'll talk to her about it."

Rob could tell Amelia was puzzled by his response and reminded himself that she didn't know anything about his relationship with Misty. It also dawned on him that if he explained things to Amelia, he was pretty sure she would not react well.

"Look, I know this is an awkward situation, Amelia, but the last thing I want is for you to be upset. I enjoy visiting with you every morning, and I still look forward to having dinner together again in the future. Sure, I have some explaining to do, but I just want you to know that none of this is your fault. After all, I've been the one driving all the way over here just so I can see you every morning. The least I can do is to ensure that you and Misty never have another confrontation. After all, our relationship has been innocent."

Rob's words calmed Amelia.

"Rob, to be fair, I want you to know that Misty did not seem angry with me. It sounds strange, but I think she and I could really get along under different circumstances."

"I think it might be best if I don't come for my morning coffee until Misty goes on the road again. Unfortunately, that could be two months this time."

Amelia pulled her cup away from her lips. The hurt in her eyes betrayed her feelings for Rob. She nodded slowly. She had expected as much—or worse—would come of her meeting with Misty.

"I'll be counting the days." Amelia leaned over and kissed Rob on the cheek and whispered, "Tell Misty it was all my fault."

Rob took Amelia's hands and gave them a gentle squeeze. "I'm going to miss you. Take care."

He walked out the door and headed to his BMW, thinking, *One down and one to go. I might as well address this with Misty as soon as I get home.*

Rob found Misty sitting in the easy chair reading a book so he took a seat in the chair next to her. *How can she act like nothing happened?* he wondered. *She's just sitting there reading?*

Misty sensed Rob staring at her so she very nonchalantly put the book down and calmly asked, "So, how is Amelia?"

Rob countered, "Why did you go visit her yesterday? You know I have every right to see her."

"My curiosity got the best of me, so I went to see what she looked like. She asked my name, and I couldn't lie." Raising an eyebrow, she said, "I see you still have an eye for pretty women."

Rob leaned back in his chair and looked at Misty. Measuring his words carefully, he replied, "She's just a friend, and I'll leave it at that. Okay?"

Misty smiled gently. "Okay. Why don't we start getting things ready for our bike ride to San Diego with Becca this weekend?"

Rob nodded. "Sounds like a good idea." He ejected himself from the La-Z-Boy with a clunk, walked over to Misty, gave her a kiss on the top of her head, and left the room.

36

THE RIDE

It was early Saturday morning when Becca's train from San Diego pulled into Union Station. Even though the train was an hour late, Misty was pleased. The goal was to pedal ninety-seven miles to Oceanside by sunset. Now the ride would need to be brisk, just the way she liked. Misty craved endorphins and was only really having fun if her heart was racing during a ride.

"Oh, there she is," Misty said. "Becca! Over here!"

Becca headed toward them, walking her bicycle alongside her. She was already dressed in racing Lycra and sported a light pack over one shoulder.

"Hi! Sorry I'm late. Maybe I should have come down last night."

"Don't sweat it, Becca," Rob said, greeting her with a hug. "If I know Misty, she's thrilled you're late. We'll have to put the pedal to the metal in order to make it to Oceanside on time."

Becca laughed nervously at the thought of a hard push down the coast. Misty grinned at her. A friend of Becca's was reopening a restaurant in Oceanside off the North Coast Highway. The Flying L Restaurant had been a mainstay and a local favorite for years.

Glancing at his watch, Rob said, "I think we might have just enough time to get there, check into our hotel, and clean up before the grand opening begins. But . . . we'd better get going."

Misty's pace was brutal, but once they cleared the Los Angeles area she slowed down a bit for the other two to catch their breath. It had been awhile since Misty had biked down to San Diego, and she had forgotten how invigorating it was to bike along the Pacific Ocean. The view was absolutely magnificent, and the cool ocean breeze blowing through her hair was pure heaven. Misty always found solace in nature and felt the great outdoors was as close as you could get to her Maker. She realized that most congregations worshiping indoors spent millions of dollars trying to create a God-like experience, but she preferred the outdoors crafted by God's own hands.

About fifteen miles outside of Oceanside, Rob said, "Well I think we are going to make it guys. It's almost five and we shouldn't have any trouble averaging fifteen miles an hour the rest of the way."

"Speak for yourself," Becca gasped. "I'm about out of gas but I don't want to miss the grand opening so I guess I don't have a choice. I just hope I have enough time to soak in a tub for a few minutes before we head to the restaurant."

Both Rob and Misty knew that Becca could get a little moody when things weren't going her way. Fortunately, they were pretty easygoing and didn't mind bending to Becca's will most of the time.

As they walked over to the ramshackle Flying L Restaurant from their motel rooms, Misty remarked, "Well, the outside doesn't look like much, but the ocean view is spectacular."

The restaurant looked like a diner from the seventies that no one had bothered to remodel. It jutted off the cliff next to a terrace, offering a great view of the inlet to the sea.

"Yes it is," Rob chimed. "I hope the food is as good as the view."

Inside, Becca caught sight of her friend Daniel and said, "Come on, I'll introduce you to the owner. He's a really great guy."

Becca caught Daniel's eye. He waved to her and they began walking toward one another. Becca greeted him with a hug and said, "Daniel, I'd like you to meet my friends, Misty and Rob. We decided to bike in from L.A. on our way to San Diego."

"That's a pretty good ride. You guys should be good and hungry by now," Daniel said. "Things are going to be crazy tonight, Becca, and I won't be able to spend much time with you, so I'm happy you brought some friends. You do understand, don't you?"

"Of course! Don't put yourself out for us on your big day."

Rob jumped in, "Nice to meet you, Daniel. Please don't trouble yourself with us. We will be just fine."

"Thanks, Rob."

Daniel escorted them to a table with a great view. He grabbed the arm of the waiter and said, "Take good care of them tonight. Becca is an old friend of the family. Don't let their glasses get empty."

Other than catching a few glimpses of Daniel from time to time, that was pretty much the last they saw of him that evening. They did not miss his company, however, as everything from the view to the conversation was perfect. That is until, weary and dehydrated, Rob excused himself for the night with an upset stomach.

"Are you sure you don't want me to come back to the motel with you?" Misty asked as Rob got up from the table.

"No need. All I'm going to do is go to bed. You and Becca stay here and catch up. The two of you haven't seen much of each other since Hawaii."

"Well, okay," Misty agreed. "I guess we do have a lot of catching up to do."

Becca had a lot to say about her new job. Misty listened intently to Becca's stories and descriptions, drinking a few too many rum and Cokes for a person who had biked so many miles.

"Hey, Becca, can you hang on for a minute? I have to take a potty break."

"Sure, Misty. Go for it."

As soon as Misty left, Becca motioned the waiter over.

"Listen, I'm trying to impress my friend so don't let her glass run dry, okay?"

"Sure thing."

"Oh, and leave out the gin in mine. Just bring tonic and lime."

"Got it."

When Misty returned, Becca continued talking about her own work until she noticed Misty beginning to slur her words. Then she asked, "So, exactly what have you been doing the past several years, Misty? Why are you away from Rob so much?"

If Misty had not had so much to drink she would have noticed the change in Becca's tone. But her guard was down and she responded as if she had just ingested truth serum.

"Well, Becca, my girl, I've been having the time of my life but shush! Don't tell anyone. Yep, I've really been having a good ole time so don't tell anybody, okay?"

"Don't worry, Misty. I'm your friend. I won't tell anybody. So just how good of a time have you been having?"

"Well, I've been having a really, really good time Becca. I've been meeting some very interesting people, you know? People with lots and lots of money. People that pay me lots and lots of money. People that give me all kinds of perks, you know? Giving lots of perks to little old Misty." Misty sat there grinning.

"So, Misty, how much money do these interesting people give you?"

The waiter refreshed Misty's drink and without thinking, she took a big gulp.

"Whoa! Is the room spinning, Becca? I think the room is spinning."

Becca came over and put her arm around Misty to support her before asking again, "So, Misty, why do these people pay you so much money?"

Misty stared into space for the next few minutes before replying. "You know, Becca, I'm not really sure why they pay me so much moola, cabula." Misty laughed. "Moola cabula. Did you hear that, Becca? Moola cabula."

"Moola cabula. That's a funny one." Becca picked up Misty's drink and put the glass in her hand before saying soothingly, "Now, take a sip and then concentrate on my question."

"Question? You're asking me a question?"

"I'm asking you why they pay you so much money."

Misty had not been this drunk since high school. When she finally remembered the question she said, "Becca? Becca?"

"Yes, Misty, I'm here."

"Becca. You want to know what? I know those peoples like me because . . ." Misty motioned for Becca to come closer before whispering, "They pays me, like, almost two hundred thousand dollars to train them for three months."

Becca was shocked into silence. She had not been prepared for a number anywhere near that large. She didn't make half that much in a year and Misty, a woman she was friends with because she enjoyed Rob's company, was making more than twice her entire year's salary in only three months. A woman not nearly as educated as she was. A woman that didn't know anything about politics, didn't read any business jour-nals, and was not the least bit sophisticated. *How in the world does Misty make that much more money than I do?* she wondered. *Surely there's something going on that I don't know about.*

"Misty," Becca prodded. "Tell me what these men like about you."

"Oh, Becca! They like me a whole bunch. I can tell they like looking at me, talking to me, and well—" Misty again motioned for Becca to come closer before whispering, "They all want to sleep with me, you know?"

Becca was so stunned she lost her composure. "Sleep with you! They want to sleep with you?"

"Hell yes, they want to sleep with me!" Misty snapped, sloshing her drink on Becca. "They all want to sleep with me. Matter of fact, most of them can't wait the entire's time."

"They can't wait the entire time? What are you talking about?"

"Well, don't tell anybodies but part of our deal is that they, you know, those interesting guys, well, they get to sleep with me. But only one time! But when they do they have to give me all the monies, and I gets to go home. Mmmhmm. I gets to go home and keep all their monies, you know? Lots and lots of monies. Can you believe it? And let me tell you a secret. Shush, you can't tell anybody. Here's the secret. Can you keep a secret?"

Becca was on the edge of her seat waiting for Misty to tell her. She wondered how Misty could be sleeping with men when she was married, how she could do that to Rob. Finally she couldn't stand it any longer. Grabbing Misty by the arms, Becca began to shake her and demand, "Tell me your secret Misty. What is your secret?"

This startled Misty and she pulled back and looked Becca in the eyes. Becca quickly went into damage control mode.

"Misty, I'm so sorry. I don't know what just got into me." When Misty's eyes began to glaze over, Becca whispered in her ear, "It's okay, Misty. Tell me the secret. I need to know."

"You know what, Becca? I'll tell you the secret. The secret is that when they can't wait to sleep with me, and when they sleep with me, and when it's over, I'm like a black widow spider. I bite them and then," she said, waiving a hand in Becca's face, "Poof, they're gone." Becca gasped sharply.

"No, no, no. I don't really kill them like a black widow does its mate. It's just that they are kaput. The training's over. And that's why my nickname is the Black Widow Trainer. But shush, don't tell anyone, okay?"

With that Misty laid her head on the table and looked like she was about to pass out. Becca talked the waiter into helping her drag Misty back to their motel adjacent to the restaurant.

Not wanting Rob to witness Misty's condition, Becca and the waiter took her to Becca's room and flopped her across the king-size bed. When Becca finally turned out the light, all she could think about before falling asleep was what she would tell Rob.

37

TATTLE AND SKEDADDLE

At 5:45 AM, a panicked Rob banged on Becca's door shouting her name. Becca had not gotten much sleep due to Misty's frequent stumbling trips to the bathroom, and she was a little groggy. She forced herself to get up and open the door.

"Rob, what are you doing up this early?"

"Becca! Have you seen Misty? I rolled over this morning to wrap my arms around her and she wasn't there. I'm really worried."

"No need to worry, Rob. Misty spent the night in my room. She's in the bathroom hugging the toilet right now."

"Oh no, is she sick? Do you think she caught the stomach flu?"

"No, Rob. Misty doesn't have the flu. Just a good old-fashioned hangover."

"Hangover? What did you girls do last night? It's not like Misty to drink heavily after an all-day bike ride. Hell, it's not like Misty to drink heavily at all."

Becca decided to create a diversion that would give her time to come up with an answer.

"Let me check on Misty to make sure she's okay. I'll be right back." But Rob followed her anyway.

With Rob standing behind her, Becca tried to open the bathroom door but something was blocking it.

"Misty! Are you in front of the door? Rob is here and we want to see how you're doing."

They heard Misty heave.

Rob yelled, "Misty, are you okay? Can you move away from the door enough for Becca and me to come in?"

Becca looked at Rob and said, "I don't think the bathroom is big enough for both of us. Why don't you let me go in first so I can help. This is my fault and I should clean up the mess. Go take a hot shower and I'll have Misty cleaned up when you get back."

"Well, okay. I won't take long."

Misty finally moved just enough to let Becca in. Misty had stopped dry heaving and had collapsed near the bathtub, leaving room for the door to open.

"Misty, are you all right? You've been up all night. I was really worried about you." Becca paused. "Do you remember anything about last night?"

"I do remember getting up to go to the bathroom but not much after that. Oh, my head hurts. I can't believe I drank so much."

That was the response Becca had hoped for. She was almost home free but wanted to ask one more question just to make sure.

"So, what's the last thing you remember talking about last night?"

"Last thing? Let's see. I remember you telling me all about your new job in San Diego. Did we stay long after that?"

"Not long. I noticed you were slurring your words so I brought you back to my room. Rob was feeling sick so I thought it might be a good idea for you to sleep with me."

"Sleep? I didn't get any sleep. I can't remember the last time I was this tired."

"Okay, why don't you get some sleep now while I go with Rob to breakfast? We can bring you back something. What sounds good?"

"Black coffee. Lots of black coffee."

Fifteen minutes later they heard Rob knocking on the door.

"Misty, Rob's here. I'll turn the lights out when I leave."

"Okay. Just don't come back without coffee."

Becca slid out the door before Rob had a chance to come in. Grabbing his arm and leading him away from the door she said, "Misty's sleeping. She said for us to go ahead and get breakfast without her."

"Are you sure? Do you think she'll be all right?"

"She will be once we bring her back some coffee. Maybe we should pick up some Gatorade as well."

"Okay, she could probably use the sleep."

After they had looked over the menu at the restaurant and placed their orders Rob said, "So, Becca, what the hell happened last night?"

"What do you mean? Misty got drunk."

"That's not like Misty. How many drinks did she have?"

"Not many, Rob. We were talking about my new job in San Diego when I noticed she was slurring her words. I became worried because she only had, like, three drinks, so I talked to our waiter while Misty was in the bathroom. I asked him how much liquor they put in their rum and Cokes because Misty seemed so loopy. The waiter laughed and said, 'That's what happens when someone drinks 151 and Coke.'"

"151? Are you both nuts? Do you know that 151 stands for one hundred and fifty one proof? No wonder she's sick!"

"Of course I do, Rob! I yelled at the waiter," Becca lied. "You should have seen me. Then, he realized the guy at the table next to us had been ordering 151s and complaining his drinks weren't strong enough. He'd messed up the tables. I feel really bad, Rob, but it's not my fault."

"Well, that guy should have been more careful. I'm sorry. I don't mean to get on you, Becca. I know you did your best. I guess I'm just upset that Misty's feeling so bad."

Soon after they were served breakfast Becca said, "Rob, you know I don't mean to get into your business, but Misty said some things last night when she was drunk that I found hard to believe."

"Things? What things?"

"Oh, just some things. Maybe I should just forget it."

Rob realized Misty could have been saying anything in her inebriated state. *God, I hope she didn't tell Becca what she's been up to.*

"Did she say anything about her work?"

"Yes, she told me about her work but it just sounded too bizarre to believe."

Rob tried to change the subject by mumbling something about the weather, but Becca was not going to let him off the hook.

"Look, Rob. I said it was none of my business but maybe you should know what Misty said. I'm friends with both of you, but I've known you a lot longer. I consider you a very good friend, and if Misty is doing something behind your back, I think you should know about it. I realize it could ruin my relationship with her, but I'll take that chance to protect you."

Rob stared out at the ocean for a moment. He felt trapped. Becca's concern for him was touching, and he had been keeping this secret for three years now. If he couldn't tell Amelia, maybe he should tell Becca. She had been a good friend for a long time, knew both of them well, and might understand. If nothing else, it would be good to get it off his chest.

Trying to get up the nerve to tell her, he reached out and grabbed her hands. Rob rarely touched her in confidence and the sudden contact excited Becca. She wanted him more than she had thought.

"Becca, did Misty say anything about her contracts with her clients?"

Becca gave him a slight nod.

"Did Misty say that they had an option to do something with her at their discretion, but only once?"

Becca was stunned. She could not believe Rob already knew. Her plan was falling apart. How could Rob be okay with what Misty was doing?

"Yes, she did."

Damn, Rob thought, *Why did that damn waiter give Misty the 151? I guess I need to go ahead and tell her.*

"Becca, I want you to know that what I am about to tell you cannot be repeated. This is very, very important to our friendship. Will you promise that you will keep it just between the two of us?"

"I promise, Rob. You know you can trust me."

Rob let out a big sigh. "Misty and I have a unique marriage. Well, I guess that's an understatement. I have agreed that Misty is allowed to sleep with other men, but we have a rule not to discuss it. It was all my idea. If I hadn't come up with the arrangement she would have left me."

Becca couldn't hide her sudden rush of emotion. "But Rob, you can't let her get away with that. You need to put your foot down and give her an ultimatum."

"And what would that ultimatum be, Becca? I told you she was going to divorce me. I had to come up with something."

"But you can do better, Rob. I'm sure you would find someone. In fact, I'm positive you would."

"Becca that is so nice of you to say but I'm just not ready to leave Misty. I realize that our relationship is more like just sharing a house, like a live-in girlfriend, not a wife, but I'm fine with that."

"So, then, if Misty can play the field, why can't you?"

Rob almost divulged that he was seeing a girl, but then he figured it wasn't any of Becca's business. The thing that distinguished Rob from others, especially from other men, was his ability to be private, withholding, and modest. It felt right to him.

"Well, Becca, maybe I will take that into consideration. I'm sure it would be something Misty would be reasonable about."

"It would only be fair!"

"Sure, but if you don't mind, I would like to drop the subject and get back to Misty. I think she could use us right now."

Becca thought about her next move and then decided she had gone far enough—for now. "Okay, Rob, but I have to tell you, this is not right. I want you to know that I'm here for you whenever you need me."

"I know, Becca. You're a good friend, and I appreciate it."

When they got back to Becca's room they found Misty huddled under the sheets with the blinds closed. Rob turned to Becca and said, "Misty doesn't look very good. I think I'm going to rent a van and drive her back home. I'm sorry we won't continue on to San Diego with you."

"Don't worry about me. San Diego isn't that far. I'll be there well before dark." Without Misty slave-driving her down the coast, Becca thought she might actually enjoy the bicycle ride.

Rob biked to the nearest rental car place and rented a minivan. When he returned, he loaded the bikes into the back while Becca helped Misty onto the bench seat.

Misty stretched out on her back and let out a long sigh. "The black coffee is helping, but I've still got a ways to go!"

"I'm so sorry this didn't work out. We'll just have to do it again next year. I hope you get to feeling better."

Becca walked to the back of the van and gave Rob a tight hug. It wasn't a friendly hug—she pressed her body fully into his when she embraced him.

Softly, she whispered, "Hang in there, Rob. Remember, I'm here if you need me."

Rob nodded his head and walked to the driver's seat. As he pulled out onto the road, he gave Becca a smile and then settled in for the drive home.

Rob chose to take the Pacific Coast Highway back to Malibu even though Interstate Five would have been faster. He had a lot to think about after his conversation with Becca. Pulling the rearview mirror down, he glanced at Misty as she slept. She looked so beautiful, her face at rest and her hair draped over her closed eyes. Rob had always appreciated the fact that she rarely wore makeup. Her beauty was so natural that makeup would have only obscured it.

But then he began to think about what Becca had said and wondered how much longer he could remain with Misty. For years he had felt as if he had a wild animal in captivity and that someday it would want to return to the wild. Releasing her for the past several years had kept her coming back, but how practical was this in the long run?

38

IT'S THAT TIME AGAIN

Rob pulled up to the departure level of the terminal. Misty's plane to Alaska would not depart for another two-and-a-half hours but she always liked to arrive early before flying out for her next assignment. Rob got out, opened the trunk, and carried her bags to the sidewalk.

"So, did you pack enough warm clothes? I know how you hate to get cold."

"I did. But I'm only going to be there until Thanksgiving, so I didn't want to get carried away. Besides, if it gets too cold I'm sure I can find some coats in Alaska that are better suited to keep me warm than anything I can find in Malibu."

"That's a good point. Heaven knows you can afford it. Maybe I need to get a gig like yours and quit my consulting job."

Misty grinned and said, "Well, you're a good-looking guy. Go for it."

"Yeah, right."

Rob stayed in relatively good shape, but he was not particularly ripped with muscle. With a slender build, wire-framed glasses, and weighing in at 170 pounds dripping wet, he looked more scholarly than athletic. Even though Misty was reflexively attracted to muscular men,

Rob's honest handsomeness and unpretentious look attracted the sensible side of her. He was, however, a tiger in bed.

After their embrace, Misty gave Rob a quick kiss and then headed off to check in. Rob watched her until she entered the terminal even though someone was honking at him from behind. He got back into the car and headed for Java Joe's. He found himself speeding to get out of the airport. He was more excited about seeing Amelia than he had expected.

When Misty boarded the plane to Anchorage she began wondering what her new client would be like. His name was Captain Kev. From the pictures in his profile, he looked like Kurt Russell but with shorter hair. Even though she was not entirely thrilled to go to frigid, wild, Alaska, the assignment seemed to be relatively easy. The real reason she was going, however, was to run away from her feelings. During the short months in Malibu, a dull ache had grown in her chest for Gabriella's friendship and company. Misty realized that she really had no friends at home, or friends at all really. The life she had chosen was a lonely one, something she had not considered when she started to pursue it. Hopefully Alaska would push aside her memories of balmy Buenos Aires.

Of course, Alaska also fit a very important criteria for Misty: it was a state rich with outdoor activities, beautiful landscapes, and untouched wilderness. Being home with Rob had not been as relaxing as she had hoped, and this trip, with three training sessions a week, seemed almost like it was going to be a vacation.

Within a few minutes, Miguel boarded the plane and took his seat next to Misty.

"Well, you beat me again. You really like to get to the airport early, don't you."

Misty smiled. Once he was settled in she said, "So, are you excited about going to Alaska?"

"Excited? Hell yeah. I've always wanted to find out if I could be an outdoors kind of guy. I think I'll do me some fishing when we get there."

"That's what I'm talking about. Why don't you go catch 'em and I'll help you eat 'em. Salmon and halibut sound really good to me right now." Misty laughed. With her companion next to her again, Misty became excited as the plane taxied toward their next adventure.

39

NORTH TO ALASKA

Their flight was smooth until about fifty miles out from the Anchorage airport, when the plane flew into a dense grey cloud. It looked like they were flying through fathomless smoke. The captain chimed in and reminded everyone to buckle their seatbelts and hold on tight. They made a rough touchdown at Ted Stevens International Airport and the captain announced their arrival, current time, and temperature. It was fifty degrees and cloudy. When they got to the baggage area, Misty saw a woman holding up a sign with her name on it. *A woman chauffeur? That's a new one. This might be nice for a change.*

"Hello there, do you work for Captain Kev?"

"Yep, Captain Kev and Miniature Mike."

"Miniature Mike? Who the heck is that?"

"Miniature Mike is Captain Kev's partner. They've been best friends and business partners for as long as they can remember. But Captain Kev is the one who hired you. Mikey is so hyper he never gets out of shape."

Miguel gave Misty a funny look and then went over to pick up their bags.

As they approached the car, they realized it was not a typical limo.

"Whoa," Miguel said under his breath. The "limo" was a hulking military-issue Humvee that had been repainted black, but still retained the roof racks, spare tire on the hood, and large imposing grill.

The chauffeur smiled. "That's what Captain Kev gave me to drive."

"So, he made you leave your limo back in Seward, right?" Misty asked.

"Limo? Oh, lord, I don't have a limo. Hell, I'm not even a chauffeur. We just learned this morning that your contract stipulated a vehicle and a driver, and that's only because I read it."

As Misty climbed into the passenger seat and brushed aside a stack of random papers she thought, *Well, this seemed like a good idea at the time but I'm beginning to wonder.*

"Better strap yourselves in, folks, 'cause we're getting ready to rumble." The driver stepped on the gas peddle and the Humvee lurched, taking it right over the curb as if it were no more than a speed bump.

"This is Awesome!" Miguel said. "This is an original military edition Hummer, just like the one Arnold Schwarzenegger used to own. It's the real deal." Misty could not believe the look of boyish glee on his face.

"Well, I'm happy someone is living out his dreams," Misty said sardonically while wondering what the big deal was. This was the bumpiest ride she had ever taken.

They muscled their way out of the airport onto a highway. Misty had seen some of the town from the air, but it looked like they would not pass any of it on their way to Seward. Around them were fir trees and golden aspen, and in the distance rolling mountains loomed. They turned onto Seward Highway and began hugging Cook Inlet, and all trace of humanity aside from the road disappeared. Misty turned to the driver.

"Um, are we going to stop for dinner?"

The woman laughed. "Dinner? I didn't bring the hunting rifle, so I guess not."

Thinking she was getting jerked around, Misty replied rather testily, "What do you mean?"

"The drive from the airport to Seward is about four hours with good weather. Did you see that mountainous wilderness with river valleys when you were descending?"

"Yeah, I guess so . . ."

"We're going right through it. That's the Chugach National Forest." Indeed, they were headed straight into the mountains. The driver mentioned something about moose jerky in the back if they needed a snack, but otherwise they would have to wait until they arrived in Seward.

As they wound their way up the snowcapped mountains, Misty studied the driver. She was a sturdy woman with an attractive face that was framed by short, sandy-blonde hair. She had an infectious smile and a beauty that increased the more you looked at her.

Misty decided to be big about the situation and not act like a spoiled girl from Malibu. It was not this woman's fault that there was nowhere to get a smoothie on the way to Seward. Besides, Misty thought she was cute. She decided to open up a little. "So, what's your name? What's your story?"

The driver brightened up. "My name is Kirima, and I'm half Eskimo. My dad was a sailor who had a one-night stand with my mother, so I have no idea what the other half is. He was probably Russian." She grinned and pulled at her blonde hair.

Miguel had been reading up on Alaska and wanted to impress everyone. "So, Kirima, why do you call yourself Eskimo? That's kind of a blanket, if not derogatory, term these days, right?"

Kirima smiled. "That is a total misconception. The word 'Eskimo' may be looked down upon in Canada, Greenland, and a few other places, but in Alaska it's different." She laughed and said, "Well, except for when Miniature Mike refers to us as Eskamonians. Sometimes I wonder about that guy."

"Aren't there different Eskimo groups?" Miguel asked.

"Yeah, there are lots of different indigenous peoples in Alaska, Canada, even Greenland and Russia. I'm Yupik, but there are also Inuit who consider themselves Indian and not Eskimo."

"Wow, I had no idea," Miguel said.

The rest of the trip was as scenic as what they had viewed from the plane. They passed through several towns that were so small they could only be called villages—Moose Pass, Crown Point, Primrose—none of which had a restaurant. The highway finally broke out of the mountains into a river valley near pristine Bear Lake and they followed Bear Creek through the valley until they reached the inlet to the sea. Soon they noticed more and more houses and then they were in Seward. Kirima drove down Main Street, which was only a block long, and then around the corner to the Hotel Murphy.

It was getting dark, and the many windows on the front of the three-story historic hotel glowed warmly against the cold blue of the mountain looming behind it. Like many of the buildings in the small marina town, the hotel was sided with white clapboard and had a red awning over the front door. It looked so inviting and warm to Misty that she could not wait to settle in, take a shower, and find a fireplace.

Once out of the Hummer, Kirima said, "Go ahead and have a seat in the lobby. I'll take care of your luggage and let Captain Kev and Miniature Mike know you've arrived. I'm sure they will be down to greet you shortly."

Once inside, Misty and Miguel marveled at all of the taxidermied animals on the hotel walls. The lady behind the desk told them that the hotel had been built in 1904, and then she was kind enough to name each of the animals. The lobby was small and so the many trophies gave the room an atmosphere of a menagerie rather than a hotel lobby. There was a full-size musk ox standing on a pedestal, a grizzly bear lunging out of a wall, and even a black bear hiding behind some potted plants.

Misty thought some of the animals were beautiful, but she was more interested in meeting her new client. Just then she heard a loud voice shout, "Nice rack!"

Misty's face turned red and she spun around. Standing before her grinning was a middle-aged man with a handsome, weatherworn face and short-cropped salt-and-pepper hair. He wore a patch over his left eye but the other was sparkling blue and looked at her intensely, as if it was looking for the other eye as well. She could tell from the file pictures that it was Captain Kev.

Misty was not about to start their meeting off like that. No one spoke to her that way.

"So, this is how you greet a lady, Captain? Nice rack?" Captain Kev's smile widened, and he let out a big laugh.

"No, you were standing under that moose head and, boy, are those horns big." Misty looked over her shoulder to find a moose head mounted on the wall, looking her in the face. She almost shrieked.

The Captain continued, "But, damn if you aren't as pretty as your picture, if you don't mind me saying. Come give Captain Kev a big ole hug."

Misty was taken aback again. A hug? Misty held her arms straight by her side as Captain Kev gave her a bear hug, lifted her off her feet, and then set her back down again. Seeing Misty lifted off the ground by this one-eyed stranger set Miguel laughing, which made Misty feel better. If Miguel did not feel threatened, then perhaps Captain Kev was okay. Then from out of nowhere, Misty felt a pair of strong arms clench around her waist and a face press itself between her breasts. Her hands were still pinned at her side and she looked down in confusion and saw a boyish face framed in floppy brown hair and a pair of burning brown eyes looking up at her.

"Uh . . ."

"I'm Michael," said her captor. "Everyone calls me Miniature Mike. You can call me Mikey, or Mike, or even Miniature Mike if you like." Misty got the impression he could go on forever like this. He was indeed small, only four feet eight in boots. He showed no signs of letting go so she smiled at him like one might smile at a toddler latched to one's leg, and wiggled her hands up over his arms and eased him off.

Captain Kev sighed, then glanced over at Miguel and then back to Misty.

"Mikey loves everybody, but especially the women. Been with him my whole life and he wouldn't hurt a fly, so don't be alarmed. He's going to behave as soon as he gets over his excitement. Right, Mikey?"

Miniature Mike frowned but nodded. Misty shook her head and then took a good look at Captain Kev. He did look a lot like Kurt Russell with short hair, just like his picture. He was cute, even with his eye patch. Then Misty noticed he had a prosthetic right arm from the elbow down. She couldn't keep from acting a little startled.

Captain Kev had become accustomed to that kind of reaction. "Noticed my arm, did ya? Actually it comes in quite handy at times. Mikey is good with machinery and has made quite a few attachments and modifications to my arm. He—"

Before the Captain could continue, Miniature Mike interrupted, looking Misty in the eye and speaking quickly in a nasally voice. "I modified the plastic housing to accept certain . . . kinds of . . . motorized attachments, you know? And then I created an independent system of artificial tendons wired into a lithium-ion battery pack. The Captain is, like, part robot now!"

Misty had no idea what any of that meant, so she just nodded and smiled at Mikey, who was grinning ear to ear.

Misty looked over at Miguel and rolled her eyes, but Miguel just shrugged his shoulders and smiled back. Turning back to Captain Kev she said, "Do you mind if Miguel and I have a private conversation for a moment?"

"Nope, don't mind at all. You two go right ahead."

It took only a second to realize that Captain Kev and Mikey were staying put, so she grabbed Miguel's arm and escorted him down the steps and behind the stuffed brown bear.

"Okay Miguel, this isn't funny. I need you to listen to me. I've never walked out on a client before but I'm tempted to right now. You've got thirty seconds to talk me out of it."

Miguel became serious. "Okay, boss. First, he's paying you 180,000 reasons not to walk out. Second, I've always wanted to go to the Pacific Northwest, and Alaska is like the Pacific Northwest on steroids. Yes, these two are definitely characters, but so what? They seem like nice guys. A little . . . different, maybe, but nice guys."

Misty stared into Miguel's eyes but she didn't really see him. She remained deep in thought for several moments before her eyes refocused. "Okay, we'll stay two weeks and then decide." When Miguel attempted to say something, Misty pointed her finger at him and said, "And that's final." This entire situation was feeling uncomfortably similar to what had happened in Buenos Aires. It was true luck that Gabriella turned out to be amazing and not a total creep. Misty was beginning to realize that, even with Miguel, this business could become more dangerous than she expected.

"Well, that's one week more than you gave Gabriella, so you must really like these guys," Miguel said, grinning.

Misty pursed her lips and pointed her finger in his face. "Not another word out of you, got it? Not another word."

Miguel ran his fingers across his lips as if to say, "Okay, I'm zipping it," but his eyes were playful.

They walked back up the stairs to the front desk where they had left the Captain and Miniature Mike.

"Okay," Misty said. "It was nice of you two to greet us, but I'm awfully tired from the trip. Why don't you let me get settled in and take a quick nap and then we can get together for dinner or something."

Captain Kev seemed a little put off. "Suit yourself," he said. "You can find me at the Fisherman's Cove Bar one street over when you are ready."

As Misty turned to walk away Miniature Mike began to follow her. Halfway down the hall she heard Captain Kev yell out, "Mikey! Get your ass back here. I'm sure Misty is capable of finding her room and taking a nap by herself."

Mikey frowned a bit and turned to follow Captain Kev out the door. Watching the little man stomp out of the hotel in his boots made Misty wonder if she should have told Miguel they would give it one week rather than two. As she approached her room, she turned to Miguel and pointed her finger again saying, "Not a word." Miguel replayed the zipper move and walked past at a brisk pace toward his room.

40

THE COVE

Misty was awakened from her sound sleep by loud banging on her hotel room door.

"Who the hell is that?" she muttered.

When she finally opened the door, Miguel was standing there in a tight shirt and jeans, looking as if he was ready to party.

"How come you're not ready, Misty? It's already nine o'clock. It's not like you to keep a new client waiting."

Misty rubbed her face and wiped the sleep from her eyes. "All right, damn it. Give me time to take a quick shower and then we'll go." The last thing she wanted to do was hang out in some smelly dive bar but she reminded herself that she needed to remain professional and she threw herself into the shower. By the time she got out, she was ready for the night.

When Misty and Miguel arrived at the Cove, the place was buzzing. As she had feared, it was something of a dive. The bar was clad in rough-hewn wooden boards; the gable above the two long narrow windows was built out of an array of wood like a sunburst—the only thing that saved the room from looking like a soggy frontier saloon. There was a lighted sign above the door with an illustration of Annie Oakley pointing a six-shooter down at whoever stood below, her eye looking down the barrel.

The walls were crammed with fishing and hunting kitsch—nets, miniature ships, oars, life preservers—lit only by neon beer signs. Miguel told Misty to wait at the door until he located Captain Kev and Miniature Mike. As Misty stood there she began to notice that every guy in the place was looking her way, and it gave her an uncomfortable feeling. *My word!* she thought, *These guys act like they've never seen a woman before.* She'd never seen such a collection of mustaches, beards, and overalls.

Miguel came back and Misty followed him to the back of the bar. Captain Kev, Miniature Mike, and Kirima were sitting at a table in the corner.

"Glad you could make it, sleepyhead," Captain Kev yelled over the noise of the bar. "I didn't realize I was hiring Sleeping Beauty."

Misty groaned and bit her lip.

"What would you like to eat? I'll have Kirima go to the restaurant down the street and get us some grub."

Misty was famished. "I would love some big King Crab legs. Is that possible?"

"Possible? You are in Alaska. We got crab legs the size of horse legs. Kirima, here's some cash. Go get us a bunch of those tasty critters and a pound of butter to dip them in. Oh yeah, don't skimp on the napkins."

Kirima jumped up and said sarcastically, "Aye, aye, Cap'n."

As Kirima left, Misty started to scoot in next to Miniature Mike but then quickly switched to Captain Kev's side of the table. Once Miguel sat down Mikey looked up at him and grinned. Miguel thought Mikey was adorable. He reminded him of a friend he had in grade school. In fact, Mikey had that kind of effect on men, which was the one reason he was tolerated. He became everyone's little brother, even though he was in his midforties. Miguel wrapped his arm around Mikey's head and gave him a noogie, like he used to do to his childhood buddy. The two were carrying on exactly like children until Misty kicked Miguel under the table and he settled down.

In an attempt to make conversation, Misty asked Captain Kev, "So, where is the local gym we're going to use and what kind of equipment does it have?"

"Gym?" He let out a belly laugh and took a drink from his glass of whiskey. "Hell, this town doesn't have a gym. Where do you think you are? Malibu?"

Captain Kev and Miniature Mike looked at each other and began laughing, which didn't sit well with Misty. Just because they were paying her did not mean they could make fun of her.

She did a good job of fighting the urge to strangle both of them before responding, "Exactly how do you suppose I'm going to get you in shape and earn my fee, Kev?"

Captain Kev winked at her.

Just then two of the local women walked up to the table.

"Hi, Captain Kev. What kind of attachments has Mikey made for you this month? We can't wait to see."

Mikey's eyes opened wide and he put on a big grin.

"Well, girls, Mikey outdid himself this time. I'm a little tied up right now but come back tomorrow night, and I'll take you for a spin."

One of the girls whispered something into the other's ear and then they both giggled. "See you tomorrow night Captain."

Misty frowned at Miguel, but he just shrugged his shoulders, looking like he was trying his best not to laugh.

But as he watched the women walk across the room, he started to chuckle.

"What are you laughing at now?"

"Misty, over there." He nodded toward the bar, where a stuffed brown bear head hung with sunglasses over its eyes and a pair of tennis shoes dangling out of its mouth by the laces. But it was the sign hanging around its neck that read "Send More Tourists" that cracked her up.

"Well, I declare," Captain Kev said too loudly, "She does have a sense of humor. I was beginning to worry about you, doll."

Misty smiled and said, "Yes, I have a sense of humor. I'm sorry. I guess I've been a little on edge since I got here. Traveling takes its toll."

Before Captain Kev could say anything that might set her off again, Miguel quickly said, "That's the spirit, Misty."

When Kirima got back they began cracking open the giant crab legs and dipping the tender white morsels in butter. Misty couldn't get enough, but finally forced herself to stop eating.

When they had all finished, Misty said, "Ok Cap-e-tan. We're going to get started bright and early so I suggest you go get some rest. Where do you want to meet in the morning?"

"There's an old building at the edge of town. It has a boxing ring, speed bag, and some dumbbells. Maybe you can figure out something we can do with that stuff."

Misty laughed under her breath and shook her head. She rose and began to walk out of the bar.

Miguel looked at Captain Kev, shrugged his shoulders, and said, "See you in the morning."

A few minutes into their walk back to the hotel, Kirima ran up behind them. "Wait up, guys. I'll walk back with you."

"Sure, Kirima," Miguel replied. "How come you scooted out of there so fast?"

Kirima rolled her eyes. "Miniature Mike was putting the moves on me again so I thought I'd take off with you."

"Why don't you say something to Captain Kev?" Misty asked. "It seems like he could make Mikey stop."

"Oh, no. No need for that. I actually kind of like Mikey but I'm just not sure I'm ready to sleep with him. I can be kind of . . . athletic in bed. He's so little I wouldn't want to hurt him."

Misty laughed and gave Kirima a friendly nudge.

41

HERE COMES THE CHAMP

The next morning, Misty and Miguel asked the hotel owner how to get to the old building, and she gave them simple directions. In a town as small as Seward, it was almost impossible to get lost. If you went too far north, you hit a mountain; too far south, and you had to swim. The building was a ramshackle old warehouse near the pier that had large, dusty glass windows and a metal chimney puffing wood smoke from the roof.

Inside there was an old boxing ring with some ancient training equipment strewn about. Shortly after they entered the building, Misty heard some music coming from outside.

Miguel looked at Misty in disbelief and said, "Is that the theme song from *Rocky*?"

A few seconds later Captain Kev jogged in. He was wearing an old silken boxing robe and had a boom box hooked on the end of his artificial arm. Miniature Mike had his legs wrapped around the Captain's waist while rubbing his neck like a trainer does a boxer. When he got into the ring, Mikey took off a bag hanging around his neck and pulled out a glove that was designed to attach to the end of Captain Kev's fake arm. When Mikey finished, the Captain began to shuffle his feet and move around the ring like he was Muhammad Ali. He was remarkably limber and seemed to know what he was doing.

Intrigued, Misty watched and thought, *Boy, these guys are really characters. Someone should put them in a book.* She took a deep breath and put on a confident smile. She would have to do the best she could with what she was given.

The rest of the morning Misty had the Captain working the punching bag and shadow boxing with Miguel. Miniature Mike was too hyper to hang around the gym so he went for a long run. When Mikey got back it was time for the dumbbells.

Misty looked at the Captain's artificial arm and tried to figure out how to balance out his workout with the weights.

"I really want you to be able to work both arms equally. What's the best way for you?"

"That bag around Mikey's neck's got all the attachments I need."

Mikey, hearing his name, rushed to the Captain's side. He pulled out a vice grip and attached it to the Captain's arm.

Captain Kev looked at Mikey while flexing his arm. "Be sure to use a few pounds less on the weights for this arm. You need to compensate for the weight of the vice grip."

Misty nodded. The Captain was more together than he looked. She wondered what other kinds of attachments he had.

At the end of the free weights session, she took everyone out for some jogging, using it as a good excuse to see the small town of a little over five thousand people. As they ran up and down the different streets, several women they passed greeted them: "Hi, Captain!" "Looking good, sweetie!" "You busy tonight?"

After about the tenth girl, Misty couldn't help but think about Captain Kev's attachments. She had several ideas about what else Mikey might have built, and not all of them were useful for lifting dumbbells. She blushed at her thoughts.

42

THE COVE, ROUND TWO

That night when she and Miguel walked into the Cove, Misty strolled to the back as if she owned the joint. She was not afraid of the good ole boys at the bar or rattled by the cramped feeling of the place. As she walked past the bar, beers were set down and conversations slowed as the patrons watched her.

Misty found Kirima and Mikey on one side of the table and the Captain on the other. When she slid in next to Captain Kev, he said matter-of-factly, "You know all the boys in here want to do you, don't you?"

Misty realized this was going to be an everyday occurrence; she might as well get used to the Captain's banter.

Deciding not to let him think it bothered her, Misty said, "That's not what's important. What's important is: Do *I* want to do any of them?"

Misty then turned and surveyed the crowd one by one.

"Hell, no! Not going to do any of them. Mangiest bunch of mutts I've ever seen." The Captain nearly spit out his drink laughing. He pounded the table and shook his head.

"That-a-girl, Misty! To hell with 'em!"

Misty looked over at Kirima who was still laughing. "How's it going, Kirima? I see Mikey is still attached to your hip."

Kirima pinched Mikey's cheek. "Yeah, the little fellow thinks he's going to get lucky tonight. Don't you, little guy?"

Mikey rolled his eyes comically, surprising Misty with his sense of humor.

Miguel was normally very relaxed, but the increased attention from the patrons toward Misty irked him, so he stationed himself in front of the table to keep an eye on the bar. As his eyes panned the room, his gaze stopped, mesmerized by a woman talking to the bartender. Although her back was turned to him, he could see her reflection in the mirror behind the bar. She was striking. She had large dark eyes, wavy light brown hair, and curves in all the right places. He thought, *Man, that woman is built for love. Uh, oh. Here she comes.*

Apparently she had already noticed Miguel looking at her and must have taken it as an invitation. "Aye, you're a lovely lad. Must have a good lookin' maw and paw," she said with a wink.

Miguel had never been approached so confidently before, and for the life of him he could not think of a reply.

The woman laughed at his silence. "You sure are a nice snatch to look at. That's a compliment, you know."

Fumbling for the first words he could grasp, Miguel replied, "Uh, oh yeah. I knew that. Nice snatch yourself." Miguel's eyes widened, and he slapped his forehead for saying something so embarrassing.

Misty had been watching from the corner of her eye and had to bury her head in her hands to keep from bursting out laughing.

The Captain said, "That's the way to talk to a woman Miguel!"

The woman stared at Miguel with a puzzled look on her face. He quickly apologized. "I'm sorry, I didn't mean you had a nice snatch. I meant it was, uh, nice to snatch you away from that guy at the bar." Miguel then put his hand out and added, "I'm Miguel."

Misty smiled and thought, *"Now he's back on his game."*

The smiling young lady took her time looking Miguel over before offering her hand in return. "I'm Amber, and the pleasure is all mine. Can I buy you a drink?"

"Of course," Miguel said.

Amber turned to the bartender and said, "Bobby, bring us a pitcher of brew so this young lad and I can get jaked!"

Miguel did not quite know what "jaked" meant but if it could be done with, or to, Amber, he was up for it.

Amber looked over at Mikey. "What a *toaty* boy. Does his mother know he's here?"

Mikey scrunched up his face and glared at Amber.

Kirima cut in. She put an arm around Mikey and said, "That's okay, you little toaty. Your mommy's right here."

The table erupted in laughter and Mikey beamed at the attention. He quickly returned to his good-natured self.

Everyone took turns buying pitchers until the noise level in the bar became deafening. Miguel learned that Amber was from Scotland. After graduating from university in the spring, she talked her father into sending her to Alaska as a reward. She spent the summer traveling around the state but came back to Seward for her last three weeks. Amber knew how to speak American English well but enjoyed reverting to Scottish slang whenever she first met cute guys. She thought it was a blast watching all of the strange expressions they made as they tried to figure out just what she meant. The only issue Amber had with Alaska was the lack of good-looking guys. Now that Miguel had showed up, she was not about to let him go.

Amber smiled at him and said, "You comin' for a wee donner doon yonder with me?"

Miguel looked up at Misty for help, but all he got was a smile and a shrug. When Amber stood up and put out her hand, Miguel was out of the seat, pronto. Off they went for a walk doon yonder.

As Miguel walked away Misty yelled out, "Be a good boy, or I'll tell your fiancé."

Amber stopped in her tracks and looked directly into Miguel's eyes. "So you have a fiancé, do you?"

"Well, not technically. We have discussed marriage but I have not formally asked her yet. I guess you could say 'yes,' but we're just going for a walk, right?"

That was all Amber wanted to hear.

"Sure, sonny boy. We're only going for a walk . . . tonight."

As the group at the table continued to cut up, the two local girls that had approached Captain Kev the night before returned.

"So Captain, did you bring your new toy?"

Without saying a word Captain Kev snapped his fingers at Miniature Mike. Mikey ran off to a room in the back of the bar. When he got back he handed the Captain something in a brown paper bag.

"Okay, girls. Time to twirl!" The girls squealed and giggled. Captain Kev excused himself from the table and walked with the two women back into the darkness of the bar.

After the three left, Misty turned to Kirima. "So, where did he take them?"

Kirima slid over next to Misty and whispered so Mikey couldn't hear her. "Captain Kev and Miniature Mike own this place. They have several bedrooms in the back fully equipped, so they say." Kirima looked back into her beer with raised eyebrows.

Misty's curiosity got the better of her. "Fully equipped? What the hell does that mean?"

"I've never been back there, so I'm not totally sure. But whatever it is, the girls sure seem to love it."

This was too much for Misty. How could Kirima not know what was going on back there? Misty was determined to get to the bottom of it. She nodded in the direction of Mikey, who was now jumping up and down at the bar, trying to get the bartender's attention.

"Kirima, there's your ticket to the back rooms. What are you waiting for? Go for it, girl."

Kirima's eyes got really big. "Are you suggesting I take Mikey back there and screw him, so we can find out what's behind the curtain?"

"Hey, you don't expect *me* to do it do you? You said yourself you like him. Look at it this way: you can do him tonight, just for fun. Try him out and see if you like him."

Kirima seemed to ponder the idea. Misty thought she could see a flicker in Kirima's eyes that indicated she might be considering it, so Misty gave her a wink for confidence when their eyes met again.

Kirima looked over at Mikey and then back at Misty. "Okay! But if I break the poor boy, it's all your fault!"

When Mikey came back to the table, Kirima whispered in his ear. A shiver passed visibly through his body and he bolted towards the back-rooms. Just before he went through the door, he looked back at Kirima and started waving for her to follow.

Kirima turned back to Misty one last time. "You owe me one after tonight. Big time."

Misty nodded in total agreement. "No problem, Kirima. Now go find out what's back there!"

It wasn't long before Misty realized she might have made a terrible mistake encouraging her friends to run off and have fun without her. Sitting alone at the table was an invite for every goofy bastard in the bar to make a pass at her. Luckily, Miguel and Amber returned from their doon before any of the leering barflies worked up the courage.

"Man, I'm glad to see you guys. Miguel, get back to work and keep these baboons off me, please."

No sooner had the words left Misty's mouth when two pitiful souls headed her way. Miguel got up slowly and walked out a few paces to form a one man barricade between Misty and her suitors.

Amber looked at Misty and said, "Work? What kind of work does Miguel do for you?"

"He didn't tell you on your walk? Miguel is my bodyguard, and I rely on him in times like this."

Ambers face brightened. "He is? How buff. That's how you say it here in the States right? Buff?"

"Yes, 'buff' will do."

"What do you do that requires you to have a bodyguard?"

"I don't want to sound impolite but it's a long story."

Amber looked at one of the guys who was now returning to his seat and made a face. "Eeeh! That wee guy is a total tink."

Misty gave Amber a puzzled look. "What?"

Amber grinned. "Oh, nothing. It's a long story."

Misty laughed and decided Amber might become her new best friend in Alaska.

Miguel was good at his job, and it didn't take long for the rest of the guys in the bar to go back to pounding down beers and talking trash. Even though Miguel was a sweetie at heart he could also be an imposing figure.

When another local came up to Miguel, Amber yelled out, "Miguel, Donny's one of the good guys. Let him through."

Donny sat down at the table and greeted Amber. "Hi Amber, I just finished my shift. What's up?"

"Just having a fine time with my new friends. Meet Misty and Miguel. They're up from Malibu, California."

"That's a long trip. Well, we could use some civilized people in Seward," he smiled. "What are you here for?"

Miguel responded, "Misty is here to train Captain Kev. He wants to get in shape."

Donny seemed surprised. "He does? I wonder if it has anything to do with that suspicious guy that has been keeping an eye on him."

"What guy?"

"He's sitting at the table over in the corner at the front of the bar. I've noticed him staring at the Captain for several days now, writing things in his little book."

Miguel peered through the cigarette smoke to the front of the bar. There was a weasel-faced man in a worn suit sitting alone at a table, thumbing through a ratty notebook.

Miguel was curious. "Donny, why haven't you said anything to the Captain?"

"I've meant to but every time I start to head his way he takes off into the back with some girls."

"Maybe I'll go have a talk with him. Hold the riffraff at bay for me." Donny laughed and watched Miguel get up from the table and walk to the front of the bar.

But as Miguel made a move in the man's direction, he closed up his book, took one more quick gulp of his beer, and hurried out of the bar. Miguel decided not to follow him into the street and resumed his guard over the table.

Misty turned to Donny, saying, "Tell me something about this town."

"Sure. Seward is a fishing town with a drinking problem."

Amber laughed. "Well I've been here for several weeks now and I'd say it's more like a drinking town with a fishing problem."

Donny laughed and replied, "Yeah, I think you're right. Guess I've never heard it put quite like that, but I'd have to say it's pretty darn accurate." Donny turned to Misty, "It's too bad you weren't here on the Fourth of July, being into physical fitness and all."

"Why's that?"

"Because that's when they race up and back down Marathon Moun-tain. It's the big mountain behind the bar."

"They race up and down a mountain? I've never heard of it."

"Well, it's pretty big. The town swells up to over twenty-five thou-sand people and things get crazy. It's kind of like the Kentucky Derby. There's all that buildup for a race that doesn't take that long to run. Actually, most do it in less than an hour."

"They can run up and down that mountain in under an hour? How big is it?"

"Marathon Mountain is 4,000 feet and they start in front of the Cove. The record is actually forty-three minutes.

Miguel jumped in. "Forty-three minutes? That's incredible!"

Donny laughed. "Yes, it's pretty amazing. There was a guy leading the race by four minutes this year only to collapse from exhaustion a block from the finish line, right down there in front of the bank. The funny part was that the guy in second place assumed that the man lead-ing the race had collapsed at the finish line and stopped running. That allowed the guy in third place to win the race."

"That . . . sucks?" Amber said cautiously.

Misty patted her on the back. "Yep, that's how we say it in the States."

"It was nice meeting y'all," Donny said as he got up from the table. "Early to bed, early to rise. Oh, the life of a fisherman."

As Donny was walking away Misty yelled out, "So, you've got a fish-ing problem?"

Laughing, Donny yelled back, "Tomorrow I do, but the next time I see you at the Cove, I promise I'll have a drinking problem."

As Misty started to take another drink of beer, she noticed Miguel staring at the backroom door with a troubled look on his face. Misty and Amber quickly turned to see what he was looking at.

"Kirima!" Misty shouted. "Are you all right honey? I had forgotten all about you."

Kirima was standing there propped up against the doorjamb. Her hair was a wreck, her clothes were disheveled, and she was wide-eyed. Both Misty and Amber rushed to her side.

"Kirima, what happened?"

Kirima did not snap to at first, but then wrapped an arm around both Misty and Amber's shoulders for support.

"Ladies, there ain't nothing miniature about Miniature Mike. I think that boy's father was a Clydesdale. If I had only known sooner I wouldn't have wasted all this time."

Mikey came walking out the door, gave Kirima a pat on the rump, and headed for the front door whistling a tune.

Amber was not totally sure what had just happened. "So, she got the ole *boaby* tonight?"

Misty laughed. "Yeah, apparently she got all the 'boaby' she could handle."

Misty and Amber got Kirima some water and then debriefed her on the back bedrooms. Kirima said each room had a bed with plush sheets, candles to see by, and dark red walls.

Misty said, "Quite the little pad, I guess. Maybe these guys really do know what they're doing. Well, that's all the excitement I can handle for one night. Who wants to walk with me back to the hotel?"

Kirima wanted to stay and rest for a bit and Amber wanted to finish her drink, so Misty and Miguel said good night and left for the hotel. As they walked through the parking lot Misty heard a squeaky voice shout, "Can you give me a hand?" Miguel had Misty stay put while he checked things out. She soon heard Miguel laughing.

"Misty, come here. You won't believe this."

Misty walked over and looked down. There was Miniature Mike pinned on the ground with a significant portion of his Harley Davidson lying across his legs. He did not seem to be in any pain and actually looked quite comfortable.

Misty relaxed once she realized that he wasn't hurt. "Taking a little nap are we, Mikey? Kirima wear you out?"

Mikey just lay on the ground grinning like a maniac. Misty turned to Miguel. "Let's get that thing off him and get going."

As they neared the hotel they could hear Mikey scream off into the night on his Harley like a bat out of hell.

43

THE BIRD CAGE BAR

Going to the Cove was getting old so Miguel asked Captain Kev if he knew of someplace else they could go. Captain Kev and Miniature Mike looked at each other and grinned.

"Sure, Miguel, I've got just the place. It's called The Bird Cage. It's outside of Anchorage, but well worth the drive. We can have Kirima drive us in the Hummer so we have a designated driver."

"The Bird Cage? That sounds kind of interesting. What should I tell Misty to wear?"

Captain Kev grinned. "Tell her to wear her finest undergarments!"

Miguel let that one slide and moved on to coordinating the trip.

"So what time should we leave? It's almost 2:00 PM now."

Captain Kev checked his watch. "As soon as we can. It will take a while to get there."

Miguel then asked the question he cared about most. "Can I invite Amber?"

"Hell, I'll ask her for you. Just go get Misty. And don't forget to tell her to wear her best lingerie."

"Huh? Um, okay." As Miguel walked toward the hotel he thought about the bizarre request.

When Misty and Miguel climbed into the back of the Hummer they found Captain Kev, Kirima, Amber, and Amber's friend Heather already there. Miguel's heart began to pound at the sight of Amber. He didn't know anything about Heather, but he was anxious to find out all about her.

Just then they all heard a deep rumble and looked out the window to see Mikey pull up alongside them on his Harley. He gave the Captain a stiff salute and held it until the Captain sighed and gestured indifferently. "Kirima wouldn't let him sit on her lap and help drive the Hummer so he decided to take his Harley," the Captian explained.

On the trip over Mikey would pass them going a hundred miles an hour only to take some back road for a while and then pass them again.

Miguel found out that Heather was an old friend of Amber's and had just come over from Scotland to be with Amber for her final days there. Heather was almost as enthralling as Amber. Her chestnut hair was straight and long. She had a cute face and an infectious smile that made her almost as seductive as Amber. But it was her stunning long legs that captivated Miguel. Heather was used to men looking at them and if she felt attracted to any of the gawkers, she would let them see more. So during the drive she teased Miguel by showing more and more thigh. She enjoyed the way he kept trying *not* to look but couldn't help himself.

Miguel had ample time to observe the girls on the way to the bar so he made a game out of it. Amber was more mysterious and a bit sultry while Heather looked outright mischievous. Amber had a confident air about her and Miguel could get mesmerized just from looking into her eyes. He found the entire experience extremely stimulating and somewhat enchanting. He couldn't remember the last time he was so turned on.

Amber was the main attraction when the two friends were out together, but Heather had become quite adept at stealing attention away from her. Both girls were playful, but Amber gave Heather the floor more often than not. Over the years, the girls had learned to play off each other for a man's attention, causing the poor guy to feel like he was getting passed from one to the other at their whim. This tag-team approach always left the target of their affections aroused. Heather and Amber had used this approach for so long they actually preferred sharing one man over each having their own. Even though Heather knew Amber was always going to be the main attraction, it was fine with her because their outings together exposed her to much more attractive men. Tonight, Miguel was the target, and he was in for the time of his life.

Just like Captain Kev had predicted, they rolled into the parking lot at a little after seven. The Bird Cage was partially sunken into the ground and had a big, blue, ugly bird statue sticking out of the exterior wall. Misty decided to postpone judgment until she'd had a few drinks. The Cove did not look like much from the outside either, but she was growing to love the place.

Once inside all she noticed was the dirty, dirty, dirty sawdust floor. When they were all seated at their table, Misty realized the walls were tilting to the left. There wasn't a level table in the place. It wasn't long before Misty heard Amber and Heather giggling. When she turned around it became obvious why. Hundreds of women's undergarments of all shapes, sizes, colors, and styles were nailed to the walls and ceiling. There were even bloomers that must have been there for decades. The Bird Cage felt weighed down by all the underwear.

She heard Captain Kev belt out, "Now that's what I call fine art, girls. Nothing finer than a vagina liner," he shouted before laughing at the top of his lungs.

Amber and Heather thought this was all hilarious but Misty wasn't as amused. She thought, *This might be the most ridiculous thing I have ever seen.* Captain Kev was pushing her patience. She was having an okay time in Alaska, but times like these reminded her she was very far away from Buenos Aires and Gabriella.

Just then Misty noticed one of the bartenders coming out from behind the bar and toward their table.

"Ladies, what brings you to The Bird Cage?"

Misty shook her head and looked the other way, but both Amber and Heather were eager to engage the bartender in conversation. He gave a spiel about the establishment's tradition of women giving up their undergarments and he assured them that they most certainly would be the best-looking birds to ever grace the bar if they decided to do so. The girls said that they would think about it and let him know later.

The barkeep must have really wanted their panties on his wall because he yelled out, "This table, drinks *on the house* until 10:00 PM."

That got the party started. Everyone in the group except for poor

Kirima was pounding down drinks, just as the bartender had planned. Misty even got into the act because to her surprise, they had her favorite rum, a seven-year Flor De Cana. After Misty got a few down, she began to relax and lighten up. Captain Kev, who had been watching Misty's drinks for the past hour, gave the bartender a signal when Misty was not looking. Soon he was on his way back to the table.

The bartender approached her. "So, ma'am, I can see you aren't interested in letting go of your panties so maybe I can interest you in some bird sightseeing."

"Bird sightseeing? What are you talking about?"

Captain Kev leaned over. "Misty, I forgot to tell you about the wild ptarmigans that run around out back."

Ptarmigans? Misty thought. *I think they had a stuffed ptarmigan in our hotel lobby.*

"Hey CK, is there a ptarmigan in our hotel lobby?"

"Actually, there is. But there is nothing better than seeing a live one running around in the wild."

This had Misty's attention as she was fond of birds. The more she drank the more she kept thinking about that cute little creature supposedly running around out back.

Finally Misty said, "Hey, barkeep. How do I see one of those cute little birdies?"

The bartender reached under the counter and pulled out some kind of instrument. When he got to the table Misty said, "What the hell is that? I just want to look at the little thing, not shoot it."

"Don't worry, this isn't a gun. It's something we use to call the birds. They are very shy and elusive little creatures. That's why we use this special trumpet to call them."

"That's the funniest looking trumpet I've ever seen. Hell, the end is pointing back at me."

"That's because it puts out a very high frequency, just like a dog whistle. Having the end of the instrument pointing away from the birds makes them think its way off in the distance. We find it works better."

"Well, okay, but you're going to have to show me how to use it."

"That's easy. Follow me." When they got to the window he said, "Put the horn out the window and I promise that within a few minutes you will see ptarmigans running around everywhere. There is a mamma ptarmigan that just had some new chicks so if you are real lucky you will see them follow her out as well."

New chicks! she thought. *Man, I hope they come running!*

Misty stuck her head out the window with the instrument as instructed but quickly popped back in and said, "Miguel, I want to make sure they hear me so will you hold onto the back of my shirt while I get as far out the window as I can?"

Miguel looked at the bartender to see if he thought this was a good idea. When the guy grinned back he took it as a sign that all systems were go.

Once Misty was way out the window the bartender said, "Be sure to blow as hard as you can so the little ones can hear it."

"Will do, Cap-e-tan. Oops, you're not the Cap-e-tan. You are the Bar-b-tan." Misty was getting a little tipsy and thought that was pretty funny. She put the horn to her lips. "Here blows nothing."

When Misty blew into the trumpet, talcum powder exploded out of the end leaving her head totally coated with the white powder. Miguel and the girls were as surprised as Misty but Captain Kev, Miniature Mike, and the rest of the bar were rolling with laughter.

"You bastards! How could I fall for this?"

When she finally got all the powder out of her eyes, she saw that everyone was standing and clapping. One by one they all came up and gave her a congratulatory hug.

One of the guys from another table said, "You're a club member now—one of us. Please don't be mad."

Misty saw the humor in the situation. Really, she should have known better. Ptarmigans? Ha! *No sense in being a party pooper*, she thought.

The bartender had been keeping an eye on Amber and Heather. From years of experience he was good at identifying the perfect time to swoop in and make his move.

"So girls, ready to take off them panties?"

Amber looked at him and said, "You'd like to get in my panties, wouldn't you barkeep? Just waiting until I'm blottered, aren't ya?"

"Well, I'm not sure what blottered is but I'm not allowed to fraternize with the patrons, beyond collecting their panties, of course."

Heather, however, was ready to party. "You're kind of cute. I'll give you my bra if you give me a nip first."

"Nip? What's a nip?"

Heather grabbed the barkeep and pulled him toward her and gave him a kiss on the mouth. He straightened back up and said, "Wow! That's even better than a nip of whisky."

By now most of the patrons had gathered around the table. The anticipation continued to build until finally Heather got up the courage to begin taking off her brassiere from underneath her blouse. Miguel became mesmerized watching how skillfully Heather removed her bra without showing a hint of skin. When her bra was finally free she pulled it up through the top of her blouse and started waiving it over her head. The whole place erupted with an applause that electrified the girls. The barkeep took the dainty thing from her hand and stapled it to the wall.

It was the first prize of the night and the crowd wanted more. Everyone in the bar began to shout out, "More, more, we want more!" They continued to pound their fists on the table in rhythm until Amber volunteered to go next. Miguel was amazed that she was just as adept as Heather at working her bra off underneath her clothes. If Miguel thought watching Heather do it was hot, watching Amber set his loins on fire. Amber finally freed the silky black beauty and began swinging it over her head. As the patrons in the bar became hypnotized by the circular motion of Amber's bra, Miguel noticed Amber's plump breasts bouncing beneath her blouse.

When Amber caught Miguel looking he covered up his eyes, but his futile attempt failed the minute the chant of "Panties, panties, panties!" began. His hands stayed over his eyes but he couldn't stop his fingers from spreading wide. Next thing he knew, the girls pulled their panties off from underneath their skirts in unison and offered them up to the bartender. When he reached out to take them the girls threw the panties over his head and spun him around. When he finally got them off, he dizzily stapled them to the wall. As he drove in the final staple, the crowd went wild.

The thought of Amber and Heather without anything underneath their clothes was too much for Miguel; his imagination went wild. He kept murmuring under his breath: "I'm almost engaged, I'm supposed to be getting engaged, I'm going to be engaged." Yet with one more look at Amber and Heather's bodies moving freely beneath their tight shirts and skirts, he began to sing a different tune. "Aw, hell! I haven't gotten engaged yet. This may be my last opportunity before I do. If I get an opportunity tonight and pass it up, I might regret it the rest of my life."

Miguel continued to struggle with his dilemma until the answer came like manna from heaven. "No penetration! I stay faithful by refusing to penetrate. Brilliant!"

With that reasoning he realized that he would never be able to talk himself out of what he was about to do, nor did he want to. He quickly looked around the crowd and spotted Misty sitting at a table on the other side of the bar.

He bent down and whispered in Captain Kev's ear, "Hey, buddy. Will you keep an eye on Misty while I politely socialize with the girls?"

Captain Kev, being Captain Kev, was happy to help out. "Sure thing, Miguel. You can't be too polite these days. Keep the girls company."

As Miguel sat down next to Amber he noticed she and Heather were rubbing noses. He looked down to find Heather's hand on the inside of Amber's thigh. When the girls realized Miguel had moved closer, Heather leaned over and whispered something in Amber's ear, which made Amber smile. Miguel couldn't stand it any longer so he tapped Amber on her shoulder.

She turned to Miguel and placed a hand on the side of his face and smiled seductively. "What is it, handsome? Were you enjoying the show?"

Amber's directness caused Miguel to lose his confidence—he felt like he'd been caught. A second later, however, Miguel's mojo came back and with a very calm voice he said, "I was wondering what Heather whispered in your ear."

"Are you sure you can handle it?"

Although he was thinking, "Fuckin'A I can!" he replied calmly, "My nickname is The Handle. I can handle anything my hands get a hold of."

That seemed to be the proper response because Amber whispered in Miguel's ear, "Heather said, 'You won't believe how much I want to eat your pussy.'"

Amber let the shock wear off Miguel's face before adding, "We're headed to the ladies' room. Would you like to join us?"

Amber placed her hands on the side of his face and moved Miguel's head up and down while saying, "Yes you do, don't you? Follow me."

When they got to the restroom door Heather said, "Stay here, and we'll come get you when the coast is clear."

Fortunately for Miguel, there were very few women in the bar. It was only a second before the girls came back. The door cracked open, and Amber's finger beckoned him inside. He followed her into the large stall at the back. Heather was leaning against an inside wall with a hungry look on her face. Once they were all in, Amber locked the door. She ripped open Miguel's shirt and began kissing his chest.

"Do I have your attention?" she asked, looking up at him.

He nodded, looking her in the eyes. Heather started running her hands over his stomach and down his thighs.

"Okay, here are the rules, Miguel. I'm going to sit on the toilet seat and you are going to watch Heather go down on me. When you can't stand it any longer, you can play with Heather's *bristols*, okay?" She noticed the quizzical look on his face. "Bristols are tits, lover boy. Don't interrupt us until I get off, or you'll get nothing." She scratched under his chin with her fingernails and pursed her lips. "*Comprende, mi amigo?*"

After she sat down, Heather hiked up Amber's skirt and exposed her dark, hairy bush. All Miguel could see was the back of Heather's head moving in a circular motion. Amber placed her hands on the back of Heather's head and helped direct her movement. Once Amber's breathing quickened she took her hands off Heather, unbuttoned her blouse, and began to massage her own breasts. By now Miguel felt like he was becoming comatose, so he leaned against the stall wall, totally enraptured in what he saw. As Amber came closer and closer to orgasm, she removed her hands so Miguel could get a good look at her beautiful breasts heaving with every breath. Right before climax, Amber grabbed the back of Heather's head and forcefully pulled her down into her. Finally Amber erupted with a shout of pleasure, and Heather backed away so she could watch her quiver in ecstasy.

A moment later Amber licked her lips sensually and looked at Miguel. "What are you waiting for, handsome? Don't you be leaving Heather out in the cold, now." Miguel felt like an idiot for not taking the opportunity to play with Heather's bristols earlier.

Being with two women was new to Miguel so he had to rely on pure primal instincts. Facing Heather, he picked her up and lifted her legs over his shoulders. Heather gave a surprised laugh and quickly grabbed the top of the stall for support. Miguel buried his face in Heather's pussy, licking and kissing hungrily.

Heather ground her hips in rhythm with Miguel's expert tongue. She was moaning more and more with every darting movement of his tongue into her wet vagina. Amber sat watching as she recuperated. Miguel looked up to see Heather's breasts bouncing out of her blouse as she moved against his tongue. Seeing this turned him on so much that he thought he might come in his pants. Suddenly he felt Amber zip open his trousers and reach in to pull out his throbbing, hot cock. The feeling of Amber's warm mouth engulfing his member sent shivers through his body and encouraged him to work on Heather even harder. As if choreographed, both Heather and Miguel erupted in unison. After Miguel shot hot semen all over the stall wall, Amber worked her hands up and down his penis, helping him drain every last drop.

When they were done, the threesome cleaned themselves up as much as possible. They were fortunate no one had walked in on them. Heather and Amber slipped out the door, but a woman walked in right before Miguel could make his escape.

When she gave Miguel a startled look he put his finger to his lips and said, "Shush, personal body guard. Don't tell anyone."

Once out the door, Miguel hoped that he would need to use that line again sometime.

From across the bar, Misty saw Miguel and the girls return to the table and decided to meet them there.

She asked, "What have you been up to Miguel?"

"Nothing, boss. I was just keeping an eye on these lovely ladies." Amber and Heather smiled demurely and giggled. "We don't want some maniac getting hot and bothered because they don't have any underwear on and trying to attack them. Right, girls?"

Amber looked at Misty and said, "Thanks for letting us borrow your hunk of a body guard. This guy will do anything to help us feel warm and safe all over. Right, Heather?"

"Right, Amber."

Misty had a feeling there was way more to the story than she was being told. She also had a pretty good buzz going and decided she didn't want to ruin it by asking too many questions. She frowned at Miguel. "I'm not sure who should be watching who anymore."

Miguel laughed confidently, implying to the girls that Misty was only joking. The laugh was enough to confuse Misty, so she started laughing as well.

They ordered another round of drinks. When the waiter walked away, Amber looked at Misty with a mischievous grin. "Okay, it's your turn to drop the knickers, Misty."

"Oh, no. You girls gave up enough knickers for the whole table, and I think you represented us pretty darn well."

But Amber and Heather wouldn't take no for an answer. A few minutes later they both said they were going to get something from the car and walked behind Misty, toward the door. As soon as they were behind her, they grabbed Misty and pulled her out of her chair and onto the sawdust floor, laughing maniacally.

"Oh no you don't!" Misty yelled, but it was too late. Heather sat on Misty's midsection while Amber slid in between her thighs to wedge Misty's legs open. Misty kept yelling for Miguel, but he just kept murmuring, "I can't hear you," and laughing.

Soon Amber had Misty's black thong pulled down around her ankles. Misty gave up and let her slide it over her feet. When Amber began to twirl it over her head, everyone in the place saw the thong and went wild. The bartender had a special case behind the bar where he placed what he thought were the primo panties. Amber bowed as she handed the thong over to the bartender. Once he closed and locked the case, Misty's thong became the prime catch of the night.

"You should be honored, Misty," Captain Kev said. "I've been here over twenty times with at least fifty women, and you are the first to have her underwear put in that case."

Misty began laughing. *Maybe I'm taking things too seriously*, she thought. *This really is a fun place with a lot of fun people. I need to just lighten up and go with the flow.*

The group had a blast all the way back to Seward.

44

WHERE IS MIKEY?

The following Wednesday, Miguel talked Misty into letting him ride the train from Seward into Anchorage with Amber and Heather. They were to stay the night and then come back the next afternoon. Misty had insisted that Miniature Mike accompany them so he could keep an eye on Miguel. Misty wasn't quite sure what had happened at The Bird Cage, but she was concerned Miguel might do something that would get him into trouble with Sylvia.

The next day, Misty and the Captain finished a good training session and walked to the train station so they would be there to meet the gang when they arrived home from Anchorage.

"So, do you feel like I'm doing you any good, CK?"

"Hell yeah. I haven't felt this good since Miniature Mike and I used to fish off the East Coast. Mikey has stayed in pretty good shape, but I've let things go a bit the last two years."

"Well, you're looking mighty fit now, Captain. Did I ever tell you that the girls think you look like Kurt Russell?"

He looked at her with a twinkle in his eye. "Do you think that's why the women love me?"

"Well that and maybe your attachments."

Captain Kev gave a short laugh. "Yes, the women do like my attachments. At least there is a bright side to losing my right forearm. It's funny how things work out sometimes."

"How did you lose your forearm, Captain?"

Captain Kev scratched his chin with his hook, wondering how much he should tell her. It wasn't that he didn't trust her; some of the information was a bit sensitive, but mainly he didn't want to expose her to any of his troubles. He finally decided he could fill her in if he was creative with what he told her.

"It's a pretty crazy story, Misty, but here it goes. Mikey and I were fishing off the coast of Maine. One day we threw our nets out and they got so loaded down with fish that it began to put a strain on our winch. When we pulled the nets in they were full of bluefin tuna."

"Bluefin? Aren't they the ones that make the best sushi?"

"Yep, they actually auction them off to the highest bidder in Japan. Some of the big ones have gone for as much as fifty thousand dollars."

"How many did you have in your nets?'

"About seventy-five. It was the mother lode."

"Hey, isn't it illegal to catch them in a net?"

Misty was smarter than she looked. He had underestimated her.

After clearing his throat he said, "Of course. It was by mistake. I felt so bad for those bluefins that I climbed onto the net with my knife in my teeth and began cutting big holes. About halfway through I got my arm twisted up in the net and the weight of one of those fish flopping around broke the bone clean off at the elbow. I watched me arm disappear into the briny deep." He said this last sentence in a raspy pirate drawl.

The Captain bowed his head and began scratching his neck with his hook while he looked out of the corner of his good eye to see if Misty was buying his story. Misty had a suspicion he might be fibbing, but she didn't care. She gave him a friendly nudge and said, "Guess we better start calling you Captain Hook from now on." In an effort to change the subject, Misty followed with, "So, how many women have you had in your private room, Captain?"

Captain Kev smiled big and pointed down to the large tarnished belt buckle securing his trousers and said proudly, "See all those notches?"

"You're kidding me. You put a notch on your belt buckle for every woman? There must be well over a hundred notches on that thing."

While the Captain basked in his glory, Misty sulked. *Damn it. I'm going to be one of those notches soon. Well, at least it won't have my name on it.*

When the train pulled into the station about an hour later, Miguel, Amber, and Heather came running toward Misty and the Captain.

"Captain! Captain!" Heather yelled. "We've looked everywhere but no one can find Miniature Mike."

Miguel added, "The last time anyone saw him he was on the caboose, hanging onto the ladder and throwing his feet out over the edge of the train. When the other passengers complained, the conductor sent someone back to stop him. The man said that when he got back there, Mikey was nowhere to be found. We're worried he swung himself off the train when we were in the mountains."

The Captain seemed unaffected by the story and kept looking calmly at the train. When everyone else turned to look, they caught a glimpse of a figure lying on the top of the caboose. Miniature Mike suddenly sat up, put his hand over his mouth, and yawned.

"Just catching some rays and a nap, I imagine," Captain Kev said. "That's nothing out of the ordinary for Mikey."

The Captain turned around and walked off. A few seconds later, Mikey jumped down from the train and followed after him.

All Misty could think was *Un-frickin' believable.*

45

HOMER SPITTOON

I t was Amber and Heather's last week in Alaska, so everyone decided to visit the small town of Homer and give them a proper send off. They booked rooms at the Just for the Halibut Hotel, which sat at the end of the Homer Spit, a narrow strip of land that jutted out two miles into Kachemak Bay. The hotel was not supposed to be fancy but Amber had heard there was something magical about being out in the middle of Kachemak Bay. Artifacts had been found there that dated all the way back to the Stone Age, so the Spit must have been a magical place for a long, long time. Everyone who came over the hill and saw the Spit surrounded by water and majestic mountains fell in love with it. It was no exception for Misty and the rest of the group.

"Unbelievable!" Heather yelled as they drove over the hilltop.

"Look at the view!"

"Spectacular!" Misty said. "Now I'm really glad we came."

Homer was a small town like Seward, so it didn't take long for the road to take them through the commercial district and directly onto the Homer Spit. The first part of the road was only wide enough for two lanes of traffic. But as the Spit widened, the group drove past what looked like a boat graveyard. All of the boats were completely ruined and half-sunken, except for one large boat sitting in dry dock, awaiting its return to the ocean.

"Holy crap! Look at that junker," Miguel said. "That's the most pathetic looking boat I've ever seen."

The boat looked to be about eighty feet long. There were metal guardrails on both the bow and the stern, making it resemble a freighter. And yet, two large wooden masts made it look like a sailboat. But it was the rounded living quarters at the stern that caused the boat to resemble a pirate's ship—that and the mismatched, dilapidated quality of the entire vessel. The quarters appeared to have been added to the ship as an afterthought and were covered with old, unpainted plywood. It was such a pitiful sight that almost everyone in the Hummer began to laugh uncontrollably.

"Hopefully there's a diesel engine on that sucker because there is no way that rusted tin can would even make it out of the harbor under sail," Miguel said.

"What the hell is it?" Misty said. "I've been around lots of boats in California but I've never seen one quite like that. If it was a dog, it would be the ugliest mutt I'd ever laid eyes on."

While everyone laughed hysterically, Captain Kev and Miniature Mike slumped down in their seats and hoped no one would notice. The ragtag ship everyone was mocking belonged to them. They had bought the boat because it had been necessary for them to make it to Alaska incognito. They assumed not many people would notice an old boat, but now they were beginning to wonder.

Amber was laughing so hard she could hardly calm down long enough to get words out of her mouth. She had the window rolled down and was pointing at the ship. "Dirty Pirates! Did you see the name of the boat? It says Dirty Pirates!"

By the time the Hummer made it down the two-mile strip and stopped in front of their hotel, everyone was light-headed from laughter.

"My side's hurting," Heather said, mascara running down her face. "I don't think I can take it anymore."

Amber got out of the car and looked at the sign resting on the roof of their hotel. Above the large sign were three life-size wooden figures. On the left was a man looking through a pair of binoculars, and next to him, a sailor holding a pole with a loop around the end. Misty assumed they were whalers. To the right of the men sat a beautiful hand-carved mermaid. Miguel was feeling clever so he pointed at the sign. "Look, it's Captain Kev and Miniature Mike scoping out Misty."

Talk about putting gasoline on the fire. Even Kirima began laughing uncontrollably. Predictably, Misty was not amused. Pointing her finger at Miguel she said, "You better behave boy, or I'm going to leave you home next trip," and then strutted into the resort.

Amber and Heather patted Miguel's back. Heather said, "That's okay, Migzee! You can come visit us in Scotland if she doesn't take you with her."

Misty liked the fact that there was something as magnificent as Homer hidden all the way out there at the end of the peninsula. She thought about all of the kidding going on and decided she was going to let her hair down tonight and not let it bother her.

As dinnertime approached, Miguel asked Captain Kev, "What do you suggest we do tonight?"

"Well, there are shops and restaurants within walking distance. If you youngsters weren't laughing so hard you would have noticed them driving in. I'm thinking about hanging out at Black Beard's Saloon with Mikey. You're welcome to join us if you get tired of all that sissy stuff."

Miguel puffed up. "Sissy stuff? You mean laughing?"

"Yeah!" Captain Kev said gruffly, his face hard. But then he broke into a laugh himself.

Amber and Heather hooked arms with Miguel and started to drag him off. Misty laughed as she followed. True to her word, she was staying loose and trying to be fun.

They all walked back down the Spit a short ways to the row of shops and restaurants located near Black Beard's. Darkness was already falling and the saloon, an old log cabin attached to a wooden lighthouse, looked warm and inviting. Captain Kev, Miniature Mike, and Kirima found a table close to the bar and settled in. Black Beard's had pretty tight quarters, but it was a great place for a couple of old salty dogs like the Captain and his little buddy to lie low.

Two hours and umpteen drinks later, the Captain had his feet up on the table while Mikey kicked back in his chair and chewed tobacco.

Kirima was not drinking and had decided to read a book. The boys thought the name Homer Spit was hilarious; every so often the Captain would yell "Homer!" and Mikey would spit on the floor. On about the tenth round of "Homer Spit," Mikey's aim got a little shaky, and he spit right on someone's boots.

The guy spun around and shouted, "What the fuck? Get over here and clean these boots off, you little turd."

The Captain and Miniature Mike slowly looked up into the sweating red face of the guy the locals called Russian Jack. He must have been over six feet eight and weighed more than three hundred pounds.

Captain Kev looked over to Mikey and said, "That's a big fuck, isn't it?"

Mikey nodded, wide-eyed.

"What part of 'clean up my boots' don't you understand, you little runt?" Russian Jack demanded.

With that, Mikey darted behind Captain Kev and squatted down. Kirima offered to clean Russian Jack's boots, but he was set on Mikey cleaning them. "Oh, he's going to lick 'em clean all right."

Captain Kev stalled for time while Mikey rooted around in the bag he always carried for the wooden, balled-up fist attachment.

When the time was right, the Captain motioned for the big guy to bend down and come closer. By now several of Russian Jack's buddies had moved in. One stayed behind to guard the front door. The bartender had seen this many times before, so he ran into the mock lighthouse that was attached to the bar. He wasn't about to risk getting hit by a flying chair or beer bottle.

Russian Jack bent over as if he were going to lift the Captain out of his seat. The Captain poked him in the eyes with his good hand. The big guy backed up, wincing in pain. With one hand rubbing his eyes, Russian Jack motioned for three of his guys to jump in. One of them wrapped his arms around Miniature Mike while Russian Jack put the Captain in a headlock. All at once fists were flying.

Kirima punched one guy in the jaw good enough to send him back against the wall. As she was moving in to get him again, one of his buddies shoved her down hard enough to put her out of the fight.

Miguel and the girls were about to enter the bar when they were stopped by a man blocking the door. "I wouldn't go in there if I were you. Russian Jack is getting ready to mop the floor with a couple of assholes."

"One of those assholes wouldn't happen to be wearing a black eye patch, would he?" Miguel asked. The man's eyes got big when he realized Miguel was a friend of the Captain's. Miguel hit him with a crushing blow to the solar plexus, and he crumpled to the ground in agony.

Once inside, Miguel saw Russian Jack and yelled, "Hey, you fat fuck! Let him go."

The big Russian began laughing, and the rest of his men joined in. Miguel kicked one of them square in the balls so hard that the guy doubled over and fell to the floor. While the other men were focused on Miguel, Captain Kev worked his prosthetic arm as high as he could get it while Miniature Mike positioned himself beneath the Captain.

The big Russian was watching his men fight Miguel when Captain Kev said, "Hey, you, big lug. Look at me when I'm talking to you. Don't you know who I am?"

Jack's face turned red and he bent down until he was nose to nose with Captain Kev. The Captain yelled, "Homer!"

As soon as he did, Miniature Mike spit a big wet wad of tobacco into Russian Jack's face, blinding him. The big Russian screamed and clawed at his eyes. The Captain turned his body to aim his arm at the Russian's face. When Captain Kev was in position, Miniature Mike kicked his feet up like he did when he was swinging from the ladder on the train. His foot hit the latch on the side of the Captain's fake arm, releasing the heavy metal spring holding the wooden fist in place. With the force of a locomotive piston, the solid wood fist smashed into Russian Jack's jaw and knocked the big guy out, stone cold.

When he bumped his head on the bar and crashed to the floor motionless, the room went silent. Jack's men released Miguel, whom they had quickly overwhelmed, and slowly backed away. The Captain and Miniature Mike broke out in laughter and began slapping each other on the back. Miguel got the bartender and told him to call 911 for an ambulance.

When the dust settled, Miguel said, "Well, I recommend we get the girls back to the safety of the inn. Sorry, but that's my job."

Captain Kev and Miniature Mike didn't look too thrilled as the night was still young, but they agreed that Miguel was right. The gang slowly left the bar.

Just before Miguel passed through the exit, his bodyguard instincts told him to turn around and get a mental picture of everyone in the bar. Only then did he notice the weasel-faced man with the notebook whom he had seen at the Cove. When the slender man noticed Miguel, he closed his notebook and slipped out the back door. Miguel thought it an unlikely coincidence that the mystery man would be in Homer at the exact same time they were.

About halfway back to the hotel they began laughing about the brawl. Kirima had a small knot on her head, but she said she would be fine once she got some ice on it. It was not the first time she had tussled with rowdy men.

Misty trailed slightly behind the group, contemplating the fight. As the rest went through the front door of the inn, Misty saw one of the strangest things she had ever seen. Two hands were massaging the breasts of the wooden mermaid that was perched atop the roof.

What the hell? Who in the world could be that perverted? In a split second, she realized there could only be one answer.

With a loud stern voice Misty yelled, "Mikey, leave that defenseless mermaid alone and get your butt down here."

A wide-eyed Mikey popped his head over the mermaid's right shoulder and stared down at Misty. She shook her finger at him, and he reluctantly came out from behind the mermaid, rolled off the roof onto the ground, and then hopped up. As he walked toward the entrance to the hotel Misty heard him say in a squeaky voice, "Can't have any fun tonight."

The next morning at breakfast, Miguel let Captain Kev know about the stranger he had seen in Black Beard's. The Captain kept a straight face but shortly afterward said, "Why don't you take the girls and go back to Seward alone. Miniature Mike and I have something we need to attend to. Tell Misty we'll have to drop our Monday workout but I should be back for the Wednesday session."

46

IF YOU LIKE TUPPERWARE PARTIES...

When Amber and Heather left for Scotland, Miguel went into a funk.

Misty wanted to cheer him up, so she said, "Come on Migs, let's go to the Cove and have a few rounds."

"I don't think so, Misty. I appreciate what you are trying to do but I'm just not up for it. Maybe tomorrow night."

"Go take a walk along Resurrection Bay, then. Maybe that will make you feel better.

"You sure you'll be okay if I leave you alone?"

"Sure, I've still got Captain Kev and Mikey. After last weekend, I think they know what they are doing. I'll be fine."

"Okay, but don't hesitate to call me; I'll come running."

Misty nodded. Miguel's comment made her think about Gabriella. It had been over four months since she had seen her and suddenly Misty had an urge to know what was going on down in Buenos Aires. *Maybe I'll just go back to the room and give her a call.*

At the Cove, Captain Kev and Miniature Mike were hoisting a few when Kirima came in.

"Hey boss and boss. You do remember I'm off tonight, don't you?"

Captain Kev looked up from his beer and said, "Sure do. By the way, what is it you do on your nights off?"

Kirima fidgeted a bit and then said, "It's kind of embarrassing. I'd rather not say."

Of course, those words perked Mikey's interest so he started repeating, "Tell me, tell me, tell me" until Kirima couldn't take it anymore.

"Okay, I'll tell you two but don't laugh. Well, I am kind of a Tupperware saleswoman on the side."

Captain Kev shot back, "What the hell? Nobody buys Tupperware anymore. You're wasting your time."

Kirima smiled and said, "I sold a thousand dollars' worth last week."

This had the Captain scratching his head because he was pretty sure Tupperware parties were a thing of the past.

"Okay, girl. Tell old Captain the truth. You're not selling your mama's Tupperware, are you?"

"No, I'm not selling my mama's Tupperware. I'm helping married women have as much fun as the women you help out."

"Hell, you're not one of those lesbians are you?"

Kirima laughed. "No, but if I were, it wouldn't be any of your business. 'One of those lesbians.' Sheesh, Captain, welcome to the twenty-first century."

Captain Kev got an idea. "Hey, Mike. Didn't you invent some kind of lubricant you wanted to sell to women? This could be your big chance."

Mikey's eyes opened wide and he jumped to attention.

"Can I, Kirima? Can I, can I, can I?"

"Man, you are the most persistent little guy I've ever known. Look, I would but I can't sell your product because the company I work for won't let me sell anything other than their products. And I can't take you with me because, well, this is a women's only party, which leaves you out."

Desperate, Mikey pulled Kirima toward him and began to whisper in her ear. The Captain could tell from her face that she was not excited about what he was saying. She just kept shaking her head no. Finally Captain Kev stepped in.

"Come on Kirima, what's his idea? Mikey comes up with some good ones, you know."

Shaking her head Kirima said, "He wants to dress up like a girl and come with me."

"Brilliant! Why didn't I think of that? Mikey will look great as a woman! Look at that baby face. He doesn't even need to shave as it is. No one will ever know."

Kirima rolled her eyes in despair but knew that when the boys got hot on an idea it was not easy to talk them out of it. Actually, she had never talked them out of an idea so she finally gave in.

"Okay, I'll let him come, but where are we going to find a dress that will fit him? Mine are way too big."

"Well, that's an easy one. Mikey, run over to Misty's room and see what you can borrow."

With that Mikey took Kirima by the hand and pulled her out the door, saying, "But first we need to go to my place and pick up the merchandise. This is great!"

Misty had just hung up the phone when she heard a knock on her door. She was in a fantastic mood after getting an update from Gabriella. Gabriella filled her in on how Tom was doing and, more importantly, how she was doing. Gabriella confessed she missed Misty, too, as a friend and companion. As Misty walked toward the door she thought, *Maybe I can figure out a way to get back to Buenos Aires. I sure miss her.*

When she opened the door, Misty was shocked to find a very excited Miniature Mike and a slightly annoyed Kirima.

"Oh, you guys! I thought it was Miguel. What's going on?"

When Kirima filled Misty in on the plans, Misty could not keep from laughing. She looked at Mikey to see if he was sharing in the comedy but, if he did, his face didn't show it. That's when Misty realized he was dead serious.

"Okay, come on, Mikey dear. Let's get you all dolled up. I have no idea what we're going to do about your hair, though."

Kirima piped up, "I have a wig I used back when people made fun of me for being an Eskimo with blonde hair. We'll stop by my place and pick it up on our way to the party," she said, slightly embarrassed.

When they got to the party, Kirima couldn't believe how cute and believable Mikey looked in his red dress, black shoes, and black wig. Just before they knocked on the door, Kirima pinched Mikey on the cheek just for fun and said, "You're so beautiful. Yes you are."

Not thrilled, Mikey grabbed her hand and placed it on his cock, which was large even when not aroused.

Kirima shook her head. "I know, but you better keep that thing in your dress or you'll get us thrown out of here."

The woman who opened the door lit up when she saw Kirima.

"Oh, good! You're here." Turning to the other women in the house she yelled out, "Kirima's here, girls." The women in the back began cheering and clapping in response.

"I hope you know what you are getting into, Kirima. These women have been drinking for the last hour and are in a raucous mood. We all told our husbands we were having a Tupperware party and suggested they all go out to the bar. They will probably be there until it closes so we've got plenty of time to try out all of your stuff!"

"I've been doing this for a while now, and there isn't much I haven't seen, so you housewives just let it all hang out! By the way, this is my helper, uh, Mary," Kirima said, motioning toward Mikey.

Mikey gave the woman a big smile and then left to get the merchandise from the car.

Once inside, Kirima surveyed the crowd. From the well-cut hair, pedicures, and expensive clothing, she figured the group must be married to the richest guys in town. They were the prettiest bunch Kirima had seen in Seward. She was pleased. Women with bodies like those would be all over her lingerie. She crossed her fingers as she thought about how much money she could make. She just had to make sure they didn't find out about Mikey first.

Kirima pointed out the cases Mikey had lined up on the kitchen table. The women tore into them immediately, holding up the lingerie and fondling the dildos and vibrators and joking with each other. It was a free-for-all.

Kirima had learned there were two kinds of crowds—those that were timid and shy and those that wanted to party. When she ran into the party girls it was better to let them just go for it instead of presenting the merchandise piece by piece.

"Ladies!" Kirima yelled. "I'm going to sit on the couch and let you sample the merchandise. Please use the demos if you must. Just don't open any of the sealed packages. Don't worry—I sanitized the demos before I came. When you are done drop them in this red bag so that no one else uses them after you do. If you have any questions, you know where to find me."

The women fell upon the merchandise with drinks in hand, fighting over the latest toys and grabbing sample packets of lubricant. It was not long before they were all heading upstairs to the bedrooms and fighting over the bathrooms downstairs. The more self-conscious women went into the rooms alone and the more adventurous went in two and three at a time.

Mikey began to slide off the couch.

"Oh no you don't!" Kirima said while grabbing his arm. "You're not going anywhere! Just sit here where I can keep my eyes on you."

Mikey sat back, crossed his arms, and tucked his hands under each armpit like a little kid pouting.

The mini orgy went on for over an hour before everyone finally worked their way back to the living room. It was a very different crowd this time. Most of the women looked a little tired and worn out, and the room was much quieter. Another round of drinks was poured.

Now that Kirima had their attention she began to show the girls the sealed merchandise, one piece at a time.

"Okay, here's one of our bestsellers. It's called the Pearl Rabbit. Who wants one of these?"

Hands flew up everywhere. Kirima knew she was going to make a mint tonight.

For the next hour, Kirima would hold up an item and then Mikey would hand it out to the women and take their money. He decided his bra could use a little more padding so every so often he would go into the bathroom and stuff the bills into his bra. After awhile they were so full he starting holding his hands under each cup and pushing them up a bit, admiring them in the mirror. Mikey got so caught up in his role as a woman that he used a tissue to touch up a few mascara smudges and applied a little more lipstick. When he felt he looked even better than before, he went back out to take in some more money.

"Okay, that's about it girls. I hope you—" Kirima stopped mid sentence because Mikey was tugging at her shirt. When she looked into his face she realized she had forgotten to let him sell his product.

"Oh, I almost forgot. We still have some lubricant to sell."

To get things started, Kirima pulled out different kinds and began to explain the difference between silicone and water-based lubricants. One of the women could not decide between silicone-based and water-based, so Mikey jumped in.

In a voice pitched only slightly higher than his own, he said, "Ladies! I have the answer for you. My lubricant is half silicone based and half water based."

Mikey grinned like a used car salesman and held up a pickling jar full of transparent gel. There was a slight murmur among the women. He then nodded to Kirima to hand out the bottles from his box. Kirima started to get an uneasy feeling about it but decided to do it anyway.

When the ladies got their bottles they read, "Miniature Mike's Lube-Ur-Cunt."

Kirima was pretty sure she heard someone gasp in horror. She put her hands over her eyes. At least they already had the money from the other merchandise. Mikey, totally oblivious to the horrified crowd, put a latex glove on his right hand, opened a jar, and dipped his middle finger into the oily substance. He held up a dripping finger and leered at the women.

"Who wants to go first?"

The room became eerily quiet and all Kirima could hear was her own heart pounding and her reputation in Seward dying.

The silence broke when an older lady said in a gruff voice, "Miniature Mike, huh!?"

She got up and began to look Mikey up and down. Mikey just stood there with a creepy grin on his face until the lady pulled his wig off.

Two more ladies jumped off the couch and ripped the top of his dress down to his waist. As petrified as Kirima was, she had to laugh at the sight of a lean masculine upper body with bulging muscles wearing a bra stuffed with money. Some of the money was actually sticking out of the two C-size cups.

All hell broke loose. Mikey bolted up the stairs and into a bedroom. He stuck a chair under the door handle just before five women tried to follow him in. Mikey pulled the sheets off the bed and tied them together. When finished, he tied the sheets to another chair and wedged it under the windowsill. Once outside, he quickly shimmied down the sheets, dropping the last six feet to the ground. He hopped up, pushed up his bra full of cash, and admired his size Cs one more time before running off into the night.

Kirima used Mikey's diversion to escape out the front door. Once in her car, she sped off down the road. When she felt she was safe, she laughed. She knew her gig was up in Seward, but she wondered if word would travel all the way to Homer.

Mikey got to Misty's room about an hour later and knocked on her door. When Misty opened the door she took one look at Mikey and shook her head.

"Sorry about your dress, Misty," Mikey said with a puppy dog look.

"I don't even want to know what you've been up to, Mikey. Well, it looks like you put my bra to good use. Got enough in there to pay for the dress you ruined?"

Mikey pulled all of the money out and set it on the bed, but when he started to give Misty some she said, "No, you give that money to Kirima. I'm sure it belongs to her. Don't worry about the dress. I'm just sorry I wasn't there to see what went down. I could have used a good laugh."

47

Now or Never

Captain Kev had seemed a little distracted over the past week. *Maybe it's because the weather is changing*, Misty told herself. A few days earlier they had gotten what they referred to in Seward as "termination dust." It was the first snow and the beginning of winter layoffs for 90 percent of Seward's workforce. After the day's training session, Captain Kev let Misty know that this night was going to be *the* night.

Looks like it's time for our termination fuck, Misty thought. She composed herself and said, "So, exactly what are you planning to do to me tonight, Captain?"

Captain Kev grinned and scratched the side of his face.

"Nothing that will leave any permanent marks on you, girl. Trust me, you'll love it!"

Misty shook her head disapprovingly and walked away.

Captain Kev yelled after her, "Wear something pretty!"

Something pretty? Miniature Mike ruined my only dress. Guess the Captain's out of luck.

Back in her hotel room, Misty surveyed her outfits. A wave of nostalgia washed over her as she remembered surveying a similar wardrobe in Hawaii before her rendezvous with the beautiful stranger. The Man, the one who had set her free. She selected tight-fitting hip-hugger jeans and a low-cut black cotton blouse. If she had nothing "pretty," the Captain would have to settle for hot.

Misty headed for the Cove. She entered and bellied up to the bar and threw down two shots of tequila, taking the bite out of them with a slice of lime. This assignment was starting to get to her. It wasn't that Captain Kev wasn't an attractive guy. His face was darling, and after all the hard work, his body was looking pretty damn good as well.

The Captain had been gracious to her even though he had a very direct way of speaking. She realized that she was just nervous about all the "attachments" she had heard about. And the thought that Miniature Mike had made them in a basement gave her reason for concern. Misty threw back a third shot of tequila and shook her head warily. Then she got up from the bar and walked to the Captain's private quarters in the back. She was lucky that the "termination dust" had kept Sewardians at home that night. Otherwise, everyone in town would be witnessing her walk to *the back* to become another notch in the Captain's belt. Tonight, she only had to face the knowing eyes of a few barflies. Still, she was nervous.

When she got to the door, a sign read: "Captain's Treasure Cove . . . Enter at your own risk."

Shit, truer words were never written, she thought.

When she cracked the door, she saw the Captain sitting in a chair with his feet propped up on the bed, listening to an iPod he had holstered onto the side of his arm. He was leaning back in a peaceful trance, his eyes closed, head gently nodding to the beat. Misty spent a few moments surveying the room. It was quite nice, actually. There were paintings of the ocean on the walls, soft lighting, and what looked like a state-of-the-art sound system. In the middle of the room was a king-size bed with pillows strewn everywhere. The fact that there were no windows, with only soft, warm lighting, made the room more inviting than she had imagined. She walked over and stroked the Captain gently on his arm.

"Well hey there, Misty. I see you're ready to brave the great unknown."

"Well, a deal is a deal, so just tell me what you want me to do," she said, forcing a smile.

"Okay, pretend you are a princess and go get comfortable on the bed." He added with a smile, "Or pretend you are a mermaid, if you prefer."

She felt another wave of nostalgia. Captain Kev's words reminded her of New Orleans. *The last time I pretended to be someone I wasn't on a balcony in New Orleans, I got the heck screwed out of me. We'll see if the Captain is anywhere near as good as Sammy.*

She arranged the pillows on the bed so that she could recline comfortably. As she lay down, she noticed several large cardboard boxes on a table against the far wall. She was suddenly reminded of the brown paper bag Mikey had handed the Captain one night at the Cove, right before he had disappeared into this very room with two women. The Captain rose from his chair, switched off the music, and walked to the boxes.

He swept his hand over them, like a salesman over a used car.

"Pick your delight. I've got over one hundred dildos in every size and style you can imagine. Just tell me your holding capacity, and I'll fill-er-up!" He laughed at his own joke, but his eye twinkled as if to suggest to Misty that he had planned this far, far in advance.

Even though it was the most unromantic thing anyone had ever said to her, she was curious about the toys.

"So, you have every size penis in those boxes?" she ventured.

"Yep, this box is organized in quarter-inch increments based on length, while the second box adjusts for girth. You can have it long and skinny, short and fat, or anywhere in between," he said, sounding proud of the technical details in a way that struck Misty as being almost nerdy.

She was perplexed by this little performance, by the decorated room, and by how all of it lured so many women into following the Captain around like kittens on catnip. So far, this was the most unsexy experience she'd ever had, and she didn't know how to proceed.

"Well, Captain, why don't you bring one of those boxes over here and let me pick my favorite," she said, more confidently than she felt.

The Captain grinned. "Good idea, girl. Now, do you want the ones made out of rubber, steel, or, most of the girls' favorite, glass?" he said in the same salesman manner, only this time Misty understood the tone in his voice a little better: he was excited. She realized now that she had never seen Captain Kev, in all their time together, genuinely excited about anything.

"Hell, I don't know, bring them all over here I guess." She didn't know what she was getting into, but was pretty sure she could handle it.

Although she had been pleasuring herself with her personal vibrator—that wonderful gift from years ago in Hawaii—Misty decided that this was the perfect opportunity to diversify. The only challenge left was coaxing the Captain into a more seductive mood. She pulled off her jeans and shirt. The room was warm despite the fall chill outside, and the bed was soft. She had purposefully not worn a bra to save a few steps and quicken the affair.

Misty wasn't exactly aroused yet, so the Captain pulled out some of Miniature Mike's lubricant, handed her the bottle, and said, "Here, you better put some of this on while we try out the different sizes."

"Damn, you make it sound like I'm trying on shoes."

When she mentioned that the lighting was too dim to read the label on the lubricant, Captain Kev told her to clap her hands lightly if she would like to brighten or dim the lighting.

Misty clapped her hands softly several times and the lights gradually came on just enough for her to be able to read the crudely written text: "Miniature Mike's Lube-Ur-Cunt."

Oh Christ! I should have known, she thought. Now, she really wanted to get this experience over with. But when the Captain drew out the first of many toys from the box and expertly attached it to his prosthetic arm, her breath caught in her throat.

Maybe all those townie girls were onto something, she thought, looking at his arm, which now terminated powerfully in a god-like sculpture of a penis. The Captain toyed around her opening delicately with several different dildos, never penetrating her completely, but teasing her sweetly, maddeningly, with a sensitivity that surprised her. It was as if the Captain could feel her through the attachment on his arm.

After giving her a taste of several and getting her good and hot, Captain Kev held up a few of his favorites from the boxes for Misty to choose from. She settled on a sexy-looking glass one seven inches long, wondering how delicious it would feel inside her.

Misty clapped her hands until the lights were low and soft. Seductive music filled the room. She lay back on the pillows and closed her eyes, ready now for the Captain to pleasure her completely. Captain Kev slowly slid the dildo into Misty and flipped a switch that caused it to vibrate. A wave of deep sensation moved through her and Misty let out a soft moan of pleasure. The glass penis not only vibrated softly inside her, but moved in and out of her, rotating slightly off center. The feeling was unlike anything she'd ever felt before: no man could give her this. Her pleasure, like mercury in a thermometer, kept rising without stop until she thought she could no longer stand the pressure. She was breathing hard and heavy, her breaths beginning to shudder with pleasure. She noticed her breasts heaving up and down, shining with a light sheen of sweat in the low light. Seeing her hot body turned her on so much she tightened around the vibrating member inside her and screamed in pleasure, throwing herself back on the bed.

Wow! So this is why the girls all like Captain Kev. He's damn good, she thought, shivering with pleasure.

When it subsided Misty said, "Oh, Captain! Can I take your arm home with me?"

Misty opened her eyes and noticed something interesting. She clapped her hands a few times until the room lit up to get a better look at Captain Kev. He was wearing earphones.

"What's up Cap-e-tan? My music not good enough for you?"

When he didn't respond she grabbed them off his head and put them up to her ears. Her brow furrowed deeply. "Why the hell are you listening to church music?"

Captain Kev was embarrassed and at a loss for words. Misty remembered how vulnerable he had seemed just a few moments before when he was showing off all his toys, and she felt sorry for accosting him.

"Hey, I'm sorry, but what's up with all this?" She took his good hand in hers. "Here, why don't you fondle my breast. That should make you feel better."

But when the Captain pulled his hand back before she could place it on her breast, Misty sat up and gathered him into a hug.

"What's the matter big guy? It's okay if you like church music."

With his head on her shoulders the Captain gradually said, "I hate church music. That's why I play it. This is really embarrassing, but I have this premature ejaculation condition and church music is the only thing that can keep me from coming early. If I'm not listening to it, bam! I shoot my wad in a matter of seconds. I think it's because I produce too much sperm for my balls to hold."

Misty fought hard to stifle a laugh. She didn't want to ruin the evening. After all, the Captain had just made her feel almost as good as her man from Hawaii. So what if it wasn't from his penis?

Misty reached down through his pants, feeling gently around his hard cock, and felt his sack.

"Why I've seen balls on a squirrel bigger than yours. No wonder you can't hold all that sperm," she said gently.

But she could tell that probably didn't make him feel better, so she began to stroke the back of his head. "Come on. Show me what else you got in those toy boxes. You were really good. I can't wait for some more."

Captain Kev pulled back with a big smile on his face. "Really? Okay, wait until you experience the clitoral tickler. It's one of the girls' favorites."

So the headphones went back on and the games began again. The Captain was not only right about the tickler but the other five toys he tried were wonderful as well.

Finally Misty, exhausted with pleasure, her body buzzing with rapture, looked at the Captain and said, "Okay, that's about all I can handle. I want you. Now."

Captain Kev put down his headphones. "Okay, but let's turn the lights off so I don't see your beautiful breasts. That will just cause me to come faster."

Misty had the Captain face her sitting up on the bed and showed him how they could hold each other while he entered her slowly in an attempt to prolong the process. After a couple of minutes, Misty decided to give the Captain a thrill by rubbing her breasts in his face. It didn't take long before he erupted, filling her up with so much semen it oozed out beneath her.

"You weren't kidding, Captain. That was a load."

When Misty clapped on the lights she saw his smiling face and messed up hair. This pleased Misty. She had grown fond of the Captain. As she stared at him, though, Misty noticed that by rubbing her breasts in his face, she had moved the black eye patch from his left eye over to his right eye. The Captain could tell she looked puzzled but had no idea what was wrong.

Finally Misty put her hand to the far left of his head and held up two fingers. "How many fingers am I holding up?"

"Why, two of course."

After a few seconds, Captain Kev caught on. His patch was on the right eye, not the left like usual, yet he could see out of his bad eye.

He laughed for a moment and said, "Oh, I just wear the patch to attract the women. Works pretty well, too."

Even though she felt a little taken aback by his trick, she embraced him warmly.

"Well, you just keep wearing that patch if it makes you happy. I think it looks good on you."

As the two embraced, Misty pondered, *Who would have thought that Captain Kev was just a big old teddy bear?*

48

THE GREAT ESCAPE

Misty was sleeping soundly when her cell phone rang at five in the morning.

"Uh, hello? Who is this?"

She heard a very quiet voice whisper, "It's the Captain. Go out on your balcony and look out into Resurrection Bay."

Misty did as she was told. There on the balcony she squinted into the early morning light to see what resembled the old boat from Homer.

"Is that the boat from the Homer Spit?" she asked groggily into the phone.

"Ha, ha. Yeah, that's the boat."

"Are you on it?"

"Yep, me and Mikey."

"How did you get it to Seward?'

"Remember when we stayed behind in Homer a few days? We got the boat out of dry dock and sailed it to Seward."

"What are you guys doing on that old boat?"

"Sneaking out of town before sunrise."

"You're what?"

"Listen, Misty. Remember all those bluefin tuna I told you about? Well, I didn't lose my arm cutting the net to free them and we didn't let them go. Mikey and I took them to auction and they went for almost three million dollars. The authorities were on our trail so we sold our fishing boat and bought this piece of crap because we didn't want to be recognized. Mikey sailed it through the canal and made it to Alaska over two years ago, and we've been hiding out ever since."

"We got word last night that the guy watching us finally put two and two together and called the authorities. Supposedly, they are on the way to Seward right now to arrest us. I just wanted to tell you good-bye and let you know I left a key to a safety deposit box at the front desk of your hotel. You will find two hundred Troy ounces of gold coins, which should be more than enough to pay your fee. Sorry I can't pay you with a check, but you understand."

Misty was too shocked for words. She struggled to play it cool, but couldn't resist asking, "Where will you guys go?"

"Don't know and wouldn't tell you if I did. I don't want you mixed up in this, so please catch the next flight home and maybe our paths will cross someday, sweetie."

"Well you take care of yourself Captain, and tell Mikey good-bye for me. And if your bucket of bolts is really seaworthy, I hear Buenos Aires is a good place to hide out. At least that's where a lot of Germans hid out after World War II."

"Hmm, you just never know. So long, Sunshine. See you when I see you."

"Okay, Captain, take care."

Misty looked out into the bay. She could hear the pistons from the diesel engine firing sporadically in the distance as she watched black smoke billow up into the dimly lit morning sky. A moment later she saw someone swinging from the mast back and forth and then side to side.

She smiled wide and thought, *Man, that little Mikey is one weird dude.*

49

BACK FROM ALASKA

Rob finished off his americano Sunday afternoon and then gave Amelia a kiss on the cheek. He had been at Java Joe's since early that morning, and it was now time to get going.

"Okay, I better get started for the airport or I might not be there to greet Misty when she gets in from Alaska. It's been a great two months, Amelia. I'm going to miss your cooking."

Amelia knew it was time to shift gears, but it was tougher this time. Her relationship with Rob had grown more intimate over the last two months. Not being able to spend quality time with him for who knows how long was going to be difficult.

"How long do you think Misty will be here this time?"

"It's hard to say. She comes and goes at whim, but she has never stayed longer than two months at a time."

Amelia prayed Misty didn't let the grass settle under her this time. Anything over two weeks would seem like eternity.

Looking at Rob with droopy eyes, she said, "Two months is a long time, Rob."

Rob was well aware that things between them were on the verge of getting out of hand, and he was beginning to feel anxious about the situation. His feelings for Amelia were beginning to usurp those for his wife. Uncertainty was difficult for someone as straightlaced as Rob. But although things were complicated, Rob knew he hadn't felt this alive in quite some time.

Trying to ease Amelia's angst, he said, "You know I will miss you as much, if not more, than you will miss me."

She smiled quickly, but was determined to hold him to his words. "You better be telling the truth."

Rob leaned in, kissing her sensually on the lips long enough for them both to forget they were in public. Amelia blushed for a moment and then quickly glanced around to make sure none of her coworkers had been watching. Rob's eyes were soft and slightly pained. His kiss had hit its mark, but instead of signaling a temporary farewell, it sealed their attraction. He wanted her, and he was running out of excuses.

Amelia watched Rob walk across the parking lot to his Beamer. She slowly put her fingers to her lips as if to verify his kiss. When he drove off, she continued to sit there deep in thought until her manager broke the silence.

Rob was five miles down the road when his cell phone rang.

"Rob, are you on your way to pick up Misty?"

"Hey, Becca. Yes, I am."

"I know this isn't any of my business, but I wanted to talk to you before you picked her up. Are you okay with that?'

Rob braced himself for Becca to bend his ear. Although Becca had always played the role of Misty's close friend, deep down he knew that her real interest was in him. Though not typically attracted to redheads, he had to admit that Becca's body was alluring. Many times he had let himself imagine what her large, full breasts might look like. He had fallen into daydreams from time to time about what it would be like to hold the full roundness of her body.

"Okay, Becca, what's on your mind?"

"I've been giving it some thought, and I came to the conclusion that your agreement with Misty is not a healthy one. It's just not natural for a man to allow his wife the freedom you are giving Misty."

Lately, and usually in the presence of Amelia, Rob had also been pondering his marital arrangement, so he acquiesced.

"Go on."

Becca wasted little time delivering her prepared script.

"I think it's time for you to have a heart-to-heart with Misty. Let her know that you think your marriage should become traditional again. Tell her it was a good experiment but it's not working out for you." Becca paused to let her words sink in before continuing. "Demand that Misty come back to Malibu and become your full-time wife again."

Becca had all the confidence in the world that Misty would refuse—that's what was so great about her plan.

Rob weighed Becca's comments carefully. He knew she was probably right, but he just wished he could come up with a fallback plan in the event that Misty refused. Becca gave him plenty of time to finish his thought process. She, of course, already had a Plan B for Rob—herself.

Rob finally said, "You've given me some sage advice, Becca. Hopefully Misty has tired of traveling and misses me enough to settle down, but if not, I need to realize that she is not the only woman out there."

That was exactly what Becca wanted to hear.

"When do you think we'll see each other again?" Becca asked.

"I'm kind of tied up with work right now but I will let you know once my calendar clears. Thanks for the call, Becca."

"You're welcome. Just remember, I'm here if you need me."

"I will."

50

TIME TO TALK

On the way home from the airport, Misty noticed that Rob was unusually subdued. "Are you okay? You seem like you have something on your mind."

Rob wanted to talk about everything right then and there, but decided it wasn't the right time.

"Yes, I have a few things on my mind but nothing that can't wait until we get you home and fed. Why don't you tell me about your trip to Alaska? I imagine it's a pretty spectacular place."

Misty was exhausted from her early morning flight so she was glad he had elected to postpone any serious discussion, which she assumed had something to do with their marriage.

"Alaska was just breathtaking. You'll have to go back with me sometime." She launched into the highlights of the trip and regaled him with tales of the fight at Black Beard's with Russian Jack and the regulars at the Cove. She was careful not to bring up her night at The Bird Cage.

Once they were home, Misty took a quick shower and then crawled into bed for a nap. Rob was glad she would be fully rested for their discussion. A full belly would be good as well, so while she was sleeping he went to the grocery store and got everything he needed to prepare a hearty spaghetti dinner. He planned on using one of Amelia's recipes.

Halfway through dinner Misty said, "Wow! This is really good. Have you been taking cooking lessons while I was away?"

Rob simply said, "You know, those cooking channels are really something. A person can learn everything they need to know about cooking from one of those."

"I hope the cooking channel becomes your new favorite channel. That was delicious," she said as she polished off her spaghetti.

Rob promised himself that if she agreed to his demands he would make every effort to actually watch the cooking channel.

After they cleaned the table and put the dirty dishes into the dishwasher, Rob said, "Why don't we finish off this bottle of Chianti in the living room, and I'll tell you what's on my mind."

"Okay," Misty agreed.

As he prepared to speak, Rob was surprised by his own calmness. He chalked it up to having both Amelia and Becca behind him.

"Misty, I would like to discuss our marriage."

Misty wasn't shocked. She had always realized that Rob's offer might not last forever, but she tried not to think about it. But that didn't seem to be an option anymore.

"Okay, what are you thinking?"

He cleared his throat. "I want you to give some serious thought to giving up your traveling and working in Malibu on a full-time basis."

Even though those were the words she expected to hear, she was having trouble grasping the fact that he had actually said them. Now that he had, she was on the spot to answer. Then she realized she didn't have an answer, so she improvised.

"I will give it some careful thought, but don't expect an answer until I'm ready. I want to make sure I make the right decision."

Misty's answer caught Rob off guard. He had hoped to resolve the issue that night. Then he realized that she admitted she didn't know what the answer was going to be. It gave him hope that she might accept.

"I appreciate you taking this seriously, but how much time do you think you'll need?"

"I can't answer that question tonight. You're asking me to choose between two things I love. As I said, I want to be sure I'm making the right decision. Don't expect an answer until I'm back from my next trip. I need to mull this over for a while."

She went over, sat on Rob's lap, and wrapped her arms around him. It was her way of letting him know that, although this was a difficult decision, he was definitely in the running. Rob was surprised that he actually had mixed emotions when she hugged him. Yes, it gave him hope that Misty would choose him over her work, but then he thought, *How would I ever tell Amelia?* For a man that preferred an uncomplicated life, Rob's was becoming complicated beyond his wildest imagination. All of a sudden he did an about-face and was very much on board with Misty's decision.

Maybe it's a good idea for Misty to decide after her next trip. That will give me time to evaluate my true feelings for Amelia. And then he thought, *How would I ever tell Misty if I chose Amelia?*

Anxious to move on, Rob asked Misty innocently, "So, how long are you home this time?"

"I'm not sure but one of my old clients left me a phone message and said it was urgent. I'll let you know after I get in touch with Peter."

That evening, Misty called Peter.

"Hey Peter, what's up?"

"Not as much as the last time I was with *you*," Peter said.

Misty caught on quickly and joked back, "I hope not. That would be uncomfortable if it had persisted this long. You do know that if the, um, symptoms last over four hours you're supposed to call your doctor?"

Laughing heartily, Peter responded, "Well, hurry up and become an MD."

"I did get a lot of experience playing doctor when I was a young girl. Does that count?"

As the bantering went back and forth, Misty remembered she had some unfinished business with Peter and realized while listening to his voice that it was something she still desired.

Peter finally got around to telling Misty what he needed.

"Misty, I have a favor to ask you. My brother Ivan is in London for the next few months, and he is in dire need of your services."

Misty was caught by surprise. *Peter's brother!* she thought. *That could be interesting—or bizarre.*

The thought of training his brother intrigued her. She asked, "When would you like me to go, if I decide to?"

"Right away."

"Right away? I just got home from Alaska! I usually hang around for a while."

"I know, but I promised him you would come. My reputation is on the line."

"You promised him? You're pretty sure of yourself, Peter. What makes you think I'm just going to drop everything and run off to England?"

"Because you're a sweetheart, and I figured you couldn't turn down anyone that looked similar to me," he said confidently, and then began to laugh.

"Similar? Just how similar?" He knew her pretty well, she decided.

"Let's just say people have a hard time telling us apart."

That was all Misty needed. "Okay, I'll take the job, but consider it a two for one. When I get back, you and I have some unfinished business left over from Beaver Creek. That is, if you think you can measure up to your brother."

Peter's voice turned more serious as he responded, "Thanks Misty, I will send you first-class tickets tomorrow. Plan on leaving in five days." He hung up before Misty could comment.

To her surprise, she was actually happy to have a new assignment so soon. If she was totally honest with herself, she liked the idea of keeping the momentum from her trip to Alaska.

Five days later, Rob was dropping Misty and Miguel off at LAX for their long journey to London. Miguel wasn't too happy leaving Sylvia

so quickly. However, his mood was somewhat tempered by the fact that London couldn't be more than a hop, skip, and a jump from Scotland and the possibility of reuniting with both Amber and Heather.

As Misty gave Rob a hug good-bye, she whispered, "No matter what I finally decide, I hope you know I do love you."

Rob squeezed her tighter and then watched her walk off. The woman he saw walking into the crowd made him more confused and conflicted than he had ever imagined he could feel: he loved her, resented her, and desired her. It was by controlling such emotions, however, that Rob had become so steady and successful. So, he kept telling himself that he would wind up a winner either way and that he was not operating out of desperation anymore. As he got back into his car and drove off, his thoughts immediately drifted to Amelia and how happy she was going to be when he told her that Misty was on a plane bound for London, England.

51

CROSSING THE POND

The flight from Los Angeles to London was brutal. Five hours to New York, and after a two hour layover, another eight hours to London. After arriving at Heathrow Airport at 8:00 AM London time, both Misty and Miguel took a comatose ride on the train into town.

On the train, the only conversation Miguel could muster consisted of mindless statements like, "Misty, did you notice in the airport they call restrooms toilets?"

"Did you notice the sign said baggage reclaim instead of baggage claim?"

"Misty, did you notice—"

"Miguel! Knock it off! I'm so tired I can hardly think straight. Get over it man, we're not in Kansas anymore."

Over the years, Miguel had gotten to know Misty just short of intimately, which gave him the confidence to lean away from her, cover his face with his hands for protection, and whisper, "Misty, did you notice?"

Misty was too tired to take a swat at Miguel so she just scrunched her nose, puckered her lips, and waved a clenched fist at him indicating he was cruising for a bruising.

The sight of the hotel reinvigorated them some. Clifford's Inn was a beautiful, grand old hotel built with eight stories of warmly lighted windows, a row of stout columns along the front of the four middle stories, and an aged mansard roof that really made Misty feel like she was in England.

Once she settled into her penthouse suite, she phoned Miguel and asked him to call her in five hours—she needed sleep. When the phone call came, Misty was famished and told Miguel to get his walking shoes on so they could go find something to eat.

Their hotel was centrally located between Fleet Street—the financial district—and what was referred to as the West End, a theater district with over forty magnificent theaters. They decided to head toward the West End. They were quickly impressed with how clean everything was for a big city. Next they noticed that there seemed to be more than ten restaurants or pubs on every block. Some blocks were populated with ethnic restaurants and others with old English pubs. After walking a ways, they finally decided the Italian restaurants looked the most promising. Just as they were getting ready to head back and pick one of them, they came across a shopping area called Covent Garden.

"Hey, look at that, Migs. Let's go check it out."

Covent Garden had several levels of quaint shops that were surrounded by a large courtyard, paved with bricks.

"Pretty cool, Misty. Let's put this on our list of places to visit."

Misty heard him but didn't respond as something else had caught her attention.

"Look Miguel, there's the gym Ivan wants me to use when I train him."

"That's interesting. The sign says they have skylights. I'm too hungry to check it out now, though. We can get there ahead of Ivan tomorrow. Let's go eat."

52

IVAN

The next morning Misty and Miguel walked through the double doors to the gym. They discovered it was on the second floor and began to climb a wide flight of stairs that took them up, up, and up to the receptionist desk. The two female receptionists were extremely friendly and outgoing, which was a comfort to Misty. But when they took them on a tour of the gym, it felt more like a Gold's Gym or YMCA in the States than the new boutiques she was used to.

"I wonder why Ivan chose this club? It's got all the basic equipment but looks like something out of the seventies."

"Not sure, but you can always ask him when he arrives. Just do it tactfully."

"Come on, Miguel. I'm not that dumb. He's paying me big bucks so I'll remain polite no matter what. You saw me keep my cool for three months in Alaska. I think after the Captain and Mikey, I can handle anything."

Unlike Peter, Ivan showed up promptly at 8:00 AM, not a minute late. Misty noticed that he indeed looked a lot like Peter. They seemed to be about the same size and had the same balding head, but Ivan had a close-cropped grey beard. Misty thought it was a nice touch. *I need to talk Peter into growing a beard*, she thought.

Also unlike Peter, there was nothing nonchalant about Ivan. He seemed to measure his every move and Misty noticed his eyes surveying the entire club as he made his way toward them. Miguel noticed as well.

When he finally reached them, Ivan said, "The girls at the front desk tell me you're Misty.

Misty answered, "That's correct. And it's obvious you are Ivan. I can't believe you look so much like your brother."

"I may look like Peter, but you will find that I am nothing like my brother."

No kidding. This is really strange, she thought. She squared up to him and replied, "I never expected you guys to share the same brain."

Ivan stared at her for a moment and then turned to Miguel and put out his hand. "I assume you are Miguel, Misty's bodyguard?"

"Yes, I am." Miguel took his hand firmly, testing the other man's strength. He found Ivan's grip to be powerful and hoped they would never have to tango.

"Good. I assume you take your job seriously. You are in a foreign country, and you never know what could happen. Please do not, as they say in America, fall asleep at the switch."

Miguel gave Ivan a serious glance before responding, "Are you expecting trouble?"

"In my profession, I always expect trouble."

Misty and Miguel exchanged quick questioning glances. Misty was shaken a bit but Miguel stayed calm.

"Ivan, will you step away with me for a moment so we can talk?"

When the two walked inside the group exercise room, Miguel said, "Ivan, I take my job seriously, and I would put my life on the line for Misty if need be."

The six-foot-four, 230-pound Ivan laid his large hand on Miguel's shoulder and said, "Perfect! That's exactly what I was hoping you would say. Don't lose any sleep over what we just discussed. I take protecting another person's life seriously and wanted to make sure you shared my feelings."

"Don't worry. Misty is like a sister to me."

"Great! Now I need to get my workout in."

When the two walked back over to Misty, Miguel gave her a little nod indicating that everything was fine.

"Okay Misty, let's get started. I hear from Peter you're an excellent trainer. Let's see if he is right."

During the two-hour workout, Misty could tell she needed to dig deeper into her bag of exercise tricks because Ivan was already in spectacular condition. This was going to be a bit more challenging but Misty was always up for a test when it came to training. Ivan lightened up during their training session and Misty began to feel more comfortable with him. He was still a very serious man, but not as intimidating as he had first appeared. When they wrapped up the session, Ivan thanked Misty, nodded to Miguel, and then left through a back door.

"That's a little strange, Miguel. I wonder why he didn't go out the front?"

"With him there's no telling. I called the security company while you were training him and asked them to e-mail me their background check on Ivan. They said you didn't ask for one. Why on earth wouldn't you do that?"

Feeling a little embarrassed, she replied, "We were short on time, and he's Peter's brother. You know Peter. He's a good guy."

Miguel stared at her silently until she said, "Oh, go ahead and have them run one anyway."

Miguel smiled. "It's already in process."

53

LONDON TOWN

For the next several weeks, Misty and Miguel used every spare moment to tour London. Several blocks east of the gym they came across a delightful area called Leicester Square. It was beautifully illuminated at night with soft yellow lighting that made the whole area come alive. There were artists sketching caricatures and the park square was lined with restaurants. The park area had some of the largest trees imaginable. The tree trunks were so big around that it would have taken three people to encircle them with their arms spread wide.

They passed by at least twenty theaters the first week. Misty wanted to see a play, but it was going to take some effort on her part to get Miguel excited about the theater. After a little arm twisting, she talked him into buying tickets to *Phantom of the Opera*.

The following day while walking in the vicinity of Leicester Square, they passed a billboard promoting *Calendar Girls*. The poster showed naked women standing around a piano.

"Hey Misty, why don't we go see that one?"

Misty laughed. "That one? Do you know anything about that one?"

He grinned. "What's to know? Seven naked ladies and a piano says it all, don't you think?"

"I don't know if it says anything about the play, but it sure says a lot about you."

The following night they made it further east to Piccadilly Circus.

When they got to the square, Miguel turned to Misty and asked, "So, where's the circus?"

Misty broke out laughing. "You're joking, right?" She could tell from Miguel's sheepish look that he wasn't.

"These are traffic circles, Migs. It's not a circus." Of course, Misty had spent a good part of the flight over reading her travel guide on London while Miguel watched movies, but she wasn't about to remind him of that.

They walked through the interchange and up Regent Street, which was lined with beautiful white stone buildings that were storefronts on the bottom, offices in the middle, and apartments on top. The buildings were so tall they looked like Las Vegas hotels. The bend in Regent Street coming directly off Piccadilly Circus was pretty significant, but the massive row of buildings followed the bend in the road perfectly. It was as if they were looking at the buildings through a fun house mirror.

"That must have been very expensive, erecting those buildings in a curve," said Miguel.

"No fooling. Have you been noticing the quality of the retail stores along the way?"

"Yep, and I knew they were quality because I didn't recognize the name of half of them."

When they got to Oxford Street they followed it to Charing Cross and then turned right in the direction of their hotel. Several blocks down the street, Miguel grabbed Misty by the arms and said, "I don't believe my eyes. I never expected to see one of those in London."

Misty's eyes focused on the building Miguel was pointing to. She read the words "Salsa Bar" on a lighted sign above a stone archway with steps leading down below the street.

"Come on, Misty. This is your chance to learn to salsa."

Misty stood there for a moment reflecting back to the time she, Gabriella, Miguel, and Tom were at the salsa bar in Rio de Janeiro and how bad she felt having to watch Gabriella and Miguel dancing without her because she didn't know the dance.

That thought quickly prompted her to say, "Okay, Migzee. Let's do it."

After finding out that the bar gave free salsa lessons, Misty and Miguel returned two nights later. Misty was hoping to get the basic steps down with the free lessons and then pay for some individual classes. The steps were pretty basic but it still took some concentration. It was made up of a series of eight counts. Move your left foot forward, rock back on your right heal, and then pause before returning to the starting position. You then repeated the same basic counts but backward. Over and over again Misty worked through the steps until she felt comfortable.

At the end of the lesson, Misty was beaming because she had mastered the steps so easily.

"What do you think, Miguel? Aren't you proud of me?" When Miguel showed little expression she asked, "What's the matter?"

"You've done a great job of learning the steps but you're just doing the footwork. I need to teach you how to strut your stuff, wiggle your hips, and move your ass. You're too tight, Blondie."

Misty's face turned red, and she began to walk back up the stairs toward the street. Miguel quickly reached out and grabbed her arm and pulled her back onto the dance floor.

"You don't think I'm going to let you off the hook that easy do you? Don't you want to impress Gabriella next time you see her?"

Miguel had just said the magic words; for the next four hours, Misty put her inhibitions aside and got to work.

As they began, Miguel said, "Don't freak out on me, but I know exactly how to shorten the process."

Misty's head followed Miguel as he moved behind her. Once in position, he reached out and put his hands on her lower back and then moved them downward to the curve of her butt.

"Watch it there, buddy," Misty said as she moved them back up.

"Don't worry, just loosen up your hips and go with the flow. Concentrate on your footwork, and I will concentrate on your ass, I mean, butt movements."

Misty swirled around quickly, and pointed her finger in Miguel's face. "If you want me to let you visit the girls in Scotland next week, you better watch it."

Miguel's face became a little more serious. "You wouldn't do that, would you?"

"Not if you behave."

"Okay, how about I pretend your ass is Amber's. Will that do?"

Misty sighed. "Go ahead and put your hands on my butt, and let's get this over with."

The tactic worked perfectly. Misty got the butt action down and was starting to feel really sexy.

As they left the club for the night she gently patted the left side of Miguel's face and said, "Amber can only hope her ass is as sexy as mine when she's my age."

Although Miguel had promised to scrub the image of Misty's ass out of his mind from the day on the beach in Rio, her comment caused him to have an unintended flashback. As he followed her up the stairs to the street he was thinking about how he would make a move if only Misty wasn't his boss and good friend. But she was, and he knew it was a thought that had no place to land, so he put it out of his mind.

54

COVENT GARDEN

As they approached the gym the next morning, Misty and Miguel noticed that the large courtyards around Covent Garden were full of people attending a festival of some kind. Tents and tables were scattered throughout the courtyards, each offering chef-prepared exotic dishes. Since Misty was pretty much a meat and potatoes girl, she showed little interest until she stumbled across a twelve-foot-long table loaded with every type of baklava one could imagine. Miguel noticed her eyes getting big as she took in the different variations of the dessert, each so sweet it would probably make one's teeth hurt. Miguel quickly grabbed Misty around the waist, picked her up, and set her back down several feet away.

"Not now. You have to train Ivan in half an hour. Those sweets will be here when you come back."

"That's what I'm afraid of. I would prefer they all get purchased before we return." Misty turned toward the gym, but Miguel grabbed her hand and said, "Hey, follow me."

"But, I thought we were going to the gym."

"Don't worry, we've still got some time before your appointment with Ivan. Let's check out that street performer over there."

They followed loud music to where a group of people were clustered around a performer. Misty didn't like the performer's looks from the moment she saw him. For the next five minutes the man worked the onlookers. He clapped his hands to the creepy music, trying to get the crowd excited and closer together to fill the gaps. If a spectator didn't do exactly as the performer wished, he would mock them. When the more timid spectators were the center of attention, they cowered and left.

What an absolute asshole, Misty thought.

Miguel, on the other hand, seemed fascinated.

Finally the creep noticed Misty. With a smirk on his face he walked up to her and held out his hand. Misty didn't cut and run like the others, but she refused to take his hand.

"Come on, Misty, take his hand," Miguel prodded while laughing.

"Oh, you think this is funny, don't you? Why don't you take his hand?"

"Me? He doesn't want me. He wants a hot-looking blonde to get the crowd riled up. Come on, if you do this I will owe you one. It'll be fun."

Misty knew it was a bad idea, but nevertheless, she took the man's hand and let him escort her into the middle of the courtyard.

The slimy street actor must have thought Misty was his ticket to drawing a bigger crowd, so he cranked up the music louder and started to dance provocatively all around her. Even Miguel was shocked at the man's actions and started to cringe.

Miguel began to sweat when Misty stared directly at him. There was no doubt in his mind that she was really pissed off.

The crowd's reaction was mixed. Some thought the performer's moves were funny and started to egg him on. Others gasped. The result was a bizarre scene, which was exactly what the man was attempting to create.

When the performer began mocking her by pretending to push up imaginary breasts with cupped hands, Misty turned several shades of red. *This little freak's making fun of my breasts!*

She glanced toward Miguel, who put his hands over his eyes and shook his head. Misty turned back to the performer, forced a sweet smile, and motioned to him with her right index finger to come closer. The actor grinned and put his hands in the air to egg the crowd on. The noise boomed through the courtyard, causing even more bystanders to come running. The performer turned back to Misty and moved in as close to her as possible. He placed his arms around her, being careful not to come into contact with her body, and gyrated his hips as if he was pretending to get very intimate with her.

The crowd went wild. Misty smirked at him and then wrapped her left arm around his body, pulling him closer.

Suddenly, the actor stopped moving. He hunched over slightly, his arms frozen in the air. His sudden stillness sent a hush over the crowd. With his full and undivided attention, Misty stared into his eyes from no more than an inch away and tightened her grip on his balls. He winced and let out a slight moan. Because Misty and the performer stood so close to each other, the crowd could only imagine what was transpiring.

After basking in her glory for a moment, Misty said, "You are one pathetic little bastard. If you ever come near me again I'll turn you into a woman."

It was obvious from the man's expression that he had raised the white flag. She gently took her vice grip off the man's genitals and began to walk away. After a few steps she turned back and said, "Cheerio!"

With that the crowd roared, laughing and chiding the actor. Misty shook her head at Miguel when she walked past. Miguel quickly followed her, but he was smart enough to keep his distance.

55

SOME THINGS ARE HARD TO FATHOM

One afternoon after a training session, Misty, Ivan, and Miguel sat at a table drinking recovery sports drinks. Miguel looked a bit queasy so Misty asked him what was wrong.

"I don't feel so good. I think I need to see a doctor."

"You just want to get out of taking me to *The Phantom of the Opera* tonight."

"Honest, that's not it at all. I feel bad that you may have to miss it."

Ivan jumped in, "Why would she have to miss it? I'll take her."

Ivan's comment took Misty completely by surprise. He was the last person she would ever expect to accompany her to a musical.

Still not convinced that he meant it, she prodded. "That would be terrific, Ivan. Are you sure you don't mind taking me?"

"Mind? *The Phantom* is my favorite. I've seen it at least forty times. *The Phantom* is in its twenty-third year, you know?"

Misty thought, *Favorite? That sounds more like an obsession to me.* She then said, "No, I didn't know that. Now I'm really excited to see it. What time should we go?"

"Let's make it our special night."

Misty made a face and asked, "Tonight?"

"No, I didn't mean our big *final* night. I meant that taking you to my favorite production when it's your first time will be very special to me. I know a nice little restaurant that's on the way, so be ready at 5:00 PM. and we'll stop for a bite first."

Misty jumped up excitedly. "Okay, then, it's a date!"

As Miguel and Misty left the club, Miguel couldn't resist teasing Misty by saying, "Wow, first time to see *The Phantom of the Opera*. Guess that makes you a virgin."

Her mood was so good that she took the ribbing from Miguel graciously. "I'm anything but a virgin, Migs."

Misty's hopes of going to a fancy dining establishment faded when Ivan walked her through the door of a small, split-level restaurant. The main restaurant was to the left, and a stairway led diners wanting privacy up to a more secluded eating area.

Of course Ivan selected the stairway. The lone waiter led them to a small table, one of two that overlooked the street. Ivan glanced up and down the street a few times and then focused his full attention on Misty.

"Are you okay with this restaurant? I know it's not fancy, but I promise the food is delicious."

Misty made a habit of never complaining about anything when with a client, so she quickly replied, "Yes, this is fine." To fill the following silence, she asked, "So, have you heard from Peter lately?"

Ivan said nonchalantly, "Peter and I don't talk much."

His response caught Misty off guard, and without thinking she blurted out, "So, you guys aren't close?"

Ivan took his time before answering, "Oh, we are close, about as close as two brothers can be."

Not wanting to give her time to continue her line of questioning, Ivan quickly added, "Enough about Peter. Tell me about yourself. Where did you grow up? What were your parents like? How big was your family?"

Ugh! I don't like to talk about my past anymore than Ivan likes to talk about Peter. This is like playing a game of chess, and now it's my move.

Misty looked at Ivan for a minute through squinted eyes.

"Okay, let's make a deal. I won't ask you about your relationship with Peter if you don't ask me about my past."

Ivan already had a dossier on Misty provided by his connections in American Intelligence; there was little about her he didn't already know. All he had wanted was to move the discussion from him to her.

"Sure, that's a deal. I guess we both get what we want this way."

The waiter brought their menus, and they dove headlong into deciding what to order. The conversation remained light from that point on. When dinner was over they took a leisurely stroll to Her Majesty's Theatre.

Once the theater was in sight, Misty's enthusiasm emerged. "The theater looks magnificent from the outside. I can't wait to see the inside."

"You'll be impressed. It was built in 1897 and is as majestic as its name. The original theater was built in 1705 and was simply named the Queen's Theatre. From 1901 through 1952 they changed the name to His Majesty's Theatre because England was ruled by a King. I assume it will revert back when Prince Charles takes the throne sometime in the future."

"Thanks for the history lesson. That was interesting, seriously."

As Ivan walked into the theater behind Misty, he couldn't take his eyes off her. She was very pretty but in a rugged, athletic sort of way. Ivan was intrigued by her every mannerism. She could be caring, pleasant, and attentive one minute but fiery and complex the next. She was always on the go, as if she had an ever so mild case of attention deficit disorder. Ivan had no doubt that these traits were the reason Misty was so popular with her clients. That and the ability to give them her undivided attention during training sessions, making them feel as if they were the only two people in the gym.

Up the stairs they went until reaching the fourth balcony, where they settled into a box he had reserved.

Misty thought the box felt isolated. *I guess I'm not surprised after the restaurant Ivan chose. This is kind of nice and cozy though.*

"So tell me again Ivan, how many times have you seen *The Phantom*? Did you say forty?"

With a soft smile Ivan replied, "Actually, I'm not exactly sure but let's just say I have been coming here to see the musical ever since it opened in 1986."

"Well if I like it half as much as you do, this is going to be exciting."

"That would please me very much."

Misty enjoyed the musical from the opening scene and was enthralled from the moment the first powerful chords of the theme of *The Phantom* played. Misty noticed that Ivan, however, watched with no obvious emotion until the Phantom appeared and the music turned haunting. He then placed his chin in his hands and was mesmerized. For almost two hours they watched as the heroine Christine was pulled between the light (her childhood sweetheart, Raoul) and the darkness (the Phantom of the Opera, known as the Opera Ghost). It was a classic tale of good versus evil, the only twist being that the heroine had a fondness for the dark side.

Though Misty enjoyed the musical, she wasn't sure her feelings quite matched those of Ivan. She made a point of acting as if it were the most spectacular performance she had ever seen so that Ivan's feelings wouldn't be hurt.

As they wound their way down the steps to the ground level, she thought about the difficult and tragic story of love in *The Phantom. I'm glad nothing like that would ever happen to me.*

56

THE CALL FROM HOME

Misty decided to take a long run the next day. Her trek took her down Fleet Street to the Saint Paul Cathedral and then back to the hotel. While on the return leg, she noticed someone about two hundred yards ahead who resembled Ivan. He turned into a passage way and disappeared from sight before she could catch up with him.

When she finally arrived at the passage, she looked down the long darkening alley. At the end was a large man in a trench coat talking on a cell phone. Just as Misty mustered the courage to approach him to see if he was Ivan, two men, also wearing black trench coats, came out of a large arched doorway at the end of the alley.

Misty backed up and moved just out of sight. She heard shouts and peered around the corner. All three men had become animated, and were yelling and pointing fingers at each other. She felt way out of her comfort zone, yet she couldn't pull her eyes away. Suddenly, the three turned to enter through the doorway the two men had come through. Just before the large man closed the door behind him, Misty got a good glimpse of his face.

My God, it is Ivan! What could he possibly be doing with those two goons?

It then dawned on Misty that she knew nothing about what Ivan did for a living. Thinking back, she realized he had been very careful to change the subject every time she brought it up. During her run back to the hotel, she promised herself never to bring up the scene in the alley with Ivan.

After a long, hot shower, she put on some casual clothes and prepared to go out to dinner with Miguel. Nothing fancy, just a nice quiet place.

When the knock finally came, she swung open the door to greet Miguel. To her shock he looked horrible.

"What's the matter buddy? Are you ill again?"

Miguel staggered over to her bed, lay on his back, and stared up at the ceiling while placing both hands on his forehead. In all the years they had been friends Misty had never known him to be in anything but an upbeat mood. Something was definitely wrong.

Finally, Miguel said, "I got a phone call from my buddy Orlando in Los Angeles. He had been at a party and noticed Sylvia with another man. They were arm in arm, so he figured something was up. Later that night he saw them making out on the couch, and then they went upstairs to a bedroom."

"Not your Sylvia, Miguel!"

"Yes, my Sylvia. Orlando has known her since grade school. He said that although he kept his distance, he was positive it was her."

"Well maybe they just went up to the bedroom to talk to another couple."

Miguel became a little agitated and popped up from the bed.

He stared at her with deadpan eyes. "Come on, Misty. I know what you're doing, and it won't work. There is no other obvious explanation, so don't try to convince me otherwise. He saw them kissing for heaven's sake!"

From Miguel's reaction Misty could tell how much pain he was in and her heart went out to him. She sat next to him on the bed and wrapped her arms around him tightly.

"I know. I guess I just don't want to believe it myself. Maybe we can sit here and sort this out."

Miguel nodded. "Okay, I'll give it a try, but not here. Let's go for a walk to talk. I need some fresh air."

After walking out the front door of the hotel and around the corner to one of the quieter streets, Misty kicked off the conversation.

"Miguel, I want you to know that I'm as much to blame for this as Sylvia."

Miguel stopped dead in his tracks and gave her a goofy stare. "What are you talking about? Are you telling me you knew she was cheating on me?"

"Oh, no! That's not what I meant. It's just that I feel partly responsible because I'm the one who talked you into being my bodyguard, which resulted in you being away from Sylvia so often. If you had stayed working at the club, you and Sylvia might be married by now."

Miguel walked to a nearby bench and sat down, placing his head in his hands. Misty felt horrible because she really did feel somewhat responsible. That and the fact that she couldn't bear seeing Miguel so hurt.

Miguel looked up at Misty. "No, you are not going to divert my attention from Sylvia and take the heat off her. All I've done is take an honest job. If she had problems with it, why hasn't she said something so we could work things out?" Miguel looked into her eyes. "The last three years with you have been the most incredible years of my life. I've gotten to see places around the world I never would have seen otherwise. If you had offered this job to anyone else and left me behind to work at the club I would have been hurt. Maybe it was a little naive of me to think I could have my cake and eat it too. I guess if I had wanted to marry Sylvia badly enough, I would have already done so. Don't blame yourself for any of this, because it was none of your doing."

"Okay, then," Misty replied. "You should catch the next flight home and deal with things now before they get out of hand."

"But what about you? I can't leave you here all by yourself."

"I'll be fine. Ivan will keep an eye on me. You're going home and that's final."

Miguel knew she was right. If there was any hope of salvaging his relationship with Sylvia he needed to address the situation immediately.

"All right, let's go back to the hotel so I can get on the Internet and book a flight home."

The two walked arm in arm back to the hotel in silence.

57

SPEAKING OF LOS ANGELES...

Amelia had gone all out preparing for Rob's next visit. She was hoping dinner in the back yard by candlelight might help take things to the next level. Over the last month she and Rob had started seeing each other on a regular basis, away from the confines of Java Joe's. Deep down, they both knew it was not a good idea, but each made up excuses in their own way to convince themselves they weren't doing anything wrong, hoping to placate their feelings of guilt.

When Amelia answered the door, Rob was standing there beaming with twelve beautiful red roses in his hand.

"Oh, Rob. Those are beautiful. You shouldn't have."

"No? You don't like to get roses?" Rob teased her.

Amelia was in tune with Rob's sense of humor by now and responded on beat, "Of course I like roses, silly. They're going to look beautiful on our dinner table. Come see what I've done." It didn't slip by him that she'd said "our table."

When Rob got a look at the candlelit table in Amelia's backyard, his whole demeanor changed from bubbly and upbeat to serious.

Amelia panicked for a moment. "Is anything wrong?"

Rob shook his head before grabbing her hand and pulling her toward him. Once she was nestled in his arms, he leaned in and gave her a long, slow kiss. It must have lasted almost a minute, but neither of them was keeping track of time. After all these months it was the first time they had kissed each other passionately. They both knew they had just broken the last barrier between themselves and the bedroom. All that was left was for one of them to make the first move.

Throughout the meal and the futile attempts at small talk, all they could think about was eating as quickly as they could and heading up to the bedroom.

As Amelia placed the final dish in the dishwasher, Rob wrapped his arms around her from the back and began kissing the nape of her neck slowly and deliberately. The kisses hit their target. Her eyes rolled back in her head as she shivered with each new moist peck. Soft and gentle, they kept coming one after another until she couldn't stand it any longer. Whipping around, Amelia gave Rob a hug and then took his hand and led him to the bedroom.

Some women took bedrooms seriously and were adept at creating the proper mood for lovemaking while others never felt the need. It was obvious to Rob which kind of woman Amelia was because once he crossed the bedroom threshold the room screamed: "Take me, I'm yours."

Amelia had been planning this night ever since she found out Misty was on her way to London. She wasn't about to let it play out in any other way than how she'd imagined it in her master plan. She had Rob sit on the bed and then slowly helped him take off his shirt. One bare chest deserved another, so Amelia backed away and slowly unbuttoned her blouse and then worked her way out of her bra. When finished, she was still wearing her blouse but the front was wide open, exposing her two delicious bosoms. She hoped Rob would consider them his dessert.

As Rob sat there mesmerized, he noticed how remarkably similar Amelia's breasts were to Misty's: a full C-cup with just the perfect lift. Amelia's cute little round nipples looked like cherries sitting on top of two mounds of freshly served vanilla ice cream.

My word! Rob thought. *Amelia and Misty could be sisters.*

Amelia playfully but firmly pushed Rob onto his back and began to systematically take off his trousers and then his underwear. As she pulled his underwear free from his waist and down to his knees, she could see he was primed and ready. It had been a long time since Amelia's divorce, and she had forgotten how delicious a man's loaded cock looked, pumped to its full capacity. Rob was not a large man and his cock was only average sized, but it was beautiful. No hooks, crooks, unseemly marks of any kind. Perfectly formed with a nice, subtle, pink tint. Had this not been their first time, Amelia would have stopped to play and admire it, but she decided to stick to the script, keep things more conventional, and save the imaginative stuff for the future.

Not wanting any more delay, she quickly took her underwear off and climbed into bed. Rob slowly moved in, waiting for Amelia to give him a clue as to what position she preferred. When she laid the back of her head on a pillow and then ever so slowly spread open her slightly bent legs, Rob knew missionary was the position *du jour*. He moved into position and eased his way into Amelia's wet vagina. They moved into and against each other, neither in a hurry, savoring every inch of the other's body and prolonging the event as long as humanly possible. Amelia came first in a long, slow orgasm that left her ready for more. To her surprise, she had a second one before Rob erupted powerfully. Watching him come helped her enjoy the final act of her well-thought-out play. Everything had gone perfectly, and she was relieved.

But as many plans have a tendency to do, this one began to develop some cracks. Of course Amelia was very aware that Rob was married going into the situation, but her physical desires had kept the thought at bay. Once the physical urge was satisfied, her demons were free to escape from bondage.

Not knowing exactly how to deal with this new feeling, Amelia strayed from her script. "Rob, I hope I haven't caused you to do something you'll regret. That was not my intention. I know you are a married man."

Rob was desperate to calm Amelia's anxieties, so he quickly shot back without thinking, "Oh, there is nothing to worry about, Amelia. Misty and I have a special arrangement. She is free to sleep with anyone, and I can sleep with anyone as long as we don't discuss it."

When he realized he had just told her what he had so painstakingly kept from her all these months, he froze.

"What did you say?"

Rob answered sheepishly, "Um, I thought I had told you that and you were okay with it." It wasn't like him to make up a lie to try and get out of a predicament, but then he very seldom ever got himself into a predicament.

When Amelia rolled over and faced the wall with her back to him, Rob felt like his world was crashing down around him. He gently put his hand on her shoulder only to have her gently brush it off.

Not good, he thought. *Not good at all*.

After what seemed like an eternity, Amelia broke the silence.

"Rob, I'm not sure I completely understand, but I'm also not sure I want to. This is all very strange to me and not something I think I feel comfortable with. I'm afraid I'm going to have to ask you to leave."

Embarrassment, guilt, and an overall urge to have someone kick his ass began to overcome Rob.

He knew those feelings were going to have to wait until he left Amelia's, because she quickly reiterated, "Please leave now and don't come back to my Java Joe's unless I ask you to. You can let yourself out. I really don't feel like getting up."

Rob's head was spinning, but he managed to get up from the bed. His instincts told him that now was not the time to further the conversation, so he honored her directive to promptly leave and not let the door hit him in the butt.

When Amelia heard the door close, she curled herself into a ball and tried to figure out the true meaning of her anger. At first her thoughts centered around how bizarre Rob's relationship with Misty was, and she tried to convince herself she was too conservative to be part of a triangle. She had always struggled with the thought of sleeping with a married man, but this was beyond her comprehension. But when her heart began to ache at the thought of not seeing Rob again, she dropped the pious attitude and delved deeper. What she came up with troubled her. Was it possible she was jealous of Rob's ability to sleep with whomever he wanted? Would their open relationship mean she would never be anything more than a mistress to Rob? She finally realized that her real motive all along was to convince Rob to leave Misty and that to do so, she was right to take a stand. Rob would have to leave Misty if he ever wanted to be with her again.

58

IN THE DARK OF NIGHT

With Miguel gone, Misty became somewhat bored, so she made a game of trying to figure out what Ivan did for a living. Over the next two training sessions, she came up with creative ways to get him to talk but to no avail. Ivan was one of the most disciplined men she had ever known. She decided that the only way to find out might be to follow him one night.

The Tuesday training session started late and darkness had set in by the time they finished. Misty had scouted out the back of the gym to try and determine just where Ivan exited when he slipped out the back door. As soon as the door closed behind him, she grabbed the dark overcoat she had stashed and bolted down the thirty steps of the stairwell, coming to a stop just outside the front door. In the alley next to the gym stood two old-fashioned red phone booths that could be found all over London. She quickly jumped into the one closest to her and pretended to be speaking on the phone.

As Misty had hoped, Ivan crossed the end of the alley heading in the direction of her hotel. When he was out of sight, she quickly exited the booth and ran to the end of the alley. Very carefully, she peeked around the corner in time to witness Ivan meeting two other men. After quickly greeting one another, the men were on the move.

Well look at me, she thought excitedly. *Little Miss Sherlock Holmes. Or should that be Shirley Holmes?*

It was a typically dreary night. A heavy mist kept the visibility to no more than a hundred yards at best. The heavy moisture in the air dimmed the yellow light from the street lamps so that there was barely enough light to see by.

Perfect! she thought. *This gives me cover. If by chance Ivan sees me, I'll just tell him I'm on my way back to my hotel.*

She pulled the hood of her overcoat over her head, breathing rapidly from the excitement as she followed the men.

This is fun. It's a good thing Miguel is gone. I'm sure he would think this was a bad idea.

She followed the men to a small Italian restaurant that was located at the corner of Catherine and Exeter Streets. Because Exeter Street was not exactly perpendicular to Catherine Street, the entryway to the restaurant was extremely narrow. The advantage was that the men could sit at a table and get excellent visibility up and down each street. She slipped into a coffee bar just across the street. Her hotel wasn't more than fifty yards away. From a tiny table in the corner, Misty watched every move the men made in total anonymity.

The men met for hours. Misty bided her time drinking too much coffee. Just when the coffee shop was getting ready to close, the men left the restaurant and began to head up Catherine Street. She followed at a safe distance but had to slip into a doorway when three other men joined the group. An animated discussion followed. When it ended, five men turned right on Travistock Street while a lone man continued to head up Catherine. As the visibility was poor, Misty assumed Ivan was one of the five men.

She made it to Travistock and peeked around the corner just in time to see the last man disappear into a courtyard. For the first time that night, Misty felt apprehensive. *How can there be any danger if Ivan is with the group? If I'm ever going to figure out what he's doing, then now is the time*, she quickly rationalized.

Misty had always been the type of person to move with authority once she made up her mind, so up the street she went. When she looked into the courtyard, she thought she had positively identified Ivan.

With her usual enthusiasm and zest, she walked towards the man she thought was Ivan and said, "Ivan, what are you guys doing?"

The large man did not immediately turn around to greet her so she glanced at the other men. It was at that moment she realized these men were not English. It was impossible to tell where they were from, but her best guess was some country in Eastern Europe. Dark hair, dark eyes, but fair skin. Just then the large man turned around and stared down at Misty. If Russian Jack had a twin brother, he would most definitely be this guy, except for the big scar that ran down the entire length of the right side of his face. As if that wasn't bad enough, Misty noticed a man lying at the big guy's feet. The man looked as if he had just been beaten. He lay there writhing in agony while blood dripped out of his mouth. It was obvious the men weren't sure exactly what to do, so they looked at each other for an answer. Misty's temperature inside her overcoat rose, and she became clammy all over. That's when panic sunk in. Just as the men seemed to resolve what to do next, Misty turned and bolted back up Travistock. She could hear the men's feet pounding the pavement closely behind her. When the men barked out instructions to each other it became pretty obvious that they were indeed from Eastern Europe.

Misty felt clumsy running in her overcoat so she began to yank it off, which slowed her pace. One of the men got close just as she pulled free, and she threw the coat in his face, causing him to lose his footing and stumble. This was all Misty needed to put some distance between herself and her pursuers as she turned right onto Christine Street. They may have been some of the scariest men on the planet, but they were no match for her as runners. A few may have been able to give her a go in the fifty yard dash but none of them had her combination of speed and stamina. Plus, she was easily able to move up the steep grade of Christine Street, adding to her lead.

As Misty passed by the Theatre Royal Opera House, she thought, *Where's a bobby when a girl needs one?*

Russell Street was fast approaching and she needed to make a quick decision. *Do I turn left and head back to Covent Garden or take a quick jog to the left and then turn right up Bow Street?* She decided that familiarity might breed confidence, and she needed all the confidence she could muster at the moment. So down Russell Street she bolted in the direction of Covent Garden. *Even the creepy street actor would be a welcome sight right now*, she thought.

As Misty made her final push, she heard the voices of her pursuers trying to figure out which way to go. It was now clear she would never make it the rest of the way without being seen, so she quickly ducked into the doorway of a store. It was only several feet deep so she had to stand with her back against the door so as not to be seen. She realized that if they had spotted her before she ducked into cover, it was all over. All she could do for now was stay put and try to keep from peeing in her pants.

The next several seconds were nerve-racking. Anxious to get moving, she took off like a bat out of hell towards Covent Garden and what she hoped would be safety. When she finally reached the brick courtyard, she realized that it was late Tuesday night and nothing was open. Seeing the gym, she ran to the two large front doors only to find them locked. Panic began to set in and for a moment she felt like she was going to hyperventilate.

She made herself stop and tried to think reasonably. *What would someone in control do?* She walked along the side of the building to the alley where the telephone booths stood. She darted inside one of the booths, closed the door, and grabbed the phone. She fumbled in her pockets until she located a credit card, which she pulled out with a trembling hand.

Oh, God! I've never used one of these. How am I ever going to be able to read the directions in the condition I'm in? Why the hell don't they just have a red phone that dials the police station directly? No, Scotland Yard would be better.

Just when Misty finally figured out how to operate the phone, she heard a tap on the glass door behind her. The sound shook her to her very core and made her want to vomit. She worked up the courage to see who was there. When Misty saw the large man with the scar on his face smiling at her, she froze. He tapped on the door again with a pistol, which he was holding in his right hand. Misty felt something similar to fear, but it was stronger than any emotion she had ever felt in her life.

A second man came into view, and she watched as the two men gave each other sinister grins. Misty slid down into a sitting position. Not daring to look the men in the eyes, she bent her head and covered her face with her hands and began to weep.

Why did I let Miguel go home? Why did I have to follow Ivan?

As she prepared for death, all Misty could think about was the day she was told her parents died in a car accident. Her last thought was, *Maybe now I will finally get to see them again.*

Just then she heard two sudden metallic clacks followed by the tinkling of brass on concrete. Her body jerked violently with each one and then she sat there, motionless, trying to figure out where she had been hit.

When she realized there was no broken glass on the floor of the phone booth, she got up enough courage to look out from the bottom of the booth. She saw the face of the large man lying on the ground staring back at her. His eyes were rolled back in his head, and his tongue hung out of his mouth. Suddenly his body slid across the ground away from the door of the telephone booth. Looking up, she saw Ivan and realized the shots were from his gun, not her pursuer's.

The sight of Ivan instantly calmed her, yet all she could do was sit there motionless until he jerked the door open and lifted her seemingly lifeless body off the ground with his powerful arms. He held her around the waist with both hands to support her dead weight.

Ivan said, "Misty, snap out of it. We need to get out of here now! I need you totally focused and doing everything I say." When Misty didn't immediately respond, he gave her a slap to the face. The slap hurt so badly she had to fight back tears. Somehow her instincts told her that if she was going to survive it was necessary to allow Ivan to be the master of her every move from this moment forward. She had never given a man total control over her before, but for now she welcomed it.

She began to speak but Ivan quickly put his hand over her mouth and shook his head. He then leaned over and whispered in her ear, "Not a sound. Follow my lead and pay close attention to my hand gestures if you want to survive."

Looking into her frightened face pained him, but this was no time to become soft. He was the consummate professional, and he knew how critical it was to maintain his composure, as well as the upper hand. He also realized that his cover was blown and that there was no way he would ever be able to infiltrate the terrorists' lair and complete his mission. His superiors would be furious with him for having Misty become his trainer, but there was no time to worry about that now. His own life was in danger, but more importantly, so was that of an innocent woman he had unintentionally exposed to danger. It seemed as if he was now the Phantom and had just dragged Misty into his underground lair.

Even though she knew she was still in grave danger, Misty felt safe with Ivan. Maybe it was the confidence he exuded, or maybe she was just grasping at any ray of hope. All she knew was her life depended on his cunning and bravery, and she was going to give him whatever support she could muster. Suddenly they heard shouts coming from down the alley. Ivan grabbed her, and they began to run.

He led her across the courtyard and down a stairway that led to the deserted Covent Garden courtyard, which made Misty feel even more afraid. When they approached what appeared to be a dead end, Ivan pulled her by the hand up a second set of steps. They were now facing the opposite end of the courtyard.

She watched him as he peered down Henrietta Street. After taking a good look in every direction, he motioned for her to stay where she was. He ran across the courtyard to the cover of the buildings lining the street. Once the coast was clear, he motioned for her to come across. Then they bolted down Henrietta, only stopping for a moment to hide in a church doorway.

After reaching Bedford Street, Ivan turned right and ran to a passageway called Bedford Court. From there they wound their way to May's Court and then on to Cecil Court. It was obvious Ivan knew his way around London well enough to avoid the main streets.

Finally they came to a street Misty and Miguel had frequented regularly during their stay. Irving Street was lined with restaurants and led directly to one of her favorite hangouts, Leicester Square. Misty had never quite learned how to pronounce it but the only thing that mattered to her now was that she was back in familiar surroundings. They took their time moving down Irving, along and through the hundreds of tables and chairs that were stacked up and chained together outside of each restaurant; Misty was glad for the cover.

When they got to the end of the street, Ivan stood motionless, looking directly across the plaza to the Hampshire Hotel. When three cabs pulled up all at once, the bustling square in front of the hotel came alive with taxi drivers, guests, and luggage being carted into the hotel. Ivan waited for the right moment and then grabbed Misty's hand and led her toward the hotel's front door.

As they passed an unattended luggage cart, he picked up a suitcase in his right hand and gathered Misty close to him with his left, and together they strode into the lobby as if they'd just exited one of the cabs. Ivan deposited the suitcase next to a chair and led Misty quickly past the front desk into a stairwell down to a lower floor. At the bottom they found two elevators and two restrooms. To her surprise, he pulled her into the women's restroom and into a toilet stall with a solid wooden door that went from floor to ceiling, locking it shut with a sliding bolt.

Ivan sat Misty on top of the toilet seat, gave her his pistol, and looked at her gravely. "They shouldn't look in here, but we can't be sure. When I leave, lock this door and hold the bolt from the inside with all your might. If anyone tries to force their way in, point the gun just to the right of the lock and halfway up the door. Don't ask who it is, don't make a noise, and don't hesitate. Shoot three times in succession.

Misty stared at Ivan with wide eyes. He could tell she was doing everything she could to hold back tears and stay brave. What he was asking her to do was so far removed from her everyday life that there was no way she could comprehend how severe the situation was.

Ivan put his hands on Misty's shoulders.

"I know this is hard for you, but you've got to trust me. Do you understand?"

She managed a small nod of her head, looking like a child who was being told for the first time never to leave her mother in a crowd.

"Good girl. I'm going to check my apartment and make sure it's safe to take you there. I'll come back to get you, one way or another." Just as she was envisioning accidentally shooting him, he added, "If it's me, I'll tap three times on the washroom mirror with a coin, then two, and then one, okay?"

Misty nodded, holding the heavy gun awkwardly in both hands. He listened at the door for a moment, then opened it carefully and slipped away.

For what seemed like an eternity, Misty sat in the stall and kept a close watch on the door, listening intently to what lay beyond. The only person to enter the restroom used a toilet stall far away, washed her hands, and then left. Misty's heart had been pounding the entire time the person was there and her hands, gripped so tightly around the gun, began to sweat. Finally, she heard the door open and shortly after, tapping on the mirror in the exact order Ivan had described. Misty cracked the door open, stuck the muzzle of the gun through the crack, and then looked to make sure it was Ivan. It was him, looking right into her eyes through the narrow slit in the door. She kneeled on the floor in relief, almost as if she were in prayer, before walking out and handing the gun over to him. He looked her over for a moment to make sure she wasn't going to faint before taking her hand and leading her to the elevator.

59

IN THE SANCTUARY OF IVAN'S ROOM

As the elevator made its way up to the top floor, Misty prayed the coast would be clear. Before the door opened, Ivan put his finger to his lips, letting her know not to say a word. He moved her to the front corner, opposite the elevator controls. All she could do was hold her hands over her eyes while he checked the hallway. Suddenly, he grabbed her arm and pulled her behind him down the hallway. She was barely looking at the numbers on the doors as they sped past. Just as suddenly as they'd started, they stopped, and Ivan pushed her through a door and began bolting it from the inside. She immediately went to the far corner of the room. With her back against the wall, she slid down until she was sitting on the floor with her knees pulled up to her chest.

She watched in amazement as Ivan slid three different bolts into the doorframe. He then grabbed a large bar that was standing in the corner and placed it onto two heavy brackets that were bolted to either side of the door. Once the door was secure, he moved to the windows and peered out into Leicester Square. The Hampshire Hotel jutted out from the middle into the square, giving the middle rooms a double set of windows. The windows angled out in opposite directions, giving Ivan not only a good view of the entire square but also a view all the way down Irving Street. When he was satisfied everything looked as it should, he set the gun on the end of the table and walked over to Misty.

From her view from the floor, Ivan looked like he was ten feet tall. Reading the look in her eyes, he kneeled down to her. "I'm sorry you had to go through this but you can rest easy now."

She put her head down and rested it between her knees, trying to understand how she felt. Her breathing slowly came back to normal and her head began to gradually clear.

When she could catch her breath and finally take in the room around her, she looked to Ivan, confused. "I saw you kill two men. Is that something you do?"

Ivan frowned. "Would you rather I let them kill you?"

His words brought back the vivid memory of being trapped in the phone booth with the two goons laughing at her. She put her face between her knees again and shook her head.

"No, but I risked my life trying to find out what you do for a living. Can you please just tell me now?"

Ivan frowned as he kneeled there looking at her, trying to frame an answer. Every inch of him wanted to tell her that he was a CIA agent on loan to England's Secret Intelligence Service, working to infiltrate a Belarusian drug trafficking ring in London that also had ties to a ring in the United States. He had thought it would be safe enough for her, but he was wrong. It would have felt good to tell her all this, but of course he knew that was not an option.

As much as he wanted to say the things that would make her brush with death feel justified, he knew better. "You know how in the movies they say: 'If I tell you, I'd have to kill you?'"

She nodded.

He paused before saying what he knew he had to say for Misty's own protection. "Don't ever ask me what I do for a living again," he said, lowering his voice to a growl and staring hard into her eyes. "I would have to kill you if I told you."

Misty's heart began to pound so hard she thought it was going to explode. Panic stricken, she slowly shimmied her way back up the wall, keeping her eyes fixed on his face. Once up, she pushed him aside and ran into the bathroom and slammed the door behind her.

60

MISTY'S WORLD TURNED UPSIDE DOWN

Misty's mind was racing. *How am I going to barricade the door? How am I going to escape?* It didn't take long for her to figure out there was no way to secure the door other than to sit with her back up against it and wedge her feet in between the door and the sink.

I can't believe Ivan said he would kill me! Would he really? I watched him shoot two men dead. He is capable of killing. Why did Peter have to call and ask me to train his brother? I should have just said no!

Suddenly she realized she had her cell phone in her pocket. She immediately dialed 999 but her finger paused over the send button.

Is this really a smart thing to do? What if they come and take Ivan into custody? Is that what I want? He did say he would kill me but didn't say he was going to kill me.

She realized Ivan had just saved her life by risking his own, and that *she* had put herself in this predicament by trailing him. She couldn't turn him in; she didn't even know his whole story. What if he was working for the government?

Misty's heart jumped at the sound of a door slamming shut. She waited, listening. Nothing. *Ivan is gone and he's left me here all by myself!*

Misty jumped up from the floor and jerked the bathroom door wide open. The room was pitch black, but that didn't stop her from rushing toward the door to try to stop Ivan before he could get all the way down the hall to the elevators. But just two short steps into her dash she slammed into something in the middle of the room. She wrapped around whatever it was in a desperate effort to regain her balance. The object reciprocated and Misty felt two powerful arms completely engulf her, to the point that she was no longer supporting her own weight.

Misty attempted to struggle until she heard a deep voice say, "It's okay, Misty, it's me."

"Ivan? I thought you had left me."

"No, I wanted to make sure the windows opened in case we needed them to. One got stuck open, and I had to force it loose. When it finally gave way, it slammed shut."

Misty was relieved. She snuggled tightly into Ivan's arms and, to her surprise, felt comforted. Once he realized she wasn't letting go, he tightened the embrace and rocked her from side to side as if she were a child and he were singing her a lullaby.

Even though Ivan had become accustomed to being in dangerous situations through the years, he had never had to worry about protecting someone he cared for deeply. Now, she was safe in his arms where he could protect her.

Misty broke the silence.

"You are nothing like your brother Peter."

Catching him off guard, Ivan replied without thinking, "So what makes you so sure I'm not Peter?"

"Peter would never treat me like this. He is a gentleman—not a killer," Misty screamed back.

"Well if it's Peter you want so badly, why don't I just leave and let him come save you." Ivan turned and started to walk toward the door.

Without thinking, Misty grabbed his arm and pulled him back to her. As she held him tight to her body she mustered up the words, "Okay, so prove you are Peter."

"Remember the night I visited you in your room in Beaver Creek? If I remember correctly, you called me an oversized gorilla."

She had to think for a moment but then remembered she had indeed called him an oversized gorilla because he had been smothering her.

Still not completely convinced, she asked, "Okay, so what did we talk about at dinner that night?"

"Why, how much you enjoy having affairs."

Misty shot back, "I did not say I liked having affairs. In fact, I never even mentioned having an affair. We just talked about why other people have affairs."

But regardless of how the conversation at Beaver Creek went, Misty realized Ivan was telling the truth, and that Ivan and Peter were indeed one and the same.

It took a little while for it to settle in, but once she accepted it as fact she said, "I'm not asking you what you do for a living, but explain to me why you have two identities if you can . . . without having to kill me."

His violent ruse was crumbling against her matter-of-fact questioning. Despite the rules he lived by, he decided he might as well tell her the truth.

"When I'm on special assignment, I am Ivan, but when I'm waiting for an assignment, I hide my identity by posing as Peter."

Misty pulled herself closer to Ivan's body and looked up at him. "So who are you really? Ivan or Peter?"

Her question must have struck a nerve because Ivan let her loose, walked over to the bed, and sat down heavily. He bent over, put his head in his hands, and started talking. "I have been switching back and forth for so long that I'm not quite sure anymore."

She suddenly felt touched by the anguish in his voice, his hidden pain revealed. It was like he was neither Ivan nor Peter but totally naked before her. She sat next to him on the bed and put her arm around him while running her hand softly through his hair. After everything Ivan had done for her it felt satisfying being able to console him.

"It's okay," she said softly. "It's just the pressure. Everything will be okay. I promise."

He shook his head and replied, "I'm not so sure. You think it would get easier the more I switch back and forth, but it only gets harder. It's not the stories that get mixed up, it's the light and dark. I am both Ivan and Peter, but Peter's the one who I long to be."

Misty closed her eyes against sudden tears. She hugged him tighter and laid her head on his shoulder. Then before she knew it, her mouth was engulfed in a slow, long kiss, and she welcomed his kiss from beginning to end. She felt so much lighter with every second that passed with her lips locked to his. It was as if Ivan were kissing away her fear and she his anguish.

61

PURGING THE DEMONS

The trance she was in faded as he pulled her blouse loose from her skirt and worked his strong hands up her back. His hands were so hot against her cold skin. As he held her confidently and kissed her passionately, she knew that what she had been denied so long ago in Colorado would be granted to her now. She pulled back slightly and began to slowly unbutton her blouse.

"Who will I be sleeping with, Peter or Ivan?" she asked with her head thrown back.

"I am whoever you want me to be."

Misty rose up and hugged Ivan, bringing her legs up around his waist, straddling him. She whispered, "Let's start out with Peter and play it by ear."

"Then Peter it shall be," he said, deftly undoing the pearl buttons of her shirt.

Misty giggled to herself and thought, *Maybe I should have asked for a threesome.*

As if by her request, everything about this man softened. His touch, his kisses, his demeanor. Inside this poor creature there were two different men who could be summoned at will.

At first, everything was wonderful. She could feel immediately that it was Peter she was with, and it was refreshing. She hoped it would transport her back to her room in Beaver Creek where they could finish what they had started the year before. As he held her in his arms, she felt as safe as if she were back in Colorado. He freed her breasts from the bra, and they embraced again. The warmth of his body released all of the tension in hers, and she went limp in his arms, completely surrendering.

Peter laid her gently onto the bed and began pulling her jeans down her legs and onto the floor. Once they were off, Misty managed to pry herself off the bed, sit up, and help Peter out of his shirt. She couldn't resist running her fingers through Peter's tight curly chest hair. It was so soft, yet his pecks underneath felt like they were filled with iron. Peter stopped to enjoy the electric touch of her hands on his skin and stare at her naked breasts. Overcome by their beauty, he couldn't resist cupping his hands underneath them and gently teasing her taut nipples.

As strange as it seemed to Misty at the time, she began to feel sorry for Ivan. After all, it was he who had saved her life that night, and it was Ivan who had taken her to see *The Phantom of the Opera* just a few nights before. But more importantly, she was losing the adrenaline rush she had been experiencing most of the night. The thrill was slipping away and she desperately wanted it back!

With a mischievous grin, she looked at him and said, "I don't want to be made love to tonight. I want to be taken."

He responded by grabbing her by the hips and thrusting his mouth on hers, but it wasn't enough.

"Please, change back to Ivan for me," she pleaded.

Peter shook his head. "I can make the change, but I can't be responsible for Ivan once I do."

"You can't be responsible?" Misty replied, confused.

"Is it Ivan you really want?"

"Yes," she said, closing her eyes, surrendering herself to him.

Ivan grabbed Misty firmly by the arms, pushing her further up the bed, and pounced on her. He leaned in and began to suck in as much of her left breast as he could get inside his mouth. At first, she was horrified when she looked down and saw her entire breast had disappeared. She felt like it was inside a large suction cup, her nipple instantly hardening when it rubbed against his massive tongue. But after a few minutes the sensation was so intense she was writhing in ecstasy. Once it began to subside, she grabbed Ivan's head, pulled him off her breast, and placed him firmly on the other.

After Ivan had sucked her so hard that she thought she was going to scream, he flipped her over onto her stomach. Misty felt like she was losing control so she immediately attempted to push herself up. She had barely made it to her elbows when his heavy hand pushed her deep into the mattress. He spread her legs apart easily despite her resistance. Face down and spread eagle, Misty was helpless against his will. Ivan thrust his large middle finger inside her so fast it made her freeze in place, afraid to move. When he began to forcefully move his finger in and out, she almost felt like she was being violated, but she also felt how wet she was. Her wetness was running down her leg onto the bed. She couldn't believe it, but his finger was almost as large as a normal penis, filling her completely. She pushed against his hand, driving his finger deeper inside over and over until she came explosively.

Misty lay there for a moment catching her breath, but just as she was getting ready to push herself up to get off her stomach, she felt Ivan's hands grab her around the ankles and lift her by her feet into the air. The top of Misty's head was hovering over the bed.

"What are you going to do to me? Put me down."

Ivan laughed and wrapped his arms around the small of her back. He pulled her up to him until her moist pussy was level with his chin and her legs dangled helplessly in the air. He brought her into his mouth, dipping his tongue inside her again and again, making her shudder with pleasure even as she was afraid of him.

Misty knew that asking him to become Ivan had been a miscalculation. She never imagined Ivan could be so barbaric.

As much as she was unwound by the deep probing of his tongue, she knew there was no telling what he would do next. She had to think of a way out and she needed to do it fast. *I set the beast loose, now I must tame it.*

Needing to do something quick, she reached down and latched onto Ivan's penis with her right hand. Once she had a firm clamp she squeezed, hard. The sensation must have been painful but Misty had no other choice. That seemed to get his attention because Ivan took his hands off her back, allowing her to fall softly to the mattress.

She crawled to her knees, pivoted toward him, and looked into his eyes. He had a confused and almost hurt look as if to say, *"What is it you want from me? I gave you Peter, but you asked for Ivan? Now what do you want?"*

Thinking fast, she grabbed onto Ivan's massive frame and pulled herself up until she was face to face with him. She stroked the side of his face and gave him a peck on the cheek before moving down and kissing his burly chest. When he began to relax, she coaxed him onto his back and propped his head up with pillows while twirling his tight curly chest hairs with her fingers. Once he was in position, she swung a leg over his side, straddling him. She grabbed the head of his cock and held it firmly as she positioned the wet lips of her pussy directly onto the soft side of his enormous penis. Gently at first and then harder and faster, she rode up and down his hot rod. Before Misty hit a rhythm, she paused to place both of Ivan's hands on her breasts to keep track of them. She raised her left hand in the air to balance herself like a cowboy breaking in a stallion as she rode him hard, up and down, over and over while praying it was working. She needed to get him off before he thought of something awful to do to her next. Ivan lay there for a while before finally starting to breathe heavily.

Thank goodness he's starting to get off. I don't think I can keep this up for much longer. Come on big boy it's time for you to come.

Misty thought that maybe he needed some coaxing, so instead of thinking these things to herself she decided to talk to him.

"Come on big guy, you can do it."

With that Ivan pulled his knees up and tilted his head back.

This was encouraging. She began to softly say, "Oh Ivan, your penis is so big. It gets me so wet just looking at it." She started to feel a real sense of power when she realized she was in complete control of this powerful man. Ivan could knock a man cold with his right fist but right now he was hers to command.

And then it happened! Ivan finally erupted and semen exploded as far as the window behind his head. When he was finished, Ivan propped himself up on his elbows and stared at Misty. Her eyes became large when she noticed a good portion of the semen dripping from his face. In a panic, she contemplated making a run for the bathroom, but before she could act, Ivan began to laugh uncontrollably. Misty was relieved but ran into the bathroom anyway, coming back with a warm washcloth to wipe his face off.

With a clean face, Ivan scooped up Misty in a big hug.

"That was incredible!"

Misty cuddled up into his arms, smiling with the secret satisfaction that she had tamed the beast within.

62

REALITY SETS IN

As Ivan lay in bed holding Misty in his arms, he knew it wouldn't be long before they would come looking for him. Things had gone horribly wrong the night before and his superiors were going to demand answers. How was he going to explain committing the cardinal sin of letting a civilian get too close to his undercover assignment? Knowing that he might never see Misty again, he put to memory every minute detail from her beautiful face to her toned, fit body. Not being able to have a true relationship due to his profession had taken its toll through the years. It was why Ivan identified with the Phantom. The tortured soul of the opera house spent his life underground, and Ivan spent most of his life undercover. Every time he saw *The Phantom of the Opera*, it eased the pain of living a double life, if only for a few hours.

He lay waiting, thinking that even if he were exiled to a far away outpost, he would have the memory of this night as long as there was breath in his body.

Shortly after daybreak, there were three knocks on the door, then two, and then one. He knew SIS agents had arrived to bring him in. He had to figure out how to convince them to get Misty out of the country and safely back to the States. Ivan knew there was a small possibility the drug cartel would try to track her down in Malibu, but he was hopeful that they would realize she would not cause them any harm.

When the two agents entered the room, the first one came walking toward him quickly with an angry look.

"What in the hell happened last night? You not only blew your cover, but the targets have vacated their safe house."

He was never one to make excuses. Just as he was about to tell him straightforwardly what had happened, the second agent interrupted, "Bloody hell, Ivan. Who's that woman? Are you nuts?"

Misty woke suddenly to the sound of the man's voice. Her eyes focused on a tall Englishman in a long coat.

"Who is this guy, and why is he in our room?"

The two agents looked at each other in disbelief.

The second agent turned to Misty with an incredulous look. "Who am I? You don't need to know—"

Ivan cut him off by grabbing his arm and giving it a hard squeeze.

The agent knew from past experience that Ivan was not someone to mess with, so he decided to calm down.

"Okay," Ivan said, looking the man in the eyes. "We're going to get a few things straight before I cooperate. Do you understand?"

Ivan gave the two SIS agents a cold look, one they had seen before and knew meant business.

The first agent sighed and tersely replied, "Okay then, get on with it. We haven't got all day. Headquarters wants you in for questioning."

Ivan looked over at Misty, and she knew by his look that she was to play quiet mouse until this whole thing was settled. Something in his eyes made all of the horrible events of her chase and brush with death come rushing back. She didn't want any more trouble. All she wanted was to go home.

Looking back at the agents, Ivan said, "Who she is and why she is here is not information you need to know. If Headquarters is interested, they can ask me. If you two hadn't of blundered in here, she would know nothing. Unless you want to explain to the American Embassy how you compromised my identity to an American citizen, I suggest you keep quiet about her."

The agent in the long coat grumbled and shifted his weight nervously, looking at the other agent.

"No, we don't want the Americans involved. What do you suggest?"

"I want you to pull in two more people and find a way to get her safely out of the country. Don't risk flying her out of Heathrow, because the cartel will be looking for her there. Get her to Ireland or Scotland and then fly her back to the States."

Ivan's words reminded Misty that her life was still in danger. She suddenly became dizzy with nausea. Even though she was scared out of her wits, she kept her mouth shut and her eyes dry. She knew Ivan was laying a lot on the line for her and felt that it was important to be strong for his sake.

The first agent pulled out his cell phone and hit the speed dial as he walked out into the hall. The other agent looked at Ivan and shook his head.

After an animated conversation, the agent in the hall reentered the room. "Headquarters has agreed. We'll have someone here within ten minutes, and they'll get her on her way." He looked at Misty and said, "Okay then, get your things together."

Misty said, "But, my things are back at my hotel."

The second agent replied flatly, "Then you have nothing."

Looking at his fellow agents, Ivan said, "I appreciate the cooperation, but leave the room and give me a few minutes alone with her."

The second agent rolled his eyes and stuck his hands in the pockets of his coat.

"Whatever. I'm writing this up in my report."

After the men left, Ivan walked over and sat on the bed. She crawled over to him and wrapped her arms around his burly chest. "I am so sorry I got you into this mess," she said. "I just feel horrible."

"Don't," Ivan shot back. "I never should have had you come to London in the first place, so it's my fault. I'm sorry you almost got killed last night and that now you have to be smuggled out of the country."

After a long silence, Ivan added, "There is no punishment I can receive that will take away last night. I will cherish it forever."

When the new agents arrived, Ivan said to Misty, "Go home. It's still dangerous for you in London. Your safety is all that matters now."

With that, Ivan rose to his feet and walked out the door without looking back.

63

TIME TO ANSWER ROB'S QUESTION

Getting Misty out of the country had become more difficult than everyone had anticipated, but it was only because the agents had promised Ivan they would take every precaution. Misty would never have guessed she would be crossing the English Channel at night in a fishing boat to get to France. Yet five days after that fateful night, Misty left on a plane bound for the United States from Amsterdam.

Once the plane was in the air, Misty felt a sense of relief. The night with Ivan now seemed like a distant memory, but the five days on the run drove home just how much danger she had been in. Even though she had thankfully suffered no physical damage, the constant rush of adrenalin made her body feel as if she'd been in a car wreck. The whole ordeal had convinced her to give Rob's plea to stop working on the road careful consideration.

I have a wonderful husband, and many interesting clients to train in beautiful, sunny California. I've had wonderful experiences seeing the world, but maybe now is a good time to quit before something bad happens to me.

By the time her plane approached JFK, Misty had made up her mind. *That's it! I'm finished being the Black Widow Trainer and I can't wait to tell Rob my decision. He is going to be so happy.*

Misty contemplated calling Rob from New York before she caught the plane to LAX but decided it would be better to surprise him. He had no way of knowing she was on her way because the SIS agents insisted that she not attempt to call anyone during her escape.

This was going to be perfect. She would come home, insist they go out for a nice dinner, and then after sharing a bottle of wine, give Rob the good news. What could be more perfect?

At 5:00 PM the taxi dropped Misty off at home.

Good, Rob's car is here. Oh my, I think my heart is actually fluttering. I feel like we're meeting for the first time.

As she entered the house, she felt relieved that Rob didn't have anything cooking on the stove. She wouldn't have to talk him into going out to dinner.

Rob was nowhere to be found on the ground floor so she climbed the stairs to their bedroom.

Maybe he had a hard day and is taking a nap. I'll just quietly crawl in next to him and be the first thing he sees when he wakes up. How romantic!

When she walked into the bedroom, she noticed the bed was made up. Then she heard water splashing in the tub.

Forget the dinner. I can tell him in the tub and we can just screw all night and wake up in each other's arms in the morning.

She took off all her clothes and pushed the bathroom door open, grinning with the excitement of surprising her husband.

It's funny how the human brain reacts when confronted with something it's totally unprepared for. It's one thing to just walk into a room and be presented with something out of the ordinary. It's totally different to walk into that room with a rock-solid image in one's head of what's going to be there, and then have it be the total opposite. This is how the brain short-circuits. Couple that with a brain that has recently been traumatized, and it's a recipe for disaster.

The shock froze Misty's brain. It was not the typical brain freeze from drinking something too cold; it was icecap cold, straight from the North Pole. As it slowly thawed, she began to hear two loud voices talking to her at the same time. For some reason they seemed far away.

As Misty began to come out of it ever so slowly, the images of two naked bodies in her tub began to emerge. One seemed to be a man and the other a woman, but the image was still too blurry to know for sure.

It was only when water splashed across Misty's face and down her bare chest that she snapped out of it. As she did, her eyes became extremely focused and the images began to come through in remarkable clarity, clarity that revealed the last thing she could have ever expected or wanted to see: Rob totally naked with his right leg over the side of their tub attempting to get out and Becca sitting there attempting to cover her rather large breasts with her rather small hands.

Becca was surprised, but there was no trace of shame on her face. It was more a look of consternation from having her little party broken up. Rob's face, on the other hand, was one of horror, shame, and guilt all rolled into one.

Rob leapt out of the bath to Misty and placed his hands on her arms.

"It's not what you think Misty. Please give me a chance to explain."

She pulled herself from Rob's grip. She staggered back, poking him hard in the chest and glaring at him.

"Don't you touch me! Do you understand?"

Having never seen her this angry, Rob realized he needed to remain passive—and find the nearest towel to cover up his pitiful looking limp dick. Throwing Misty a towel to cover up might be a good idea as well but if Rob was a betting man he'd bet Misty was so upset she couldn't care less about being naked.

While Rob retreated to the towel rack, Misty yelled, "You better throw this bitch a towel while you're at it. I don't want the neighbors to see her big fat boobs when I'm running her ass off down the street."

The fact that Misty was naked and didn't care only scared Rob more.

Becca had had enough of Misty. She felt like she had every right to be there, given Rob and Misty's "arrangement," and had no intention of leaving. She looked at Rob in disbelief.

"Are you going to let that whore talk to me like that? I mean, really? Rob, we talked about this."

There was a whine in her voice that Rob suddenly recognized had bent his ear toward her too many times—manipulated his pain into false affection for her. He was suddenly filled with loathing and resentment for the woman who sat there dripping wet in his bathtub. He tore a towel off the rack and tossed it at Becca.

"Get out of our house."

His words hit Becca like a slap in the face. The towel followed. She pulled it out of the water pathetically, her face a confusion of pain and anger. She climbed out of the tub half covering herself with the soaked towel and began to cry.

"Rob, why are you treating me this way? I'm the one who really cares about you. She's just using you."

She's just using you. How many times had Becca said that over the past few months? She'd said it enough that he began to believe it, but seeing Misty here, fierce even in her nakedness, made him remember how much he loved her. *Misty never tried to use me. She was always honest with me about her job. She didn't have to tell me that she cheated on me that first time, and I didn't have to accept her for who she is.*

He looked at Becca. Her freckled skin was red from the bath and her eyes were puffy, her red hair hung in wet tangles around her face. He knew that he'd never been attracted to her and had gone to her out of desperation. He then looked at Misty, who had traveled across the world to come home to him and was now looking at him expectantly, waiting for him to make a decision.

Rob stepped out of the way of the door and motioned to Becca.

"It's time for you to go. You're not allowed in our lives anymore."

Speechless, Becca walked numbly out of the bathroom, half covered, gathered her things in the bedroom and walked out.

Misty felt a surge of pride seeing Rob be so decisive—it even turned her on a little—but that was soon overcome by the reality of the situation.

"I came home to tell you I was quitting my job and would be your wife—your real wife. I thought you were in the tub so I took my clothes off to join you. Now look at how ridiculous I am. How could you do this to me?"

Now that Becca was gone and his tiny victory complete, Rob could not believe this was all actually happening. Within the course of ten days, he had blown his relationship with Amelia and possibly ruined his marriage. Any feelings of triumph he'd had telling off the manipulative Becca in front of Misty were now as shriveled as his embarrassed penis.

"Let me explain, Misty. We can work this out once you know the whole story."

"No, Rob. You blew it. I could have forgiven you if you were sleeping with Amelia, but *Becca?* She was our mutual friend and, I had thought, my girlfriend. Becca is the only person on the face of this earth you could have screwed that would ruin our marriage. How could you!"

"That's what I want to explain, if you'll let me."

"Rob, there was no question mark after 'how could you.' There was an exclamation point. I don't want to hear your excuse because that's all it would be, an excuse."

When she got a grip and noticed the pain on Rob's face she softened her demeanor.

In a low voice she said, "I'm hurt right now. Let me have a few days by myself to think things over. I'll call you when I'm ready to talk," she sighed. "Stop looking at my naked body, and throw me a towel."

Misty pulled her clothes back on, fighting to get the material over her damp skin. She quickly snatched her keys off the bedside table, grabbed her purse, rushed to her car, and drove off. A few blocks down the road she pulled over and put the car in park.

What now? she thought as she put her hands over her face and cried. *What am I going to do now?* Her iPhone was buzzing in her purse. Rob texting apologies, no doubt.

She heard the rhythmic pounding of a jogger's approaching footsteps and quickly pulled out to check into a hotel. It was to be Misty's home for the next few days.

64

THINGS TO CONTEMPLATE

The past week had been too much to handle. Even thinking about it made her want to go to sleep. Ivan. The chase. The escape. Now Rob and Becca. To be holed up in a hotel room just sleeping and eating room service for two days went against every fiber in Misty's body. She craved movement and exercise and had not watched television in so long that she had no idea what was going on. It seemed like it was all reality TV shows that chronicled the sordid lives of cheating spouses. She watched them with a masochistic interest, but they only deepened her depression.

From somewhere in the haze of images from the past week flowing darkly through her mind, she heard the phone ringing. She looked in the direction of the sound but never made a move to get up and answer. The phone rang every fifteen minutes for the next two hours before she heard a knock on the door.

When Misty opened it, a lady from the front desk was standing there.

"Ma'am, I apologize, but a Miguel has been trying to contact you for the past two hours. He found out you were here, but as hotel policy we never give out guest room numbers. He's been calling from the house phone downstairs for several hours. If you like, we can have him escorted from the building."

In her grief, Misty had forgotten all about Miguel. It was not very thoughtful of her considering he had his own set of issues he was dealing with.

"No, go ahead and give Miguel my room number and have him come up."

A few minutes later there was another knock on the door. When Misty opened it, Miguel was standing there, as strong and handsome as ever. Seeing her best friend and adventure partner made her feel better than anything had in the past couple of days. She greeted him with a tight hug that made him wince.

"Careful there, girly. You're stronger than you think."

"Oh, Miguel! I'm so sorry. You would not believe what's happened to me if I told you. But what's more important is that I've been back two whole days and haven't even called to ask how things worked out between you and Sylvia. Can you forgive me?"

"Of course, Misty. Rob called me and said you two had a blow up. It sounds like we're going through the same thing."

"Did he tell you what happened?"

"No, but he said it was one hundred percent his fault."

Misty was relieved that she didn't have to retell the story of finding Rob and Becca in the bath—and that Rob had owned up to it. That took a lot of guts.

"Yes, he was to blame for our fight, but I wouldn't say it was his fault. I'm just as much to blame. I left him alone too long."

"Does that mean you will forgive him and get back together?"

Misty had been trying to feel a different way about it than she did, had tried to find a way to make it work for her, but she could not. She didn't have to think too hard when she answered, "No. We won't be getting back together. I've put him through enough. Rob needs to find a woman who will be there for him. He is a good man and deserves someone who can share a conventional lifestyle with him. I'm just not that person."

Miguel probably knew Misty better than anyone, and he had a hard time refuting what she had just said. Even though she was as loving a person as any woman he had ever known, she was just too much for Rob to handle. It's not that he thought Rob was inadequate. It's just that

Miguel wasn't sure there was a man alive who could handle Misty. She was best experienced, not owned. Miguel was thankful that his relationship with her had never become physical—it would have ended everything between them. He knew that he probably had more of her than any other man, specifically because he'd never tried to own her. He accepted her totally and completely and showed her by embracing her warmly.

When she felt better she said, "So Migs, enough about me. Did you work things out with Sylvia?"

Miguel shrugged.

"No, it was too late. Sylvia decided that she's better off with another dude, and I guess I can't blame her. I haven't given her the time she deserves. And if I'm being honest with myself, I should have known that if I was really in love with her, I would never have been so attracted to Amber and Heather."

"Fair enough, but she wouldn't even stay with you if you took another job?"

Miguel got a puzzled look on his face and replied, "Another job? Are you nuts? I love this job. Don't worry! I'm going to be fine. Just tell me where we're going next."

Misty put her hands on Miguel's shoulders and said, "I've decided not to take another job until I'm ready, and I'm not exactly sure when that will be."

Miguel's face fell. It was one thing losing Sylvia but another to be told by Misty that she didn't know when she would take another assignment. He knew he had invested too much in his work, using it as an escape from his troubles at home. Now he was really going to have to face reality.

"I've decided to go back to Buenos Aires. That is unless Gabriella won't have me. When I left, she said I was welcome any time, so I hope she meant it. I've decided to call Gabriella tonight to let her know I will be coming home—" Misty stopped before correcting herself. "I mean, coming back to Buenos Aires for a long stay."

Miguel's eyes lit up. "But what about me?"

"Well, I was just thinking about that. If you and Sylvia aren't together anymore, maybe you would like to come to Buenos Aires and live with your brother while we both sort things out. I have saved up a lot of money over the years and would be happy to pay you forty percent of your salary while I decide what to do next."

"Hell yes, I'll take that deal. I don't have anything holding me in Los Angeles anymore. My brother is the closest family I have left. When do we leave?"

Hearing Miguel's enthusiastic response lifted her spirits and forced a huge grin to her face. It felt like it had been ages since she'd smiled so brightly.

"Pack your stuff, buddy. We'll leave as soon as I do one final thing."

"You got it. I'll get packing right away."

65

SETTING THINGS STRAIGHT WITH ROB

When Misty called, Rob was sitting at the kitchen table over a cold cup of coffee, trying to work through things in his head, but getting nowhere. When he saw her number on the caller ID, he felt panic and relief all at the same time. She sounded good—great, in fact—and wanted to meet to talk. She gave him the details and then hung up, leaving Rob happy but confused.

As thrilled as he was to have the opportunity to explain things to her, he could not understand why she insisted it take place at Amelia's Java Joe's. He was very uncomfortable with the thought of showing up there with Misty, but she said she would not meet with him unless it was there. He even thought of calling ahead to see if Amelia was working, but the thought of her picking up terrified him even more, so he went along with the plan, certain he was in for another awful day.

When they met in the parking lot, Misty said, "I know this bothers you, but you are just going to have to deal with it. You owe me that much."

Rob nodded in agreement, although he was upset and scared about what might happen. He didn't like going into unknown situations; he didn't adapt quickly and often said the wrong thing when he had to think on his feet. They walked in and stood in line in silence. Rob was praying Amelia had maybe gotten sick or something and would not be working today. No luck. There she was, operating the howling espresso machine. If she had noticed them, she betrayed no emotion.

At the counter, Misty ordered a latte and Rob ordered his usual americano. When the cashier yelled to Amelia, "He'll have the usual," she made no reply and went about her business with her head down. Amelia placed Misty's drink on the counter first and walked away.

I hope my drink isn't as cold as Amelia, Misty thought. When she set Rob's drink on the counter, it was a tall latte. Rob picked it up without looking and took a sip. He immediately scrunched his nose and looked back at Amelia as if to say, "What's up?"

Amelia walked over, threw his drink in the trash, and then made him his usual venti americano.

When she set it down, she said, "Sorry, I didn't recognize you," and walked off.

Misty and Rob sat down at a corner table and Misty started talking. "Rob, I've been giving this a great deal of thought, and here's what I have come up with. I don't want to hate you, and I don't want you to hate me. It's not your fault things turned out the way they did. I'm just not capable of commitment, and I tried to tell you that three years ago. You convinced me to stay because you said you didn't want to own me, you just wanted to be by my side. You touched me with that statement, and it made me want to give it a try. Well, we've both tried to make it work, but I think we know that the way we are attempting to live our marriage is just not the natural order of things." And then she looked over at Amelia. "That's the kind of woman you need, not someone like me."

Rob looked sick.

"What's the matter? Has she totally turned you away?" Misty asked.

For the next thirty minutes, he filled in Misty on what had happened between him and Amelia over the last year. While Rob was talking, Misty could tell Amelia kept trying to disguise her glances in their direction. It was obvious she wished she could hear every word they were saying.

When Rob finished talking about Amelia, he continued with, "As for Becca—"

Rob stopped when he got an icy stare from Misty.

"Now hear me out. I know Becca is a sore topic, but please give me a chance to explain."

She reluctantly let him continue.

"I was devastated when Amelia threw me out. I had no idea what you were going to do, whether you would decide to stay with me or leave, so I went into a funk thinking I could wind up without either of you." Rob shook his head. "How prophetic was that? Look, Becca found out the predicament I was in and chose to come visit me on her own. I guess she just got to me when I was vulnerable. It started out with a little neck massage and went from there. I have always liked Becca as a friend, but have never thought of her as anything more. Yes, I was possibly on my way to sleeping with her, but hey, we will never know for sure. It was stupid, and I know that now."

Misty smiled. "So, you haven't slept with her?"

Rob shook his head vigorously. "No Misty, you've got to believe me."

She was filled with relief. She didn't know why, but knowing that Rob had not slept with Becca made things easier to swallow.

"Good, she doesn't deserve someone like you. If she's not ashamed of herself, I hope she's just plain frustrated."

"Oh, she's frustrated all right. She called me after you left, and I told her to go to hell and that I don't want to ever see her again."

Misty exploded with laughter, causing Amelia to drop the drink she was making. Misty heard the commotion and smiled at Amelia before turning back to Rob.

"You said that to Becca? You? Mild-mannered Rob?"

"Well sure. I didn't like the way Becca responded when you walked in on us. She should have shown more shame and been apologetic. When she showed disdain I knew her motives had been wrong all along. I don't have a place for her in my life anymore."

Misty beamed and began to feel like her old self again. It was time to tell Rob about her plans to go to Argentina.

"I've decided to go back to Buenos Aires for a while. It's not right for me to stand in the way between you and Amelia."

Rob looked confused. "What do you mean stand in the way? Amelia has basically told me to go to hell. Of course, she's just too classy a lady to actually say it that way, but I got the message loud and clear."

"Rob, listen to me. I'm a woman, and I know other women. Amelia is over there dying to hear every word we are saying. If she truly wanted you to go to hell she wouldn't be paying any attention to us. Trust me, she still likes you."

For the first time Rob got a little color back in his cheeks and began to perk up. "Are you sure?"

When Rob saw the look on Misty's face he realized she was absolutely certain.

And then Misty put her hands out and reached for his.

"We need to get a separation, but I want you to know that I will always consider you a dear friend. I want you in my life."

Misty's words gave Rob back his dignity and sense of self-worth. After looking into her eyes for a moment he responded, "I would like that very much, Misty. I will always adore you, you know."

"A part of me will always be in love with you."

"And me you. What do we do now?"

"What now? Well, you go home and leave Amelia to me. I'm going to make things right before I leave."

Rob became a little nervous.

"Are you sure?"

"Rob, I've never been so sure about anything in my life. Now get out of here and let me do my work. I'll look you up before I leave so I can give you a proper kiss good-bye."

That brought a smile to his face, and he said, "Promise?"

"I promise."

When he left, she went up to the counter and ordered a tall americano. Amelia handed it to her with a puzzled look on her face.

"I thought you liked lattes."

Misty smiled. "Yes, but since Rob and I are splitting up, I thought I would check out what he's been drinking all of these years."

Amelia tried to act unfazed but when Misty began to walk toward the door she yelled out, "Misty!"

Misty turned around and walked back to the counter. "Yes?"

Misty kept constant eye contact and made sure to keep a smile on her face. Finally, Amelia asked her to hang around ten minutes so she could visit with her on her break.

"I'd love to," Misty said with a smile.

When Amelia sat down she asked, "Are you two breaking up because of me? I would feel horrible if that were the case."

Misty grabbed her hand and replied, "No Amelia, we're breaking up because I'm no good for Rob. I've been unable to give him what he needs, and I am standing in the way of him having a quality relationship with someone better suited for him than I am. Rob needs someone who's a good cook, someone who'll be there for him every night. Rob wanted to be with me so bad that he put aside everything he believes in to let me be who he knows I am—but despite all that, we've only grown farther and farther apart."

Amelia didn't know what to say. She had never been spoken to so honestly by someone, especially the wife of the man she loved.

Misty gave her a moment and then continued, "Rob is the best man I know. He's better than I am, that's for sure. You're luckier than you know to have him."

Amelia finally broke down and cracked a smile. "So you say he needs someone who's a good cook?"

"After living with me he deserves a good cook. Do you think you know someone who might fit the bill?"

"Maybe. Just maybe I do."

When the two stood up they gave each other a hug without pause. It only felt natural. While still in their embrace, Misty whispered, "Well, next time Rob is in for his americano, tell her to invite him to dinner so he can check out her cooking, will you?"

Amelia hugged Misty tighter.

"Yes, I will make sure she invites him over for dinner. She just hopes he comes back."

"Tell her not to worry; I'll make sure he does."

66

Looking for a Little Peace of Mind

When Misty called Gabriella to tell her that she and Miguel were coming to visit her in Buenos Aires, she could tell from Gabriella's voice that she was absolutely thrilled. Gabriella had wanted to send her private plane to pick them up, but Misty informed her that she already had tickets, leaving the next day. She and Miguel had built up enough frequent flyer points to fly first class. All she had to do now was pack. As she began to fill her suitcase, she decided to take only clothes that Gabriella had given her. She knew she was taking a pretty bold step but kept thinking, *Today is the beginning of the rest of my life. I don't know exactly where it will take me, but I want to make sure I don't bring any old baggage.*

On the flight down, Misty and Miguel remained silent as they each contemplated the bold move they were making. They were both excited and apprehensive at the same time. Miguel felt secure in knowing that his brother would receive him with open arms, and that his fluency in Spanish would make it easy to find work, but he had no idea how easy or how hard it would be to up and move to another country.

Misty, on the other hand, had no reservations about leaving Malibu. Her wandering had led her to that city long ago, and her wandering the past several years had been leading her away again. The path she'd chosen with Rob felt entirely natural to her. Her sexual awakening in Hawaii had forced her to admit that she wasn't made for committing to a partner, and she saw now that her business as the Black Widow Trainer was only a way of helping her further find herself—and she had. She spent much of the flight looking out into the clouds, her mind blissfully clear of uncertainty or regret. Miguel, seated next to her, was similarly entranced by their sudden transit from America to a foreign land, and he spent the long flight daydreaming about what his new life might have in store for him.

It wasn't until the captain notified the passengers to prepare for landing that the two sprang to life. Misty's heart was beating a hundred miles an hour while Miguel bounced his knees up and down and nervously looked out the window. When the plane finally touched down Misty let out a sigh of relief and thought, *It's hard to believe, but I'm really here. I can't wait to see everyone.*

When Misty stepped outside the baggage claim toward the curb, she nervously looked around for Gabriella's limo. Just as she was starting to fear that Gabriella had forgotten about them, Miguel said, "There's the limo Misty! Let's go."

When the car pulled over to the curb, Misty could see Tom's smiling face through the open window. He gave her a wink, but she stood motionless until Gabriella emerged from the back seat. She was wearing a sleek black suit tailored very tight around her waist. Misty thought her straight, dark hair was as stunning as ever and her breath caught in her chest.

Gabriella Marquez walked assertively over to Misty and the two embraced. They stood there, holding one another without saying anything while Miguel and Tom loaded the luggage into the car.

When Tom finally gave the signal to go, Gabriella whispered hotly into Misty's ear, "Welcome home, dear."

"Home . . . I kind of like the sound of that."

After Misty and Gabriella released each other, Misty was greeted by Tom, who opened his arms for her. Her normal enthusiasm came back, and she ran over and gave him a big hug.

"Oh Tom, it's so good to see you again."

"It's good to see you too, Misty."

Misty backed away to get a good look at the aging German.

"Look at you! You look terrific! What have you been doing while I was away?"

Tom puffed his chest out and smiled proudly. "I decided it was time to take a page out of your book and hire a personal trainer! I've never felt better."

Miguel punched him on the arm playfully.

"Does this mean you're not going to pass out if we have to take a little jog?"

"Watch it, boy," Tom said, tensing his arm.

"Wow, feel those guns! I might need you to protect me instead of the other way around."

"What makes you think—"

"Okay you boys, behave," Gabriella interrupted, rolling her eyes. "You've got all the time in the world to prove to each other who is the biggest stud. Let's just be nice to one another right now."

Tom and Miguel gave each other a grin and then a quick embrace before Miguel said, "Okay, the old man and I can pick up where we left off later."

When they drove through the gates of Gabriella's seaside compound, Misty was almost overcome with emotion at seeing the old Marquez mansion once again. *This is just what I need to unwind and get my life back together.*

When she stepped out onto the driveway, Gabriella took her hand and began to lead her to the mansion.

"I know just the thing for you. You need to see the ocean."

As they walked through the house and approached the patio, Misty's nostrils filled with ocean air from the Atlantic. She felt like the warm Argentinean sun could help purge the memories of her damp cold night in London. Looking out at the sea, Misty was certain that she'd come to the right place.

When the boys finished with the luggage, everyone had lunch on the patio and chatted. Gabriella had instructed the kitchen to prepare a grand Argentinean feast with local wine. Both Misty and Miguel felt like they hadn't eaten in months once they started digging into the fresh breads and cheeses and sipping the delicious wine.

Once lunch was over Gabriella said, "Tom, why don't you take Miguel to his brother's house, and I will show Misty to her room so she can settle in."

Miguel was happy to hear that because he was getting anxious to see his brother. Tom nodded, and the two men said their good-byes and left.

As Misty and Gabriella entered the main house, Misty realized it was even more magnificent than she had remembered. But when she made it to her room, she was so taken aback she had to sit down. She took her time looking over every detail: high ceilings with crown moldings and large, beautiful, arched, wood-framed windows that gave a spectacular view of the Atlantic. Antique wood furniture from the late 1800s made the room feel old and timeless. Misty walked up to the old music box that sat on her dresser and lifted the lid. The music that softly came out reminded her of her childhood. *This really does feel like home.*

Gabriella stood quietly, enjoying the expression on Misty's face as she continued to explore her large sitting room and massive bathroom.

Finally Misty gave Gabriella a big hug and said, "I don't know what to say. You are so kind to me. This is everything I have ever dreamed of."

"You don't know how happy that makes me, dear. Now put your things up and join me out back at the swimming pool. I've arranged for dinner to be served poolside when the sun sets. Until then, let's have a little swim. What do you say?" Gabriella smiled and turned smartly on her heel, exiting the room and giving Misty no chance to object.

Typical Gabriella, she thought, smiling. She quickly changed into her suit, noting as she put it on that it was the one that Gabriella had bought her for their trip to Rio. Nothing sounded better at that moment than a swim in the beautiful fresh water of the mansion's pool.

Gabriella greeted her at the pool in a stunning black two-piece. As Misty approached, Gabriella leapt playfully in a perfect graceful arch into the pool, just out of reach. Misty didn't hesitate to follow.

67

DINNER IS SERVED

Over a luscious dinner of grilled salmon and more delicious wine, Misty filled Gabriella in on what had transpired after leaving Argentina. It was a long story, and Gabriella sat there empathetically listening to every detail while wishing she could have been around to help protect her friend. She was confident Misty had the character and mental fortitude to rebound, but she also realized the process should not be rushed. Everyone heals at a different rate, and she wanted to make sure Misty did at her own pace. Although Gabriella felt like holding Misty in her arms and telling her how sorry she was, she was astute enough to know that a better strategy would be to take Misty's mind off of her troubles.

"I want you to know," Gabriella said with a smile, "that you are welcome to stay for as long as you like. In fact, I would love for you to make this your home base. Now that you are a single woman, it will be easier for you to settle back into your role as the Black Widow Trainer."

Misty was surprised that Gabriella would talk about work so suddenly, but figured she was only trying to help.

"Black Widow Trainer . . . I'm not certain I will ever be the Black Widow Trainer again."

Gabriella smiled knowingly. "You may have gone through a rough spell, but this is no time to throw in the towel. I'm going to help you do a better job screening your clients so trips like London never happen again. Besides, you are happiest when training clients and you would be bored doing it in one place. Take all the time you need, but let me know when you get the itch to travel again, and I'll help you make all of the arrangements. I will never tie you down. You have my promise. All I want is for you to be happy."

After listening to her, Misty began to realize that she was probably right. *Gabriella knows me well. It's not like me to just stay in one place. But for now I want to spend time with her. Just being around her gives me strength.*

Now that Misty was feeling a little spunkier, she decided to tease Gabriella. "So, when are you going to go on one of my excursions with me?"

For someone that is used to being one step ahead of everyone, Misty's comment took Gabriella by surprise. She thought about it for a moment and then began to grin.

"I think I just might like that idea. What do you have in mind?"

"Well, let's see. We could both take on a client and tag-team him," Misty said provocatively.

"Or tag team her?" Gabriella quickly replied.

Misty laughed. "Or we could train a couple of brothers?"

"How do you feel about some threesome action?"

Misty thought the last few words sounded hilarious in Gabriella's Spanish accent and started laughing.

"Well, you just never know. Maybe we will have to give it a try sometime."

Then Misty remembered that she had a secret she hadn't told her.

"You'll never guess what I did in London."

Gabriella could tell from the look in Misty's eyes that she couldn't wait to tell her.

"I have no idea, tell me!"

Misty began to move her hips and shimmy to the salsa beat in her head.

"Ohh!" Gabriella said slowly, smiling and moving to the same beat as Misty. "Oh Misty, I know the greatest salsa instructor that works at the Club Cuba Mia. You are really close right now but Gregorlo will teach you how to stop moving your arms and concentrate more on your hips."

Misty kept smiling. Gabriella was always a teacher.

"Let's go dancing tomorrow night. What do you say, Misty?"

"I'm not sure. You know what happened the last time we went dancing," Misty said playfully, giving her a sidelong glance.

"Yes I do indeed. Maybe we should go dancing tonight!"

Misty shimmied her way over to Gabriella and untied her robe before saying, "Oh, I don't know. Maybe there are a few things you can teach me before Gregorlo gets his hands on me."

Reaching out and pulling Misty to her, Gabriella said, "Honey, you have no idea the things I'm going to teach you tonight. Just wait until I get my hands all over you."

Misty held her tighter, and for the first time since London, she realized that everything was going to work out just fine.

About the Author

Steven Craig Odanovich grew up in Flour Bluff, Texas, only minutes from the beaches of Padre Island. His creative roots are firmly grounded in the muscle car culture of the seventies. As a young music business entrepreneur, Odanovich launched a successful record store at a time when neighborhood record stores were still a prime point of connection between popular music and the public. His genuine affinity for the music and the fans helped Craig's Record Factory build huge customer loyalty, keeping regional and national competition at bay.

Rising to the executive level in the video and home entertainment division of H-E-B, a regional grocery and retail chain, Odanovich led growth for the company in an emerging market space. Later, applying his leadership abilities and insight to other highly competitive business arenas, he built value and increased market share for each of the companies he subsequently served, both in executive posts and as a key consultant.

Through his many stages of career evolution, Odanovich has maintained a constant interest in popular music and film. Three decades of avidly collecting music and seeing movies has provided a wellspring of inspiration for the author. Odanovich currently pursues his writing career in San Antonio, Texas. He and his wife Cathie have four children.

THE BLACK WIDOW TRAINER
CAPTURED PREY

ON VACATION

Misty stood statuesque as soothing warm water cascaded over every voluptuous curve of her well-honed body, washing away the salty sweat left over from yoga class. Tonight she would dine with her best friend, Gabriella, in the quaint little town of Lahaina. Maui offered the girls a sunny escape from the cold June days in Buenos Aires. The next two weeks would be filled with beautiful beaches, exotic tours, fabulous food, and everything else paradise could provide.

"Misty, dear! I'm going downstairs to the bar for a drink so take your time getting ready."

"Okay, Gabriella. I won't take long."

Misty finished showering, toweled off, and then lay on the bed for a short respite.

"Maid service! Do you need anything?"

Misty groggily reached for her cell phone to check the time and then panicked.

"No thanks! I don't need anything," Misty shouted as she frantically jumped to the floor. *I've been sleeping for ninety minutes! Gabriella must be worried sick. I'll send her a text.*

As she hurriedly threw on some clothes, she wrote, "So sorry Gabby! I fell asleep. I'll be down in a jiff!" Within a minute she heard a beep with Gabby's reply: "Take your time. I met the most amazing man."

Oh really? Well good for her.

On her way to the lobby Misty couldn't help but wonder what Gabriella's mystery man looked like. *Knowing Gabriella, he's smart as well as attractive.*

Misty spotted the two as she walked into the bar. As she drew nearer, she stopped dead in her tracks. The strikingly handsome man looked incredibly similar to an old acquaintance she'd had drinks with at this very same bar over three years ago. *"It can't be. What are the chances of running into him after all these years?"*

Broad shoulders, silky, smooth brown skin, and long, thick black hair. Whoever he was, her old acquaintance was still one of the most magnificent creatures she had ever laid eyes on. His exotic blend of possibly half Hawaiian and maybe half Asian or Polynesian still made him the most intriguing-looking man she had ever known—and the last time she had known him it had been in the biblical sense.

Gabriella said, "Oh, Misty, I would like you to meet—"

Gabriella quickly glanced back at her new acquaintance and said, "I'm sorry, what did you say your name was?"

"I didn't say."

Misty remembered how the man she knew long ago had never divulged his name to her, which in an insidious way had made him all the more intriguing.

As she took a seat she studied his every feature before asking, "We've met before, haven't we?"

"Possibly. You remind me of someone I met several years ago in this very same bar."

"So you two already know each other?" Gabriella asked.

They both nodded without taking their eyes off of each other.

The night in his hotel room long ago had been a sexual awakening and was instrumental in setting her free. The thought of that night caused her to cross her legs and pump her right leg up and down vigorously. Now both mentally and physically aroused, she fought the impulse to drag him up to her room and hold him hostage for a repeat performance. *If only Gabriella were not here.*

Bemused, Gabriella stared at the two in disbelief. "So you two really know each other?"

"A chance encounter," Misty said.

The man added, "Yes, and what's the chance of being with two beautiful women this time?" He rose from the table as if sensing it would be best to let the women sort this out in privacy. "I'll be right back. Please order another round of drinks when our waitress returns and put it on my tab."

When he was gone, Gabby asked, "So what's going on, Misty? There seems to be history between you two."

"Remember me telling you about the man I had an affair with that led to my break up with Rob? It's him!"

"No way," Gabriella replied. "So what is his name?"

"My friend at the time, Becca, referred to him as The Man."

"'The Man!' That has a nice ring to it," Gabriella said. "Then that's what we will call him."

A glassy-eyed Misty said, "Yes, and what a man he turned out to be. I accompanied him that night, to his room. I can still remember him stopping me before we entered and saying, *this is no place for little girls.* I went in anyway. If there was still any little girl in me I was all big girl when I left."

Now that Misty had confirmed his prowess in the bedroom, Gabriella's pulse quickened. She had fallen under his spell while waiting for Misty and found him off-the-charts handsome and oozing with charisma. But being the practical one, something began to trouble her. Assuming only one of them could score, which one of them would it be?"

"Misty, we need to talk. I'm as enamored with this man as you are, but if we fight for his affections I'm worried one of us will get hurt."

"So what do you suggest we do?"

Gabriella thought it over for a moment before saying, "Why don't we invite him to dinner and see how it all plays out?"

"I'm down with that!" Misty said with a mischievous grin. "After all, we are on vacation, so a little adventure is in order."

When The Man returned to the table he said, "Hey, why the long faces? This is my last night on Maui. What do you say we all go get some dinner?"

Misty winked at Gabriella as she replied, "Gee, why didn't we think of that."

On the way out the door Misty said, "Hey, we still don't know your name. We can't spend a night on the town with a nameless man. Now come on, give it up."

The Man contemplated long and hard before saying, "Teakie. My given name is Teakie."

The girls looked at each other in astonishment before Misty laughingly blurted out, "Teakie? Oh, how darling, we're going out with little Teakie tonight."

Misty realized her remark had embarrassed him, so she quickly put her arm around him and patted his chest. "I'm so sorry for laughing at you. I was just joshing you."

A warm smile spread over his face that showed off his perfect row of sparkling white teeth. "That's okay. Now you know why I hesitate to give women my name."

The quality of the food at their restaurant was matched by the quality of conversation. After eating a little too much they decided to take a long walk along the beach to walk off dessert. Gabriella found Teakie to be charming, not a charmer. From her past experiences, a man this good-looking had a propensity to be somewhat conceited. She now understood why Misty had trusted him enough to go to his room without even knowing his name. Seeing how well Misty and Teakie were getting along, Gabriella decided that she would not compete for his affections. Now if Teakie chose her on his own without her trying, that might be another story.

The girls hung all over Teakie as they climbed the steps to their hotel. The message in their body language was clear: "You're not going anywhere tonight without one of us, Buddy." Once in the main lobby, Gabriella reached around Teakie's back to pinch Misty as she said to Teakie, "Why don't you sit on that comfy sofa while Misty and I visit the ladies' room?" Teakie shrugged his shoulders and plopped on the couch.

Once safely inside the ladies' room, Misty asked, "What's up, Gabby?"

"What's up? Teakie's penis is up. I accidentally brushed it while we were walking up the stairs. Well okay, maybe not accidentally." She grinned. "That man is primed and ready for action!"

Feeling excited and a bit silly, Misty said, "They taught us in school that teak is a brown hardwood. Maybe they gave him his name because he's brown skinned and his penis is as hard as wood."

"Cute, Misty," Gabriella said while shaking her head. "Why don't you and I discuss which one of us gets to mount that hardwood and which one retires to the room to be *bored* out of her mind?"

Misty turned on the faucet and splashed some water onto her face. "That's quite the dilemma my friend."

Trying to delicately deal with their predicament, the girls spent the next five minutes coming up with reasons why the other should spend the night with Teakie.

"Gabby, it's only fair you get to experience Teakie firsthand. I've had my opportunity."

"No, Misty. I could tell during our walk on the beach that you guys have a lot of catching up to do. I should be the one to bow out."

They eventually agreed it was ultimately Teakie's decision to choose, and the unlucky one would gracefully exile herself to the boredom of their room.

Misty hugged her friend tightly. "Now, let's go let the cards fall where they may."

When they arrived at the couch they panicked. Teakie was nowhere to be found. A pall fell over the girls as the disappointment set in. Misty and Gabby held hands in an attempt to console one another, feeling like brides left standing at the altar after the groom got cold feet and bailed.

Suddenly, their trance was broken as two powerful arms wrapped around them from behind. A friendly, seductive voice asked, "Why the long faces? Did you get some bad news?"

When the girls realized it was Teakie, their moods lifted and each breathed a sigh of relief.

Teakie said, "I've got an idea. Why don't we all three go up to my room and get to know each other better?" Giving the girls a little squeeze, he added, "Misty knows what I mean, don't you Misty?"

Misty looked at Gabriella with a twinkle in her eye as she said softly under her breath, "Are you up for it?" Gabriella's smile indicated she was.

When Teakie unlocked the door to his room, Misty took him by the arm and said, "I hope you know this room is only for *big boys*."

Teakie replied, "You can be the judge of that."